THE FLOWERS OF THE FOREST

Elizabeth Byrd was born in St Louis, Missouri, but now lives in a fifteenth-century cottage outside Edinburgh. Her highly successful novels include *Immortal Queen*, *The Famished Land* and *The Long Enchantment*. Her most recent book is a novel about the nineteenth-century Edinburgh murderers Burke and Hare.

THE FLOWERS OF THE FOREST

ELIZABETH BYRD

Pan Books Ltd London and Sydney

First published 1962 by Constable & Co Ltd
This edition published 1966 by Pan Books Ltd,
Cavaye Place, London SW10 9PG
ISBN 0 330 02401 9
6th printing 1975

Printed in Great Britain by
Richard Clay (The Chaucer Press) Ltd, Bungay, Suffolk

Prologue

August 18th, 1513

SMOULDY WEATHER, the crofters called it, sultry and windless, charged with storm. In the Firth of Forth the war fleet lay at anchor, banners motionless, sails limp. Only a few cod boats ventured to sea followed by screaming gulls.

All day sun had brutalized Edinburgh. As it set the sky was gashed red as a wound and the heat endured. The moon rose, lighting parched gardens. In the forests boars rooted stubble and carcasses of small animals were picked clean by the wolves.

This night the town was tense with fear. Men shivered awake, hearing the watchman call the hours, feeling soft arms clasp them and the drip of tears on their shoulders. Their weapons lay ready – spears and broadswords and dirks. In castles new-polished armour stood like propped corpses. In hovels bows and arrows were wrapped in cutting scarves to keep them dry against the rain.

Midnight. The High Street stretched a pale ribbon between the darkness of wynds and closes where timbered houses clung to the spine of the Rock. High above them hulked the Castle, a crouched monster pinpricked by torches. Sentries paced its battlements, staring southwards. Soldiers removed the Seven Sisters – great, black-snouted cannon that had defended Edinburgh for generations and soon once more would face the English in the field.

Few folk were abroad. A servant and her lover watched the Nor' Loch as moonlight silvered its water. A merchant, solemnly drunk, weaved homeward. A sobbing slut crept from a house in the Cowgate. A white witch stalked a cat, needing its blood for a potion. A thief slunk through Candlemaker's Row with silver plate under his cloak. Two farmers in the shadows of the Netherbow Port haggled the price of a bull. From the Church of St Giles a tired priest shuffled towards Holyrood Abbey, sandals slapping the dust.

At the Tron where butter and cheese were weighed by day the stalls were empty under stretched canvas, but the booths still reeked of haddock and vegetables rotted in the gutters. An old woman filled her skirt with soft, browning carrots. Her bare feet slid over sheeps' entrails which she picked up.

A town watchman pacing the High Street swung his lantern into dark crannies where rats feasted on refuse. 'Twelve o'clock,' he chanted to the closed grey houses. 'Twelve of a Friday morn and all's well . . .'

'All's well,' mimicked a passing fop. 'All's ill, you old fool, and well you know it.'

The air was heavy as though it might be grasped hot in the hand. A kailwife, stifled and sleepless, risked the poisons of the night air and opened her casement. She stared idly at the Market Cross which stood in mid-High Street in the shadow of St Giles. It was a turreted stone pedestal, high as a pulpit, shaped like an octagon. For fifty-five years she had witnessed tragedies and celebrations at the Cross. Here the doomsters hanged criminals and burned black witches. Here from a fountain flowed brooks of claret on feast days. She had drunk to James III on his birthdays; toasted the present James IV and his English bride. Here but a few days ago she had heard the proclamation of war with England and loyal Scots summoned to arms. Dear King, she thought, dear to me as my own son, and as reckless. She felt the need to mother him in his folly and then laughed silently. Imagine her wanting to tell the King what to do! She must be growing daft with years.

She was turning from her window to seek her bed when she heard the shrill of a trumpet and stared, stunned, at the Market Cross. For there was no trumpeter, no herald, no torches. Only moonlight brightened the bare pedestal.

I *am* daft, she thought.

Then a voice spoke loudly from the Cross – a man's voice, but sepulchral as if dragged up from the depths of the earth.

'Hear ye! Ye who are to die, take heed! As herald of Pluto, Ruler of the Lower World, I command thee to listen.'

The thief heard it, the fop and the farmers. The priest made the sign of the cross. The merchant paused, one foot on his gallery stairs.

Again the trumpet sounded and the voice spoke. 'Hear ye – ye who are about to die!'

Candles flared and heads poked from windows.

'Ye women who will mourn, gather thy woe-weeds!'

The kailwife shivered in the heat. The slut whimpered, clinging to the wall of a house as blood trickled through her bodice.

'Hear, then, the roll call of they who shall die in battle!'

Again the trumpet sounded, but muffled as though dirged through grave dirt.

'Hear ye . . . James Stuart, King of Scotland . . .

'Adam, Earl of Bothwell . . .

'Alexander Stuart, Archbishop of St Andrews . . .'

There followed a long list of nobles and high clergy.

'. . . and hear ye common folk the names of those who shall perish . . . to rue their part . . .'

The slut moaned. 'Not he! Holy Mary, spare him!'

'Robert Lawson . . .'

The merchant cried out, 'I am Robert Lawson!'

The voice continued with name after name. 'And these men shall appear before the tribunal of Pluto within forty days.'

Lawson shouted, his words drink-slurred, 'From that summons and sentence I appeal me, body and soul, to the mercy of God!'

The voice at the Cross was silent. Only moonlight moved from the pedestal, pooling the earth below.

Half-clad people carrying torches swarmed into the street seeking solace from one another; weeping, speaking of relatives and friends doomed for death.

'Look!' The priest pointed towards St Giles. 'Corpse lights!'

Blue flames flickered through the churchyard, hovered pale upon the graves, licked along the earth and disappeared through the trees.

The crowd murmured in horror, for more than any other omen blue flames presaged death.

The priest, Father Duncan, clutched his crucifix and prayed aloud. The people knelt wherever they stood – some in the clean ridge, or 'crown' that ran through the middle of the street, others in filth.

'We beg thee to deliver us from evil . . . into thy care and the care of thy Son, Jesus Christ. Amen.'

He blessed them. As the crowd rose he said, 'I trust I've not failed you, for I know little of exorcism and have not the means of it handy.'

'You did noble,' said a cooper. 'But tell us, Father – who is Pluto?'

'A fiend.'

'English?' asked a pastryman.

'Nay, I think not,' Humbly Father Duncan added, 'I'm not learned. I'd best ask my bishop. But I think Pluto is a Greek.'

'Yet,' said a weaver, 'his herald spoke honest Scots.'

'The Devil speaks all tongues, my son.'

A magistrate said, 'Perchance it was a hoax. There are many close to the King who would discourage this enterprise. Or it may be that the English themselves seek to prevent war by trickery.'

'Trickery?' The kailwife spoke on a sob. 'Twas no trick. I looked down at the Cross for moments before the trumpet blew – no man was there. And what of the corpse lights?'

The crowd discussed whether the dark miracle would dissuade the King from war. Most agreed it would not. Though marked for death James IV was stubborn as he was brave, and bound to his word – Lord love him. They spoke of his goodness, mourning already the loss of a precious friend. For had he not walked among them giving largesse, comforting the sick, cuddling the little bairns? True, it might be foolhardy to invade England but by Christ, Scotland would not grind under Henry VIII's boot.

They recalled that Henry's hatred of Scotland had simmered through years of peace. As a lad of eleven, learning that his sister Margaret was betrothed to James, rage heated his body to fever and physicians were called to attend him. After the marriage – the union of 'The Thistle and the Rose' that pledged eternal friendship between Scotland and England – Henry had broken his bond. He permitted the slaughter and imprisonment of Scots on the Border. Despite Margaret's entreaties he refused to send her legacy of jewels, gold and silver. A year ago he had joined Pope Julius II, Ferdinand of Spain and the Venetians in their Holy League against France, Scotland's ally. And now Henry had marched into France with an invading army.

'It's not mere politics,' said a sailor. 'Our King has a man's need for revenge. You mind how he loved Captain Barton? So Henry orders Barton murdered at sea, captures our ships and artillery.'

'Let us be fair,' said the magistrate. 'Barton was a pirate.'

'A damned fine one,' said the sailor. 'Likely the best we had.'

Father Duncan said, 'You forget a spiritual grievance. It was Henry who persuaded the Pope to excommunicate our King.'

'Can it be,' asked the kailwife, shocked, 'that if the King dies in battle he'll die heretic?'

'Aye, dame. And he so devout that he'd rather make a holy pilgrimage than hunt.' Father Duncan struggled with his conscience. 'I mean, he would *almost* rather.'

The magistrate said, 'We should patch our quarrels with England. Revenge is a child's way—'

The crowd shouted him down. It was unthinkable to allow Henry further depredations. Not yet twenty-two, his arrogance was said to stagger foreign envoys. He ever bragged that he owned Scotland and that James was a rebel against his authority.

The pastryman said, 'Master Lawson! You're the only man here named for death yet you're calm as curd. Will you still follow the King if he marches?'

'Aye. I warrant he and God are stronger than the Devil.'

The crowd cheered him.

'My brother John was named, he who lives in Peebles.' A girl hid her face on a neighbour's shoulder. 'But I'd not hinder his marching.'

Women wept softly, in resignation. They would not question the King's judgement but they dreaded losing him for he was the brightest skein in the dour wool of their lives. In their various secret minds he was father, friend, lover, god.

'You'd best go to your beds,' Father Duncan said, and blessed them again. Strange, he thought, as they dispersed – by day in their rags of coloured homespun they were his own familiar flock. Now, half-clad or in long-flowing night-robes, they were spectres slipping through the wynds, shadows moving against the blood-glow of torchlight. He sighed, feeling the weight of his inadequacy. He had not the learning to advise and comfort, only the heart to try. It seemed to him ironic that he, of all the monks and friars of Edinburgh, should have heard the Devil and raised his own puny voice in prayer. But had the prayer been heard? Was he not too young and bumbly? He thought of himself as little Father Duncan though he stood six feet in his sandals.

He went to Robert Lawson who lingered at the foot of his forestairs. 'My son,' he said, 'you were brave to defy the Devil and wise to trust God.'

Lawson shook his head. 'I'm drunk, mizzled with spirits.'

'The spirits in a flagon are not so evil as that which we heard tonight. But God will comfort you.'

'Perchance by death.'

'Peace, son. And a good night to you.'

Father Duncan walked on down the street. He passed the

slut, then turned back and stared at her. Head bent, she was stumbling, and he gasped at the sight of blood on her gown, trickling from bodice to hem.

He went to her, peering at her face which was half-hidden by her unbound hair. 'Are you not Dame Dart? Bess Dart?'

She paused. 'Aye, Father.'

'What has befallen you?'

She chewed her lips.

'God help us – did someone seek to kill you?'

Bess shook her head, hair swinging gold in the moonlight.

'Speak, child. What happened? Who did this to you?'

Her mouth clamped tight. He questioned her futilely. Finally he said, 'I'll see you to a surgeon and then I'll rouse your husband—'

Each whispered word seemed wrenched from her. 'I beg you not to tell my husband.'

'But he should know, and soon or late he will know. Likely he's seeking you now. He'll want to find the rogue who hurt you.'

'You don't ken my meaning,' she said. 'It's not my pain I'd keep from him but what we heard at the Cross. Don't tell him of that, I pray you!'

Gently he said, 'You're ill, else you'd realize that by morn the whole town will have the news.'

'And why,' he asked the hair-shrouded face, 'should he not know?'

'Because his name was called!' Bess tossed back her hair and faced him, her face so pain-twisted that he found it a stranger's. 'He is to die, but I must be the one to tell him.'

'Come now, I don't recall Hugh Dart's name was spoken. I could swear to it.'

'It was! It was the first one called of the common folk. I heard it plain.'

He realized her addlement and humoured her. 'There, lass, I'll not tell him. I'll take you to a surgeon.'

She tried to walk a few steps, but crumpled. Carefully he

picked her up and she nestled her head against his shoulder, her hair spilling down his cassock. They turned off the High Street and entered Cap and Feather Lane. He stopped at the door which bore the barber-surgeon's symbol of a pole bandaged with ribbon.

'Master Geddes will heal you, never fear.'

He drew on the iron tirling pin and they waited.

'You are good,' she murmured. 'If you were really a man I'd reward you – if I could.'

He flushed, then smiled. The poor child meant no harm. Strange how one sometimes found good in evil, evil in good. Just this morning he had been shocked to perceive evil in the Archbishop, for pride was a grevious sin. How could a man of God curse a beggar in his path, drawing aside his robes as though contaminated by the pleading hand? But Bess Dart had evened matters. She had offered him the only gift she had – or thought she had. He said, 'I thank you, but you owe me nothing.'

The door opened and Geddes, in nightclothes blinked at them sleepily across the candle he held. He was a tall, grey man, thin as his own pole, eyes and mouth narrowed to slits.

'I found Dame Dart sore hurt.' Father Duncan started to move through the door but Geddes blocked his way.

'Can she pay?'

'I'd guess she can. You mind she has a trade.'

'Sit her down.'

They placed her on a broad oak bench. Geddes lit candles on a nearby table. They cast long shadows on white plastered walls that rose to a ceiling of oak beams.

Geddes knelt beside Bess, removed the bloody cord at her waist and examined the pouch that hung from it.

'Not a penny,' he said. 'You'd best take her to the Abbey.'

'But the monks are not' – Father Duncan swallowed the words, 'as skilled as you.' Instead he said, 'The monks are too far. She might bleed to death on the way.'

'She must pay.'

'You're not in need of money.' He looked about the room. Lute strings strung with pulled teeth festooned the walls, testifying to years of customers. There were expensive citterns for men to play while they awaited shaves or leeching and an elegant copper bleeding basin stood in a corner. That basin alone brought a mint of money for the Town Council rented it often to cart she-bawds to the Tolbooth. He marvelled that Bess had escaped that fate. It was a sad thing to see a woman huddled in the basin and carried through the streets naked to flung dung and stones and spittle. True, bawds required punishment, but it should be left to the will of God and the mercy of Our Lady.

'She must pay,' Geddes repeated.

'Have you no conscience? What of your vow to help the sick?'

'I'm a poor man—'

'You are indeed.' Father Duncan took a coin from his purse and placed it on the table. 'Today I collected alms for the poor, and since you are a wretched sort of man it befits you to have this.'

'I'll see to her.'

Geddes took a dagger from his cabinet and slit Bess's bodice. Both men gasped at sight of her right breast. Geddes touched it and raised sticky red fingers.

'Who did this?'

'I don't know. She won't speak.'

'Her husband? Even he must know she's a whore. He was weary of being cuckolded, so he—'

'Nay,' Bess moaned, 'he loves me.'

Geddes shrugged and brought vials from the cabinet. He placed agrimony leaves and mandrake juice and yarrow in a wooden bowl, mixed them with wine and hog lard. As he worked he glanced at Bess and grimaced. 'It could be the judgement of God. What man will want her now?'

Father Duncan glared at him. 'Hold your tongue. Such words salt her wounds.'

Geddes brought an angelica root to prevent infection,

pushed it into her mouth and told her to chew it while he finished the poultice. 'When you heal you'll need a philtre. I charge only sixpence. . . .'

Bess's forehead poured sweat. Her hands clawed the bench as he probed the wound. She screamed through the root and spat it out.

'My husband will want me—'

'Aye, child.' Father Duncan turned away, retching.

'—as long as he lives.'

I

Bess Dart

AT DAWN SHE lay at home on her straw pallet feeling the fire of pain, seeing the fire of the sun gather behind the lattice. She looked at her husband sleeping beside her. Soon, unless the King heeded the ghostly prophecy, Hugh must start the long march south over hills and wild moors, a scorching nightmare for one unused to soldiering. She had tried to dissuade him but he had insisted on joining the men who were to mass at Boroughmuir within the week. Captain Ramsay had signed him up, reminding him to be ready with weapons and provisions for forty days.

Forty days, she thought – the exact time mentioned by the voice at the Cross.

Unable to prevent his going, she had planned to join the camp followers so that she might nurse Hugh were he wounded. But now she lay helpless, herself wounded in body and spirit. Her husband was doomed; she had lost her beauty, her potential earnings, her hope – and all in one scant hour.

But she knew herself for a practical woman. Self-pity meant waste, nor would she clutter her brain with hot, half-formed plans for revenge. There was no hurry; she would bide her time. Country-bred, she reflected that nature moved in slow, inexorable rhythm. There was a season for birth and harvest, a season for death. As surely as rain would fall on Edinburgh, so would the man pay for his crime.

She was not considering vengeance now but she hated the man, and she hated the city that spawned him. Four years in Edinburgh had not inured her to its filth, its clatter, nor to the snarling competition of its tradespeople. Often she dreamed of returning to Kirkcudbright, her village in

Galloway, to the sleepy grey-green peace of the Border hills. How lovesome to hear birdsong in the oaks, sheep bells on the slopes and a woodcutter's axe breaking a summer's silence. She remembered the thatched cottage of her youth where rooks and magpies built in the straw; the hollyhock walk and the hawthorn hedge and a stile berried red in the back end o' the year. She visioned herself there with Hugh, a vastly different lass from her city self. In white ruffled coif and linen apron she would tend her herb garden, spin and weave, pillow the down of their own geese. Sometimes she fancied she could smell lavender on her sheets, sniff apples sputtering on her hearth. If once she were back she would never take such things for granted; she would hold the black earth in her hands as though it were gold, and revel in leaf smoke. She and Hugh would – but no, he would not. He would never leave Edinburgh, save for this pesky war.

Yet until he met her the city had brought him only misery and she marvelled at its hold on him. He would not imagine a better life than this. Poor Hugh – he was proud of their stall, unaware that people laughed behind his back, amused that a foggie owned property. Back home in Kirkcudbright they would not laugh. They cherished simples and old folk as a natural part of life. The witless and the helpless, like the lambs, were gently cared for.

Hugh turned in his sleep. As his body thrust towards hers she moved over, murmuring in pain.

He opened his eyes and sat up. 'Why, Bess! You are still in your kirtle.'

'You forget what happened,' she said, and repeated the lie she had told him last night. 'Someone had left a dirk in the street and I stumbled and fell on it.'

'Mass! Now I remember.'

He bent to caress her but she said, 'Don't joggle me.'

'Poor Bess. But the priest said you will heal.'

'I'd heal faster if you would stay home from war and care for me.'

He shook his head. 'I am pledged to go. It's like I've

given my word to the King. Besides,' he said, in a rush of reason that surprised her, 'what could I do but not joggle you? Folk will bring you food and drink.'

But she had no friends, and she wondered how even Hugh could live with her a year and not perceive the slights she endured. Respectable matrons did not appear to see her when they bought fish. Bawds had always been jealous, and her married state enraged them. Only Guilie MacIver, the White Witch, condescended to her company.

'And the priest will help you,' Hugh said.

She used her illness to protect him from death. 'You cannot leave me. Suppose I should die, and you away?'

'I've no power to keep you from death,' he said, and again his logic surprised her. 'There's naught I can do that others can't, save loving you. And that I can do from Spain.'

'England,' she said gently. 'It's England we're to fight.'

'I can love you from any land.'

He stroked her hair, soft and curly, golden as butter. 'I'll be back, Bess, and likely with plunder. We'll be rich, hire an apprentice and open another stall—'

'Heed me,' she said in the tone that always hushed him. 'I'd spare you this if I could. You dare not go to war, for you're marked to die. Last night at the Cross . . .'

As she told him she realized he was not listening. His eyes deadened, his face slackened as though a curtain pulled over his brain. He had a way of never hearing evil or ill tidings.

'Are you not afraid of the Devil?' she asked hopelessly.

'Aye,' He frowned. 'Why, Bess?'

'I just told you—' She broke off in despair. It was never before so needful that she reach his mind but he sat beside her, remote, walled in innocence.

She tried once more. 'I cannot work for a while. Who's to tend the stall with you away?'

'We'll close it. There's plenty of coins in the trencher.'

There were plenty because her own earnings had supplemented their trade. But now . . . she closed her eyes, tears slipping under the lids. No man would want her now, the surgeon had said. Even Hugh's love must change when he saw her bare. Child-like, he could never hide his feelings; he would show his revulsion plain. As time passed he would treat her as a sister and spend his lust on others.

She must prepare him for the day when he would see her unbandaged. 'You ken what my wound is? My – the dirk slashed my chest.'

'A mercy you weren't killed.'

Would I had been . . . but that was a sinful thought. She had Hugh to live for, to care for. Without her he would be cheated of what little they owned and likely become a public charge.

'But do you understand?' She touched the linen wrapping that showed above her low bodice. 'One of my—' She lost courage. 'I have hurt my breast.'

He said nothing but bent and kissed her, a soft wisp of a kiss, the sort she might expect, she thought bitterly, from now on. Other women wanted his kisses; even fine ladies stared at him in hunger, eyeing the heavy chestnut curls, the great shoulders, the long-limbed body carried so proudly despite its poor covering. Only last week the Countess of Bothwell had come to the stall to buy salmon, and glimpsing Hugh had said to her maids, 'Jesu! Apollo comes to earth in strange disguise.' Later when Bess had asked Guilie what the countess meant, the witch had explained that in olden times Apollo was the fairest of gods.

Bess was furious at the way the countess looked at Hugh – sidewise, eyes slanty under kohl-painted lashes. But now she remembered that the Earl of Bothwell was marked for death too, and she felt sudden kinship with his wife. It was so startling to pity a countess that she mentioned the fact to Hugh, more to expand the thought than to seek his understanding.

'It's queer-like that a fishwife and an earl's wife should face the same grief. And likely we're the same age. She looked about eighteen.'

She explained. 'You mind the lady with the great show of

maids and pages and trainbearers who was at the stall last week?'

'Aye. She was even fairer than the Queen. She wore a red taffety hat, and a perky patch next her mouth.'

Curtly, she said, 'You've memory when you wish. You can't recall the price of cod but you mind a woman's face.'

He seemed hurt. 'She was fair, was she not? You said so yourself.'

'She should be fair, with all that paint. But a snisty wench by the look of her.' Her feeling of kinship had vanished. 'I doubt *she'll* mourn her husband long.'

'Is he dead?'

Wearily she shook her head. 'You'd best feed us and open the stall.'

He rose, padded naked to the clothes hook and dressed in brown belted tunic, cloth hose and rush-woven shoes. He bent to build a fire at the hearth but she said, 'The heat would swelter us. We'll eat cold.'

Obediently he filled trenchers with cold barley bannocks and salted herring. Then he tipped the ale jug and poured two mugs.

Poor fare, she thought, forcing herself to eat, and a poor room. Hugh had caught a hog in the street and tied it in the corner where it ate piled refuse. The floor was of earth, littered with fragments of food. There was a scarred pine table, two beer barrels that served as seats, a chamber pot and basin and this bed of straw and rags. She had planned changes. Each coin saved meant a clothes chest, chairs, a painted cloth to hang against the crumbling wall. Flesh instead of fish, and fruit not picked from the gutter.

Sometimes, slutting in fine homes, she had eaten beef roasted in madeira. She had looked into a long mirror of polished metal, seeing for the first time the slender grace of her body. Twice she had shared a bed with brocaded hangings. She had even used an inside privy and walked on a carpet of cloth. It seemed sad that she could not tell Hugh of these marvels. Poor love, he knew nothing of the world beyond his native hills, the murky, fish-stinking lane, this shabby room. And now his humble days were numbered.

By the Virgin, she thought, I'll not let him go to slaughter. I'll find some means to stop him.

'Are you finished eating, Bess?'

She gave him the trencher and he dumped the fish bones out of the window with the chamber slops and pig dung. 'Now heed me,' she said, 'when you open the stall, hawk the herring first . . . take care you're not cheated . . . mind thieves.' She reminded him of prices and he repeated them after her. She warned him to hasten stall-troublers who loitered but did not buy. 'Should some fine folk want a fish dressed, dare not do it yourself for fear of the law and tell them the flesher will charge tuppence to dress a salmon. Hide any fish that's rotting and bring it home else the Town Council will seize it for the lepers.' She sighed. 'I wish I was able to cook, for you can't disguise ill fish.'

'I can, Bess. With onions.'

She was astonished that Hugh remembered. But of course in the passage of hours he would forget.

'I'll be back at noon to fix your dinner,' he said. 'Maybe I'll find you a pear.'

She tried to stretch her arms towards him but winced and let them fall to her sides. 'You love me?'

'That you know,' he said, sounding puzzled. 'I've told you afore.'

'Tell me again. I must, I *must* know.'

'I love you.'

'You'd not love another?'

'I know no other.'

It was not the reply she required but she realized that none would satisfy her need. Because of Hugh's witlessness she had often been lonely but their bodies had bridged the mental void. Now she must find some other way of warmth.

He touched her lips, traced her straight little nose. 'You are bonny, Bess.'

'But suppose I was not?'

She waited and his silence grew long. 'No matter,' she said fearfully. A man-child's thoughts could be cruel . . .

'But you are bonny,' he said finally, 'else I'd not have wed you.'

She wondered why she tormented herself. 'Am I not a good wife? Thrifty, and helpful at the stall? Don't such things count more than beauty?'

'Nay. Any woman can work and save. You don't ken a man's need, Bess.'

She wanted to laugh, to weep. But she said, 'You'd best hurry, the sun's high. Leave off the door latch, and if you see Guilie, send her to me.'

After he had gone she lay sweating, and the pain seemed worse, hot needles in her flesh. She tried to think of happy things – rain, cool air. She clung to the hope that when the King heard what had happened last night at the Cross he would change his mind about war.

She dozed. The door creaked open.

'Guilie.'

The witch came to her swiftly and knelt beside the pallet. 'What ails you, dove? Hugh said you were ill but couldn't remember why.'

Bess told her the truth and Guilie shuddered. Then she said, 'The monster!'

'That he is.'

'I've a means to deal with him, and I will.'

'But you never brew bad, Guilie.'

'I never have. But I know how.'

'Peace, you cannot risk such. You'd be burned.'

'But I want to help—'

'It's too dangerous.'

'None would ever know but us two.'

Guilie rose and paced the room, a tall, spear-thin woman in berry-brown gown and clean white kirtle. Her face was ill-arranged, Bess thought, as if God had his mind elsewhere when he made her. Under the coif her hair was white, though she was not yet thirty. Her nose was too long, her eyes small and sooty, her chin a tiny ledge supporting a huge mouth. But one forgot her ugliness for her tenderness and the caress of her voice. And she was gifted, even able to read and write.

Now the soft voice snarled. 'Get me something of his! Anything of his body – hair or nail scrapings.'

'I can't. I dare not go back.'

'You must, when you heal. Then I'll make a tallow doll in his image and each hour I'll run a blade through the heart until his own heart fails.'

That would work, Bess knew, for Guilie had the magic power. But she said, 'Life can be worse than death. He is only twenty. I'd have him live to old age – in pain.'

'Then I'll torment him. He'll live with the pain in his heart or his head or wherever you wish.'

Bess mused. 'He is fair in looks and women want him, so—'

'Ho!' Guilie scoffed. 'If women want him why did he need to hire you?'

'I was new to him. He said he'd seen me before, but not so close as when we chanced to meet in the Lawnmarket, and he thought me beautiful. He asked me to his house . . . but what I'm getting to, he is bonny as I – as I was. I want that he shall not be.'

Guilie nodded. 'But I must have some waste of his body, I cannot work a spell without nails or hair or blood. You must go back, Bess. You dare not face him bold but you could sneak into his lodgings.'

'With servants about thick as rats? And even if I could, I'm not like to find such waste.'

'I wonder,' Guilie said, 'who pulls his teeth?'

'I'd vow he has them all.'

'Few men of twenty have all their teeth. No matter, we'll find a way. But where should I pain him? Heart, head, belly . . .?'

Bess looked up at the fire-blackened ceiling. Through the

open lattice they could hear the clatter of horsemen and bells for early Mass.

'He is handsomer even than Hugh,' Bess said. 'He is vain of it.'

'So?'

'I want that no woman shall ever love him again. I'd take from him what he took from me. His manhood.'

They looked at one another and smiled and were silent.

* * *

Hugh returned at noon, greatly excited. 'Captain Ramsay summoned me, Bess! I'm to be at Boroughmuir before dusk. We march at dawn.'

Bess half-rose from the pallet, then lay back trembling. 'For the love of Christ send word you cannot go! Captain Ramsay' – she thought of the many nights she had lain with him – 'is generous and kind. He will understand that I need care.'

'Nay, I told you – it's like I'd promised the King.'

So the King was determined to march. Now she could hear the jangle-clatter as troops of horsemen galloped by, raising clouds of dust high to her window.

'I'm sad to leave you,' Hugh said, but his face belied his words. Against the plump brown beard his cheeks were flushed, his eyes expectant. She realized what the war meant to him – a chance to prove his strength, the only step towards glory he would ever take. Already he was hovering over his one weapon, testing the blade of his dirk.

'They'll give me a great colin clout to fight with and a two-handed sword as tall as myself...'

'You've forgotten me,' she said.

'I've not forgotten!' Triumphantly he went to the door and lugged in a wooden bucket, dumping its contents on the table. There was spoiled fish – mackerel and ling and herring; onions, turnips and oat flour. 'There's enough ale in the keg for a week,' he said. 'Guilie can make your bread. You'll not want.'

'What of your own provisions?' she asked. 'Mind you need enough for forty days.'

'I've packed a fardel – it's at the stall. There's not much but we'll find game on the march.'

'Game? In this drouth?' The land would be littered with carcasses of birds and rabbits, the vultures gorged. 'You must take enough. Kill the hog.'

'You wanted to save it for Twelfth Night.'

But there might be no Twelfth Night for either of them. 'Kill it,' she said sharply. 'You can leave a slab for me.'

He stared at the hog which lay roped to a ring in the wall.

'Nay, he's not fat enough.'

'How can I feed him?'

'Guilie will—'

'She has her own concerns. Kill him.'

'Nay!' she said as he eyed his knife, 'not here! Take him to the street, I'll not have blood and screams, 'twould sicken me the more.'

Hugh led the hog out and Bess lay drenched in sweat, listening to the street sounds – the cries of hawkers, 'What do ye lack?', and the hoofbeats of mules and horses raising the hot yellow dust. Here she must lie in the noisy, ugly boundaries of this room, for days, perhaps for weeks. But there was one escape.

Closing her eyes she slipped into daydream. She was in some sweet Border village in a bed sheeted with fresh hop-harlot. New-mown hay carpeted the floor and the willow walls were glossy from scrubbing. A neighbour woman brought her a mug of brook-chilled cider, crusty barley bread, honey and pears. She could smell the rain and the salt of the sea (for the village lay on the west coast) and the dried gilliflowers that powdered her pillow. Then Hugh came in, shaking the rain from his coat, boasting of a new lamb or a great catch from the sea. He was still witless (for who would change her beloved, even in dream?) but he sensed what to do without being told, and their sheep prospered. His judgement was simple but she could lean on it, and he knew how to tell of his love. 'How bonny you are, Bess – you don't look ill at all.'

But she was sneezing, hoarse with the Quacks. Beneath the sheet her breasts thrust full and fair.

Then the neighbour woman left, and Hugh sat down beside her. 'Have you ever kissed another man, Bess?'

'Nay, never.'

For in the dream Bess never had. She went to confession every week with no sins on her soul beyond, perhaps, too much pride. Pride in her home, in her domestic skills and in her beauty. Or she might be cross with her children (there were eight) when they pranked.

'Kiss me, Bess. I love you so . . .'

Hugh lay beside her and gathered her close. She nuzzled the rain in his curls, laughing, teasing to swallow a raindrop. They kissed, lips on chest and breast, thigh and belly. He burrowed in the warm little coves of her throat and shoulders. She kissed his feet which smelled of trampled thyme. Dusk stretched a slow grey paw through the casement. No sounds but rain patting the roof-reeds and drumbeats on the shore, guiding the boats to haven.

The door creaked and the dream ended. Hugh came in and placed a bloody ham on the table. 'I've packed the rest. Are you hungry?'

She felt that she would never be hungry again. 'Just give me sops.'

He dipped bread in ale and brought her a bowl of it. While she ate he removed his tunic and put on a homespun shirt and belted leather doublet. He drew on sturdy leather shoes that reached his ankle.

She watched in despair, wishing that he had armour, but that was only for the rich.

'I saw Tom McGregor just now. He said I might leave with him and his brothers!'

Like marching with the King himself, she thought, so greatly was Hugh honoured. For normal men had scant respect for him. But now, in common danger, they ignored his lame mind and noted the strength of his body. Her compassion for him piled, constricting her throat. He had never been courted, only hooted or humoured. Not for him the lazy hours at the Golden Hawk, sipping bastard and swapping lies. But now in war he had stumbled on salvation. It had sprung from blood and bleakness but it lit his face.

Quietly, she said, 'Come. Kiss me goodbye.'

His lips on hers were warm but the kiss was hurried. She stroked the brown ringlets that fell to the edge of his shirt.

'I'll be back with loot, Bess.'

'Come back,' she said, her eyes flooding tears. 'Only come back. I'd follow you if I could.'

'I saw a mass of women gathered at the Tron, ready to follow us.'

'Few follow their own men,' she said. 'Most are dirty jades.'

'Aye, I saw Catherine the Pig. She goes in style, on a mule, and she has a great hat to shade her.'

'You could take the yaws from looking at her,' she said angrily.

'She is too fat.'

She felt a shiver of fear. 'You'll not take up with any woman? Promise me.'

He promised, but impatiently, as if the vow were of little consequence. He kissed her again. 'I must go. Tom will be waiting.'

'I will pray,' she said, 'every morn, every night.'

He went to the door then paused, frowning, looking about the room as though suddenly lost.

'Bess, I – I—'

She had a vision of Hugh as a child, round-eyed, puzzled, trapped in some adult maze.

'Oh, love!' She tried to stretch her arms towards him. Easing her body to the edge of the pallet she rose slowly, arms limp, afraid to take a deep breath lest the pain slash too fiercely. She crept a few steps and he came to her swiftly, pressing her close and she clung to him through waves of pain and nausea.

'You *do* love me, Hugh?'

'Aye.'

She wondered why, after more than a year of happy marriage she was still unsure of his love. Was there some strangeness in her that mistrusted the most obvious devotion? Or were all women unsure? Men seemed quickly sated by both spiritual and physical love. But women were ever-greedy and if starved built on the frailest foundations. Guilie, now, was a wise woman yet she twisted Robert Lawson's indifference to awe. 'I am a witch and he only a corn merchant. He cannot imagine that I'd be pleased at his courting. That's why he never calls on me save for a remedy . . .' Men did not twist so, they perceived clearly. And they needed love like a cut of pie – often, not constantly. But they wanted the pie safe in the cupboard.

'God keep you, Bess.'

Hugh pulled away and was gone.

Slowly she moved back towards the pallet. On the table she saw the fish, the flour, the vegetables and a pear.

She picked up the pear. It was soft and brown-spotted, unsold at market, unwanted, discarded. She cherished it hard against her cheek, feeling the juice run down. Today Hugh had been alone at the stall, his mind stretched to its limits. He had battled weights and prices and haggling customers. He had probably suffered the ridicule folk dared not display when she was there. She knew his sensitivity and she knew how gallantly he strove to hide his hurts, to be a man. Today, brief as it was, must have been anguish for Hugh. He had probably forgotten most of her instructions and surely had had no thoughts of his own. She must stop the fish deliveries from Leith . . .

But somehow during the rattle and clatter of sale, through fear of failure and mockery and malice, his thoughts had been of her. Thoughts like a slow-flowing river – but thoughts none the less. He remembered that she liked pears and had plucked one from the dust. And that was love.

* * *

The day drew to a close and Guilie came to light the rushes in their wooden holders. She said that thousands of men were massing at Boroughmuir, nobles to be led by the King himself.

'It's an eerie thing to be on the streets, Bess. You see no men save greybeards and bairns. You could not have picked a better time to be ill.'

'Has Flutter marched?'

'Aye. They've given him pipes to play and he'll merry the men with his ballads. He asked me to tell you he thinks of you in love.'

'And I of him,' Bess said.

'The King's not afeard of the Devil,' Guilie said. 'Because he's never met him.'

'Have you, Guilie?'

'Aye.'

'God! You never told me.'

'It's not for chatter.'

'Do I chatter? And do I have a gossip save yourself?'

'Even so, I'd not tell you, save to take your mind off your pain.' Guilie sat down on a barrel, removed her coif and bundled up her hair to cool her neck. 'It happened when I was a lass in Kelso. I was only fifteen, ugly then as I am now – a skinny, snow-haired scarebird. My hair was white as birth. Still, there was less of me then to appal the eye.'

'You have fine hands,' Bess said, 'a good body – if a puckle narrow – and the most pleasing voice I ever heard.'

'I pleased no one. I was shy as a mole and tunnelled inward, seeking lone places because none in the village cared for my company.'

'Surely your parents . . ?'

'They'd wanted a son to work the land and I was frail, fit

only for spinning and brewing. But the priest was kind. He taught me to read and write and said I had a lad's mind. But there was no school, of course, not even for gentry. And I had no friends because I looked so strange. I'd wander the hills alone, pretending . . .'

'I know,' Bess said. 'I still pretend.'

'I was a queen or a princess. I made crowns of primroses, bracelets of violets. I had a cat-tail sceptre. Rocks were my thrones. Once I knighted a young sapling and it bowed in the wind.

'Then on All Hallows Eve I went to the market square where the young folk were fashioning spookie scares and masks. Someone had seen Jack O'Lantern slying through the fields and they dared one another to go to the churchyard and meet him, but none had the courage. So I thought, for once I'll be noticed and admired and I came forward and said, "I'll go! I'm not afeared!"

'They stared at me in silence and I thought them awed by my bravery. I turned, shouting for them to follow, and raced off, clean in the face of the wind, my gown slapping like a sail.

'But, Bess, no one followed. I paused at the stile and listened for footbeats but no one came. I told myself that they were testing my courage so I went on to the churchyard. It was pitch black there and I rammed into gravestones and bruised me. But all the while I was listening, sure that they would come. And I worried that Jack O'Lantern might be in evil mood. It's said he can change moods fast as autumn frosts his hide.

'Now I was frightened, with the dead all around. It seemed they were moving like sea under the grass. Then I heard footsteps. Jack O'Lantern wisps over the ground, so I knew it was not he but the young folk. "I'm here!" I called, relieved and happy.

'But no one answered. The footsteps came closer and I screamed.

'I was seized and flung to the earth – and possessed. He

said not one word and I could not see him but I knew it was the Devil.'

Bess shuddered, crossed herself. 'How did you know? Perchance one of the village lads followed you.'

'Did you ever feel manhood cold as ice? So cold it froze your loins and chilled your belly?'

'No. Not ever.'

'God grant you never will.'

'Did you touch goat's hide or wolf's pelt?'

'Nay, he wore cloth. He'd assumed a man's guise.'

'What did he want of you?'

'Merely sport, I think, for he never spoke. After a while he vanished, and I stumbled home. I told no one but the priest. He bade me pray and said the Devil would never return if I set my thoughts on God – which I did. But from that time there must have been some magic on me, for folk began to call me a witch. They remembered I'd gone to the graveyard when others feared to. They thought my hair unnatural for my age. When a crop failed or a cow sickened I was blamed. They wore amulets against me. For five years the priest defended me, then he died. When the plague came and struck down sixteen people I was stoned out of town.'

Bess reached for her hand. 'So that's why you came here.'

'I walked here, begging my way. For a year I was servant to a surgeon in the Cowgate, learned of healing herbs and medicines. Then we heard of a black witch who was ill of dropsy. The surgeon was frightened and refused to attend her so I went in his place. Poor creature, I could scarce relieve her suffering. With all my skills I was only an apprentice. Week by week she wasted but in hours when the pain diminished she taught me her arts, from love potions to the darkest spells. I learned more of surgery from her than from my master – I can heal a tumor by the touch of a dead hand . . . When she died she left me her house and thirty crowns.'

'I wondered how you came by your house.'

'Rest her soul. It grieved me they burned her corpse on Calton Hill and planted her in unhallowed ground. I set a cross of rowan twigs there . . . Enough, you know the rest. I've prospered. Folk trust me with their secrets and I've not brewed ill.'

'If you do, the Devil might return. We'd best forget John Gordon.'

'Likely he's gone – marched with the King.'

'Then he may be killed, and no sin on us.'

'But if he's not killed,' Guilie said, and the phrase trailed off.

Bess said, 'I love Hugh so much that my hate for John Gordon is weak as watered wine. You know love, Guilie. You love Robert Lawson.'

'Aye, but love feeds on a man's desire and none but the Devil ever desired me. You mind it was so dark he couldn't see me.'

'Nonsense! Of course he could, the Evil Eye sees sharply as God. Think of all the lusty wenches in hell – yet he chose you.'

Guilie laughed. 'That is a friendly thought; only a woman could reason so deviously.'

'Has Master Lawson marched?'

'I passed his house and saw his mule packed. I've been a fool, Bess. He cares nothing for me.'

'I marvel you care for him. He drinks—'

She paused. She herself was so vulnerable to attack. *He has no mind, he cannot care for you with gold or groats nor ever will.*

'Aye, he drinks for some soreness of heart. I wish I could cure it. I've given him mare's milk, and mint plucked by moonlight but still he mizzles himself. I cannot take another payment from him. I tried tansy and bitchblood and honey with toadshead – all I know. Still he drinks. He will lose his trade if he keeps his life.'

'You are wry. At the Cross he put his life in God's hands.'

'God's hands are busy now – busier now than ever before in Scotland. No one knows how many troops are moving –

some say one hundred thousand, some say only half that many. But I can tell you this – the streets are empty of men. You walk along and you feel a spine-chill. A man-child runs out from an alley and a mother clutches him back as though he were precious – he that was slapped or spat on at dawn. It gives you a gash in your stomach to think that this very night all over Scotland men are pouring out of villages like flood-water, leaving no dikes but women and children, and if the English should attack . . .'

'Ifs and buts,' Bess said. 'I marvel that I'm hungry. Would you cook that fish afore it rots?'

'Aye, it's a miracle that you—'

'And a mite of turnip. A big mite, Guilie.'

Guilie lit the fire in the clay hearth and smoke puffed through a hole in the wall. She moved deftly, tidying the table while she heated a cauldron of water. After they ate she took a bucket to the well at the end of the lane, returned with fresh water and washed the trenchers. Then she bathed Bess's face and hands, combed her hair and wrapped a clean rag on the log pillow.

'Now you're eating you'll heal fast, Bess. Likely you can open the stall in a week or two. Then the men will return with loot and you'll prosper as never before.'

'Men!' Bess said. 'Are you daft?'

'You've only to lower your price a bit.'

'I've earned as high as a crown, sometimes with food and wine.' She added, honestly, 'But mostly two to four groats.'

'Could you not take two groats?'

It would be humiliating. 'I don't know. Somehow I can't think on it now.' She twisted her wedding ring. 'It's strange that now Hugh is gone I long to be faithful. It never mattered before but now I feel like a wife, like other wives.' She sighed. 'It's late to start.'

'Think on it later, then,' Guilie said. 'Tomorrow I'll roast the ham and bake your bread. Sleep well.'

But after Guilie left Bess lay awake hearing the bells of St Giles and Holyrood Abbey. Women were at Mass, praying for the men who had left. Far off in the moor-kirks other bells joined in; sad-sounding, she thought, silvery and sad. As she prayed for Hugh she fancied that she swelled the vast tide of prayer that was rising this night from the farthest reaches of Scotland. Women in desolate peel towers, in regal bed-chambers and in hovels like this. Likely Queen Margaret was at her prie-dieu in a chapel hazy with incense and crowded with priests, yet her prayer no different from others:

'God, spare him. Holy Mary, comfort him . . .'

* * *

Soon after midnight rain thrashed the city, drumming against the massive iron gates of West Port, Bristo and the Netherbow; battering the Castle, drowning its gardens and tilting fields. It beat like a sea, snatching the dust from eaves and gables, soaking thatched roofs. Lightning sizzled across Salisbury Crags, the high hump of Arthur's Seat and Calton Hill. At Boroughmuir wind bowed tall oaks, bent saplings, crumpled the pavilions of the nobles and the tents of the officers.

Bess awakened, awed by the force of the rain. The coolness was exquisite but she worried about Hugh on his bed of puddled earth. Worse, he must march at dawn over roads scarcely passable in dry weather. Flooded burns and rivers, boot-deep mud, mildewed clothing, sour grain – and perhaps the terrible, ravenous camp fever. The King, it was said, had vowed to penetrate three feet into English soil and there make his stand. As the crow flew, it was about fifty miles to Northumberland, but the men must take a devious, winding way over steep hills, so the march would be many miles longer.

She remembered Father Duncan's admonition, 'Be prudent in your prayer lest it be answered.' Too many folk had prayed for rain so it came in deluge – and at the wrong time. What should have been a blessing might prove a curse.

The rain pounded her casement all night. In the afternoon Guilie brought fragments of news. The Queen was at

Linlithgow Palace; the King on the march, preceded by pipers, trailed by earls and knights, archbishops and bishops, lairds, gentlemen and the trade guildsmen of Edinburgh bearing their blue banner. The main body of the army travelled towards Coldstream, magnificently equipped. The guns had been sent out in three units and five cannon were already at the Border near Norham Castle. Altogether there were seventeen big guns, each with twenty workmen to service it, drawn by four hundred oxen. Oxen also pulled tons of food – beef, mutton, salt fish, cheese; sixteen hundred hogsheads of beer – nearly eighty-seven thousand gallons, besides ale and wine. Horses carried small firearms such as dags and hackbuts, drew powder carts and baskets of yew-bows in waterproof cases.

'From what the old men say there's never been an army like it,' Guilie said. 'You'll need no mourning ring, dove.'

'I'd not buy one if I did.'

'Hawkers are already selling them, of jet and purple stones, and fine ladies are buying them lest they be caught lacking. Jean MacKenzie says the Countess of Bothwell bought one not an hour ago.'

'So! I guessed she was a cold bitch.'

'She's not the only one. The chandlers do a lively trade in black candles, the drapers in woe-weeds . . .'

'Some women doom their men in thought. It's not every shebawd sidles the streets.'

'You're healing. You've the strength for anger.'

Her days passed much alike. Guilie came and went, the rain stopped and resumed. Then Father Duncan visited, bringing apples from Holyrood Orchard. Bess had not had a fresh apple since she left Kirkcudbright and she ate it with delight.

He said, 'I'd have come sooner save for a flurry of confessions. It seems every woman in Edinburgh is searching her heart now that her man is gone. Regrets, remorse . . .' He chuckled. 'One goodwife even repented burnt tartlets and lazy-made suckets. I told her that careless cookery was a very minor sin, but I warrant when her husband returns she'll set a better table.'

'I wish I had such small sins to repent.'

He drew his barrel-seat closer to her pallet. 'You've never confessed to me.'

'But I've told you why – I'd not mock God, nor you. I knew I'd floss right out and sin again.'

'But now?'

She hesitated.

'I think you've no love for that life. What led you to it?'

She sighed. 'It's a long story, Father.'

'I'd be glad to listen.'

The room greyed with twilight. Father Duncan leaned forward, his hands caressing a crucifix. He had the awkwardness of a farm lad despite the dark dignity of his robe. Under his full sleeves she imagined sharp elbows and bony wrists. His face was bony too, narrow and sunburned from throat to sandy hair. A young face, she thought, but with wise grey eyes that held a touch of sadness.

She said, 'I scarce know where to begin. I was born in Kirkcudbright...'

She told him of the Border village on the south coast. Less than a hundred folk lived there, fishermen and sheep farmers. 'It's beautiful – the boats float like gulls on the sea and there's surely no bluer sky in heaven. Even the bracken is shiny and brown as a maid's hair and the dew has a perfume to it. You should see the lambs in April, so sweet, so silly! You should see—'

'Is this a confession,' he smiled, 'or a love song?'

'Both,' she said.

* * *

She was born in a turf cottage that faced the sea. It was sheltered on three sides by an oak grove and guarded by magpies – always a lucky omen. They nested in the reeds that thatched the roof and their chatter, like women's, was sometimes friendly, sometimes querulous or hotly scolding.

She had thought all magpies were female until her father said nonsense, all birds had mates. He said you had only to loiter at the Black Bull to know that men gossiped as much as women.

Thomas Andersen was of Viking ancestry, big and blond-bearded, often storm-tossed as his own fishing boats but quick to make amends for a hasty temper. Whatever he ventured thrived and he was the wealthiest man in town. Besides his two boats he had a hirsel of sheep, nearly two hundred yowes, two fine tups to service them and a shepherd to tend them. Bess and her young brothers, Thomas and Andrew, wore good wool in winter and damask on summer Sundays. Each had a pair of worsted stockings and leather shoes for occasions such as funerals, weddings and the festival of Twelfth Night and Easter. Bess's mother, Anne, took pride in a spotless cottage. 'If cleanliness is next to godliness,' Thomas said, 'your mother will scrub her way to heaven.'

Anne was tall and fair, a quiet, rigid woman. Even on her knees with her skirts bunched up for scrubbing she seemed straight-spined as a tree. She would spend hours polishing a table until the wood glowed like amber but she never had time to kiss a child goodnight. Objects meant more to her than people, Bess thought. Fish, wool, herbs – all were handled lovingly and skilfully. But human flesh was rarely touched.

Often Bess would try to snuggle against her mother's shoulder or burrow in her lap but was gently pushed away. 'You're no babe. Get to your bed.'

Or to your loom, or your cook-fire, or your dairy . . . At ten, Bess could churn and make cheese; she could card, spin, weave and dye cloth. She brewed vinegar of roses, ground malt for drink, boiled sea water and bottled its salt. Her summer and winter gardens thrived and she learned to cook what Thomas and the boys brought in – fish, gull, quail and moorfowl. On holidays she would bake a kid with a pudding in its belly, dress a capon with prunes and apples, fashion

Yule tarts into the shape of stars. Anne taught her to handle money and keep accounts and she found pleasure in thrift. Ale-brewing was a major expense in most households but she estimated she spent only twenty shillings a year, three half-pence a gallon for two hundred gallons. She learned remedies for common family ills – boiled ravens' eggs or a live spider swallowed in porridge cured the ague, and a lizard skin soothed sunburn. If anyone ate too much and fell ill of the Hickop she could relieve them with green ginger root and a draught of malmsey. From the roots of elecampane she brewed a cure to fasten wagging teeth.

Anne never praised Bess but neither did she scold. A sweetmeat was good, not delicious. Or it lacked, it was never poor. One Yule day after Anne's calm acceptance of what Bess knew to be a superbly roasted goose she ran to her father in tears.

'That goose,' she sobbed, 'I spent months on it, fattened it, cozzened it, spared no tending. Today I killed and plucked it, gilded the bill, stuffed it with pudding and made it as handsome a goose as ever—'

'As ever I ate. What ails you?'

'Mother said nothing!'

'She ate, didn't she?'

'As though it were *any* goose.'

'It's your mother's way. You mind she's English.'

'From only ten miles across the Border!'

Thomas shrugged his huge shoulders. 'English folk clamp their tongues. But when they do speak the truth is in it. She knew it to be the finest goose this side of the King's own table but she could not say so. It's a sort of shyness.'

Or indifference, Bess thought. Anne was remote, tolerant only because she had no strong convictions. That spring, when she sickened of a cough, she did not even struggle to live. In her last hours, with the family at her bedside she asked Father MacDonald, 'Shall I go to heaven?' much as she would ask, 'Will you stay to supper?'

'Aye, dame. You've lived a good life.'

As he spoke of the joys of paradise Anne's face reflected neither joy nor wonder. She would endure heaven, Bess thought, as she had endured earth.

Bess wept for Anne's passing not in deep grief but as one weeps on the threshold of change. At thirteen she sensed that her childhood was over. From now on she would have complete responsibility of their home.

She moved between cottage and fowl yard and dairy as she had done for years. The sequence of the seasons repeated the same events – the April lambing, the sheep clipping in early summer, the breeding in autumn when the ugly, prancing tups were released on the hirsel. As always, Bess pitied the 'cast yowes', the unwanted grandmothers who were butted out of the flock by the younger yowes. She took them off the hill, in bye, and fed them on turnips and petted them. No one clipped them, for their heavy wool was worthless; some fell of the weight and died, and Bess mourned them. When Tam the old shepherd died she threw a handful of wool in his coffin for surely he'd know no peace in heaven without some warmth of his sheep. She buried old collies under the grass of the in-bye, for who knew what dogs felt after death? She hoped that they heard the old yowes' hoofs above them and were comforted in the knowledge that some day, up some green hill of heaven the flock would wander again, full and complete, shepherd and sheep and dogs.

So, with her mother's death there was little outward change, but the rhythms of change beat in her own body. She laughed and wept easily. A fit of giggles would end in tears, tears would provoke laughter and laughter more weeping. Within an hour she could cuff her brothers, hug them, hate them. All in a day she would adore her father, resent him as a muddy-booted nuisance, turn again from contempt to worship. With her gossips, Eleynor and Kate Drummond, she might be heart-sworn at noon and hair pulling by dusk. When folk were most kind she fancied they pitied her, and sensed mockery in compliments. There was no mid-path in her judgement of people. They were saints or rogues, fools or sages. But all of them had one common fault – none understood her, though Thomas came close to it.

Her happiest hours were spent with him after the boys were asleep. She was too old for dolls but she still required stories and Thomas told thrilling ones. One August evening she plumped into his lap and demanded her favourite. 'Tell me about the time you sailed to Iona.'

'Not again, lass?' he asked in mock-horror.

'Please!'

'Well, the voyage was ill-starred from the start, being a Friday. Mist rose, thick and queer-like . . .'

She shivered happily.

'We hit a rock. It cleaved us like a knife slicing mutton . . .'

She dreamed through the moth-filmed taperlight, adventuring with him as she had done so often.

'. . . but I was able to clutch a spar . . .'

She snuggled close, cradling her head on his shoulder, and thanked God for his rescue.

'And I – damn it, Bess, get up!'

She was suddenly sprawled on the floor in the rough hay.

'Get up. Tidy yourself!'

She sat, limp with astonishment. She patted her hair.

'Your skirt!'

She pulled it down. 'But I – what did I—?'

'Get *up*!'

She rose. 'But what did I do?'

He stared down at his big hands. 'It's hot, your clasp was like fire. I'm staled to a nub with that tale, you've heard it a hundred times. Did I escape drowning only to die of boredom?'

She was contrite, and apologized.

'And a lass your age should not climb all over folk, it's not seemly.'

She was hurt and bewildered. He flushed and would not meet her glance. She said, 'May I never sit in your lap again?'

'You're no child to behave so.'

She crept to her room in loneliness and desolation. Her moods grew more variable and by autumn Thomas hovered between anxiety and exasperation. She would sit at the fire mutely, tears spotting her apron.

One night Thomas said, 'I don't ken my own daughter.'

Bess looked up from her sewing. 'What do you mean, Papa?'

'You're becalmed one moment, squally the next. I think it's a strap you need – or a mother.'

She felt a stab of grief – not for Anne but because some words had the power to hurt and exalt. Mother . . . Mass . . . God . . . Love.

'It takes a bitch to handle a pup,' he said. 'I'd best wed again.'

She stared at him, aghast.

'You need a woman's guidance.'

'You mean you need a woman! Is it Moll Pitts?'

'Quiet, saucebox!'

She faced the blue sparks of his eyes and lowered her own.

'Sometimes,' he added more gently, 'you are too harsh with your brothers and sometimes pamper them to jelly. Tom and Andrew are no longer babes – seven and ten years old, not to be muddled and puzzled by your whim. You goad them to mischief, then slap them for the very sins you sowed. This house needs a steady hand.'

'Your hand is—'

'Is not here when it's needed. The sea is not for sleep-heads. I rise at dawn, return at dusk and bed at nine. And what do I find in my few hours here? Screaming, bickering or, at best, sullenness. I chide you and you turn daft and run to the woods—'

'Because you shout at me!'

' – or you dream with wide eyes, deaf to a simple question. A man needs peace and if it's not in his own home he'd best bring it in.'

'You'd not bring in Moll Pitts!'

He glared at her. 'I said quiet! Do you want the lash on your back?'

Bess knew he would never strike her but she assumed timidity. Papa must feel that he was behaving as a proper father should. She was learning that males were pleased by the image of themselves as they wished to be. Thus her helplessness with heavy chares made Tom and Andrew feel strong and mature.

'I must have peace,' Thomas repeated.

'I, too, want peace, Papa.' When he did not silence her she continued. 'But I do not have it. I clean and sweep and spread new rushes. The lads drag in playmates, the dogs dirty the reeds and all the work must be done again. I trust Andrew to turn the spit while I gather the herbs but he plays with the kittens and the meat chars black. If I slap him he yowls as though I'd dirked him – and Tom is as bad! As to mischief, do *I* suggest they play me tricks? I dare not enter my bed without looking for a frog in the sheets or a turtle. And they spy on me when my gossips come and babble every word.'

'Mass, girl! All boys tease and idle and trample. You're making a sea of a stream. Your mother had no brawling.'

'Because they respected her age. But it's not just the boys who plague me.'

'Then what does?'

'I don't – I don't know.'

He groaned. 'Why don't you know? Answer me.'

But she couldn't. Ever since the night he had tumbled her off his lap she had felt bereaved, almost as though he were dead.

He smashed his fist into his hand. 'For God's sake, you have a snug home, warm clothes on your back. You're never a day ill and fair to look upon.'

Folk said she was the prettiest maid in the village. Even in a shadowy room her hair gleamed as though sun smouldered there, trapped in thick braids that fell to her thighs. Her eyes, intensely blue as her father's, dominated an oval face – dreamy, sleepy-lidded eyes fringed with heavy lashes. Boys pleaded to kiss her mouth and vowed she stained it red with berry juice. But she'd kiss none of them, nor ever would. All she wanted from them was admiration.

'What ails me matters little,' she said. 'I'd count it as nothing if I knew you wouldn't wed again.'

He was silent and she said, 'I vow I'll be calm as a nun and raise the boys wisely.' She longed to run to him, to feel the comfort of his arms, but held herself taut on her bench. 'You'd not forsake me for Moll?'

'She's a good woman. She'd be a true mother to you. Eh? You know that, don't you?'

Reluctantly, Bess nodded. Moll would be gentle and forbearing: half of Bess's work would be done swiftly and efficiently. Doubtless Moll would be compassionate, having herself known pain with a husband and brother lost at sea.

Thomas said, 'You'd have hours to yourself for visiting and frivoling. Moll thinks you're tied too much to your work.'

'She'd say anything to sly her way in here. She's after a husband.'

'What woman is not? But it's I who've done the courting. Mark you, it's we who will profit. She brings two boats.'

'So that's the bait,' Bess blurted. 'You don't love her!'

'Blood of Jesus!' Thomas bellowed, 'is my honour questioned by my own daughter? What do you know of love? Get to your bed and give thanks for your blessings.'

Through a flood of tears she saw him rise. He pulled her to her feet. 'We'll not talk of this again. If Moll agrees I'll wed her after Yule.'

Bess turned wordlessly and went to her room. She undressed and slipped into her heatherbed, burying her face in the rough pillow, smelling the sweet herbs of its case. She had taken pride in her housekeeping, in the fresh cleanliness of linens and quilts. But she would no more. Moll would supplant her; she would not be needed.

'What do you know of love?' Thomas had asked.

Love was an ache to be close to him and to care for him.

It had never occurred to her that they would be separated save by death. Her friends looked forward to marriage but she would never leave Thomas. Yet now he had left her as irrevocably as if he had moved miles away.

Outside her casement the November wind whirled dead leaves through the garden and Bess thought of the chill days ahead. There would be no more nights alone with Thomas by the fire. This year, and always, she must share the ingle-nook seat with Moll.

I cannot bear it, she thought – but I must.

* * *

Bess hoped for comfort from her friends but when Kate and Eleynor Drummond came by the next afternoon her news excited them.

'A wedding!' Kate spread her plump hands in rapture and wriggled off the kitchen stool. 'We've not had a wedding in three years! I'll wear my green—'

'And I my crimson,' Eleynor said.

Bess, smoothing linen at the table dropped the sleek-stone with a clatter. 'All you think of is your frippery, not my suffering. How would you feel to have a stepmother?'

Eleynor said, 'Dame Pitts is no dragon. Your papa is right. She will share your work and tend the brats. And likely help you marry.'

'I've told you I'll never marry.'

Kate spoke with the wisdom of fifteen. 'You'll sing another tune when you ripen.'

Eleynor said, 'Why, a year ago I could not bear John to touch my hand – now I thirst for his lips. It's odd how we change.'

'But I am different.'

'You lap the lads' flattery.'

'So I do, as I lap kind words from you. Not that I get them,' Bess added bitterly. 'You give me no comfort now.'

'Pox!' Kate said. 'One would think you mourned a lover, not a father. Do you know what *really* ails you?'

'Jealousy,' Bess said.

'Aye, but you've been tossed for months, ever since your bleeding began. But the whimseys will pass when you're our age.'

They were wiser than she. 'Perhaps,' she sighed.

Bess envied them their placidity. Perhaps it went with plumpness. The sisters never fretted about anything more vital than some silly lad.

Bess finished pressing the linen and sprinkled it with dried lavender and woodruff. The sisters helped fold it and stacked it neatly in the cupboard.

'Where are the brats?' Eleynor asked.

'Andrew's fishing with Papa, Tom is building a stell to keep the sheep from snowdrifts.'

'Brats they are, but growing useful,' Kate said. 'How do they take to the marriage?'

'I doubt if Papa's told them for he hasn't yet asked Moll.'

'Perhaps she will refuse him,' Kate said.

'Refuse *Papa*?' Bess asked incredulously.

'They'll make a pretty pair,' Eleynor said, 'he so fair and she so – ah, Bess, I'm sorry . . . But think of the hours you'll have to yourself when she is here. Mind all the picnics you missed since your mother died, the harvest feasts and hay-rides, because you were bound here with chares?'

But after the girls had left Bess reflected that keeping house for her father had been more rewarding than any village revel. She was not needed outside nor even missed save by a couple of moony lads. Here she had been essential as hearth and taper-light. Thomas was no oaf; he appreciated what she did. He always remarked flowers on the table, plants on the sill, juniper burning in his room which overpowered the fish smell of his clothes. She spent her happiest hours creating new dishes for him and learning new skills. She pounced on peddlers who had travelled widely, asking the latest in men's styles so that Thomas's shirts and doubtlets could be fashioned so; and when the apothecary returned from Dumfries or Annan she pestered him for news of new remedies. Just last week, though the stench sickened her, she burned a rabbit's head for its powder and mixed it with mastic and myrrh so that Thomas's teeth would be white. She loaded him with amulets against sea-storm, plague, scrofula, blindness and witchcraft. He was thirty but if he could survive another five years likely he'd live to old age.

'What do you know of love?' Thomas had asked. My work is the measure of my love, she thought, as she filled a cauldron at the well and hung it on its hook at the fire. These turnips and onions – this mutton – all were tiny offerings. But Moll has more to offer – her body. Few men wed for more nor less.

The kitchen glowed with sunset now, warm rose light blooming on stone walls and ceiling beams. In the fireplace, hooded with clay and wattles, oak logs blazed above iron firedogs. Bess turned the spit, watching the grease from the mutton hiss on to the trough in smoking amber bubbles. She tested it with a dagger and stirred the vegetables. Then she laid the table with four trenchers, and dirks to cut the meat. In the back garden, while the dogs frisked around her, she spaded up the butter pot from the frosted earth and transferred some to a bowl. Replacing the pot she stood for a moment sniffing the autumn. Across the browning hedgerows drifted the smell of burning leaves and a coil of blue smoke spiralled above the meadows. Far off a cow lowed, sheep bells tinkled. Out on the Solway Firth sails moved along the horizon. She strained her eyes for the sight of Thomas's boats and when she saw them murmured a prayer of thanks to St Cuthbert. It was enough, for the moment, that her father was coming home.

* * *

Her brothers burst into the kitchen, separate explosions from the hill and the sea. They looked alike – blond, stocky, with grimy red cheeks. She made them wash at the well and they cursed the waste of time. Before Thomas could mutter grace they were reaching across the table for bread and salt.

They ate for a while in silence. Then Thomas said, 'A fine joint, Bess.' He wiped his beard on his sleeve and teetered back on his stool. 'Eh, lads?'

Andrew shrugged and grinned. 'She cooks good – for a woman.'

'For a woman!' Bess was quickly defiant. 'I'd like to see a man try to cook.'

'Then you'd best go to court,' Andrew mumbled, his mouth full. 'We had it from a Leith sailor we met on the wharf – he says the King's cooks are Frenchmen.'

'Ho,' Bess jeered, 'you'd believe anything.' She cleared the table and brought hot apple pasties. 'What man could do this?'

'Or what other woman?' Thomas asked gallantly. He pinched the crusted fruit and sniffed. 'Cloves?'

'And a pinch of red sage.'

He ate hurriedly. 'Heat me some water, Bess. I want a bath.'

His children stared at him.

'You had a bath in April,' Andrew said, 'when you got bloody from the lambing.'

'So? Tonight I want a bath. And Bess, the new doublet and knitted hose.'

Heartsick, she understood. He would call on Moll and ask her to wed him.

'A bath's like to kill you in this weather,' Tom said.

Bess spoke sharply. 'Our father has a reason. You'll not question it. Andrew, go to the well while I fetch his clothes.' She turned to Tom. 'Did you replace the coin in the pail after you milked?'

'Aye, but why do the fairies never take it?'

'They are properly thrifty, but they like to know it is there should they need it.'

'What do fairies need? What do they buy?'

'How should I know?' Bess asked impatiently. 'But

you've seen milk sour for lack of a bribe. Now get to your chares.'

The boys left, carrying water barrels. Thomas went to his room and emerged in a short strip of homespun. 'Well, Bess – shall I tell the lads before I'm sure of Moll?'

'Use your judgement,' she said coldly, and turned away.

'Come, Bess, you're no child. Moll will be good for this house – but I've a man's need too.'

'Don't talk of it!'

'Faugh, you're no prisshittie. You know how it is with animals—'

'But you are no animal!'

'I am, as we all are, and we'd best enjoy the blessing. But folk tend to sneer at their very foundations, at the very gift of life. You mind what Father MacDonald said in kirk last week? "We sin – we are only human." *Only* human? By Christ, what more can we be?'

'But to be animal—'

'Is part of our humanity, and the part least cruel. I'd sooner see Tabby torment a mouse than a woman torment a woman.'

'Yet we are placed higher than animals.'

'Only as petals top the stem of a flower. The two are indivisible, one needs the other. The bloom sucks the root. Never be shamed by your roots.'

The boys lugged in the water. Bess heated it and filled the iron washtub. Thomas dropped his homespun and squeezed into the bath, legs out, while they rubbed his back with wood ash.

'I'll tell you why I bathe,' he said. 'I go a-wooing tonight.'

'Why bathe for that?' Tom asked.

Thomas thrust out his wet hand and whacked his son playfully. 'I'm not tumbling on the moor. I'm asking Moll Pitts in holy matrimony.'

The boys stared at him in silence. Perhaps, Bess thought, they are hurt as I. But she soon realized that only surprise had stunned them. Bright-eyed they stood by the bath and hurled questions. Did Moll know his intention? Would she come here to live? Would they own her cottage? Did she wear a wig?

'Stop shouting!' Thomas bellowed. He shifted his body and water sloshed on to the floor. 'Wig? It's her own bonny hair . . . she'll live here, and we'll own her cottage and boats.'

The boys discussed her boats – sturdy, well-made. Then Tom asked, 'Suppose she doesn't agree?'

'She will,' Thomas said confidently. 'Not many men would overlook her age – she's twenty-four.' He preened his beard and puffed out his chest in mock-conceit. 'She'll never have a better offer.'

Her brothers shrilled in laughter and Bess turned away, feeling doubly betrayed. She hated their assumption that this situation was acceptable, even pleasurable. Andrew's next remark shook her towards tears.

'Dame Pitts is a fine cook,' he said. 'Last week when we went to chop wood for her she gave us quince pasties—' He rubbed his stomach and licked his lips. 'I could eat a dozen now!'

After my apple pasty . . .

'She promised to restring her husband's bow for us,' Tom added. He glanced at Bess. 'And *she* didn't mind the dogs in the house.'

'There'll be no dogs in this house,' Bess said grimly.

Thomas sent her a long, even stare. 'If Moll will have me, then it's she who orders this house. Set your mind to that. Now fetch me a drying cloth.'

Mutely she obeyed. Thomas slipped into a clean cambric shirt, hose and sandals and his new sheepskin tunic with its wide Sunday belt. Facing the circle of polished metal that hung on the wall he brushed his beard and combed his hair. Then he strode to the door.

'May we wait up to hear what happened?' Tom asked.

'Nay, you'll bed as usual, for I may be late.'

Bess watched him walk down the garden path. Then she turned to her chares, tidying the kitchen slowly, prolonging each task against the time she must be alone. Finally she helped the boys set up their pallets near the fire and ordered them to bed. She would wait up for Thomas.

At twelve o'clock she sat on a bench in the common-room watching the hour glass, stroking Tabby who fluffed beside her. She had never been up so late save at her mother's death-bed and she imagined that midnight had its own smells – must and moles and sleeping plants that expelled a breath unknown to sunlight. And assuredly midnight had its own sounds. Mice scuttered in the walls and Tabby stretched, flopped off the bench and prowled in the rushes. The cottage creaked from the wind in its joints. Bess thought of spookies and felt a prickle of fear up her back.

Rubbing her amulet – a spider trapped in a walnut – she recited a psalm and felt calmer. Surely Thomas would be home soon, for he must rise at four. But time meant nothing to lovers – so folk said.

She rose and paced the oak-beamed room. If Thomas married then she must accept a new life with what grace she could. She clutched at the thought that, however much he denied it, Thomas wanted Moll's property more than her love. Why else had he chosen a comfortable widow rather than a young beauty? Moll was fair enough but she did not compare to others in town. Certainly he was not seeking a housekeeper when he had one in his own home.

She laughed softly. How men deluded themselves – and their daughters. Papa, quite rightly, wanted a larger fleet. She should not be jealous of a woman he used as a convenience.

She heard the thump of feet outside. As she opened the door wind whipped her skirts and flung her hair.

'Bess! You should be abed.'

'But I had to know if she—'

She knew from his face that Moll was his.

'We'll have the banns read this week.' He went to the fire

and warmed his hands. 'But she wants to wait until late January to give her time to stitch her attire.'

Bess bent her head. 'I wish you happiness.'

'Come, lass, once you know Moll better you'll like her well. She wants you to visit her tomorrow, for she says she'll need your advice. It's not too soon to think on the feast and the revels.'

She'll not need my advice, Bess thought. But it is clever of her to say so.

Thomas stretched out on the hearth rushes. 'I'm not wedding as a lad would, with the dust of dreams on my eyes. I know no woman is perfect.' In the firelight his eyes twinkled blue. 'It's said that a good woman is like an eel put in a bag among five hundred snakes, and if a man should have the luck to grope out that one eel from all the snakes, yet at best he has a wet eel by the tail.'

Bess smiled. Surely a man in love did not talk so of his intended wife. 'What of the wet eel's cottage? Will she sell it?'

'We discussed that. It will be your dowry when you wed.' As she started to speak he said, 'Peace, you're too young to know your mind. Moll says girls change moods overnight – of course you will marry.'

She wants me off her hands and out of this house . . . The thought that had sustained Bess vanished; for even though Thomas might not love Moll, Moll's love for him could tear all other ties. She had lost her father as truly as though he lay under the pear tree, cold by her mother's side.

* * *

The next morning Bess went to visit Moll. The day was wind-wild and black smudges of clouds scudded across a slate sky. From the sea came the penetrating, bone-curdling cold that no clothes, however warm, could repel. Clutching her cloak tight about her, Bess scuttled along the High Street past dumpy, whitewashed houses towards the hoar-frost of the fields. She climbed three stiles, cursing the briars that clawed her skirts. Dead bracken tangled underfoot and a rabbit fled her footsteps. There was the smell of leaf mould and sea salt and, as she approached Moll's cottage, of baking oat bannocks.

Bess frowned. *She* had baked bread three hours ago. Perhaps Moll was a slug-abed.

Moll welcomed her with a kiss, removed her cloak and led her into the common-room. 'Come to the fire. I'll bring a potion to warm you.'

While Moll was gone Bess looked about the room. This was her dowry, hated as such, but admired. Fresh evergreens strewed the floor and the hearthstone was clean as her own. There were odd and lovely objects, for Colin Pitts had journeyed afar on galleys and brought back treasures: a chair with arms, the only one in town, a teakwood casket, a brocaded lute. There was a sea-chest covered by a painted cloth embroidered with fire-eating dragons. And the grey cat that rolled in the greens was assuredly foreign, sleek as a seal, and tailless.

Moll returned with mugs of mulled ale, warm bannocks and a spicy apple spread. Bess tasted and thought, She is as good a baker as I, and her preserve is better than mine.

Moll drew her stool close to Bess's. 'I hope you favour this marriage.'

Bess spoke stiffly. 'My father's wish is mine.'

Moll was silent and Bess studied her. She was not pretty but her face was arresting. The cheek bones were high and finely moulded and her skin was moist and cream-toned. Below a broad forehead her brows were glossy brown arcs, and her mouth was full and smile-ready. A blue cap hid her hair but Bess remembered it as unusually beautiful, brown with reddish sparkles. Her figure was strong and broad-hipped but her hands and feet were dainty.

'I wouldn't wish you less dutiful,' Moll said finally, 'but I do wish you would speak your mind. Chained thoughts brew mischief.'

'I think only of my father's happiness,' Bess said coldly.

Moll's voice caressed her. 'That I believe. I've never known a daughter so devoted. But I hope to share in that devotion.'

Bess inclined her head.

'I've always wanted a lass of my own to – to—' The lovely hands stretched towards Bess, shyly retreated as they were ignored. Softly she asked, 'Am I so hateful?'

'Nay, Dame,' Bess said, chillingly polite.

Moll sighed. 'I have tried to put myself in your place. Perhaps I, too, would be resentful. But if you truly want your father's happiness you must not merely tolerate me.'

She rose and stood behind Bess, her hands on the rigid shoulders. 'I've no wish to take your father's love from you, nor could I – it's rooted deep. And you should not fret on his love for me, for it has a different quality. There is room for both.'

'Aye.'

Moll's hands fell to her sides and she moved back to her stool.

Wind tugged the shutters. It mourns through the hills, Bess thought, like funeral lutes . . .

Moll battled the encroaching silence. 'I hear Catherine MacIntosh is with child – her ninth.'

Bess said nothing.

'Due in May.' Moll refilled Bess's mug and handed it to her. 'A pity she must forego meat during Lent, and she so frail.'

Bess murmured agreement.

'Did you know that Sir John's ward has arrived from Edinburgh?'

Despite her resolution to remain formidably cool, Bess leaned forward. Few strangers came to Kircudbrightshire, and this was an event much discussed. 'Is he at the castle? Had anyone seen him?'

Moll smiled. 'Aye, he's been at the castle since yesterday. Dame Preston saw him on the road. She says he's a tall, bonny lad of about sixteen with yellow hair '

Wise in the ways of the local gentry, Bess asked. 'Do you think he's really the laird's ward, or his bastard?'

'His ward. You mind Dame Preston has a tongue like an adder but she said the lad does not resemble any of the Dunbars.'

'Shall he come to kirk Sunday?'

'Threave has its own chapel. Why should he ride so far?'

How romantic, Bess thought – to be Sir John's ward, to live at Castle Threave and learn from books and perhaps go to France to study. Boys had all the luck; no one ever heard of a girl so privileged.

Moll said, 'I hear you have the lads a-dream. Do you fancy any?'

'Nay, I shall never wed.' She faced Moll defiantly. '*Never*.'

If she knows she'll not be rid of me she may think twice about marriage . . .

But Moll seemed unperturbed. 'Once I felt as you do. I waited until seventeen, determined on my freedom. But sometimes love strikes swift as lightning, as it did when I met Colin Pitts.'

'If you loved him so,' Bess said, 'how can you love my father now?'

In the firelight Moll's turned cheek was softly rounded as a child's. 'There is no limit to one's loves, Bess.'

'But the church says—'

'The church blesses second bloomings.'

'And third? Suppose my father died, would you take another husband?'

Moll lifted her chin. 'I'll not lie to you. Who knows what I might do?'

Bess wriggled uncomfortably, torn between disapproval and admiration. Moll and Papa were alike, their minds were suited.

Longing to leave, she said, 'Papa said you wished to discuss bridal plans.'

'Time enough for that. Today I wanted to probe your

feelings. If I cannot be a mother to you, will you think of me as a true friend? Will it be so difficult?'

It will be impossible . . . But Bess forced a smile and as Moll brought her cloak, turned obediently to be kissed. There was no middle course. She must accept the situation or run away.

Walking the wind-grey miles to her house she pondered how she might prevent the marriage, but her thoughts went in circles, tiredly, hopelessly. And she could not run away. Even if some haven existed, she could not leave her father.

A curlew cried in the wood and a flock of crows beat up from a turnip stack. Her depression deepened to a point beyond tears. I am dead, she thought, but without the peace of death.

* * *

Yule passed into Twelfth Night. The people of Kirkcudbright knelt in prayer, stumbled in ale-fever, danced and feasted and returned to sober living. Icy rain thrashed the village and filled the brown pockets of the hills. The storms of January kept boats in harbour; folk mended nets and stitched sails in huts shuttered against the cold. Rushes mildewed and sheepskins steamed by the fires. Only shepherds ventured out, groping through mists that swept from the Irish Sea, seeking the summits for grass and bringing back yowes whose stiff-frozen fleeces thawed, dripping, on hearthstones.

On January 28th, with the omen of sunlight, Thomas and Moll were married. For Bess the ceremony and day-long fête culminated weeks of heart-stabbing duties. She helped to embroider the yards of Moll's blue damask gown; baked the nuptial sweetmeats, decorated the bridal chamber with spruce and holy images. As she fitted the Marriage Wreath on Moll's dark hair her fingers trembled so that the garland split and holly berries rattled to the floor. Trapped in the draughty stone of St Cuthbert's Kirk she stood corpse-cold as Moll made her vows:

'I do promise to love and honour . . . to be bonny and buxom at bed and at board . . . if Holy Kirk will so ordeign . . .'

To Bess, the revels at home seemed interminable. At midnight when the last guest had lurched through the door she went into the garden and looked up at the scattered sheen of stars. Work awaited her inside and she longed to tire herself to sleep. But she could not disturb the newly-weds with clean-up clatter. Their candles still glowed through the casement.

Memories of the day trooped relentlessly. Thomas's face as he placed the shiny new ring on Moll's finger, her radiant lifted eyes and the ardour of their kiss. ('A wanton shame,' old Mistress Pym had whispered.) Thomas was no play-actor. Assuredly he had not contrived passion when he caught Moll by the hips as she served him bridal cake and carried her off to their room, muffling her mouth with his so that she could not even bid the guests, 'Stay late and make merry.'

Papa will give me warmth, Bess thought, but only as a log drops a cinder. In Moll's care the boys will not need me. Kate and Eleynor will marry and fence their affection round husbands and children. I shall be for ever alone.

Wind soughed through the bracken and bent prickly-sloe thickets. Clouds obscured the stars. Bess turned and looked back at Thomas's casement. The candles were snuffed.

She crept up the path and entered the cottage on tiptoe, passing the closed door, the dying fire, the platter-strewn tables. Tabby mewed and rubbed against her. She picked her up and held her close, but Tabby squirmed from her grasp and plopped into the cedar, shaking herself free.

* * *

As the weeks passed Bess found that Moll was generous, asking advice but rarely giving it, behaving as though they were equals. She was tactful. Rather than say, 'It's time to plant,' she would ask, 'What do you fancy to plant next week?' and left the garden in Bess's grateful hands.

The garden was escape and creation and here at least she was needed. She mothered it, fighting weeds, bribing the fairies' goodwill with gifts of sweetmeats tucked in the sod. On March 1st by gusty moonlight she sowed flax and hemp, planted beds of hyssop, sage, thyme and rosemary. She asked the Virgin's blessing on peonies and cowslips, pinks and patience, for flowers must always bloom beneath her image in Bess's room.

In the house she felt stifled. Her jealousy thrust deep when Thomas praised Moll's cooking or peacocked in clothes she had made. More painful were intercepted glances, an embrace glimpsed through a half-opened door, soft secret laughter in the night. She came to feel that she, not Moll, was the intruder.

One morning in mid-April Bess was clearing the breakfast trenchers when Moll left her loom, ran outside and was violently sick in the grass. Bess rushed after her.

'What ails you?'

Moll straightened and leaned against a tree.

'Was it the strawberries?' Bess asked.

'Nay, lass.' Moll took deep breaths. 'I'm with child.'

Bess gasped. She had never imagined that Moll might bear children but now she realized what it would mean, Moll and Thomas and the baby would form a new, impervious closeness.

Moll's voice was hushed with awe. 'To have a child! Ah, Bess, I've prayed—'

Bess ran across the garden into the bluebelled meadows. She heard Moll call out but she ran on until her breath failed and then she sank on to a sponge of heather. She had no plan beyond flight. Rising, she stumbled on into the gloom of Black Morrow Wood where oaks shut out the sun. Her face pressed in dew-wet moss, she wept until her throat ached. Then, exhausted, she stretched out on her side, head pillowed in her arms. For a while she stared at the lacy young ferns that hedged her like an infant forest. Then her eyelids grew heavy and she dozed.

She awoke with a start as a hawk zoomed down through the oaks and dived on a hare. There was a heavy stir in the thicket and she sat up fearfully. Wolves prowled here, and bears. Frantically, she considered running but Papa had warned to be still as a statue lest an animal scent one's terror.

A young man crashed through the brush dragging a game bag and Bess slumped with relief. He bent and bagged the hare. From a bright string he swung the carcass of a small bird, luring the red-taloned hawk to his wrist. As he replaced a jess on its leg he turned and saw Bess.

'Jesu!' Then he smiled. 'Good day.'

'Good day.' Though he was a stranger she was not frightened for he had the look of a gentleman, tall and lithe in a green damask jerkin and darker green hose. Sun piercing the thick foliage glinted on straight fair hair and sparkled the silver chain at his throat. Beardless, he looked about sixteen.

Suddenly she guessed his identity. 'Are you not the laird's ward?'

'Aye, mistress.' He hooded the hawk. 'How did you know?'

'Because,' she blurted, 'folk have talked of little else since we heard of your coming.'

He looked amused and she blushed. 'New folk rarely come to the shire, and your doing so seemed—'

'Unusual?'

'Aye, and romantic too.'

Pox, she thought, I am prattling as if he were just another lad. Suddenly she was aware of her wretched appearance – tear-puffed eyes and undone coif strings. Her pink gown was old and faded from many washings, her apron patched.

'Romantic? Why?'

'To live in a castle.'

He laughed. 'I'd find a pudge more romantic – and warmer. Where do you live?'

'In Kirkcudbright.'

'I've been there but never seen you. You were not at the frolic Shrove Tuesday nor Egg Saturday.'

'Nay, sir – sire,' she corrected, unsure how to address a knight's ward. She knew his name – Giles Thorn – but to call him Master Thorn seemed overly familiar. 'I rarely frolic.'

'Why not?'

Because I have no heart for them, she thought. But she said, 'My duties keep me much at home.'

He seemed flatteringly interested and led her to talk of Thomas and the boys. She spoke of the new marriage but she did not confide her misery. Instead she stressed her housewifely skills, anxious to impress him without seeming immodest. She concluded on an intellectual note: 'Father Macdonald has taught me to write my name.'

'Indeed? And what is it?'

'Bess Andersen, sire.'

'Likely you'll be changing it soon.'

To her surprise she said airily, 'I have my pick of lads.'

'Are you handfasted?'

'Nay, there's none I like well enough.'

His grey eyes, long and lazy-lidded, were speculative. He stroked the hawk that clung to his leather-bound wrist and whistled a soundless little tune. She fidgeted under his glance.

'You've said nothing of yourself, sire. Do you read from books and study the stars?'

'When Sir John forces me. But it's sport I love. I train his goshawks and order his falconers.'

'And do you live in painted chambers with gold cloth on the floor?'

'Christ, no! Have you never been in Threave?'

'Who would let me past the gates?'

'I would. You shall see Threave in all its elegance – smoking, stinking, dilapidated, crumbling. I warrant you live in more comfort than we.'

'You would really invite me there?'

'Any time you wish.'

What a marvel to tell Kate and Eleynor and Papa!

No, she thought, Papa would not care. He would listen, but he would not care.

'What frets you?' Giles asked. 'Have I burst an illusion about Threave?'

'Nay, I was thinking I must get home.' She rose and brushed grass from her skirts.

He rose too. 'You've no blossom basket, no trowel. What were you doing here?'

'Nothing. Sometimes I just walk.'

'And weep?' His voice was gentle. 'I think you are lonely. Is your father's bride the nub of it, Bess?'

He spoke with the grave concern of an old friend and she told him, haltingly, of her love for her father and her loss of him. '. . . today I learned she's with child. It will bind him even closer and I will matter even less.'

She sensed his warm sympathy. 'But some day you, too, will bind yourself in love and forsake your father.'

She shook her head.

'We change. When you were a bairn could you imagine that you'd ever put aside your playthings?'

'No, sire.' She thought of a beloved doll deserted in the rag chest.

'But you did, and without a pang.'

'Aye.'

He smiled and went to her and took her hand. 'Come, my horse is tethered in the clearing. I'll see you home.'

Astonished by such an honour, she followed him a few yards into the wood. Mounted before him, bending to avoid low-hanging branches, she had a swift surge of happiness. As they trotted out of the forest into the meadows she said, 'I've no words to thank you.'

'For what?'

For being tender as Papa used to be . . . 'For heeding my troubles, sire.'

'You shall call me Giles. We're friends, are we not?' He took one hand from the reins and turning up her face, kissed her cheek. She rested her head against his shoulder feeling cherished and safe. It was like leaning against Papa save that the shoulder was harder, thinner. He smelled of horse and wood-scent.

As they rode into the field behind the cottage the dogs set up a clamour and Moll hurried out. She ran to Bess as Giles lifted her from the saddle.

'Lass, I've been nearly frantic!' She clutched Bess close. 'Where have you been?'

'With Master Thorn.' Bess disengaged herself and performed introductions.

Moll's face was a puzzle of awe and amazement. 'So you are Master Thorn? You honour us. But where did you meet Bess?'

'She was walking in the forest. I was hunting.'

Moll glanced at Bess, a long, slow scrutiny of face and gown. Then she smiled. 'It's nearly noon. Will you dine with us, Master Thorn? Bess boiled a fine turbot this morning and I warrant even you have never tasted a berrydough pert as hers.'

Bess stared at Moll. It was she who had boiled and baked.

'She's a fine cook,' Moll said.

Giles regretted that he must dine at the castle. 'May I come again?'

'It will be our pleasure,' Moll said.

'It would be my pleasure to take Mistress Bess a-Maying.'

Bess was exultant. May Eve was the gayest frolic of all the year, gayer even than New Year's, for one had no duties, no penances. She had not been a-Maying since childhood – had not even cared to go – but now she could scarcely wait the two weeks.

Moll hesitated. 'I must ask her father.'

Bess flared. 'Why? Papa let me go when I was six!'

'But now,' Moll said dryly, 'you are fourteen.'

Giles broke in. 'Mistress Bess misunderstands your wisdom

but I admire it. Rest assured she'll be safe with me. I'd allow no mischief.'

Moll's voice wavered. 'Perhaps. But I must ask her father.'

Bess burst out furiously. 'I'm no child!'

'But your father must decide,' Giles said. 'I'll return to ask his permission.'

He bowed, swung on his horse and was gone.

Bess said. 'Do you think me stupid or do you insult me? Babes are brewed on May Eve, but only by jades!'

'Last year nineteen maids went to the woods and three returned with child-seed. None, I think, were jades but magicked by springtime – as you could be.'

'You may not trust me, but Giles is a gentleman.'

Moll chuckled. 'Gentlemen are neither passionless nor impotent. Our King is the prime example. You'd best not pursue that point if you wish to persuade your father.'

Bess sulked, then considered. Moll might be helpful – had she not kindly lied about the turbot and berrydough? 'How can I best persuade him?'

'By not persuading at all. If he thinks you too eager he will wonder what fire kindled you in the woods. As I do.'

'As God's my witness, no fire at all! Only the spark of friendship.'

'But why does Master Thorn seek a friend of your station?'

Bess had no answer. Yet she knew he was truly her friend and in the security of that knowledge she was invulnerable. Moll could snipe but she could not spoil. New and swift the friendship might be, but it was not flip nor fragile and it would not bend to cynicism.

'Mark you,' Moll said, 'I like him – he would draw any lass. I hope to God that he proves himself. If he does I'll do all in my power to help you snare him.'

'Snare him! Holy Mary, none of you believe me, you pin me to your own patterns. Snare him? I want no husband!'

She flounced into the house and shut herself in her room.

No one understood her; not even Giles perceived that she was unlike other girls. But there must be others who shuddered at thought of marriage. Nuns, perhaps. Doubtless many entered convents as much to escape passion as to render spiritual service. The world pushed one to conformity but she would not betray her own nature.

Recreating the morning, she remembered Giles's words. '*Could you imagine you'd ever put aside your playthings?*'

She bent to the rag chest. From under a pile of tattered homespun she brought out the old doll. It was loose-limbed, a battered crumple of sheepskin and hemp. One raisin eye remained and it seemed accusing.

'Grizel.' Bess held the doll close. 'Forgive me . . .'

* * *

Several days passed but Giles did not return. To Bess's relief Moll and Thomas made no comment but Kate and Eleynor slid from peaks of excitement to impatience to dreary certainty that he would never come. Yet each afternoon when they visited her one or the other was never far from the casement.

They could not lure Bess from the cottage lest she miss him. She would not budge for Robin Hay's name-day feast nor Sarah MacLean's confirmation. Each morning she dressed in her next-to-Sunday gown and kirtle of beauti-coloured cambric, a violet fillet on her loose-flowing hair. Each day she wore shoes and stockings. At her waist the Book of Hours dangled on her prettiest girdle cord and it bolstered her faith.

But as the days passed her faith wavered. Most of the girls in the village were spoken for May Eve and some had stitched new finery. Kate and Eleynor were going with John Sinclair and each had a new and becoming ruffled coif. Bess listened to their prattle and tried hard to join in it. Aye, it was against custom for Jane Bliss to go – only the young should celebrate springtime, and she was twenty. True, no maid should dream of going alone . . .

Thomas was unusually attentive to Bess and his new concern hurt her as much as Giles's absence, for she suspected Moll urged it. She could imagine Moll saying, 'The poor child has been jilted. Be doubly kind.'

One night after supper when the boys were abed Thomas said, 'Moll and I—' He glanced at his wife and cleared his throat. 'It's only four days 'til May. We think you should go with the Drummond girls since – since it seems as though—'

He paused and scowled and Moll sprang to his rescue. 'Likely Master Thorn was called away on the laird's business and unable to return. He will understand if you make other arrangements.' She held up a length of pale green lawn. 'I found this in my box. There's time to make you a gown.'

'Thank you. I should like the gown.' Bess's chin trembled. 'But if Giles doesn't come I'll stay home.'

Thomas started to speak but Moll said, 'As you wish, you need a gown in any case. Thomas, hand me my sew-chest, there's a love . . . Bess, shall the neck be round or square?'

'Square is more the fashion.' A tear rolled down Bess's nose.

'By Christ!' Thomas roared. 'Do you both feed on dreams?'

'Hush!' Moll shook her shears at him. 'If you can't stomach kirtle-talk you'd best go to the inn.'

Grumbling, he subsided. Moll measured Bess and cut the cloth and pinned it about her. The sleeves would be long and full with a tiny cuff, the bodice laced tight to a point.

'I hear that Sir John's falcons come from France,' Moll said. 'Perhaps Master Thorn went there to bring a shipment.'

'Perhaps,' Bess said. She knows full well he's forgotten me but she seeks to spare me hurt, she even bullies Papa for my sake.

Moll said, 'If we take great care we can piece enough fabric for a coif and frill and we'll vein the bodice with white.'

Impulsively, Bess bent and kissed her cheek. Moll looked up, a pin in her mouth. Her eyes held the same soft radiance Bess had seen in church. Shyly she extended her hand and Bess clapsed it tight.

'Well now,' Thomas's voice was over-loud. 'I think I'll see how the bowling goes.' He pulled his cap from a hook. 'The champion from Whithorn – what's that? Hoof-beats?'

He opened the door and went out. Trailing the half-pinned gown, tripping over its length, Bess ran to the casement. In the moonlight she saw Giles dismount. Thomas met him and tethered his horse to the yew. Moll, pressing behind her said, 'Quick, tidy yourself.'

Bess plucked off the fabric, ran to her room, combed her hair and bit her lips for colour. Then she stood at the door willing herself to calmness. She must try to seem casual, he must not guess how she had longed for his visit. She would say, 'Why, a good eve to you, sir,' simulating surprise. Or, 'How good of you to come.' No, that would sound false. Thomas had taught her to scorn common folk who put on gentry airs.

I shall say nothing. I shall curtsy and smile.

But when she opened the door to the common-room Moll was alone at the casement.

'Where are they?' Bess asked, alarmed.

'Still by the tree.'

Bess peered anxiously but their backs were turned. 'If only we could see their faces! Do you think Papa is forbidding him to come in?'

'If so, you must trust his judgement.'

'If he won't let me go a-Maying I'll never forgive him!'

'Look you, lass, May Eve is not the sum of life. Perhaps next year . . .'

But a year could bring havoc – the sweating sickness, the plague, the pox. Giles might journey afar or marry and, like Papa, desert her.

'Thomas is right in protecting you.'

'From what?' Bess asked. 'I've told you a dozen times I'm not in love!'

'Love is clothed in many guises. It may even seem hate, yet hate has bedded countless pairs. And sometimes love masks as friendship.'

'But I swear to you—' Bess paused in despair. Giles was mounting his horse. Papa was coming up the path.

'I beg you,' Moll said, 'trust your father.'

I hate my father. Not content with depriving me of his love he denies me Giles's comfort. Trust him? Aye, if I were in bodily danger he'd risk his life to pull me from sea or swamp but he'd not lift my heart to keep it from breaking . . .

Thomas came in. 'Master Thorn was here. He said he'd been on a hunt clear to Liddesdale and just returned. They brought in enough game to—'

'Papa! Did he ask me a-Maying?'

'Aye. I spoke out plain and probed his mind. He says he's lorn at the castle with few young friends, and that I believe. For a schooled man he speaks an honest tongue.'

'So—'

'You may go a-Maying.'

'Papa!'

'But not for the night. He will be here after supper and bring you back by midnight.'

Bess argued through her delight. 'But everyone stays till dawn, even the tiniest bairns curl up and sleep in the leaves—'

'You'll sleep on your bed 'till you're wed.'

Moll said, 'A lass who leaves a revel early whets interest. He will miss you and thus his – friendship – will deepen.'

'He'll court you properly,' Thomas said, 'or not at all.'

'Court!' Her happiness was drowned in a tide of loneliness. 'Do you want me to wed and leave you?'

'Of course,' he said heartily, 'when the right lad appears. What man but longs for grandchildren on his knee?'

In the years since her mother's death she had held two deep, unshakable convictions: The Virgin protected her.

Thomas needed her. His love had seemed eternal as the sea itself, moody at times, but always strong beneath the currents of stress.

Yet all the time I deluded myself. I was only a convenience. Now that he has Moll he would shunt me to the first man who came along. Even a poor one would suffice for he contrived Moll's cottage for my dowry, to be rid of me the sooner.

'What is a "right lad"?' she asked bitterly.

'Why, one who'd not laze or loiter or beat you. But why cook the mutton before the lamb is dropped? We've a year or more to measure the lads.'

Moll glanced at Bess and spoke hurriedly. 'Thomas, if you're going to the Green—'

'Nay, I'll not.' He yawned and replaced his cap on the hook. 'What's about, Bess? A bit of cold fowl?'

How often she had sprinted to forage a late supper, how lovingly she had served it with a flower tucked next the trencher or a young lettuce opened to cradle the meat. But tonight she went to the kitchen and heaped cold gull on a plate without a touch of garnish. The boys stirred on their pallets, sighed in their sleep. She returned to the common room and watched Thomas eat.

'Fine,' he said.

He had noticed nothing different.

* * *

On May Eve the forest was bursting with bloom, the plump, pink-tipped buds still wet from rain. Girls held torches while boys stripped hawthorn boughs to garland village houses, and groping deeper into the woods, raised the flames high to hunt the Maypole. But though dozens of trees were marked it was slyly understood that the tallest and slenderest would not be found until dawn.

Courting couples scattered through the forest while the younger folk ran in rowdy packs. As the moon rose, children cried and were quieted. Brothers and sisters blanketed them on grassy mounds where they slept under drifting petals. Bess easily evaded Tom and Andrew; they were more concerned with hunting a Maypole than with gathering flowers, for whoever found the perfect tree won the honour of driving it by oxcart to the Market Square at sunrise through throngs of cheering people who waited to twine it with streamers.

At the edge of the wood she introduced Giles to Kate and Eleynor but by mutual agreement they did not linger together and took their separate ways into the forest. Each blooming bush seemed lovelier than the last. Soon Bess's basket was heavy with heatherbell, gilliflower and wild pinks. Giles carried it while her torch searched a tangle of dark trees.

'I've never been this deep in the wood,' she said.

'There's finer hawthorn there. Look!' He cut a bough lush with bloom. 'It's fair enough to garland your kirk. And here's more for your doorway.'

She exclaimed as he daggered another spray.

'And for your roof.'

He eased the boughs into a basket.

Faint in the distance she heard singing. 'Giles, we're so far – perhaps we should go back.'

'Come, just a few yards farther.'

She followed him into a clearing, marvelling at the contrast of black tree trunks with emerald grass and the achingly tender yellow-green of saplings. Cobwebs filmed old tree stumps like silver lace and white blossoms showered her hair.

'Look at the moon, Bess – round as a Spanish orange.'

As she looked up he took the torch from her hand and set it down. 'Now you can see it clearer.'

'There's a fat man in it for sure with a mouth like a little O.'

'But the moon's a lady, or so the poets say.' He removed his doublet and placed it on a mossy bank. Bess sat down, fluffing out her skirts.

'Do you know poems?' she asked.

He sat at her feet. 'A few, hard-learned in Latin.'

'I've never heard one.'

'You're hearing one now.'

She glanced at him, puzzled.

'Listen. It's rare in these parts.'

At first she heard nothing. But gradually the wood was full of sighs, of leaf-shift and wing-flutter and vague, mysterious movement. And then she heard what he had heard – a nightingale in tremulous trill, a golden-coloured sound that gathered the spring to its heart and soared to shimmering peaks. She sat with tight-clasped hands, fearful of breathing lest it stop. She thought, I shall never forget this moment of music and slow-dropping blossoms, the smell of crushed violets, wild strawberries and wet earth.

In the faint torchlight she could discern the shadowed planes of Giles's face but not the face itself. His shoulders were a dark bulk against the soft, surrounding green.

The song slipped into silence. Plunged swiftly to reality she felt bereft and isolated.

Giles reached for her hand. 'You seem sad.'

She hesitated for fear he would think her stupid. 'Sometimes I feel so near to heaven, as I did just now. And then the world moves between.'

'We can't often hear nightingales.'

'But we should feel closer to heaven.'

'How do you know there's a heaven?'

'I can't tell you. You'd think me daft.'

'No, Bess. Tell me.'

'Well, when Mother died I thought about heaven a great deal but I could not feel it – it was only a happy word. Weeks passed and I ceased to brood on it. One day I was home, in the kitchen pounding oats. Suddenly I felt a wave of such glory as I cannot describe. It was as if all the love in the world beamed on me for a few brief moments. Then it passed.'

'Has it never returned?'

'No. Sometimes alone on the hill or in the woods I try for it but nothing happens.'

'A sort of ecstasy,' he mused. 'I envy you.'

She said, 'I know so little about you. You've never mentioned your parents.'

'There's little to say. I was orphaned at birth. My mother was a cousin to Sir John and he had me raised and schooled in Edinburgh, then sent to him. That's my history.'

'That can't be all!'

'Nearly all. The family who raised me were well paid for their kindness. As a lad, when the goodwife kissed me goodnight I tried to figure the price of it – a penny, a groat? And the monks who taught me were patient though I often ran off to hunt instead of tending my lessons. They could not dismiss me without losing the laird's gold.'

'Surely you were loved for yourself,' she said.

'When payment is involved one is never sure.'

'But now that you're with Sir John—?'

'He brought me here out of duty, as he often remarks.'

'Is he cruel to you?'

Giles chuckled. 'You imagine a drama I can't provide. I scarcely see him save at meals. He orders his estate, sits in Justice Court and travels on the King's business. He leaves me free in the stables and mews, which is all I require. I'm a sort of gentleman Hunt Master paid in food and clothing.'

Her hand tightened on his. 'It sounds a chill sort of life.'

He shrugged. 'I could fare far worse. From the moment I popped the womb folk have been dutiful.'

He released her hand. In the half-dark she saw him slash the earth with his dagger.

Poor Giles, she thought, caged in suspicion.

'What of the future?' she asked. 'Shall you inherit the castle?'

'God, no, it reverts to the Crown, for the laird is merely its steward.'

'But you'll live there for life?'

'Who knows?'

She sensed reproof and was silent. A moth brushed her cheek, then drifted towards the torchlight and she watched its flirtation with death.

'It's best not to probe the future, Bess. A gipsy begged at the castle last night and Sir John let her read his hand. She saw him in a bloody spew on a hill – a battle, she said – and she crossed herself with rowan and ran from the hall before we could question her. And the odd thing is, she'd not even wait for bread and meat but went wailing out as hungry as she'd come.'

Bess shivered. 'I'd never have my fortune told.'

'Yours is plain to foresee. Marriage and children.'

'No,' she said. 'I'll never marry.'

'You can't remain a child for ever.'

'I'm no child!'

'You are until you wish to leave the nest. Would you linger at home, growing dry as a nut while others bloom in wifehood? Is your father the boundary of your hopes?'

'Aye. This is a wee town, Giles. I know every young gawky for miles about and I'd sooner die than wed one of them. No strangers ever come here.'

He leaned towards her, lightly kissed her cheek. 'How small and serious you are, gosling. And how little you know of yourself. Do you know, you make me feel full eighty years old?'

She laughed as he rose and hobbled towards one of the baskets. 'Are you hungry, Bess? I brought a bit to eat and drink.'

She was perversely pleased that the castle cook was inferior to herself. The swan was tough and the cheese sour but the claret was better than most. Pleasantly drowsy, she lay back on his outspread doublet. The trees arched blackly above her, gradually brightening downwards through the torchlight to the wild green of low boughs, the trunks of birches silvering through moss and mayflowers.

Giles sat beside her, pulled off her coif and freed her hair. His hands were big and gentle and she remembered without hurt how Thomas used to stroke her hair like this.

'You will always be my friend?' she asked.

'Always.'

'And you'll not leave me?'

'Not for long.'

'I want to make you happy,' she said, and floundered for the words she sought. She wanted to mend his thinking and heal his bitterness. She thought of the little lad who mistrusted the goodwife's kiss and who still mistrusted . . .

'You do make me happy, Bess.'

'If only I could tell you—'

'Hush,' he said, and took her in his arms and kissed her mouth.

She had not known that a kiss could be more than a meeting of lips. But this was a long, slow plunge into depths where there was neither light nor darkness, only a perfect state of being. He needs me, she thought, he loves me, and I must not fail him.

She had heard the frank talk of women at lying-in gatherings when, with neighbours, she had brought food and gossip to liven a confinement. But the ribald chatter had nothing to do with this. His hands on her body brought no thrill but there was deep delight in his closeness; no desire but an aching need to please him. She would confess to the priest a sin in name only for this was not lust but the very essence of love.

Suddenly she was knifed by pain and her screams tore under his mouth but still he kissed her. Even in torment she would not struggle nor beg release lest she break the bond between them.

Giles kissed her wet eyes and sat up, fastening his clothes. 'Forgive me, gosling. You know I'd not hurt you, except in love.'

She cuddled close, thankful for the ebb of pain. 'Now you must know how much I love you.'

He patted her shoulder and reached for the jug in the basket. 'Drink, it will ease you.'

She shook her head. She wanted to be close in his arms again, and waited patiently while he drank. But when he capped the jug he sat a few feet away, picked up a stick and whittled it with his dagger.

'Giles.' She went to him and put her arms around him. 'You must know how much, how very much . . .' But she had no words for the depth of her love. 'I'd die for you, truly.'

'No need for that.' Again he patted her. 'Now be a good lass and tidy yourself.'

But she clung to him. 'Kiss me.'

He kissed her cheek and resumed his whittling.

'Ah, love, hold me close and kiss me as you did before!'

'Women!' he said good-humouredly. 'You wear a man out and then beg more.'

She drew back, bewildered. 'I'm begging nothing, only to be close.'

But he seemed abstracted. 'A few weeks ago I saw an abandoned well near these woods. Could you find it?'

'Aye, but Giles, what's amiss? Why are you so cold? Do you think me a jade?'

'Nay,' he said impatiently, 'but your father will if he sees blood on you. We must find the well and wash the spots from your skirt.'

'But I'm not ashamed. I'll tell Papa the truth.'

He stared at her increduously. 'You're daft as a blue hare. He might kill you.'

'Not when I explain that we love one another, that we'll marry.'

'Marry?' He tossed away the stick. 'You said you'd never marry.'

'That was before. Now we belong together.'

'But folk don't marry because of a May-tumble.'

Dazedly she said, 'Was it not more than that?'

'You're lovely, Bess, and I'm fond of you. But I promised you nothing but friendship.'

'But after this—' She was almost incoherent with shock. 'We are one person. Surely you feel that?'

'No,' he said gently, 'that's a poet's fable.'

'Then – you do not love me.'

He took her hand. 'I'm sorry, Bess. Believe me, I meant no trickery.'

Tearless, trembling, she moved away from him. In her ignorance she had tricked herself, presuming that they shared an identical depth of emotion, believing that men and women were alike in love. But it seemed they were far apart as life and death.

She caught back the hair that tangled to her hips and picked up her coif. 'Take me home.'

'Come, gosling, don't make me feel like a rogue.'

'It's worse to feel like a fool.'

'But you aren't. Any young maid can be swept by passion.'

'It was not passion.'

'What was it, then?'

But she could not explain what he seemed incapable of feeling. 'No matter. You'd not understand.'

'Don't hate me,' he said.

She stared bleakly at the hawthorn boughs so joyously gathered an hour ago. She had always looked forward to May Day. It was fun to ribbon the Maypole and gild its trunk, to help the girls fashion a huge daisy turban for the top. But this year would have been memorable for she had hoped Giles would escort her to the Green. She had visioned them laughing at the antics of Jack i' the Green frisking on his hobby horse. They would watch the bear-baiting, the wrestling and the archers. Even the May Queen (always some lady from the castle) in her crown of Canterbury bells would not cause such a stir as Bess with Giles at her side. People would whisper how handsome a couple they were, she in her green lawn gown and a coif of yellow violets . . .

But the dream was smashed. She covered her face with her hands.

'Bess, if there should be a child I'd wed you.'

But not for love. Wearily she rose. 'I want to go home.'

They took a circuitous path out of the woods, avoiding others.

At the old ivy-covered well Bess scrubbed her petticoat and replaced it, holding her kirtle and gown above the wet cambric. As they neared home she smoothed her skirts and stuffed her hair under her coif.

'I'll ride by at eight and take you to the Green,' Giles said. 'Better, I'll borrow a little cart and you can drive it. We'll garland the horse and braid the reins with blossoms.'

'I'm no child to be pacified. I'll not see you again.'

He put his arms around her but she pulled away and they walked on in silence. The cottage was candlelit and Thomas called a greeting from the casement, then retreated from view.

Giles placed the flower baskets at the door. 'You worry me. You make me somehow fearful.'

'Don't fret,' she said. 'I'll not tell Papa.'

'That's not what I meant.' He studied her face. 'You look ill. And – strange.'

'Good-bye.'

'You can't mean that. I'll wonder how you fare and what you're feeling. I'd want to share any burdens.'

'You can't.'

The wind mourned through the trees, listed and littered the new green leaves. She turned and went into the house. My burden is love, she thought, but no one wants it.

* * *

Bess told Moll and Thomas that May Eve had proved disappointing, for Giles was humourless and dull; she would not see him again. After their initial surprise the explanation seemed to satisfy them and though the boys teased her about rejecting the last suitor she'd ever have, she was too apathetic to retort and they soon lost interest in baiting her.

During the next two weeks she missed Giles desperately

and was tempted to see him on any basis but her pride overcame her loneliness. Had she lived alone she could have relaxed in tears and even found comfort in indulging her misery, whereas the effort of appearing cheerful was a constant strain, a never-ending struggle from dawn until bed time.

The need for privacy became obsessive. Finally she asked Thomas if she might move to her dowry-cottage.

'Why?'

'I'd like my own home to tend. I miss the responsibility I had.'

'Tell the truth,' he said sharply. 'You're jealous of Moll and you can't abide her authority – she who's so good to you. You should be ashamed''

She tried to protest but he shouted her down. 'What would folk think if you moved away? That Moll was harsh, that you fled cruelty. I'll not have you stir malice against her. You'll stay here until you wed – should any man want a selfish, ill-tempered ingrate.'

'Papa—'

'Of late you've grown so sullen that you're losing your looks. Your mouth hangs down as long as your hair.'

'Can I help how I look?'

'Aye, by taking interest in someone besides yourself. Did you visit Dame MacIntosh when she was delivered still-born? You did not. Would you go with Moll to her cousin's frolic? No, you sulked at home. You'd not even join the May Day revel – it was Moll who wreathed the house . . .'

To soften his wrath and avoid further scenes Bess dragged herself to occasional frolics, always repelling the clumsy advances of the boys who brought her home. One June afternoon she visited Kate and Eleynor who asked hopefully is she had changed her opinion of Giles.

'No.'

'It's not for the likes of you to find him dull,' Eleynor said. 'You'll never do better – that is, if he'd marry below him.'

I would marry you if there were a child.

'What's amiss, Bess? I didn't mean to offend you, but none of us are gently born.'

Bess managed some reply but her thoughts were in sudden turmoil. She had heard women discuss pregnancy but, disinterested, had scarcely listened. Now she was eager for knowledge. To have a child would be her salvation, and his. For though he married her in duty he seemed sincerely affectionate. And in time he would learn to love her.

She sought for a way to broach the subject of pregnancy. Taking a devious course she asked what had caused Dame MacIntosh's still birth and gradually led up to her question.

'I wonder how she knew she was with child.'

The sisters exchanged superior smiles. 'What a goose you are!' Kate said. 'She was sick to her stomach.'

'Oh – like Moll,' Bess said, disappointed.

'And she began to swell.'

'Is that all that happens?'

'Well, of course first she stopped bleeding.'

Bess felt the race of her heartbeat. It was June 7th. She was surely five weeks with child.

Lightly she said, '*I'll* not sicken and swell, that joy is all for you if you're silly enough to marry.'

Gaily she left them and stopped at the apothecary's on the High Street to buy cloves. Master Craik was an old friend and he left his counter and drew up stools for a chat.

'How is Dame Andersen?'

'Moll is better. Your medicine eased her.'

'Good, And you? You look thin.'

She longed to confide in him for another question nagged her. Could one stop bleeding yet not be with child?

'I am well,' she said, 'but worried. A lass I know – not Kate nor Eleynor,' she added quickly, 'was caught on May Eve. She's not bled as she should have last week.'

His plump face with its wise brown eyes wrinkled sympathetically. 'Poor lass – but it's far too early to be sure. Was it her first frolic?'

'Aye, so she says.'

'She should not fret for another week or two.

'You mean, she may *not* be with child?'

'She may not be. Especially if she had the wit to cough and jump and run about afterwards.'

'She didn't,' Bess said happily.

'Will he marry her?'

'I think so, aye I'm sure of it. You see, he said—' She broke off, fearful that he might suspect the truth. But Master Craik for all his skill and knowledge was not shrewd. Countless times her brothers had snitched spice sticks from his barrels but he always welcomed them cordially, never perceiving the theft.

'Let me know how she fares, Bess, and before too long. I go to Edinburgh at the end of the month.'

'All the way to Edinburgh! How lucky you are!'

She wondered why folk called him 'Poor Master Craik.' True, he was a childless widower with no woman to tend him but he travelled widely, braving the pathless hills and miserable roads to barter for supplies in market towns. Yet despite his adventurous life he was not a romantic figure; dumpy, round-shouldered, with a wild shock of grizzled hair that sheep grease could not tame. 'Poor Master Craik' owned his own house and shop and wanted for nothing material.

She bought the cloves and he followed her out to the street. 'Now mind I'll be waiting to hear of the maid. Does she love the man?'

'More than – aye, she tells me so.'

She thought he looked sad. Perhaps the mention of May Eve had revived memories; perhaps at forty he mourned his youth. Or in his kindliness he worried about the lass and wondered whom she might be.

Impulsively Bess kissed his cheek and left him standing among the dust motes that danced in the doorway. Glancing back to wave she saw that his hand was raised to his cheek as though it had been hurt.

* * *

A week passed in a flurry of cleaning. Old reeds were swept out and fresh-mown hay spread on the cottage floors. Moll and Bess scoured and polished. But once the chares were done Moll slipped into an odd listlessness, drumbling aimlessly about the house. One afternoon she left the churning to sit outside on the grass, her back against a tree, hands idle and eyes half-closed.

Bess followed her. 'Does the child move?'

Moll lifted a tranquil face. 'Ah, no, not yet. I'm just a-dreaming.'

Bess sat down, crushing daisies and clover. 'Dreaming of what?'

'Of the child. Of how he will look and talk.'

'He?'

'Aye. I have a daughter.'

I am a poor daughter, Bess thought. I feel gusts of warmth towards her but no sustaining glow.

Yet now she felt close to Moll. 'If I – when I am with child shall I dream too?'

'It's needful to dream. Your fancy will form him. You will vision him as you want him to be.'

He would, of course, be the image of Giles, but chubby at first as babies should be . . . She lay back on the grass watching the flight of a gull through clouds and the sun's slow decline. She was sure that she was with child. All day she had had a back ache which seemed significant because it was unusual.

She hugged the pain happily. Tomorrow she would find a way to see Giles at Castle Threave. Together they would return to tell Thomas. The banns would be read. She and Moll would stitch a white bridal gown with slashed sleeves . . .

'Will you fetch ale?' Moll asked.

Bess rose and started towards the cottage. The sleeves would be pale blue, perhaps embroidered in white . . .

Moll called after her. 'Change your gown. There's blood on it.'

* * *

She had no hope that Giles would marry her now but she clung to the thought that if she sought him and shed her pride he might, in time, come to love her. She would be gay and undemanding, one with his moods. She had been incredibly foolish to relinquish him, spiting only herself. Crumbs of love were better than none.

But she could not go to him without arousing Moll's anxiety. She could not disappear for most of a day without explanation and the journey itself would be difficult. She must follow the River Dee that snaked for twelve miles to the island fortress where someone must row her across from the mainland. Once there she must risk the chance that Giles might be hunting miles away.

She dared not involve Kate and Eleynor in a lie to account for her absence. Better to simply vanish and explain 'a long walk' when she returned. Moll would be panicked. Thomas would rage. But she, God willing, would be reunited with Giles.

So, on a Thursday morning when Thomas and the boys had left and Moll was in the dairy, Bess took buttered bannocks tied in a strip of homespun and slipped out through the front garden. Mindful of briars she wore an old gown and sturdy leather shoes to prevent blisters.

The sun was warm on her shoulders and she hummed a tune to ease her over stiles – a high note, up, a low note, down. Grouse rose in the fields, beating their wings, and gulls fled the turnip heaps. Hills topped with fir trees billowed in blue scallops speckled white with sheep.

She followed the sullen, slow-flowing Dee past miles of alders and larches, meeting no one. At noon she paused in the shade of willows and ate her barley cakes. Clambering down to the river bank she took off her shoes and cooled her feet in the water, toes teasing the trout that rose to the surface.

Another mile. Two . . . three. She was tiring but calm with confidence. She must be near Castle Douglas and Threave was only two miles west.

Hearing the sudden pound of hoofs she stood aside as a

horseman rounded the bend and, seeing her, drew rein in a cloud of dust. As it cleared she recognized the blue and crimson of the laird's livery and greeted the man with delight.

'Sir, am I near Threave Castle?'

He stared at her with an old man's suspicion. 'About four miles. But if you've come begging justice the laird's holding assizes at Douglas.'

'I'm seeking Master Giles Thorn.'

'Then you'd best walk east.' He smiled, thin-lipped, at some private amusement and she waited impatiently but he said nothing more.

'Where east, sir? How far?'

'Seventy miles.'

She gasped. 'But *where*?'

'He's in Edinburgh.'

She was suddenly weary to faintness, almost too tired to shape a question. 'When does he return?'

His voice was less harsh. 'Do you know him?'

'Aye.' She looked down at her dusty shoes. 'I've come from Kirkcudbright to see him.'

'You'd best hurry home before it storms.'

She glanced at the sky indifferently. Clouds were piling darkly to the west. 'How long will he be gone?'

'Who know? He's gone for schooling.'

'But he is schooled.'

'The laird grooms him to manage the estate.'

Despite her own despair she imagined Giles's. He who loved the freedom of the woods was trapped in a life of ink pots and quills.

She stared at the man helplessly.

'Go home, lass.' Again he glanced at the sky. 'And hurry.'

She turned and shuffled back along the path as he spurred ahead out of her sight.

For a while she was mercifully thoughtless, moving one foot beyond the other. There was an ominous stillness without breeze or birdsong. Now on the river appeared a flotilla of ducklings and an anxious old collie ran barking along the bank. He was rounding up the ducks as he once had tended sheep, trying to force their direction. Threatening stragglers, he charged into the water and retreated in a frenzy of barking. Briefly he peered at Bess through rheumy eyes, then turned to enforce his authority. But the ducklings sailed on, pert and oblivious.

Rain began, trickling on her hair, gathering power, pooling peatholes and levelling grass. Her shoes squished through sodden, clasping bracken and she cringed in terror as lightning hissed across the hills. She stumbled on and on, her hair a wet rope, her eyes narrowed against the blur of rain.

She found the storm providential. Neither Moll nor Thomas blamed her for being drenched on a walk. And both were alarmed because for three days she shivered in delirious fever.

Moll sat by her bed. 'What dog, lass? Why do you weep?'

'She's dreaming,' Thomas said.

But the old dog was no dream. She saw it on the river bank tending sheep that had vanished over the hills of time, longing to take charge, but no longer needed.

* * *

After a week when Bess was well she visited Master Craik. Bluntly she said, 'I want you to take me to Edinburgh.'

He did not seem surprised. 'Wait,' he said, and bolted the door of his shop, turning the hands of the paper clock to signify that he would reopen at noon.

'Now, Bess.'

She told him everything. 'I'm sorry I tricked you.'

'You didn't. I've known too many lasses who fretted about their "friends". It's an old tale and a sad one.'

'But when I see Giles again in Edinburgh—'

'A sadder one, I fear.'

'Why! It's but a step from liking to love.'

'It's a thousand steps, and if not taken swiftly, then never climbed. I doubt that men, nor women either, ever grow into love. Respect, aye, and pity and affection. But hot love is born at once, as it came to you in his arms.'

'But surely when I see Giles again—'

'Bess!' He threw up his hands and his wide brown sleeves swept back to reveal hairy arms. 'In my two-score years I have marvelled at the innocent conceit of women. I've heard pox-scarred, flabby-breasted, raddle-faced spinsters sigh, "If only I could meet the King." As if their lives would change! As if by mere meeting they could win his heart and kingdom! And they believe it, God help them, they believe it.'

'But Giles is no stranger and he's not that far above me.'

'If you'd stirred his love he'd never have let you go or by now he'd have sent you a message. Don't feed on fancy. Don't dream of going to Edinburgh.'

'But I must.' She leaned forward on her stool, locking her eyes with his. 'I think Our Lady directs me. She has given me faith.'

'Such faith is only hope in mask.'

He is ageing, she thought, and the old see disaster in every venture.

'Father MacDonald urged me to have faith. I've not lusted but only loved and though he gave me stern penances he also offers his prayers.'

'For this journey?'

'I've not told him. I've not seen him since my illness.'

Craik shifted his heavy body on the stool. 'Consider facts, not faith. If you went to Edinburgh and Master Thorn refused to wed you you'd live in hell. The city crushes young girls with bestiality, or at best, poverty. You think you are unhappy here – God, girl, it seems heaven when you leave it. And you cannot come back. How could you explain your absence?'

'I couldn't,' she said, 'and I'd not risk disgracing my family. But I don't want to return.'

'So I said – once. As a young man I was frantic to leave here. But as the miles slipped by and the weeks passed Kirkcudbright became, how can I tell you – like a grey landscape that gradually brightened until it was more vivid than the streets of Dumfries or the moors of Liddesdale or even the spires of Edinburgh. I was haunted by faces and voices. When I glimpsed the Queen in procession I thought, with a twist of my heart, "She looks like Dame Applewaite." When a bishop spoke at the Market Cross I was hearing Father MacDonald's voice. Never a warming fire but I longed for my own hearth, and this shop—' He looked about the low-raftered room with its brown-bottled shelves – 'I could smell the costmary and iris and even bitter-scented vials seemed perfumed and precious.'

Bess listened politely. 'What's true for one is not for another. I have few pleasant memories to take with me. Papa is all I love here.'

'You want to punish him, but I think you punish yourself.'

'I only know I must go. Please take me with you!'

'No, Bess.'

'Then I'll go alone.'

'Good God! It's more than seventy terrible miles.'

'I can walk ten miles a day.'

'Mud, heat, storm, swamp – how would you eat, shelter yourself?'

'I have a crown and three groats saved but I'd beg my way if need be. I'd sleep where I found a haystack or heather-bank.'

'Are you mad? There are thieves on the road, strange men roam the hills, wild dogs . . . I'd sooner tell your father to lock you up than let you go.'

'You'd not break my confidence, but even if you did he can't lock me up for ever. I swear I'll go and nothing shall stop me.'

He argued, scolded, pleaded. 'Don't put this on my conscience.'

'It will be on your conscience if you let me go alone, for you could make my journey safe.'

'And suppose I did? And Master Thorn rejects you? What then? How would you live?'

'In service to some family. There's nothing I can't do about a house.'

He studied her from perky coif to slender, girdled waist. 'No good wife in her right mind would have you in her service.'

She was hurt and indignant. 'Why?'

'In almost every house there's a husband and sons – and beds.'

'I'm no wanton!'

'But others are.'

'You invent grief.'

'Think on my own grief if I took you. How often do two people leave Kirkcudbright? Folk would be sure to connect our disappearance. And I must return here in honour. I've a respectable trade and I'll not lose it through your wilfulness.'

'I've thought of that. I have a plan.'

'Aye,' he groaned, 'I might have known you would.'

'You'll leave of a noon when the whole town is astir to see you off and you'll spend the night nearby – perhaps at Dundrennan Abbey. I'd slip out the following dawn and meet you on the road. We'd avoid towns where you're known and once in Edinburgh I vow I'd never bother you. You could return here and pretend astonishment at my disappearance. Or,' she dimpled, 'by then I'll have sent word to Papa that Giles and I are married.'

Someone hammered on the door but he ignored it. 'You put an impossible weight on me.'

'I know. But you'll be in my prayers, 'til I die.'

How old he looks, she thought, ruts in the plump folds of his face, thick lips taut.

'If you won't take me I'll not blame you. But you'll see me footsore in Edinburgh before you leave there.'

He expelled his breath on a long sigh. 'I believe you. So be it, I'll take you.'

She jumped up to kiss him but he shouted, 'Don't! Don't *do* that!'

'But I only wanted to thank—'

'I want no thanks! Don't sweet me and don't slobber! Now I'll meet you at the Abbey Burnfoot next Thursday morning. If you're not there by seven I'll know you've come to your senses, and I pray God you do.'

He led her out the back way lest someone see her. 'Confess this plan to Father MacDonald. His holy power may stop you.'

'There are priests in Edinburgh.' She smiled and turned with a swing of her skirts. 'I'll confess when I get there.'

* * *

Now that it was imminent Bess dreaded the journey. That week, ironically, the boys seemed unusually tractable and Tom even brought her a pretty shell. She realized she would miss Moll and worry about her condition.

Thomas was the double-edged sword. She loved and hated him, craved his attention and scorned her craving. To make her leaving easier she whetted his anger, storing resentment to bolster her courage, dwelling on his indifference and hoarding that too lest she soften. And she hoarded supplies for the journey. Under her pallet, in a fardel, were her four gowns and kirtles, shifts and hose and cloak – all she owned save what she would wear. In another bundle were a pair of sleeves secretly embroidered for Master Craik; and for their first dinner, a young baked moor hen and green cheese to eat on the road.

After supper on Wednesday evening when the last chares were done the family gathered for prayer in the common room. Thomas's voice was deep and sleepy:

'*Bless us and guide us in Thy Spirit . . .*'

His prayer was always the same; the words never changed. Night after night since she was three Bess had knelt in this same spot near the casement and in summertime the lingering light upon her had seemed like a benediction.

'*Chasten us . . .*'

She thought of how often she had been punished for some mischief and later crushed in Thomas's arms, soothed and crooned to, the chest-hair through his open shirt tickling her nose. Years of cuddling that had ended so strangely, so abruptly.

'*Guide us and abide in us . . .*'

Abide . . . Bess raised a tear-drenched face. She could not leave here, much as she loved Giles. For Thomas was rock and root, hill and seabed, God himself.

'. . . *Amen.*'

He ordered the boys to bed and they went to their pallets in the kitchen. Moll went outside and Thomas started towards his room.

Bess followed him. 'Papa – kiss me goodnight.'

He brushed her cheek with his beard. 'Why, your face is wet.' He peered at her. 'Weeping? What is it now?'

She clung to him, knowing that if he held her close for only a moment she would never leave; that the brief moment would suffice for the years and that even Giles would not matter. She would take what crumbs Moll let fall and be content.

'For God's sake, Bess, what ails you?' He pulled her arms from his neck and frowned. 'Well?'

'I love you so much.'

She waited for him to reach out to her.

He smiled, tweaked her chin and, yawning, snuffed the candles.

The horse jogged over the hills, huge panniers slapping its sides. Bess rode behind Craik, his body shielding her from sun and dust

Skirting Dumfries they followed the River Nith, then turned east towards the Tweed. Travelling as father and daughter they stopped for food at remote farmhouses and often the food was free. Here in the lonely Borderlands people were starved for company, thirsty for news, and they shared what they had despite their poverty.

Bess was shocked by the poverty. Kirkcudbright, with its fishing plenty seemed rich in comparison to these inland villages which were often no more than three or four wretched huts surrounded by turnip and oat fields. Often a large family occupied one room. She realized that she had lived in luxury.

The weather was unusually pleasant and they slept beneath hedgerows wrapped in their cloaks against the dew. At dawn they were off again through miles of pink and white heatherbell bloom, climbing across rumpled hills made passable only by sheep ruts. Here lonely peel towers, pitted with archers' slits, guarded the high slopes and they were welcomed by sentries who rarely saw a stranger from year to year. On the third night they were offered shelter in Elliott's Tower and slept on hides in the guardroom.

Winding northwards through dark glens, past chuckling burns, they travelled miles of bright gold gorse, heather and whin. Always the curlews cried, and the gulls, and crow-flocks blackened the sky like thunderheads. Bess was bone-weary, 'saddle-sick', Craik called it; and though she did not admit it, desperately homesick. She pictured her family's distress at her disappearance and tried to savour Thomas's worry. But her own despair, she knew, was greater than his. He would search for her with hounds through the woods and along the shore. Perhaps he would mourn her as dead. But within a few weeks he would resume his life, more mystified than miserable. And gradually she would be forgotten.

Near Lauder a storm roared in on an east wind and she blessed Craik's foresight in bringing heavy blankets. They rode huddled under the woolly tent until they reached a cottage at midnight. The family roused to welcome them. Bess slept on the floor, warmed by a dying fire and a young yowe which lay beside her.

At dawn they moved on through mist and spent the night at a hostel. The next day was clear and in the afternoon, far in the distance, Bess saw a golden hill speared by sun-shafts, criss-crossed by spires and turrets.

Craik drew rein and pointed with his whip. 'There's Edinburgh, high as the sky, low as dung. Filth and splendour and squalor and shine. I pray you'll find the best of it.'

Giles was somewhere in that golden beehive. 'Likely I'll meet him this very night.'

'Nay, Bess. Not in a town of ten thousand.'

'Ten *thousand*?'

'Maybe more since I was here six years ago.' He spurred the horse. 'If Thorn is a student you'd best inquire of him at the monasteries. Meanwhile I'll take you to a lodging. You must find work at once.'

'Aye,' she said obediently. But first she would search for Giles.

As they approached the city she saw smoke rising against the sun. The air was rank and grew steadily worse so that she covered her nose with her hand and swallowed against illness. The city was an open midden, Craik said. Folk used the alleys as privies and dumped slops from their casements. Pigs ate tons of refuse; what they left was carted to the swollen brown waters of the Nor' Loch which served as a moat for the Castle.

They rode towards the West Port whose rough stone turrets rose in the shadow of the Castle. Bess stared up at the fortress in awe that was tinged by fear. High on its massive rock it seemed ominous, a crouched mammoth grey with years. When a cannon boomed from the battlements, rousing echoes from hill to hill, she squealed in terror.

'Don't fret,' Craik said. 'It's a salute to some entering ship, or perhaps to His Majesty.'

She had imagined the Castle to be all glitter and grace. 'How awful to have to live there. Poor King!'

'Poor King,' he scoffed. 'He lives at Holyrood Palace a mile east of here – and don't be pitying your betters.'

A town watchman permitted them through the West Port. Looking back, Bess felt a recurrence of nausea. Above the gate, resting on a ledge, was a row of human heads, some newly cut.

As they rode into the great quadrangle of the Grassmarket, Craik pointed out the bannered tilting yard where the King held tournaments; and to the left the Greyfriar's Monastery cuddled in beds of flowers. She willed herself to remember the route ahead so that she could return tonight and inquire for Giles.

On either side of the street were low stone houses with projecting timber fronts and crow-stepped gables. Smoke rose from holes in the roofs – roofs shaped, Bess thought, like little peaked hats. Despite the width of the street she had a sense of oppression. The Castle cast its overhanging shadow so that colours seemed muted, watered. A woman's red shawl appeared a sickly pink, green grass was pallid save in rare shafts of sun.

She mentioned this strangeness to Craik. 'The Castle is too big, too fierce, too—'

As she searched for a word he said, 'Aye, I felt as you do when I saw it the first time. But the rock supports the houses, it's the spine of the town and the Castle protects it. The city wall is a jest, crumbled with age. But as long as we have the Castle we're safe.'

'We?' She smiled wanly. 'It's not your town.'

'It is when I'm here.'

'But you hate it.'

'Too bitterly not to love it a little.'

'How could one love it? Stench and shabbiness.'

'You'll see differently. This is a poor part, where horses and cattle are sold on market days.'

He paused at sight of a crowd gathering ahead of them. Men and women pushed and jostled towards a high wooden platform and Bess peered forward excitedly.

'Is it the King?'

'Nay, we'd hear his trumpeters and pipers. There'd be a horse guard.'

As they drew closer she could see a dark-robed man on

the platform. He raised his hand for silence and the crowd quieted.

'In the name of our sovereign lord, James, King of Scotland . . . on this day, the twenty-eighth of July, in this year of 1509 . . . that justice be done and the innocent avenged . . . shall John Tippet, candlemaker, be put to the crown for the cruel and odious murder of his wife, Janet . . .'

Craik checked the horse.

'Will they kill him?' Bess whispered. 'Here?'

'Aye.'

'I can't watch. I can't! Please ride on!'

'Through that mob?'

People were spilling out of the houses ahead, running from the West Port and forming a dense mass in their path. Children climbed trees for a better view and the low, overhanging galleries of houses were jammed with spectators.

'Does John Tippet have aught to say before he dies?'

Bess watched a small grey-bearded man hauled up to the scaffold, his arms roped behind him.

He spoke out boldly. 'As God's my witness I've broken no law. I thrashed her with a cudgel and none can deny that's a husband's legal right.'

The magistrate said, 'Aye. But you also crushed her with an iron bar and that's illegal.'

'She sauced me and I lost me temper—'

'Quiet! The court has found you guilty. You're not here to speak in your defence but to say your last prayers.'

Tippet knelt and bowed his head. His lips moved soundlessly. Sweat dripped from his forehead. A monk came up to pray beside him. Finally the magistrate tapped the monk on the arm and they left Tippet alone. He fingered a crucifix and kissed it.

Bess prayed too, begging his life. Perhaps the King would send a reprieve as had happened on the Border last year when a horse-thief was pardoned in the very shadow of Gallow's Oak . . .

A burly man in a brown apron mounted the scaffold

carrying a smoking iron pot. Tippet, still kneeling, began to shiver violently. Bess tried to turn her head but was magnetized. The big man, clasping pincers, dipped into the pot and lifted out a circle of red hot iron.

Tippet wobbled to his feet and lunged to the far edge of the scaffold. Long spears pricked him backward towards the executioner. The crown dropped to his forehead with a hiss.

Through the screams and the smell of burning flesh Bess sat rigidly, fearful of being ill. She buried her face in Craik's back and he turned and patted her awkwardly.

'The wretch deserves it, lass.'

But no one deserved this, no human being however wicked, no devil, no one . . .

'Come, he's quieted – fainted. Likely he'll die before they can revive him.'

But they did revive him. Ten minutes passed, fifteen. Bess flinched at each muffled scream. Her arms ached from covering her ears.

Craik said, 'It's over,' and she let her hands fall and heard the pronouncement of death and the priest's chanting.

Boys climbed down from the trees and the crowd slowly dispersed. As Craik urged the horse on she heard snatches of talk:

'. . . should have shaved his head first.'

'. . . man last week drawn and quartered but not a yowl 'til they cut his liver.'

'. . . we'll have a nice eel for supper.'

Vendors, like vultures, hovered on the edge of the crowd selling curds and whey and sweetmeats. Beggars swarmed, boasting their sores, and a gipsy had set up a fortune tent.

As the blare of voices grew faint with distance Bess said, 'All I have seen is blood, blood, blood! I hate it here!'

'He didn't bleed,' Craik said mildly.

'It was worse! And those heads on the gate – it's a horrible town!'

'I warned you. I hope to God you find Thorn and that

he'll wed you, or at least protect you. You've noticed men staring?'

'Staring? At me?'

He nodded and she said angrily. 'I may be from the country but I'm no gawky, my gown's decent and so is my kirtle, I see no women hereabout so fancy!'

She sputtered on. 'I'm dusty, aye, but my braids are neat in my cap. I've hose on and shoes. Why should folk stare?'

'Because,' Craik said, 'you're bonny.'

She thought he was trying to humour her and brooded on her appearance, wondering if Giles would be ashamed of her. In sudden panic she worried that he might have found a sweetheart.

Now they were twisting steeply up the West Bow, a dark, narrow passage of houses grimed by the years. As they circled into the Lawnmarket, Bess tensed at the sudden swell of voices and stared, astonished at the masses of people who, milling about the canvas stalls, made the street nearly impassable. Here at last in this grey city was colour – the scarlet and green of Flemish tapestry displayed in wooden booths, the flame of Spanish shawls, Turkey work, bolts of purple velvet. Vendors hawked cutlery, eggs, fish, sweet oils, amulets. Men drank at the brew-stalls and women swarmed round the tall, spired Weigh House buying cheese and butter. Hogs blundered among the marketers or wallowed in the muck that trenched both sides of the street. There was the smell of haddock, spice, civet, urine and the hot dust that swirled under cart wheels and horses' hooves.

On the wide-bosomed High Street Bess marvelled at the numbers of tradesmen – goldsmiths, locksmiths, glovers, perfumers, wigmakers, bakers, fleshers, skinners, saddlers. She stared up at the Great Kirk of St Giles with its golden crown, and at the Tolbooth where Parliament met. In its shadow were live poultry booths, the cackle and gabble of hens and geese. Here the din of buying and selling was so strident that Bess was glad when they turned east through the shady lane of Blackfriar's Wynd. Now for the first time she saw elegantly dressed ladies in pale silks and flowing veils, trailed by their pages and tiring women. She admired the small but stately grey stone houses with turnpike towers and pigeon entrances below the gables. Behind them stretched tiny, tidy farms. She sniffed grass and cabbages and felt a stab of homesickness.

At the new city gate – the Cowgate Port – Bess again saw human heads spiked on the fortified turrets. As they rode on her depression deepened. The sky was slowly darkening in the strange, long twilight of summer and violet shadows filtered through the lanes that crossed the South Back Canongate.

'This is the poorest part of town,' Craik said, 'but the cheapest.'

The houses were crumbled with age, many with broken stairs and sagging roofs. Men, patched and ragged, went shuffling homeward from work. Some, sprawled in doorways, were blind or crippled. Even the urchins looked old, Bess thought, and their play was quiet and mirthless. Hard-faced women sat on their forestairs nursing babies, grinding oats, gossiping. Outside one of the houses Craik checked the horse.

'I'll leave you here, Bess.'

'Here!' Dismayed, she glanced at the house with its rotting timber gallery. The casements were small and slanty, like goblin eyes, and the garden grew high with weeds. A cat slunk through the bracken, raised its head and spat.

'It's Baillie's Lodging.' Craik pointed to a sign that swung from a rusted hinge. 'Mistress Baillie is a good soul, she'll not cheat you and likely she'll know where you can find work.'

He helped her down from the horse and pushed her fardel into her arms. 'Well, Bess – may God keep you.'

Aghast, she said, 'You're leaving me here? Won't you even come in with me?'

Mindful of the women who watched from the nearby stairs he spoke softly. 'I can't risk talk – Mistress Baillie knows me and gossip travels. Tell her that you come from Dumfries and that I picked you up at the Cowgate Port and brought you here. You never saw me before.'

Bess glanced again at the house. 'Suppose she has moved away or died? The place looks deserted.'

Craik called to the nearest woman. 'Is Mistress Baillie at home?'

'Aye.'

'Go, now, Bess.'

She wanted to ask where he would lodge and if she would see him again but pride clamped her mouth. He had brought her here against his better judgement, he had been kind and even brave. For less than this men had been whipped from their towns and stripped of their goods.

She thanked him for all he had done but he cut her short, put a crown in her hand and left her. She stood forlornly in the road watching as he and the horse disappeared in the haze of twilight.

Uneasily she turned and walked slowly through the weeds to the door and pulled on the tirling pin.

A pinch-faced girl of eleven took Bess's fardel and led her into a low-beamed room. In the middle under a hole cut through the roof a steaming pot swung from its crane.

'What's the price of a room, with food?' Bess asked.

'Two groats a day.'

Bess thought it robbery but she had no choice. 'Is Mistress Baillie home?'

'Aye, but she's ill. I'll take you to your chamber.'

They climbed rickety stairs to a tiny room. The bed was a pallet of rags. There was a table with a candle and wall hooks for clothing.

'Is there no better room?' Bess asked.

'They're all alike,' the child said wearily. 'I'll bring your supper.'

Bess unpacked her fardel and hung up her gowns. Presently the child returned with a tray and set it on the table. She lit a candle. In its flare her face seemed haggard and Bess stared at her curiously.

'Do you work here,' she asked, 'or live here?'

'Both. I'm Mistress Baillie's niece.'

She turned to leave.

'Wait,' Bess said. She could not bear to be alone. 'Sit down and talk to me.' She patted the bed. 'What's your name?'

'Lucy.' She sat down gingerly and wriggled her thin, bare feet.

Bess tasted the haddock stew. It was watery and herbless but she complimented it, hoping to see Lucy smile. 'Did you make it?'

'Aye.'

'Do you have many lodgers?'

'Only you.'

'And who lives here besides you and your aunt?'

'No one.'

'Is your aunt very ill?'

'Aye, it's been months. She has the coughing sickness.'

'My mother' – Bess began, than realized the blunder she would make – 'says that the best cure is hearty food and rest.'

'Hearty food?' Lucy's tired smile came. 'Beef and mutton cost. I do the best I can.'

'I'm sure of it,' Bess said. 'And your food refreshed me. I wish to go out tonight and I'll need to take the stink off, for I've travelled clear from the Border. Where do I wash?'

'At the public well at the foot of the next lane. A bucket will cost you a plack.'

A third of a penny for water! But she must be clean for Giles.

Lucy gave her a door key from the string at her waist. 'When you cross the garden, mind the cat. He hates folk. He kills things.'

'Ah, but all cats kill, it's their nature. I'm not afraid.'

She saw a sudden spark of interest in the sallow little face. 'You're not? Not of anything?'

She was afraid this moment – that she might not find Giles, that she would be unable to bear the loneliness and homesickness. But she said, 'I'm afraid of lightning, of course, and the pest and the Evil Eye.'

'I am afraid of death,' Lucy said.

Somewhere in the house there was the merest rustle of sound and Lucy jumped up. 'Leave the tray here. I'll bring your breakfast at five.'

She was gone before Bess could speak.

That night, in her new green gown, Bess walked the devious, ill-lit mile back towards Greyfriar's Monastery. Arms pulled her towards doorways but she broke free and ran; voices wheedled or mocked, and a blowsy woman followed her down the West Bow promising gold if she'd come to her house. It was a stumbling nightmare through patches of torchlight and shadow, dodging muck thrown from windows, slipping and sliding over wet dung and fish guts and vegetable rot. The sight of the Castle guided her and its lighted battlements brought her at last to the monastery.

She walked through the sweet, sleeping fragrance of roses to the arched gate where a lay brother admitted her into a cool stone ante-chamber. He would search the records. If Giles Thorn were a student his lodging would be known.

But there was no record of Giles.

'There are other monasteries, child. Try Holyrood Abbey at the end of town.'

He gave her directions and she began the walk back, made long not by distance, but fear. Again she evaded arms and insults and the fierce dogs that lunged out from darkened kailyards. A watchman permitted her through the Netherbow Port and she entered the Burgh of the Canongate.

Parallel to the south was her own slum but this street she found beautiful. The houses bore armorial carvings above the doors, the gardens were formal with fountains and sun dials. In the moonlight she could see a forest and a high green hump of hills – Arthur's Seat and the Salisbury Crags.

Ahead, pewtered by moonglow, Holyrood Palace rose in graceful dunce-cap spires. To its left stood the abbey, like grey lace hardened to stone. It vaulted from bright green gardens and ivy climbed to its peaks. She approached the gate, announced her mission to a sentry and entered a huge courtyard. For a moment she stared up at the palace windows, wondering which was the King's chamber. Candles shone from several and she heard music and stood entranced. But guards at the door were watching her curiously and she went to the abbey porch and pulled on the bell rope.

A monk greeted her kindly and seated her on a bench while he searched the records. She waited for a long time, hearing from somewhere inside the deep, reverberating chant of psalms.

The monk returned. 'Aye, Master Thorn studies here. He lodges at Grimm's Hostel in St Mary's Wynd.'

'Thank God! And where is that?'

'Betwixt the Netherbow and Cowgate Ports.'

She walked back, relieved that she did not have to return through the ravening High Street. At the Netherbow the watchman directed her, and though she could not read it she saw a swinging sign and tapped the door knocker.

But Giles was not there, said a crone. He was likely at the Cock and Stag, a tavern beyond the Cowgate Port.

Bess did not realize her exhaustion until she had trudged another half-mile through dark, rock-broken lanes. At the pictured sign of the Cock and Stag she paused and tidied her hair. Than, timidly, she opened the door and peered into dim, candle-sputtering light.

She saw Giles at once sitting at a table with two young men. As she went to him a babble of talk sickened and died. Benches scraped as men turned to look at her.

'Giles!' she said.

He lowered his ale mug with a clump. His face drained of colour.

She stood smiling. 'I'm here!'

'So,' said one of Giles's companions in drawling delight, 'she's here. But' – he beckoned her playfully – 'not close enough.'

Giles rose dazedly. 'Bess.'

'Get her a stool, you dolt,' said the other young man.

But Giles took her arm and led her out to the street, away from the lights of the inn.

'For God's sake,' he said, 'are you with child?'

'Nay,' She leaned against him, her chin in the haven of his shoulder. 'I came to you because I love you.'

'You're *not* with child?'

'I told you I'm not.'

She felt his tense body slacken. He drew back. His face was still pallid. 'Why did you come?'

'I was too unhappy at home . . .' She told him about the journey with Craik. 'I'm hoping you've missed me too, that you've changed to love of me.'

Against the chill of his silence she asked, 'Folk do change, don't they?'

He turned his head and she longed to touch the glossy hair that swept back from a peak at his forehead. His fingers curled into fists, then slowly eased.

A sudden wind rose, swinging the tavern sign, ballooning her skirts.

'Giles – then you don't love me. You won't wed me.'

Mutely he shook his head.

She took a deep, shuddering breath. 'I've lost my pride. I lost it miles ago. I'll do anything you wish. We could lodge together. I'd cook and sew and wash for you. I'd work and earn my keep.'

He said nothing. The tavern sign swung and creaked.

'Just to be near you – I'd ask nothing more.'

He walked towards the Cowgate and she trotted along beside him. 'Lodgings are dismal, the food so poor. You'd like my cooking and I'd make your friends welcome. I'd be mute as a cod when you're studying—'

He stopped walking and turned on her savagely. 'What

have you done? What have you done to your life? You know you can't go back, you could never explain this folly . . . May God damn that apothecary!'

'I'd have come anyway.'

'You've torn yourself from all that's safe and sweet—'

'Sweet?'

'Secure, then. In time you'd have had your own home, children—'

'I've told you I'd not marry one of those snot-faced lads!'

'There are worse things.'

They walked on in silence. Her throat ached with the need to weep, her body was chilled as though fevered. They turned up the South Back Canongate and she paused outside her lodging.

'Giles, take me with you. Please.' She looked at the old ruined house. 'Don't leave me to this – this—'

Strangeness, loneliness, bleakness.

He drew two crowns from his purse. 'It's all I can spare. If you're desperate go to St Catherine's Convent across the Loch. The nuns would never turn you away.'

She straightened. Pride rushed through her, a hot, reviving current. 'I ask no charity.'

He clasped her shoulder, hurting her. 'Believe me, if I could – but, Bess, try as we may we can't take fire from another's spark. Some day a man will love you and you'll not return his love. That too will be pain and you'll know what I'm feeling now.'

He slipped the coins in her hand. She let them fall to the ground and turned from him and walked towards the house. The cat stalked her through the weeds mewing through a bloodied mouth.

* * *

At dawn when Lucy brought her porridge Bess said, 'I must find work. Perhaps your aunt can advise me.'

'She knows nothing of what goes on now, she's too ill. You might try the High Street vendors.'

But she hated the squabble and stench there. Surely someone in the Canongate needed a housekeeper.

That week she knocked on every door from the Netherbow to the palace edge but pert maids sauced her and sent her away. She tried Greyfriar's Wynd, the Cowgate, and finally the poorer streets. She begged to do any work, however menial. But housewives seemed hostile and she remembered what Craik had said and wondered if they could be jealous.

Now she was sharply aware of her beauty. Wherever she went men stared. Some handled her boldly but she learned to spit such venom that they retreated. Others whispered compliments, urged trysts, and these she ignored. She was beginning to hate all men. Her father and Giles had failed her; these others were ruttish, leering louts. The fine gentlemen who accosted her were no different than the rabble, sharing the same lust.

She came, defeatedly, to work on the High Street at Donald MacNiff's fish stall. She learned how to skin and bone without breaking the fish, how to price and weigh and cheat. Careful cheating, MacNiff said, made the difference between profit and loss. She must forget her prisshittie country ethics.

She worked for a month until Dame McNiff climbed out of childbed, went to the stall and dismissed her.

There came a series of early autumn storms that brought trade to a standstill. The roads were impassable so that farmers could not cart their produce to market. The High Street flooded. Fish and vegetables rotted in the scanty shelter of open stalls. There was no work to seek.

Bess sat in her room staring out at the never-ending rain. Even when it stopped she could not expect trade to resume until mud had hardened on the roads.

By mid-September she owed Lucy two weeks' board. She had not a penny to have her shoes cobbled nor a plack for water. She thought of the two crowns Giles had offered and cursed herself for a toplofty fool.

Another week passed, and she roamed the dark, silent house, hearing Mistress Baillie's cough, and the rain, the rain. Sun crept out one noon, then vanished in clouds. At dusk the rain resumed.

She talked to Lucy. 'How do you bear it so patiently?'

'I've my aunt to care for. She's like a little bairn.'

Restless, unable to spend another hour in the dismal rain-drummed house, Bess went to St Giles.

The church was crowded with panicked people but it was scant comfort to face starvation with others. In the incense-fogged shadows she closed her eyes and thought of home with such longing that she wondered if she were meant to return there. She would walk back, aye, even in flood. But she could not shame her family – or could she?

She knelt before the image of the Virgin, looking up into the calm, marble face. 'Would it shame them too much? Could I tell my father the truth? Could we find some means of settling village gossip?'

Tapers flickered on either side of the statue. The painted blue eyes were cold.

'May I go home? Give me a sign.'

But there was no sign.

She left the church. Rain splashed from eaves and gables, folk sloshed through alleys of mud. As she stood in the shelter of the door a man came out of the church behind her.

'Your pardon, mistress. May I speak with you?'

She turned away, frowning.

'Please, I mean no offence. I saw you kneeling by Our Lady and I thought you resembled her. I would like to paint you.'

He smiled into her round eyes. 'You know, paint your portrait.'

She could not help but be flattered. 'You are an artist?'

'Aye. But I've never found a model for Our Lady. I think of her with golden hair and a face holding peace – as yours does.'

'Does it?' she asked, astonished that it should.

'Aye, mistress. I could pay you a crown each time you pose.'

'Pose?'

'Each time I did a bit of painting.'

'A *crown*?'

'That's generous. You have only to sit.'

'A crown!' she said, exultant. He did look prosperous, a gold cloth collar banding his dark damask cloak, a jewel on the hat he held. He was perhaps thirty, with a high forehead and long, delicate nose, a balding head and dark beard trimmed to a point. She trusted his eyes – blue and forthright.

'You would earn several crowns,' he said, 'depending on how long the work should take.'

Perhaps four crowns, five! 'Could you start soon?' she asked. 'Truly, sir, I need a crown tonight.'

'Come, then.' He took her arm. 'My house is not far.'

He led her off the High Street through Candlemaker's Row to a narrow, twisting lane. His house was not handsome but solid and neat in its storm-crumpled garden. An old woman opened the door, hung their cloaks in a press, replenished the fire and left them.

Bess glanced about in delight. The room was panelled in white wood, the table was of marble and the chairs carved oak with blue velvet cushions. A woman's portrait, framed in silver, dominated one wall and Bess said, 'Please make me as beautiful!' and capered across the room to admire a tapestry.

'I've neglected to ask your name, mistress. Mine's James Villard.'

'I'm Bess Andersen.' She sat down, her wet, muddy shoes squishing the rushes. She sneezed.

'You are chilled.' Villard poured a decanter of wine into a pot on the hearth, plunged a poker into the fire and thence into the pot. As he brought her a hot mug he bent and slipped the fillet from her hair.

'It must be unbound.'

Obediently she took the pins from her hair and it rippled

to her thighs. Timidly she said, 'I'll do as you please, but wouldn't Our Lady look tidy?'

'She would wear no headdress. Though perhaps a veil...' He sat down opposite her. 'Tell me of yourself.'

Cautiously, for she was careful not to involve Master Craik, she said, 'I came up from the Border in July.'

'Why did you work at the fish stall – a lovely lass like you?'

Surprised, she asked, 'You saw me there?'

'I've seen you often. And each time I was more entranced.'

She spoke hopefully against her sudden instinct. 'I marvel you wanted to paint me, seeing me aproned and bare-foot.'

'I didn't,' he said, and smiled.

She clung to her hope. 'You mean, you didn't want to paint me until today?'

'I am no artist. That was a little ruse. I want your company.'

She sat in silence, too disappointed for anger. The loss of the crowns was shattering but it hurt her too that her vanity had tricked her. Of course she did not resemble Our Lady, and now she was paying for blasphemy.

'Come, now, forgive me and smile and drink. Later we'll share a roasted fowl and a ginger pudding.'

She scooped up the hairpins and bundled her hair into the fillet. The dream was dead. Supper would be a wake for it.

As she rose he came to her and caught her about the waist. She turned her face from his lips and pulled free.

'Sweeting, you said you needed a crown. I'll pay it for your love.'

She hurried to the door and snatched her cloak from the press. Villard followed her, pleading, but she opened the door and ran out to the street.

Rain lashed her and she put on the cloak and hooded her hair. A few doors away she stood uncertainly, confused and witless, wondering how to get home.

How to get home – and to what? A dreary room she

could not even pay for. Food given kindly but sparingly. And if the rain continued there would be no food for the poor. Smoked fish, bacon and oats were hoarded by merchants and sold at exorbitant prices.

In the chill of autumn she thought of May Eve in Giles's arms. How long had he loved her, measured in minutes? Ten, fifteen. In fifteen minutes, then, she could earn a crown that would keep her safe for three weeks. She had felt no disgust in Villard's embrace, only faint repugnance. She did not even blame him for trickery. Perhaps, she thought, one could not summon hate from an empty stomach, nor love nor any emotion.

She had had only thin porridge at dawn, a bowl of cabbage at noon without butter or cream. The thought of roasted fowl was tempting but she hurried down the street hoping for a familiar landmark. Rounding a corner she looked up and saw the black blur of the Castle against a watery grey sky. Sure of her bearings she walked north.

As she walked she thought of Father McDonald's retort when she told him about Giles: 'Your body should have been sacred until marriage.' Now it was sacred no longer. It needed food. Beyond all sin was the lust to survive. And there was her pride. She could not go on taking the remnants of Lucy's ruined garden. And yet she was hurrying home.

Lucy met her at the door. She took Bess's cloak and draped it over the hearth stool. 'I've taken another roomer.' Her eyes pleaded. 'I had to give him your supper.'

'No matter,' Bess said, miserably embarrassed. 'It's nothing.'

'What else could I do? Aunt Mary must eat and now I can buy her food.' She glanced about the room. 'There is nothing left worth a herring. Once she had a chest and a chair, but when hard times come you sell what you have.'

Mistress Baillie called from the next room.

'I'll go and bed her. Then we'll eat – there's still cheese, and ale dulls the appetite.'

Alone, Bess wandered the room. Wind from the window chinks flared the candle stubs. She smelled the ghosts of cabbage and cod, the wet wood of old beams, and creeping mould.

She put on her cloak, drew it close and opened the door to the wind and the rain.

She awakened the next morning in the unaccustomed darkness of a curtained bed and pulled back the hangings. Dawn greyed the room and she ran naked to the window and looked out. The lane was a lake of mud; rain splashed from gables and eaves. Shivering, she returned to the bed, drew out the crown from under her pillow and treasured it in her hand.

As she dressed she reflected briefly on the past hours, then dusted the night from her thoughts like dirt from a sill. To be debased one must feel debased. She felt wholly herself. A woman's core, she thought, lies beyond any man's handling.

At a small table beneath a square of polished metal she braided her hair and fluffed her wilted coif. Again she must confess a lust she had not shared and the priest would give penances and urge her to return to 'the good life'.

She thought of the fish stall, of moving ankle-deep in guts and heads and slippery scales. But when trade resumed there was other work; a flesher might hire her to clean carcasses or she could wring necks in the fowl market. She could not hope for apprenticeship in the shops. Such winsome tasks as curling wigs or brewing scents went to men.

One must balance 'the good life' against the bad. As she used to keep household accounts she now held an accounting. Last night, oddly detached, looking on at herself, she had seen a hungry girl eating, accepting a man, sleeping on soft linen, waking again to lovemaking. She was grateful to John Villard for money and food but she sensed that he was no measure of her future. She could not expect such considerate treatment from others, nor such luxury. For the first and perhaps the last time in her life she had slept on a bed instead of a pallet. Likely never again would a servant bring her breakfast on a silver-edged tray covered with fine linen. She had eaten, then slept again with her face deep in a rose-scented pillow. Villard had given her good advice: 'To please a man you must pert yourself, be gay, feign ardour.' But he had made it clear that only novelty interested him. He would not want her again.

So this was what her father had called 'first fortune', like a young fisherman's first net-heavy catch, a farmer's first lush harvest. She must not hope for so much hereafter in 'the bad life'.

But what could be worse than the markets, what work more degrading or less secure? If she worked for herself she could not be dismissed on the whim of some jealous woman; she could earn more in a day than she did in a week at the stalls.

Again she went to the window. Even here in this snug room the carved oaken shutters smelled of mould. She thought of the rain rotting the city, starving its people.

Lucy was right. When hard times came, one sold what one had.

* * *

Times were hard. Bess never earned as much as a crown but a four-groat hour paid two days' board and sometimes the man furnished supper. She saved her money, spending only what was necessary for shoes and a warmer cloak. Unlike the sluts who strutted the High Street, she strolled demurely, never soliciting, luring obliquely with her eyes. With sunlight, when trade resumed, her own trade improved. Soon she could move from Lucy's to lodgings of her own.

She was neither happy nor sad, for her mind was numb as though poppy-drugged. There was no remorse, for always she seemed a remote observer to another woman's actions. No man stirred her and this did not surprise her; she had always suspected herself passionless and had proven it even in Giles's arms. But passion was easy to simulate and no man ever complained that she was cold.

Within a few months she achieved a weary worldliness. The variety of masculine behaviour ceased to astonish her. She learned their strange love-needs and that beauty was not essential. Fat Catherine the Pig and Zelda, a bony Blackamoor, did a lively trade. Young lads often preferred old crones and children had their customers. A man, she reasoned, was formed of his past and if the woman there in the shadows of memory had been crippled or plain or beautiful, then he sought her image. Bess was sometimes rejected for curious reasons; her chest was not flat or she lacked the desired pockmarks. One man complained that her hair was too thick and wavy, another objected to her small feet. Often in the darkness a man murmured a name strange to her and she marvelled that love could glow through sordidness, through the murk of absence or estrangement. No one had ever loved her, none would ever speak her name like a prayer.

She felt bitter pleasure that she was no longer knifed by memory of Giles and her father. When time passed without thought of either she would reflect: 'A whole hour has passed and I haven't once remembered . . .' But often sleep betrayed her and she awakened weeping from a dream.

She moved from Lucy's to a lodging in a narrow lane off the High Street where she could receive visitors, paying rent to the goldsmith whose shop was below. She had a rock-walled room with a hearth, a pallet and a clothes chest that served as table and seat. Her savings were slowly mounting. With luck, she would not be forced to the whining miseries of old bawds.

The bawds whom she knew by sight were hostile to a 'foreign' competitor with the bloom of the country still on her. Often they joined forces to revile her, warning men that she had 'The English Yaws' brought from the south. She ignored them, secure in her health and youth and superior beauty.

She tried to ignore the goodwives but their silent contempt hurt her. Even now she felt one of them, respectable as they in her secret mind, longing to join in their prattle on forestairs or in gardens. Once, hearing an argument on pie-making she could not resist and paused at a public well where the conflict shrilled.

Timidly she said, 'I couldn't help but hear. It's best *not* to belabour the dough but to handle it light as you can.' She smiled at a tall, blue-kirtled woman. 'You are right, mistress.'

Eight pairs of eyes narrowed. Faces tensed. No one spoke. They resumed laundering, dipping their clothes in pails and scrubbing them against the rough sides of the well. A small boy ran out of an alley with his bucket and when he explained that his mother was thirsty from fever they stood aside and let him draw up water. They never looked at Bess. She felt disembodied, invisible. But when she walked on she was aware of their eyes prodding like sharpened dirks.

Occasionally she glimpsed Giles in crowds but scuttled off before he recognized her. After a year she no longer saw him. Evidently his studies were completed and he was back at Threave.

Though memories of Giles and her father ceased to hurt, the vision of Kirkcudbright probed and nagged, as Craik had said it would. When it rained she walked the green skirts of town, closed her eyes, sniffed the fields, and was only a heartache from home.

Gradually she learned Edinburgh like a dark, unfolding picture book. From Castle Hill to the Royal Park she knew each steep-pitched wynd and crooked passage. By day she strolled elegant areas – the Cowgate and the Canongate – where she sought leisured gentlemen. But when dusk approached she hurried to the markets where men were leaving their shops and stalls. Visitors were a boon. When she heard the drumbeats of docking ships she walked the two miles to Leith. Sailors were usually generous. But she preferred men in the retinues of foreign ambassadors for the

French, Italians and Spaniards were gently mannered. Sometimes they even escorted her to a cock fight or bear-baiting as though courting a sweetheart. Conversely, she liked the rough, honest 'Redshanks' – Highlanders from the isles and the mountains. Most sluts cheated them, pretending a difference in northern and Midlothian currency. Bess's honesty was rewarding. Chiefs praised her to their clansmen and rarely a Campbell or a Cameron came to Edinburgh but he sought her out.

A few of her customers became her friends. Blind Robin, a street singer, always accompanied her to Sunday Mass. Captain Colin Ramsay filched food for her from the barracks stores and often stayed for supper. But she felt no depth to their affection. Both were self-sufficient, neither needed her.

Through loneliness and compassion she befriended an old man whom she found starving and freezing in an alley. She rented a room for him on the floor above her, cooked his meals and bought him warm clothes. She thought of him as her grandfather and though he was deaf, poured out her heart, sure that he understood. In hours when she was free he dozed by her hearth or sat whittling, smiling and serene. In her transient world he became her family, her solace, and she thanked God for placing this gentle feeble creature in her trust.

One January night in his room he murmured that a cross had appeared on the casement; he saw bright visions of saints and heard Easter bells carolling across the silent, snow-clasped city. Bess humoured him and tucked him in his pallet, snuffed the tapers and left him. Some time during the night he wandered off and though she searched for months she never found him.

Without him her loneliness was intensified. She brought an orphan girl to live in the upstairs room, a puny, black-haired child who begged in the taverns. Janet was nine, soft-voiced and quick to obey. Bess called her 'Daughter' and they spent a week cooking together and sewing and refurbishing Janet's scant wardrobe. Bess explained her plans for the future. Janet would never beg again, but learn a decent trade . . . That night Janet vanished, and with her Bess's warm new cloak and four shillings.

Loneliness drove Bess to the taverns. Sometimes late at night she stopped at the Golden Hawk to gossip and rest her feet. Here she met pallid-faced folk who rarely saw the sun – purse-picks, house thieves, jades. It was not gay company, for most were weary as she. But they accepted her and lent her brief warmth.

One night, sharing a table with a young drab, she saw a man staring at her from the doorway. He was small and scarfaced and his eyes, searing her, seemed yellow as a cat's. His mouth, curved in a smile, was a cruel gash in a beardless pallor.

Bess looked away. 'Who is that man at the door?'

The drab followed her glance. 'That's Flutter. You take him, I'd sooner starve.'

'Why? Have you had him?'

'Na, but I've heard of him. Neither Catherine nor Zelda will take him again and you ken *their* greed.' She drew her stool closer and whispered. 'They say he . . .'

Bess listened, sickened. 'He must hate women.'

'But he needs them to hate.'

Against her will Bess glanced again at Flutter, drawn and repelled by the strange amber eyes. He was still staring at her. Now she saw that he held a lute. He plucked one string, a curious low note that he repeated once . . . twice . . . three times.

Bess shuddered. 'Even his music is hateful.'

'Aye.' The drab pulled off her cap and scratched, cursing the lice. 'I've heard him called Satan.'

Bess tried to ignore him but the plucked lute string was insistent, insidious. She noticed that others too were uneasy for chatter died. Colin, the tavern host, sidled up to Flutter timidly and said, 'We'd be honoured if you'd play, sir.'

Flutter scowled. 'For what?'

'For wine, for the finest claret.' Colin called a wench who brought a brimming cup. 'Drink, sir, in good health.'

Flutter tasted the claret, then flung it in Colin's face. 'Slop,' he said, 'fit only for swine like yourself.'

Bess watched in astonishment as Colin, famed as a blustering bully, wiped his face on his sleeve and squeaked an apology. Voice trembling, he said, 'You'd prefer sack?' and hurried off to the cellar.

Flutter swaggered into the centre of the room and men made way for him. He stood under the oaken candelabra and Bess saw that the yellow eyes were sheenless, dead. His face, slashed by old scars, was sharp to emaciation. Though his body was a mere ruckle of bones he carried it proudly, gracefully, and she guessed he was not yet thirty.

He spoke to the men nearest him. 'Do you know what's said about dogs?'

There were smiles, abashed, uneasy, fatuous.

'It's said that dogs can hear sounds humans cannot. So when I've finished playing, I'd welcome your impressions.'

No one spoke. The room was so quiet that Bess could hear the clank below as Colin opened the cellar door. Bewildered, she thought, any one of these men, insulted as they are, could crush him with one hand. Yet they cringe like cuffed pups.

He tuned his lute, looked up at the dusky rafters and began a song in doggerel verse – news of the countryside, gossip of the city. Though she hated his insolent manner and the raspy, insinuating voice, Bess was charmed – he was the most amusing ballad pedlar she had ever heard. When he sang of court intrigues she leaned forward, her foot tapping in rhythm:

> '*The Earl of Buchan's bastard lass*
> (*Fair Agnes is her name*)
> *Shall wed the Earl of Bothwell*
> *And gather greater fame.*

'But will poor Adam Bothwell ken
After the banns are said
How oft she'll truffle with the King
Within the royal bed?'

He grasped an ale mug from the nearest table and drank. Over its rim he stared at Bess, eyes mocking. Then he continued:

'A prissmedainty lady
Can be so doxy-bold
She'd sell her soul for a kingly roll
And a garter worked in gold.'

Before the applause died his mood changed, and his lute dirged. He sang of the political struggle between France and England and of its danger to Scotland. Scots were bound by both traditional alliance to France and the peace treaty with England made nine years ago when King James married Margaret Tudor. If diplomats bungled and if Henry VIII continued to allow the molesting of Scots on the Border it could mean war.

He broke off abruptly, Colin appeared with a jug and Flutter drank from it while the crowd stamped and cheered and demanded more ballads.

'Nay,' Flutter said, 'I thirst.'

Blind Robin, the street singer, spoke. 'You've travelled far and know more than we. But we've had peace these many years. Surely our King is too wise to be tricked between two powers.'

'Our King,' said Flutter, 'is a fine gallant gentleman—'

Men shouted agreement.

'– and a fool.'

Bess expected the men to rise, lunging daggers but no one moved. Eyes glittered angrily but steel remained in dirk-sheaths. A gipsy woman pulled rowan from her bosom and kissed it against evil.

Evil engulfs this room, Bess thought; it spreads from his

body, it is dark in his face. She would not look at his shoes for fear they were misshapen, hiding cloven hooves.

'I'll eat now,' Flutter said, and Colin led him towards the kitchen, prattling of a roasted joint he hoped would please so discriminating a palate.

'They are all afraid of him,' Bess whispered, herself afraid.

'Aye. He killed a man in here last month.'

But killing was common. 'So?'

'Not for hate nor for gold – for pleasure. He kills as other men drink or game or wench.'

'God! But why have I never seen him before?'

'He's not often in town. He travels from Border to Highlands gathering news.' Reluctantly she added, 'He's clever. Even the Queen receives him in her bower.'

'He *is* merry, for all his fearsomeness.'

The drab smiled, showing stained teeth. 'I think he fetches you.'

'Then you're daft. I am only curious. Flutter,' she mused, 'what a foppy name for a man like that.'

'It's a German name none can speak.' The drab tucked her hair into her cap. 'I go to the West Bow. Mind you keep from my way.'

'I'll try the upper High Street.' Bess glanced at the fog-filmed casements. Few men would be abroad. It had been a poor day.

The drab reached for her shoes under the table and put them on. 'This life is terrible hard on the feet.'

'Aye.'

'I worn out two pairs of good rush shoes since March.'

'Leather costs but it lasts.'

The drab left and Bess lingered over her ale, postponing the long, probably futile, walk. Then Flutter emerged from the kitchen and moved towards her slowly, smiling his gash of a smile. She felt for a moment as though she were impaled on his glance, trapped and helpless. Then she rose, threw a coin on the table and hurried out to the street, fearful that he would follow. There were no pursuing footsteps but she started to run and did not pause until she saw the town watchman at the Netherbow Port.

As she approached he swung his lantern into her face. 'Eh, it's you. What's amiss?'

She glanced behind her through the swirling fog. 'Naught's amiss. I'm eager to get home.'

'Poor pickings, eh?'

'Aye, it's rooky weather.'

The mist was thickening as she groped into her alley. She went past the goldsmith's door and climbed the spiral stairs to her room. Insidc, she latched the door and dragged the clothes chest against it. Her lodgings were well known; Flutter had only to ask the tavern folk where she lived.

She waited, fully dressed, listening at her casement that faced the street. Finally she went to her pallet and fell into uneasy sleep.

She saw Flutter often and always with nerve-jerking suddenness. Rounding a corner one midnight she encountered him in a doorway, waiting there as if he expected her. She remembered her father's admonition, 'Be still as a statue if you come on an animal in the wood . . .'

He held a lantern low and the light streamed up through the shadows, gleaming the yellow eyes and the harsh, sandy hair. His lips were folded tight, his eyes unflickering. She longed to run but she forced herself to walk past him slowly, slowly . . . No one was in sight. The houses were dark and shuttered. She listened for his footsteps behind her and heard nothing but the thump of her heart.

Once she saw him on horseback riding out of the Bristo Port. The mare was packed with provisions and she realized thankfully that Flutter was leaving town. But a month later he was back, leaning against the Town Wall, quiet and rooted as the lichen there. Hurriedly she crossed the street towards a group of playing children. She thought she heard him laugh.

He seemed to know her destination before she did and she walked the streets in terror, shunning the darker alleys. It would be easier, she thought, if she knew what he wanted of her, at least less gruesome than this silent stalking. And yet, he did not stalk – he waited.

One night she heard drumbeats announcing a ship and at dawn she walked to Leith. Mist was lifting and the sky was pearly pink as she reached the landing. Far out a tall ship rocked at anchor. Bess leaned against a warehouse wall, watching sailors launch boats to bring in passengers and cargo.

She glanced to her left. Ten yards away Flutter stood motionless, staring straight ahead. She saw him in profile – the arrogant, hatless head, the sharp-jutted chin, the loop of lute ribbons at his thigh. Why was he here? Men on the incoming ship sought bawds, not ballads.

She measured the distance to the wharf. Slowly she moved over the tar-splattered planks. Behind her she heard the pluck of the lute. The strange, low note followed her, repeated at intervals – unresolved, relentless, pushing her close to hysteria.

Safe at the dock among the sailors she glanced back. Flutter had gone. Perhaps, she thought, he had never been there at all. Perhaps the Devil had thrust his image into her mind. Perhaps her mind was sickening . . .

That night to a big Dane's astonishment, she begged him to stay and sleep in her room. And she kept all the rushlights burning.

A few nights later at the Golden Hawk she learned that Flutter had left for England. But she sensed she was not free of him, only reprieved.

* * *

Once a month Bess washed her clothes on the banks of the Nor' Loch and there she met Guilie McIver. During that summer they talked pleasant trivia, never confiding but sliding around the edges of one another's lives. Bess respected

Guilie's obvious education. Here, she knew, was a lady – sensitive, courteous, infinitely kind. She speculated on Guilie's reserve and imagined her background: a spinster living on a moderate inheritance. Her laundry basket held simple, well-stitched clothes. There was never a man's or child's garment and Guilie never mentioned a family. When they left the Loch they went separate ways, agreeing to meet 'the first fair day of next month'.

Because she needed a woman friend, Bess thought of Guilie often and wistfully. She hoped that Guilie had not seen her prowling the streets, for assuredly no lady would consort with a slut. It was a slim hope but it fattened on Guilie's reappearances at the Loch. For Bess, wash days became the happiest of the month. She brought oatcakes and cheese and they ate together, making a picnic of their labour. Guilie provided seeded loaves or suckets or preserves. In her company, Bess was herself – a housewife, respectable as any in Edinburgh, and full of chatter as a pyecake of raisins.

One morning as they stretched their wet clothes on a line between two trees Guilie said, casually, 'You've uncommonly pretty shifts. But I warrant you need them in your trade.'

Bess's heart lurched painfully. She stared at the lace-edged red-ribboned shifts that had betrayed her.

Guilie said, 'Women come to me for various love potions to rouse men and were I honest I'd say, "Wear pretty shifts and a smile and gentle your manner and you'll not need a witch's brew."'

Bess stepped back. 'A witch!'

'Aye, I'm a witch, but not a black one. Truly, I don't brew death or vengeance, only love. But shifts and smiles are not always sufficient, especially if the woman is ugly as I.'

Bess shook her head. 'You are not ugly.' She had seemed so at first, with her huge mouth and sparse chin and small, narrow-set blue eyes. But now Bess saw the tenderness of mouth and eyes and heard infinite tenderness in the voice.

'I am so ugly I avoid mirrors . . . Once I drank my own potion, a philtre. Not six hours later a man stopped me in the street and tried to bed me. But I turned prideful and perverse, I wished love for its own sake, and I loathed my own trickery, and I'd not even speak with him.'

Bess was silent, anxious to comfort Guilie, but knowing that words would not suffice. One could not heal a wound by patting.

'Bess—' Guilie's eyes begged. 'I should not have told you of my craft. But what friendship can there be without truth?'

Impulsively Bess went to her and hugged the gaunt shoulders. 'I was shocked, but only by the word. I'm sure white witches do good. But what I was thinking – you must have known about me all this time. But you never said, nor hinted . . . and you always came back.'

They clung for a moment in the windy sunlight, skirts flapping, Guilie's strange white hair blowing free of her cap. A gown fell from the line and Guilie secured it with string.

'It's good to have a friend,' she said. 'Will you sup at my house tonight?'

'If I may come late. I must see a soldier at six, and he may linger.' Bess blushed. 'I'm sorry, I—'

'Never think me a prude! I marvel at you.'

'Why?'

'I warrant I'm twice your age but you know so much of love.'

Bess said, 'I've never been loved in my life . . .'

They met often, usually at Guilie's little house near the West Port. They agreed to dismiss the past and rarely spoke of it, but they planned for the future. When they had saved enough they would return to the Border where Guilie had also lived, choosing some town where neither was known. There they would buy a cottage. Bess would plant and keep house; Guilie would practise the respectable arts of healing to insure security in their old age.

Guilie argued that Bess must not feel constrained by such plans. Some day she might want to marry. Bess laughed at this innocence. Who would marry her?

'Some honest lad.'

'Even the dullest would guess my trade.' Despite her scorn of imitating other bawds she walked differently now, swaying her hips, thrusting out her chest. 'At a merchant's house the other night I saw myself reflected full length, and I look what I am. Even my eyes are pawky.'

'It's only your fancy,' Guilie said. 'You've eyes like a little bairn, and it's your sweet look attracts men. Compared to the sluts I see, you're like a snowdrop. But you're wasting your gifts. You're fairer than any court ladies, for all their prinks of fur and velvet. Why don't you linger about the palace gates, and at the castle?'

Old in superior wisdom, Bess said, 'Court ladies behave like wantons. Noblemen don't need me.'

'Who knows? You might lure the King himself.'

'He has no need,' Bess repeated. 'The Queen is young and perky. And there's Lady Bothwell.'

Guilie spoke softly, though they were snug in her parlour with the shutters drawn. 'Suppose I told you that Lady Bothwell is so unsure of His Majesty that she came to me not two months ago for a philtre?'

'She *did*?'

'Aye, I mixed her my headiest brew, with diamond dust to spark passion and unicorn shavings to insure fidelity. She was to pour a drop into his wine and I warrant it worked or she'd have returned to berate me and demand her angel back. She's a bitch, that one.'

'I hear the Queen is too.'

'Aye, he must be shrew-tossed. It's said he plans a pilgrimage clear to Jerusalem – and no wonder . . .'

They gossiped through the June afternoon for Bess never worked on a Sunday. At sunset she left Guilie and strolled aimlessly down the Canongate. A blush of rose light lay across Salisbury Crags and blurred into the lingering blue above Arthur's Seat. It was pleasant to loiter without purpose, to reflect on Guilie's friendship and on their plans.

Beyond the Canongate Tolbooth, behind stately houses,

she caught glimpses of bright silks and heard the hum of chatter – hosts and hostesses entertaining in their gardens. She walked on, dreaming of the garden she and Guilie would have in some Border nook. They too would entertain guests – the goodwives of the village. There were no men in her imagined future.

Suddenly she heard pounding footsteps behind her, and a yell: 'Stop, thief!' She stepped off the causeway and stood aside, watching the familiar sight of a ragged man pursued by a bailiff. If the man were able to reach the Sanctuary of Holyrood Abbey he was safe from the law for twenty-four hours between Saturday and Sunday midnights; safe from all crimes but treason and sacrilege.

Bess cheered the panting thief and hurried on to learn his fate. Heads poked out of windows and a small crowd followed, most of them betting on the bailiff, who was always in racing practice. His long arm shot out just as the fugitive, in a final spurt of speed, sprawled face down in the dust, safely across the earth-set stones that marked the Sanctuary. He lay gasping for breath and the bailiff gasped too, cursing him, cursing the jeering crowd. Beyond the Girth Cross outside a cluster of hovels a group of Sanctuary criminals, some wearing the yellow bonnets of debtors, shouted obscenities at the bailiff, who turned and stalked back through the crowd.

From the Abbey a bell rang for vespers and the men in Sanctuary quieted and dispersed. The crowd in the Canongate drifted away. As Bess was about to leave, the thief who lay on the stones turned over and sat up. Grimy sweat dripped from his face. His arms and deep chest revealed by a torn shirt were darkly bronzed. Despite his filth and rags she thought him the handsomest young man she had ever seen.

He scratched his brown, curly head. Brilliant blue eyes, large and luminous, looked into hers.

She asked, 'Are you hurt?' and went close to him.

'Nay.' He stood up – tall, slender, with massive shoulders.

He mopped his face on a fragment of sleeve. Then he reached into his belt and drew out a little image of St Peter carved in wood.

She said, 'You've robbed a church!'

He shrugged. 'What else can a poor man do?'

'Who would buy it and risk God's wrath? What could you hope to gain?'

He fondled it in his big hand. 'I could take the jewels from the eyes.'

She bent to examine it. 'They're buttons,' she scoffed, 'not a pricksworth of value. And for this you've committed sacrilege! Why did the bailiff permit you Sanctuary? He could have dragged you to the Tolbooth.'

'He doesn't know I have this. But' – he reached under his belt and extracted a piece of mutton – 'he knows I took this.'

Bess could not help but laugh. 'From where? The stalls are closed.'

'From the kitchen of the Golden Hawk. The cook chased me to the street and then the bailiff roused.' As she continued laughing he said defensively, 'It's a fine big chop,' and replaced it under his belt.

'Never mind the chop. Now heed me. If the monks find the holy image on you they are bound to give you over to the law. You might be branded or your ear severed, or worse.'

He frowned. 'Are you sure?'

'Of course I am!' It seemed preposterous that he did not know the punishments for crime. 'Give me the image and I'll return it. Is it from St Giles's?'

'Aye.' Obediently he handed it to her and she hid it in her shawl. For all he knew she would keep it herself. What an odd fellow – surely the most guileless thief in Edinburgh.

'You must be a stranger here,' she said.

'I am from Elgin.'

'Have you been in Sanctuary before?'

He shook his head.

'The monks will give you supper and you have the freedom of the Royal Park until midnight. Then you must go.'

'Will the bailiff be waiting when I come out?'

'Aye, bailiffs wait at the gates, but for bigger prey than you. Still, you'd best avoid the busy streets for a while. And stop thieving,' she added sternly.

'But it's all I know to do.'

'Have you no trade?'

He bent his head. 'Nay, no one wants me. At home I tended sheep but they always strayed and my brother sent me away. Then I worked for a charcoal burner in Drumsheugh Forest but he said I was stupid and made me go. The merchants won't have me for I cannot count.'

A gull, she thought – a poor dim-wit.

Gently she asked, 'Where do you lodge?'

'I sleep by the Nor' Loch. Sometimes I catch enough fish for a meal. Once' – he extended his arms – 'I caught a fish this big.'

In her pity for him she pretended to be impressed and encouraged him to talk of his fishing. But all the while she was wondering how he could survive in a cheating, sharp-witted world where even the shrewdest battled for existence. Hunger, abuse, ridicule – yet there was pride in every man, even the dullest. At home folk like this were cared for in the almshouse or petted by relatives. Border people felt that harmless simples were closer to God than any of his creatures.

Impulsively she said, 'I'll try to find work for you. I'll help you as best I can.'

He stared at her as though seeing her for the first time, appraising her speculatively as other men did. But there was also wonderment in his face. She thought he was like a child trying to fathom adult intentions, wanting to trust but prepared for betrayal.

'I mean it,' she said. 'You mustn't go hungry or you'll steal again and mire in trouble. I want you to come to see me.' Carefully she explained the location of her house. 'I live above the goldsmith's shop, and my name is Bess Andersen.'

He was silent, studying her face.

'What is your name?' she asked.

'Hugh Dart.'

'And you will come to see me?'

'Aye.'

'I am always home at noon. You won't forget?'

He smiled for the first time, a smile of such radiant sweetness that she was swept by sudden happiness. 'I won't forget, Bess Andersen.'

'You'll not go hungry tonight and you have the chop for tomorrow but you'll need money.' She opened the purse that swung from a cord at her waist. 'Here's a shilling.'

As he took the shilling hc grabbed her hand and kissed it. Startled, embarrassed, oddly excited, she turned and hurried up the Canongate, her hand still tingling from the press of his lips. No one had ever kissed her hand. Only great ladies received such honour. When Catherine the Pig waddled out of a lane and shouted an insult Bess poked her nose in the air so haughtily and passed with such arrogant swish of skirts that the slut gaped and stood looking after her. Bess giggled. Perhaps Catherine thought she had come from the palace!

That evening Bess returned the image to a niche in St Giles, then went to the barracks to seek Captain Ramsay. An orderly brought him out to the gate and she told him about Hugh Dart.

'. . . so could you find him work? He could fell trees or haul stones. He's young and strong, you see, but simple.'

Ramsay groaned. 'You are the simple one. First you tend a crazy old codger, then a thieving child, now a foggie. What can he bring you but trouble? What can you expect from such a man?'

'He's – he pleases me.'

She flushed and he said, 'Oho. So *that's* it.'

'It is not! I fret for him, that's all; he's helpless as a babe.'

Tiredly he pushed his hand through the lifeless grey of his hair. 'Very well, I'll inquire about work. The fleet is still a-building. He might haul timber to Newhaven. Do you think he could drive oxen?'

'I'll ask him. And bless you.' She stood on tiptoe and kissed his cheek above the grizzled beard. 'Shall I send him here to you?'

'Aye, any day, I should like to see this lovesome lad of yours.'

'I never said he was lovesome and he's not mine, he means nothing to me!'

He laughed, tweaked a curl from her cap and chided her for lying on the Sabbath.

* * *

Hugh Dart worked for two days hauling wood to Newhaven. On the third day, returning to Edinburgh, he miscalled his command and the oxen overset the wagon into a ditch. Hugh walked eight miles back to the city, told the lumber yard master what had happened and prudently fled. Bess comforted him. Oxen, she said, were famous for stupidity.

Captain Ramsay, grumbling at his own stupidity, sent Hugh to work at a quarry but after a week he was dismissed as clumsy and slow. When Ramsay refused further involvement, Bess found Hugh work in a High Street bakery where he kneaded dough, washed pans and did other simple chares. The baker was pleased with him – slyly pleased, Bess suspected, and lest he was being underpaid she went each wage-day and watched the money counted.

She found Hugh a room near the bakery and made him a soft rag pallet. He gave her his earnings and she bought his food, cooked it, sewed him new clothes. One wash day in September as she hung his jerkin and shirts on the line Guilie said, 'So that's the reason I see you so rarely now – but I'm glad for you.'

Bess had not told her much about Hugh, save that she had befriended a dim-wit. Guilie had asked no questions and Bess had been relieved for she would have felt impelled to defend her behaviour. Likely Captain Ramsay was right. She was a fool to spend every free moment on a man who could never take care of her. But fool or not, she was happy.

'I don't mean to pry,' Guilie said, 'but I can't help but note the change in you. You sing while you wash, you laugh at nothing, and your eyes hold secrets.'

'There'll be no secrets from you,' Bess said, ashamed that she had not confided in Guilie before. 'It's Hugh Dart, the dim-wit.'

Bess was prepared for a shocked expression, or for polite resignation. But Guilie smiled. 'He's no dim-wit to love you, dove.'

'But I'm not sure he *does* love me. He's not one for words. He has never even kissed me.'

'Then kiss him out of his shyness.'

'Mass no! He might think me bold.'

'Oh,' Guilie said. 'I see.'

'He must do the courting.'

'Of course,' Guilie said. 'Only proper.'

'Once he said I was the fairest maid he had ever seen, and I think he misses me sorely when we're apart. When I'm with him the hours speed. He loves to watch me cook and you'd never ken a narrow man could put so much food in his belly . . . He is so good, so trusting of me. It's as though he lived in a sweet haze, blind to evil.'

'He does not guess your trade?'

'Oh, no! He thinks I take in sewing and work strange hours. He visited me only once, for I told him the goldsmith's wife allows no men above stairs. Such lies sicken me, but I'd sicken worse if I lost him. Thank God he's no tavern-tarrier else he'd surely hear talk of me.' Wryly, she added, 'Captain Ramsay says I'm safe on that score, that Hugh is too dull to grasp anything. He says I waste a good mind on a gull, that I'm a star-eyed fool.'

Guilie spoke violently. 'Who is he to judge you a fool? By Christ, how I loathe folk who blandly tear at one's happiness while offering nothing in its place. Vultures! Confide in no one, Bess. If you do you give them the right to spread ruin.'

'I can confide in you.'

'Because you know your happiness is mine. But tell me – how could you live with Hugh and ply your trade? Men must visit you.'

'When I lived at Lucy's I visited men. I could do that again.' She paused and glanced at Guilie indignantly. 'Did you say how could I *live* with Hugh? Indeed, I'd not live with him unless we were properly wed!'

'I meant no harm,' Guilie said.

'Nay,' Bess said, 'of course you didn't.' Primly she smoothed her cap. 'I must go, whether the clothes are dry or not.' She went to the line and dropped the clothing into her basket. 'The Campbells are in town, I hear. I'd best hurry home . . .'

Late that night she lay on her pallet near the fire and stared into the embers. Sleepily, she thought of Hugh and pondered a way to coax him into love talk. To be a wedded wife . . . how the sluts would gabble and the goodwives gawk? She would move to Hugh's room; she could not risk men coming here . . .

She dozed, then awakened abruptly. Someone was rapping on her door.

Pesk take it, she thought – another Campbell. But she slipped into her shift, smoothed the pallet and went to the door.

'Who is it?' she called.

There was silence.

'Who is it?' she repeated.

'Hans Pfludder.'

She did not recall him though the name was vaguely familiar. Too late, as she loosened the latch she knew whom she would see, and tried with all her strength to close the door.

But he pushed in effortlessly.

'Go!' she said. 'Go at once!'

He shut the door and stood against it. 'Why?'

'Because I—' She strained desperately to conceal her fear. 'I want to sleep.'

He latched the door and ignoring her, walked about the room. 'I've wondered how you live. It's tidy enough.'

She stood chilled, horrified. 'What do you want?'

He placed his lute on the clothes chest. 'Now, that's a mad question.'

'Please, *please* go!'

He strolled to the window, his back to her.

'I've the Yaws,' she lied.

He turned and smiled and she cringed back at sight of the sharp rat's teeth. 'Scots call it "The English Yaws", and the English call it "The Scots Yaws". King Henry has it. You'd be in high company.'

He shed his doublet and tossed it on the floor. 'But I don't believe you.'

'It's true,' she said, shaking but summoning her wit. 'You've been away, you don't know how ill I am. I've lost most of my trade—'

'Look, lass, I live on gossip, it's my bread and meat. Your trade thrives. But if you did have the Yaws, what matter? Soon or late we all rot.'

She pleaded. 'For God's sake, go!'

But he seized her and threw her on the pallet. Her body stiffened in a paralysis of panic. There was nothing to gain by screaming for cautious neighbours would never come to her aid. And it might goad him to frenzy.

She tensed, remembering what the drab had said . . .

She felt Flutter's hands, in terror of what they might hold. They were empty so she waited for blows.

Gradually she relaxed. This was just another man. Then, incredulously she realized the difference. The part of herself that looked on laughed silently.

He cursed and moved from her across the rough sheet.

Then he sat up and clenched her shoulder so hard that she moaned.

'You'll not prattle of this.'

'No.' She sat on the side of the pallet and smoothed down her shift. 'I never talk.'

'How do I know you won't?'

'Because it's nothing to me.'

'It would merry the town.'

'To my hurt,' she said.

'To *your* hurt?' He laughed harshly.

'Aye. I'd not boast of failing a man, would I?'

He drew back his fist and hit her on the jaw. She reeled and lay back whimpering.

'That's to warn you. I frequent the taverns and streets and my ears and eyes miss nothing. If I hear one hint of this, see one sneer on a face . . .'

She felt her teeth. Thank God they were safe, but her head throbbed painfully.

'Look at me, Bess.'

She raised on an elbow, looked into the narrow yellow eyes.

'What do other sluts say of me?'

'They say—' What would soothe him, please him? Could she lie to that shrewd face, and her brain so addled she could scarce speak? 'They say you're a lusty man.'

He said bitterly, 'So they keep their pacts. What else do they say of me?'

'They seem affrighted.'

'With reason. I'd kill the woman who told the truth of me.'

She struggled against loss of consciousness. She must remain alert, use her poor, pain-racked brain as best she could.

His silence seemed menacing. To break it she said, 'You are so manly, no one could possibly guess . . .'

'I do a man's work, fight and drink. But when I lust, I'm a spurdie. Why?' He gripped her shoulder and she winced but dared not move. '*Why?*'

His question seemed wrenched from him, throttled rather than spoken freely. Even through her fear and revulsion she felt a glimmer of compassion. Her jaw would heal, her headache pass, and her terror. He would be tortured always, for ever slashed by shame.

'Why?' he repeated. His throat seemed constricted and she wondered if a sob were caught there.

'I don't know,' she said. 'Some men, many men are like you.' She hoped he believed her, for this happened rarely, save with greybeards. 'But I don't know why.'

He was silent, staring so long at the dead embers in the fireplace that she wondered if he slept in a sitting position. The fat candle she always kept burning at night sputtered and died. She saw daylight move slowly, catlike, through the casement. Outside there was the early flurry of merchants setting up their stalls. Bells rang for sunrise Mass.

He turned and bent and touched her purpling cheek. 'I had to. I take no risks.'

'I am no risk.'

He rose abruptly and put on his doublet. 'What is your price?'

Boldly, she raised it high. 'I'll be bruised, I'll not be able to walk the streets until I'm healed.' Nor could she see Hugh. She must send him a message explaining that she had left for a few days in the country. The messenger alone would cost tuppence . . . 'You owe me two crowns.'

He threw three crowns on the pallet. 'I'll see you tonight.'

She wanted to protest but dared not.

'Never fear,' he said, biting out the words. 'I'll not try.'

'Then why should you come here?'

He shrugged his thin shoulders. 'I can talk to you.'

She felt trapped by the crowns, and pushed one towards him. 'I'm not paid for talk. I want to sleep, and rest.'

'Rest, then, and sleep.'

He bent towards her and she drew back, both hands protecting her face. He caught her hands in his, kissed her bruised cheek, and left her.

He arrived at dusk as she was stirring mutton stew for supper. He held out a poke. 'Look inside; a bit of fluff to keep you company.'

Bess cried out as the poke moved in her hands, then laughed in delight as a tiny, plump-pawed kitten dropped to the floor and scurried behind the chest.

She caught it and clasped it close, thinking she had not held a cat since Tabby. Its fur was long and soft and golden and she said, 'This is no wynd-wretch. Where did you find it?'

'I bought her off a sailorman. She's Persian – a breed from a far country. The Queen has one. She binds its neck in jewels.'

'She does?' Bess motioned towards a stool. 'Sit down Tell me about the Queen.'

Stroking the kitten, she listened entranced as he talked of Queen Margaret, for he knew the most intimate details – the unguents and paints and amulets she fancied, the perfumes. He described her gowns minutely as a woman would; he even knew her moods and whims and the dreams she told her astrologer. 'She loves her astrologer, though I doubt she daffs with him. He's put a charm on her teeth, and they've not pained her since . . .'

An hour passed. Bess said, 'The meat! I'd clean forgot it!' and ran to the boiling pot. As she added onions and barley she asked, to her own surprise, 'You'll stay and sup?'

'With pleasure.' He sniffed appreciatively. 'Scots can cook, but the English can't. I sat at King Henry's table—'

'You *did!*' She stood by the hearth, heedless of the stew-spoon that dripped from her hand.

'I sat below the salt, of course. But it was the second-best food in the realm and the meat was maggoty. I warrant the King and his nobles above the salt fared little better for I saw him spit beef on the floor. Later when I sang I stood close to him as I am to you and he was crunching marchpane dry as autumn heather. He's fond of saffron in his food and forbids his ladies to waste it as hair-dye . . .'

He talked as the barley cooked, he talked through the meal, and when he paused Bess pressed him for more gossip. She had never been so entertained. When he left and she washed the trenchers and mugs she marvelled at her new knowledge. Imagine, young Lady Bothwell bathing her breasts in snow to make them perk! Imagine her runking her husband so soon after marriage without a thought for the poor man's feelings, and casting spells and enchantment to keep the King from other women. The life of a royal mistress must be competitive as a slut's, and far more dangerous . . .

For a while she played with the kitten, coaxing its confidence so that finally it slept cuddled on the pallet against her shoulder.

The Tolbooth clock struck and the town watchman called out, 'One o'clock of an October morn, and all is well . . .'

All was well, Bess thought. The messenger had returned word that Hugh would miss her during her country sojourn. Surely he loved her . . . Counting her blessings she thought, I have Guilie's friendship, perhaps even Flutter's. He was strange and moody but now at least she could walk the nights without fear of him.

She snuggled her cheek against the warm throb of the kitten. 'And I have you, pert-paws.'

* * *

Flutter proved his friendship through many kindnesses. He brought her gifts – wine, a Flemish shawl, French essence. Through his uncanny knowledge of people and events she learned of incoming ships before drumbeats announced them, before other bawds had wiped the sleep from their eyes. He would say, 'Be at the West Port Tuesday morning, the Argylls are riding south,' and she would meet the clansmen as they arrived. Or 'The English Ambassador left London yesterday with a retinue of two hundred,' and she would be waiting at the designated gate. He knew what hostels lodged foreign visitors, their names, occupations and gold-worth.

She tried to repay Flutter with suppers and dinners during the odd hours when she was not working or with Hugh. She cared for his clothes, polished his boots and his lutes, but this was not enough. He had made her virtually free of the streets; she could pick and choose and her savings were mounting.

'What can I do for you?' she asked one night as they shared a late supper in her room.

He did not pretend to misunderstand. 'What you are doing, Bess. I weary of tavern food and the truffy folk one meets there. I find this home.'

'What of your own home?' she asked.

The thin mouth tightened. Abruptly he said, 'You can serve me more of those turnips. What in the name of heaven do you do to deify a turnip?'

She scolded as she served him, calling him blasphemous, and he grinned and ate. She leaned her elbows on the table. 'Flutter—'

'Aye?'

'You're a man—'

'Ho!'

'Don't jest. I've a puzzle. How does one wile a man to speak of love?'

Another man might have quipped or laughed. He took a draught of ale and said, 'Who is it? The baker's lad?'

'Aye, it's Hugh. I want to wed him but he hasn't spoken of love.'

'Why wed a sloupe, Bess? You could dally.'

'No.'

'Won't he dally?'

'Nay, he's never handled me. But I'm glad. I want to be pure when we—' She blushed, saw Flutter's quickly-concealed smile and said angrily, 'Well, there's no cause for merriment. Marriage is holy!'

'But, Bess,' he said, 'what if the bairns are fogs, or mad?'

'I doubt I can have children. In three years I've not conceived.'

'You don't use candle wax?'

She stared at him, shocked. 'A sin against the church!'

He leaned forward and kissed her cheek. 'Ah, Bess, I love you.'

'Then if you do, help me, I'm near the end of my wits. I've done all a modest lass can, but still he does not speak.'

He sighed and shook his head. 'I've no advice, Bess. What of your friend, the witch? Has she no spell for you?'

But she remembered how Guilie had drunk her own potion and saddened with success. 'It would be false,' she said. 'I want no magic but his own words, his own feelings.'

'You believe in God,' he said, and was silent, moving his empty cup along the table.

'Aye.'

'I don't.'

She shivered, fearful for him.

'But if you do, ask God what to do. He's a man – of a sort.'

She ignored the banter in his voice, and the underlying self-contempt. Quietly she rose and cleared the table, forgetting Hugh for a moment and thinking of Flutter, longing to comfort him, but unable. He sat staring into the rushlight, face taut, one hand clenched, the other beating a soft tattoo on the bare pine board. A grey mood was on him, she knew, and she must change his humour lest it turn black. She was not afraid for herself but his fury could brew murder in some tavern, some alley.

She eyed a bottle of brandywine he had brought her – precious, expensive, mellowing. Perhaps it would soothe him. . . .

'Don't fret,' he said, turning to smile at her. 'Give the lad time. All men shy at marriage.'

So his thought had been of her, as hers had been for him. She went to him and stroked the shaggy, sandy hair in wordless gratitude.

* * *

Dead leaves crisped on the High Street and the woods of the Royal Park flamed like a gaudy plaid. Bess and Hugh stood outside the bakery and he pointed to the Castle that thrust black battlements against a fierce gold sunset.

'Look,' he said. 'How beautiful!'

'Aye,' she said dubiously. The Castle was still a monster and the skies of Edinburgh seemed unnatural. They were never pastel-pretty as the Border skies but violent, moody, cloud-torn. Perhaps the many wood fires caused strange effects.

Now he was looking up at the spire of St Giles. 'It's like it was afire, Bess.'

She marvelled that he found beauty in every grubby street, every steep tip-tilted lane. He had a poet's heart if not a poet's words. He could stare for long moments at a torch set in a darkened doorway and see figures flowing upwards in the light – dogs and elves and saints. After Mass on Sundays they climbed Arthur's Seat and he never wearied of the view. Each time the city seemed reborn for him. Each time he said, 'I will never leave here.'

The city was a passion in him, she thought. He loved it as men loved hard, unyielding and merciless women. If only he could love her with an ounce of this ardour . . .

They left the bakery and walked towards his lodging, moving through the heavy press of homing workers. At the Butter Tron Bess came suddenly face to face with Zelda, the blackamoor bawd.

Zelda stopped, hands on hips, and shrilled obscenities. Bess hurried on, nearly running, praying that Hugh had not understood.

'Aye,' Zelda shouted after her, 'run, you runking paikie!'

Hugh cursed and turned to go back.

'No!' Bess grabbed his hand. 'Please! It often happens. Some women, mad or drunk, envy me – my looks.' She tightened her hold on his hand. 'And sometimes men flirt or whisper but you must not mind that either, it's part of the street filth like the slops and the dung.'

She was shaking. 'Do you understand? You must ignore such folk.'

'But she called you a—'

'No matter. Promise me, Hugh, that you'll not heed such talk. It could only mean trouble.'

'Aye?' His eyes were troubled, trusting.

'Truly.'

'They envy you,' he said, as though repeating a lesson.

'Some do.'

'Why?'

Sometimes his mind was so plagued slow! 'I told you. Because I'm fair.'

He thought for a while. 'She was black. How is it that some folk are black, Bess?'

Relieved, she said, 'Guilie says they come from the east where the hot sun scorched them.'

They walked on to his lodging and climbed the turnpike stairs. Bess had been there earlier and left a turf fire burning. He exclaimed in astonishment at sight of the room.

She had worked all week to surprise him. At home, with a carpenter's help, she had fashioned a table of pine boards and today while Hugh was out she had had it carted here, with two smoothed ale barrels to serve as seats. A length of brown sacking hid a broken wall and sacking covered the window. On Hugh's pallet she had spread a red blanket.

'A table!' he said. 'How did it come here?'

She told him and he shook his head in wonderment. The table was set for supper. In an earthen cup, between pegged rushlights, white asters nodded shaggy heads. She had snitched them from a Canongate garden at dawn.

'Is it Yule?' he asked.

'Foggie,' she said fondly. 'It's only October. Daft-days are in December.'

He could never count days nor months nor money though she had tried to teach him. He roamed about the room, admiring it.

'How did you come to do this?' he asked.

She could not tell him that she thought of this room as their bridal home. She would shed her own shabby things, bringing only the clothes chest, and little by little she would add dainties – a painted cloth for the wall, cushions for the pallet, a spread. In a year or two the luxury of chairs, though that was the far reach of daydream . . .

'I did this for you,' she said, 'for your comfort. Besides, we are celebrating. It's just four months today that we met.'

His smile was vague. Time meant nothing to him.

She pointed to a tall brown jug on the table. 'That's Spanish wine. Drink.'

And may it loosen your tongue to love-talk!

As he drank she removed her cloak, revealing a new gown of crimson wool laced at the waist with strips of black braid. It was the costliest dress she had ever sewn, full-skirted, cut low at the square neck.

He wiped his mouth and put the bottle down. 'It's good wine, Bess, but I like ale better.'

'Then fetch it,' she said, disappointed. Wine perked, ale dulled. She twirled in the gown. 'Do you fancy it?'

'Aye.' But he scarcely glanced at her, though she wore a matching fillet on her shiny, new-washed hair. 'Where's the ale?'

'In the cask,' she said impatiently, 'where it always is.'

While he drank she served rabbit stew from a kettle on the hearth. They sat on the barrels and ate at the flowery table.

'I hear the King eats sitting,' Hugh said, 'Like this.'

'We shall always eat so.'

'When I am here,' she added quickly.

He said nothing, eating hungrily. When she had tidied the table and replenished the fire he sighed contentedly. 'That was good. Must you sew tonight, Bess?'

'Not tonight.'

'It's lone when you're not here.'

'Aye?' She resumed her seat on the barrel. 'Tell me?'

'I did.'

She wriggled the tip of her shoe. 'Why is it lonely?'

'Because I am here by myself.'

She nodded encouragingly. 'And you miss me?'

'Aye.'

She waited, but he said nothing more. She took a work basket on to her lap and began to darn a pair of his trench hose.

The turf spat and crumbled. Wind screamed, slapping the broken shutter and stirring the sacking. It was cosy here, she thought, closed in with him against the whirling dark, serene and safe. This room was home to her, as hers was home to Flutter, a fortress against the world.

Guilie was right; she must not let the world intrude. When she came here she shed all thought of the past years, the past hours. She did not shrink in horror of those hours, but they were mean and monotonous, the dismal pattern of paid passion. There were few incidents worth repeating to Guilie or Flutter, and even those paltry. A man haggled price or became abusive or told an amusing jest or spewed out drunken endearments or spoke of some lost love. Most were lonely, and she thought of her own loneliness before she had met Hugh.

She said, 'Where would you be now if we'd not met?'

He seemed bewildered.

'Stealing? Hiding? Shivering on the Loch-side?'

He shook his head. 'I don't know. I might be in an almshouse, as I was at Blairgowrie. We lived on turnips except when someone had kittens or pups to drown.'

'You ate *pups*?'

'Aye, or cats. The cook stewed them for us. That was the only meat we ever had.'

She grimaced. 'Aren't you happy that you have your own home, good food, work?'

'Aye.'

She wanted him to say, 'And it's all your doing,' but he had heard a rat scuttering in the wall and told her of the rats in the almshouse who had killed a sleeping man. 'They only kill when they're starved,' he said. 'But they don't starve here in town. There's food a-plenty thrown to the streets.'

'I know,' she said, biting off a thread. Dear heaven, how did one lead a man to speak of love? She dared not be too obvious for Hugh was sometimes surprisingly perceptive. Foggies had curious insight, like children and witches and holy folk.

'. . . and rats are smarter than ferrets . . .'

Holy Mary, the time a-wasting, my love a-wasting and he prates of rats!

'. . . I saw a pack scrambling down Castle Hill, their eyes like little red torches, fat as May-puddings. They—'

'Hugh,' she said. 'Tell me, of all the things you might have in this life, what do you wish for most?'

'Eh?'

'What do you want more than anything in the world?'

He thought for a long time, head bent, heavy curls flowing over his forehead. Then he looked at her. His glance travelled from her round-toed shoes up to her eyes. She put down the stocking and leaned forward.

'Well?' she asked softly, 'What would be most precious to you?'

Against his silence the wind soared and screamed and she heard a crash in the street, perhaps some swinging sign blown from its hook.

'What, Hugh? What do you want most?'

He said, 'A fish stall.'

'Oh, *Hugh*!'

'Across from the bakery I watch McNith and envy him sore. The bonny colours of those fish—'

'Ugly, slimy things! I worked there and hated it! They smell vile!'

'Fish cannot help that, Bess.'

'And when they rot they stink clear to Holyrood. Fish! It's not so bad to catch them as my father did, out in clean air, but to live with dead ones! You don't know how it is in a stall!'

His great shoulders straightened and he smashed his hand on the table. 'You asked me and I told you. *I like fish.*'

Mass! she thought proudly. He knows his own mind. He's not a babe to be led by my shiftcord.

'At noon I take my dinner basket out to the street and watch McNith while I eat. I know I could learn to clean fish . . .'

He could learn more than that, Bess thought. Perhaps he was no foggie at all, only slow minded. He had learned how to mix dough and Master Pirk was training him to bake.

'I'd like to work at a fish stall, Bess.'

Ah, well, if his heart lay in fish-dealing she would help him, teach him to sell and weigh and count. They would save their wages and buy a stall. Perhaps a year or two after their marriage she could quit her trade, secure in his competence. They would move to a primsie little house with a garden and dovecote and goodwives would pause at her forestairs to glib-gabbet. Hugh, too, would have friends, nor would she deny him tavern-talk for that was a husband's due. As a respected merchant men would seek his company and value his opinions.

'. . . MacNith says cats steal more fish than folk do. If I had a stall I'd keep a dog to chase away the cats.'

She marvelled – no foggie could figure a clever scheme like that! But she wished he would change the subject. Some girls, she thought contemptuously, would force his attention by lifted skirt or lowered bodice or simply say, 'I love you, I want to wed you.' For her such conduct was unthinkable. To beg marriage would be degrading, unwomanly. And even if he accepted her she would feel for ever cheated if the thought were not his own.

Perhaps, she thought, the Virgin will help me for assuredly she would want me to wed and achieve at least that much respectability. Please, she prayed, if Thou hast even a puckle of pity, show me some way to divert him from prattle of fish to proposal of marriage. I do not ask this in lust, Thou knowest, though I love the very look of his body.

She remembered the day last summer when, preparing to go to the Loch, she had told Hugh his clothes needed washing. He slid from his tunic and handed it to her, gravely waiting for her to put it in the basket with the other soiled clothes. She had not dreamed a man's body could be so beautiful, flawless from plump curls to big feet, and she ached with tenderness for his tall, bright innocence as he stood in the flooding sunlight. She loved every cove and niche of him, the proud puff of his brown-fluffed chest, the shadowed underarm revealed as he extended the tunic, the long, slender legs and round kneecaps. And his face – could so strong a face be called sweet? It seemed so to her, for the full mouth was smile-ready and the eyes soft with light.

He had asked if she would be long at the Loch and she shook her head, moved beyond speech. She longed to touch his rosy brown skin, to lean her head on his shoulder and ruffle the frill of chest hair. In love, she reminded the Virgin again. Only in love.

Help me, she begged. Months have wasted since I met him and likely years could pass and he'd never even think of marriage.

'. . . I'd feed the dog fish guts,' Hugh said happily, 'so his food would cost nothing.'

Softly she sighed and closed her eyes. Mark you, she said to the Virgin, I'm near the end of my wits. If only you would inspire me, put some thought in my head or a few words to wile him.

She waited tensely, hearing the wind try the shutters. Hugh rose and stirred the fire with a stick, still talking of the fish stall.

Suddenly it seemed that the Virgin spoke. Bess opened her eyes, sat up straight and echoed the divine hint: 'I don't feel well,' she said.

Hugh paused in mid-sentence. 'What? Why?'

'It's not that I'm ill,' she said. 'But tired. Mind, I am seventeen.'

He nodded.

'My mother said women of seventeen waste to bones unless they marry.'

'They do? Why, Bess?'

'I know not, but it's true. A husband blooms a woman.'

He sat down on the stool. 'How?'

'By just being there. By caring for her.'

She nodded again but said nothing. She resumed her darning, watching him from the corner of her eye. He stared up at the ceiling, hands limp at his sides.

'Bess,' he said, 'I think that we should—'

'Aye?' she asked eagerly.

'– stuff some tuffcl into yon hole there above us. That's where the rats come through.'

'Holy Mary!' she said, 'you're back to rats again! Have you no thought for me? I tell you I am wasting but you speak of other matters, I tell you I need a husband, but you do not' – she felt her face flush – 'advise me.'

His glance fell from the ceiling to her face. 'You need a husband.'

'There's Flutter,' she said, 'but he is too often away. Robin is blind. Captain Ramsay is already wed.'

Her hands trembled clumsily with needle and thread. 'Who is there for me to marry?'

Hugh frowned and bent his head; he always frowned when thinking.

The wind turned lunatic, raving and screaming and she rose, pressing the sacking against wall and window. At the table she tipped the bottle of Spanish wine and drank to ease the chill of his silence.

Hugh understood, she knew – she had made the matter plain, too plain; she had ventured beyond modesty. A woman could sink no lower than this flagrant hinting. She must leave now, quickly and with dignity, for it was clear that he did not love her. She was merely a lass to wash and sew and cook for him. He took no spark from her presence, only the warmth of mothering.

She must go with a casual 'God keep you' as if it were

any other leavetaking. But she would not appear at the bakery tomorrow to walk home with him. She would never come here again, nor would he seek her for she had told him too often that the goldsmith's wife permitted no men to visit her room. Perhaps for a morn or a night he might wait in her alley but he had no knowledge of her ways and soon he would give up – if indeed he sought her at all.

Wistfully, she tried to build on his remembered words, words that had glowed for her as though illuminated on parchment: 'You are the fairest maid I've ever seen.' But so he might admire clouds or blossoms.

Wind whisked out the candle nearest the window and she pictured the wind-shredded banners on the Castle battlements and the high wind-battered reeds on the banks of the Nor' Loch and hostel signs blown about the city – the Cock and Stag, The Bull, The Black Knight, flung metal and paper hurled in the dung and leaves of the streets. And she thought of her walk through those streets and up the stairs to her room. Soon she would lie on her pallet, listening to the wind, listening for man-steps on the stairs that would never be Hugh's.

She picked up her cloak and clasped it about her shoulders.

'Must you go, Bess?'

'Aye.'

She looked around for the last time. He had more comforts than she; – she was leaving him secure. Unless the baker and the landlord cheated him he would neither starve nor freeze. His future would be safe.

She looked into her own future, grey as Edinburgh, grey as its spires and skies, grey as the cats that slunk the wynds. She turned her face into the wool of her hood and felt it damp.

'God keep you,' she said.

She heard the creak of the stool as he rose, felt his hands on the back of her shoulders.

'Bess, you could marry me.'

She turned and looked up at him but his face was a blur through her tears.

'Why do you weep?' he asked, and pulled her into his arms.

She clung to him, rapt and wordless. He kissed her cheek, then her mouth and she felt a strange, plunging sensation as though she were falling through space. Never before had she known this desire for obliteration under another's lips, this need to crawl into another's belly and be locked there.

It was not seemly, she knew, this shivering, scorching flood of feeling. It required all of her will to break the kiss but she could not force herself to leave his arms.

'Hugh,' she said, nestling closer, 'let me go!'

He kissed her throat.

'You'll show proper respect—'

He parted her cloak, bent and kissed the silky skin that plumped at the edge of her bodice.

'– or I'll leave this instant!'

He released her and she drew back.

'Do you' – she knew that her voice wobbled childishly – 'do you wish to wed me?'

'Aye.'

'I shall have to think on it.'

He reached for her but she evaded him. 'I'll not be handled like a jade!'

'I meant no harm, Bess.'

'Of course it is proper to *woo* a lass.'

She waited.

'What should I do?' He sounded patient and puzzled and eager.

'A man should speak of love. Of course, if you don't love me—'

'But I do!'

'Then tell me.'

'I love you.'

'Much?'

'Aye.'

'How much?'

He spread his hands helplessly, moved his lips, but no

words came. Dear Hugh, she thought, he cannot estimate. I shouldn't have burdened him.

'Then if you love me,' she said, 'I shall accept your proposal of marriage.'

He smiled.

'You may kiss me again. Now mind,' she said, 'gently.'

But it was she who deepened the kiss, recklessly, wantonly, and again she pulled free. Lest she further disgrace herself she fled across the room to the table and poured two cups of wine.

'Come,' she said. 'We'll drink to our betrothal.'

As they clinked cups and drank she vowed to the Virgin that she would be a faithful wife just as soon as her earnings permitted.

'When shall we wed?' Hugh asked.

'Soon.'

'You'll be Dame Dart.'

He could have said nothing to please her more. She went to him, cautiously on guard against her passion. Lightly she kissed him. 'I'll be off now, love.'

'May I see you home?'

But she might meet a man on the way home and she needed every penny for their future. 'Nay, I'll be safe.'

She sang down the dark, winding stairs. On the street she walked proudly, lost in dreams. She was nearly home when she realized that men had glanced at her with interest but had said nothing. It seemed Dame Dart was stamped on her already, and she was glad. For this one night she would allow herself the luxury of solitude.

There were knocks on her door which she ignored. But at two in the morning when she heard Flutter's four taps she roused from sleep to admit him.

'I've so much to tell you!' she said. 'Hugh—'

'Was prodded towards marriage.'

'Now, how did you know?'

'By your face, your voice. Here.' He handed her a small fardel. 'I knew in my bones we should celebrate.'

She opened the bag. 'A duckling! Sack!' She patted the jug, then groped to the bottom of the bag. 'A tartlet. Where did you get all this?'

He stretched his lank body on the pallet. 'I was called to merry the guests at Holyrood tonight. Later I supped in the kitchen and coaxed the cook. So you've a betrothal feast.'

She had no idea how hungry she was. The duckling, roasted in a plum sauce, was fit for the Queen's own table.

'And now your marriage gift,' he said. 'I'm still a-gathering bits of it.'

He took a box from his belt and when she opened it she saw a great cuddle of keys, keys of all shapes and sizes, the sort that goodwives wore dangling from their waistcords – the very badge of respectability.

'Flutter.'

'And the cord for them, there at the bottom.'

A cord of crimson velvet laced with gold and buckled with ivory.

Keys on a cord! She stroked them; she made them jingle.

'I never thought to have keys save for my own latch,' she said.

'You don't ask what they open.'

'Who cares what they open? It's the look of them on a woman, and the lovely sound they make.' But she humoured him. 'What do they open?'

'Doors of my past. Old lodgings, wine cupboards, ale cellars, gates. One I stole when the Netherbow sentry was asleep, another from a drunken magistrate. I'd thought to have them melted for money but I fancied you wearing them with your nose a-tilt and your skirts a-flounce—'

'I love them.' She looped the beautiful cord around her waist, over her shift. 'And where did you get this?'

'From Lady Bothwell's bower. It lay on her beauty cabinet in a clutter of paint pots. She'll never miss it.'

'It's just my size! And I warrant the King himself gave it to her!' She took it off and slipped the keys on it but her pleasure was tinged by wistfulness. She could bear this mark of goodwife only in private lest men on the street mistake her for virtuous.

'What's amiss?' Flutter asked.

She told him. 'And I cannot even wear my hair up as proper wives do, until I quit my trade.' She confided her hope of someday owning a fish stall. 'Does it seem mad?'

'Aye, but most dreams are.'

She thought about that after he left. Not for long could she trick herself – Hugh was like a little bairn and likely would always be so. To save enough to buy a stall would be immensely difficult and even if they prospered from the start she dared not retire from the streets for three years, four. Now in her youth she must hoard for the future.

She removed her shift, knelt naked by her pallet and thanked God and the Virgin for Hugh. No matter what happened, she had attained the grandeur of a woman loved, a woman betrothed.

She snuffed the rushlight, fastened the key cord about her waist and lay down to sleep.

Early the next morning Bess visited Guilie's house to tell her the happy news and then went to Holyrood Abbey to ask that the banns be posted so that she and Hugh might be married within forty days. The young priest looked at her thoughtfully; perhaps he had seen her in the streets but he made no comment, only asked when she wished the ceremony to take place.

'The second Sunday in November,' she said. 'And I want to be married proper, even if it costs me.'

Father Duncan smiled. 'It's only your attire that will cost you and the merry-making after. The Church asks nothing save that you provide your own wax candles.'

She glanced around the chapel that vaulted to a ceiling of ornamented stone. A pity she could not have flowers for the altar but since it was go-summer she must be content with herbs and leaves.

'Shall there be many guests?' he asked.

Bess shook her head. 'Just four.'

He seemed distressed. 'They'll be lost in this place. Surely you have more family and friends than that?'

'Nay,' she said. 'I've no family.'

'Then who shall give you away?'

She had not considered that. Flutter, Captain Ramsay and Blind Robin had been her customers; it seemed indecent for them to take part in holy ritual. 'May a woman give me away – a friend?'

He asked, 'Is there no one else?'

'No one.' Bess sought to impress him. 'She has her own house and a garden. She will merry my guests afterwards with a vast cake and suckets and wine. She is Mistress Guilie McIver.'

'The witch!'

'A white witch, truly. She brews love spells, healing herbs and fair winds for mariners.'

'White or not,' he said grimly, 'no witch may enter the house of God.'

'But she does, Father. She slips into St Giles often and prays like anyone else.'

'She defiles a holy sanctuary – she's bride of the Devil. Let me tell you, child, what manner of woman she is . . .'

But she only half listened. Guilie was lovely, Guilie was gallant. Bess's marriage would wreck their plan of retiring to some Border village to live in spinster harmony, yet Guilie's joy in Bess's happiness was shiningly sincere. Not a trace of selfishness shadowed her love, but it would tear her heart not to be at the wedding – both our hearts, Bess thought.

'. . . so you must promise you'll not ask her here.'

Bess bent her head.

'Else I'll not perform the marriage.'

She promised.

'You say you have three other friends. Why cannot one of them give you away?'

'Because they have been my lovers.'

He stared at her as though puzzled.

'I'm a slut, Father.'

As he turned slowly towards the candlelight she saw grief in the grey eyes, a hardening of the long jaw. She expected a stream of scorn but he said nothing, looking off down the aisle blue-clouded by incense.

'You asked me, Father, and I told you true.'

He faced her. 'Do you go to confession?'

'I haven't been for three years. I would mock both God and the priest.'

His eyes were suddenly merry. 'I've heard many an excuse; yours is new. Why should your confession mock God?'

'Because he knows my heart. When folk confess they intend to change their ways. I cannot change else I'd starve.'

'But you are willing to mock God by taking marriage vows which you do not intend to keep.'

Hopelessly, she thought, my honesty has trapped me. Now he will refuse to perform the ceremony, perhaps warn other priests hereabouts. Hugh and I will have to slink to some country kirk miles away, a costly and awkward business, and bleak without our friends.

She said, 'Does it make no difference to you that I marry for love? I warrant you bless many a fine lady who weds only for wealth or title, and who in her heart is evil as I – or worse. If you refuse to wed us you force me to seek some other priest, conceal my trade from him, deceive him, and thus be doubly false.'

He shook his head, a little smile tugging the corners of his mouth. 'I'm no match for you, mistress. And I'll not let you pile sin on sin. I will marry you.'

She dropped to her knees and kissed the hem of his robe. Quickly he bade her rise, his face pink with embarrassment. 'There is still the matter of who shall give you away.'

'The baker,' she said in sudden delight. 'Master Pirk! If I pay him to bake the church-cake he'll surely agree.'

'That is well. Now, heed me. There are two promises I require of you. First, to seek honest work.'

'I have.' She told him about her early struggles. 'Since

the city has fattened matters are worse for men come here to seek work. They've even pushed women from the poultry market. Trade is a family concern or else folk hire their friends. I am friendless.'

He mused. 'There must be something . . . I shall make inquiries.' His voice sharpened. 'Do you *want* to change your life?'

'On my word,' she said.

'And do I have your vow you'll not consort with this witch?'

She hesitated.

'Your vow before God.'

'Aye,' she said softly. 'I promise before God . . .'

May God forgive the lie.

* * *

On her wedding day Bess awakened to a murky dawn. She took the rags from the air holes and looked down. Brown, drifting fog obscured the peaks of the houses and the street below. Far off, drumbeats of ships announced their positions on the Forth In the wynd the watchman called the hour.

Shivering towards the hearth she stirred the fire and heated water for a bath. Queen Margaret, Flutter said, bathed once a month whether she required it or not. Bess had reminded Hugh that he too must bathe – it was part of the bridal ritual – and she imagined him now beside his own hearth, rubbing his body with wood ash, kneeling beside a wooden cask just as she was kneeling, splashing and sponging. She hoped he would not forget to wash his head; and she smiled, thinking how pertly his wet hair sprang to curls after a rainstorm while her own took hours to dry.

She brushed her teeth with evergreen bark. Then, in a clean white shift she sat down on the hearthstone, dried her hair and combed it. She heated kail-broth but could not eat. Jumping at the sound of a rat in the walls, she thought, 'I'm queer as a quail.'

It was too early to dress, but she put on the new gown of sheep's russet and a white cambric kirtle. Then she tied on the bride's laces, white ribbons which fluttered from her sleeves, bodice and skirt. She must wear her old shoes and patched hose but her garters were new and her headdress elegant – a garland of gilded wheat ears from which her hair hung in braids below her waist.

She wished for a mirror, for she felt beautiful and longed to see herself as a bride, storing the image against the years. No matter, she thought, Hugh would see her and perhaps he would remember . . .

The room was bare. Most of her scant furnishings had been moved to Hugh's, together with the kitten and her clothes. Tomorrow she would return for what little remained.

The watchman called the hour of six and she paced restlessly, waiting for the bridal party. She could hear street noises, but today they were muted. In such a fog folk groped warily and horsemen rode slowly, half-blinded. Looking down from the air hole she could see lanterns moving eerily across a sea of mist.

There were heavy footsteps on the stairs and she ran to the door, unlatched it and opened it wide. But it was not Hugh. A handsome young stranger stood on the steps below, holding his tartan bonnet in a huge hand.

'Bess Andersen?' he asked.

'Aye,' she said, 'but I'm not for hire today. I'm to be wed this morn.'

'Wed?' His tufty black brows met in a frown.

'Aye.' She couldn't keep the pride from her voice. 'At Holyrood Kirk.'

He shook his head as though to clear it of drink or dreams. 'I'd hoped . . . I've heard much of you in France.'

'In France?'

'Aye, from my brothers. I'm Dougal Campbell. Donald and Ian and I have been studying in Paris. I've just returned.'

She loved the entire clan, the roistering, generous, black-browed lot of them. 'I mourn I cannot serve you, but if you'll meet me somewhere Tuesday I'll be happy to oblige you.'

'But you said you're being wed.'

'I'm no dowered bride. What I bring to my husband I must earn.'

He moved up a step. 'Does he know that?'

'Mass, no!'

'He doesn't know you whore?'

She shook her head.

He laughed scornfully. 'Then what manner of fool can he be?'

'What manner of oaf are you to pry?'

She slammed the door, latched it and stood with her back to it, aghast at her anger – and stupidity. Now she had lost the clan. He would tell his kin of the insult and word would spread like balefire through Argyllshire, clear to France. She had tossed away one-tenth of her income, nay, perhaps more, for the blood-bonded Campbells were related to other powerful clans. I am a fool, she thought, so deep in love I'm daft.

There was sudden clamour outside and again she stripped the hole of rags and looked out. She could see nothing but she heard the bridal music – Flutter's lute, Robin's voice in song:

'Come thee to kirk, mistress fair,
Perk thy laces and come ye doun . . .'

Kettledrums drowned out his voice, there was shouting and stomping as though the entire neighbourhood had massed in her honour. Thrilled, she grasped her bouquet of oak leaves and hurried down the narrow stone stairs to the street. Wind swept the fog, and she gasped.

For there was a crowd fit for the Queen herself, pushing and shoving and cheering at sight of her. More wondrous still was a mule garlanded with broom, pink plumes tied to his ears. An old brown mule, shrivelled to carcass, but a mule to ride in dignity. The miracle of the mule held her so entranced that she did not even notice Hugh until he touched her arm.

He was wearing the new red doublet she had made him, with a sprig of rosemary in his belt to signify manliness. Behind him stood Master Pirk, holding aloft a great golden cake. Flutter and Captain Ramsay guarded the ale barrel, its shafts adorned with a fat white bow.

She stood in a delighted daze while the kettledrums banged and the crowd bellowed. She could not believe that the mule was not an illusion of fog. Yet it moved its hoofs, it lifted its head, tossing the plumes.

Flutter came to her side. 'Let's be off.'

'The mule – how did it come here?'

'I dragged it. It wanted to die in peace.'

'You jest.'

'Only a little. I was bringing my own mule but it cast a shoe so I hired this one from the blacksmith for a penny the hour. I warrant he'll last to the Kirk.'

She patted the bony haunches. Hugh helped her on to the mule, which he led, and the procession moved off down the High Street towards the Abbey, Flutter and Ramsay trundling the barrel, Robin tapping along with his stick, and the crowd following, swelling at each wynd. Bess sat erect, proud despite the fact that she knew she had no cause for it – any wedding, however humble, was an event to the poor, breaking the wretched monotony of their lives. These folk who shouted and beat their hands and sang with Robin – these urchins who frisked ahead of the mule – none were her friends. They sought only excitement and perhaps a crumb of cake for luck.

The fog thickened; she could see nothing save green broom, pink plumes and Hugh's scarlet tunic. Nearby colours shifted from blue to green, and a brown cap flung high in the air fell like a leaf at her side. She fancied she could smell poverty trapped close in the windless mist – sweat, mould, rotting wood, sour sheepgrease and steamy wool. Turning her head she saw a stream of tapers behind her, briefly illuminating the peaks and eaves of Canongate houses.

'But the bride all laced in white
Will untie them in the night . . .'

The crowd, like happy hogs, wallowed from verse to bawdy verse. She tried to ignore the words, to reflect on other matters. Her future with Hugh . . .

What future? scoffed her mind. Even in poverty, most women could lean on a husband's mind; but Hugh's was like this haar, sometimes lifting briefly only to descend again. She must rely on herself, alone in marriage as she had been alone these past years. True, Hugh would bring his small wage each week but she must make the decisions, shaping their lives as best she could.

She had the strange fancy that Hugh, leading her through the fog, was leading her nowhere. Through the far torch-light ghost houses slipped past and white-cragged trees. Pox, she chided herself, you have the bride-humours and the evil weather worsens them. Nothing is amiss.

But she thought of the Campbell and her loss of his clan.

'So the bridegroom said, Aye,
It's a locksmith I'll find
For to trust this lewd wench
I'd be out of my mind . . .'

The Abbey bells rang out, slowly, solemnly, from great iron throats and the crowd silenced abruptly. Suddenly it occurred to her that they intended to enter the church and she prayed they would comport themselves decently. The Abbey was open to everyone provided the women covered their hair and the men were sober enough to stand. Father Duncan need not have fretted – the chapel would be packed.

For a moment wind parted the fog and she caught a glimpse of the dunce-cap spires of Holyrood Palace ahead and the huge stone hulk of the Abbey to its left. Dark clouds drifted over the high hills of Arthur's Seat and the Salisbury crags. Then the haar resettled, thick and ochre as they moved into the courtyard.

Hugh checked the mule and lifted her from it. A great carved door creaked and swung wide. She could see welcoming monks, and beyond them the shadowy blue vistas of the chapel, her wax candles alight at the far end like stars flickering in the gloaming.

She stood aside while the ale barrel was rolled in, Master Pirk following with the cake. For a moment she stood beside Hugh, holding his hand. Then a monk beckoned her inside and escorted her to the same stone anteroom where she had inquired of Giles so long ago. He gave her a crucifix and bade her pray until he returned for her.

She tried to pray but her mind was too muddled. At a time when she should reflect on the spirit she found herself concerned with the material – her fatal blunder with the Campbell would tie her to the streets an additional year. She pondered the omen of a dour wedding day. In the gloom of one tall rushlight fixed to the floor the high window slits were dark as though it were midnight.

Presently the door opened and a nun entered.

'I am Dame Mary,' she said, 'Prioress of St Catherine's.'

Awed, Bess bobbed a curtsy. Dame Mary was wimpled as other nuns but her robes were of black velvet stamped with gold, her beads were gold, and the cross at her girdle was filigreed. In the dim light, Bess could have sworn her little mouth was painted, and the dark eyebrows were plucked as thin as any fashionable lady's.

Mary sat down on the stone bench and patted the seat, motioning for Bess to join her. As Bess obeyed she caught a whiff of scent and a glimpse of a dainty foot in an embroidered slipper.

'Well, my dear, I hope you'll not mind another guest. I was about to leave Bishop Tutberry's study when I heard the bridal bells, and since I *cannot* resist a wedding, why, here I am.'

Bess murmured that she was deeply honoured.

'I trust I do not disturb your prayers.'

Bess said contritely, 'I could not pray.'

'I am not surprised.' Mary smiled and a cluster of dimples appeared. 'A bride is laden with all manner of wonderment and worry – will the ring fit, will her shoes creak as she kneels, or worse, will the bridegroom scurry off at the last moment.' She put her hand on Bess's. 'But you've no need to fret about yon long lad, he sits on a bench guarded by his friends – and what a handsome fellow!' She studied Bess. 'You are lovely, child, but your wheat's a bit askew.'

Deftly, she rearranged the garland. 'Now, before you walk the aisle, bite down on this prayerbook.' She offered a crimson morocco volume. ''Twill colour your lips and holy you as well. Keep it as a gift from me.'

'Oh!' Bess opened the little book. 'Thank you, but I cannot read.'

'No matter, 'tis a comfort to touch.' Again she studied Bess. 'I've never seen a sweeter bride. Have you looked in a mirror?'

'Nay,' Bess said. 'I have seen myself in mirrors, but not today.'

From her vestment pocket Mary extracted a little round of metal and Bess peered into it. Aye, she *was* beautiful – the wheat ears became her.

'We are not allowed mirrors,' Mary said, returning it to her pocket, 'so I confess this sin four times a year.' She sighed. 'It does seem unfair, for I never use it in vanity, only for neatness. When I travel dusty roads how else am I to know of smudges on the face? The Bishop says my attendants would tell me but that's absurd, they are far too respectful.'

'So the Bishop knows you have a mirror?'

'Indeed, it is he who hears my confession, I maintain that far from being the Devil's invention, mirrors are instruments for good. For example, when a lass looks into a mirror for the first time and perceives herself ugly, why then she gives up hope of a worldly marriage and often takes religious vows, thus creating more nuns for the church.'

'That could not have happened to you,' Bess said shyly. 'You are comely.'

Overplump, Bess thought, but pink cheeks cushioned the nest of dimples and her eyes were round and sparkly, the colour of robin's eggs. The nose was snub, the mouth a tiny heart rounded at the underlip. Bess could not guess her age but surmised that a prioress must be at least forty.

'Thank you, child. I was comely as a lass but I had six sisters fairer than I and as time passed it became apparent I'd never wed, for gentlemen were scarce in Blinkbonny. I could not wed below me – we were gentlefolk, my father was a scholar and bookbinder for the monastery. It became needful to choose between spinsterhood and the church. Our priest suggested I'd be happier near Edinburgh in a convent rich with books – I read and write three languages. So I came to St Catherine's. 'Twas a wise decision. My life is full.'

And yet, Bess thought, she cannot resist weddings . . .

'The only wasp in the pudding,' Mary said, 'is that the Bishop, God keep him, fails to understand women. He thinks me frivolous. When I defend mirrors he accuses me of sophistry. Holy Mother! Whenever a man loses an argument he charges a woman with deviousness; be she reasonable as Justitia. I should not weight you with my troubles—'

'Nay, I'm honoured to listen.'

' – but there's no one to confide in. It would never do to tell the nuns of the scoldings I endure. He summoned me here this morn, I was rowed across the Nor' Loch in that pesky fog, and I'd no sooner entered his study than he says, "I smell musk," and though my scent is only dried lavender he wrinkled his nose and said it was not seemly to flaunt fragrance. I reminded him that our kirks are fragrant with incense but he said the incense is blessed, so I said, "You yourself blessed my herb gardens during the drouth." Once again he was bested and once again branded me as a sophist.' She looked up as the door opened. 'Ah, here's Brother John come to fetch you.'

Bess said, 'Please, Dame, tarry afterwards and seal us with ale.'

'With pleasure.' She trailed to the door, smaller of stature than Bess had realized. 'And mind, if you ever cross the Loch, come to see me.' Then, with a little wave, she was gone.

Father John said, 'I regret the delay. The crowd was unsettled.'

'Unruly?'

'They pushed one another to be close to the altar but no bones were broken. Now they've quieted.'

He led her through the door to the vestibule where Master Pirk awaited her. Beyond the mass of standing people the altar seemed miles distant, a blur of golden light below a ruby crucifix.

Father John motioned to Bess. She took Pirk's arm and they walked slowly up the aisle. She forgot Dame Mary's instructions about the prayer book, moving in awe towards the great cross that flamed blood-red above the flare of candles.

Timidly she approached the altar rail where Father Duncan stood in his white robes. Pirk released her arm and Hugh came to her side. At a sign from the priest, they knelt. The silence was absolute save for the rustle of her leafy bouquet as it touched the stone floor.

The Nuptial Mass began and she remembered a wedding she had attended in Kirkcudbright. She had been seven years old, proud to scatter roses in Maggie McKenzie's path, but bored and restless through the interminable chanting. Later she had asked her mother why the ceremony need be so long and Anne had said, 'Because marriage is for ever, unto death and beyond.'

With each word Father Duncan was binding her close, closer to Hugh in chains of prayer – the Pater Noster, the Agnus Dei. Captain Ramsay handed Hugh the ring which he slipped on her finger. It was only a poor goose thropple but now, blessed, sacred as one of purest gold.

'*Et Verbum Caro factum est.*'

The holy oil was rubbed on her forehead. The congregation genuflected. Bess nudged Hugh, who rose and helped her to her feet. 'You may kiss me,' she whispered.

Suddenly they were separated by the rush of the mob. Men fought for bridal trophies, snatching off the white laces from her sleeves and skirt, and lifting her petticoat to pull off her ribbon garters. They plucked at her bouquet, grabbing the leaves and placing them in their hats. She squealed and laughed and ran towards the nave where the ale cask stood ready. Pirk poured a giant cup which Bess tasted with Hugh; then they passed it and it travelled the length of the chapel, each guest touching it with his lips, sealing the solemn contract of marriage. Bess sold small cups to the thirty who plunked pennies and groats atop the barrel for the Bride's Gift. She cut the cake, surrounded by the shoving, pushing crowd who grabbed crumbs for luck. She was hot and dishevelled. Sugar frosted her skirt and her hose hung loose about her ankles. Mercifully, the mob began to move to the front of the church.

Hugh romped with some urchins, wresting a bride lace from them. Briefly alone, she bent to pour ale for herself, glad of the sudden respite.

A man spoke softly. 'You've something headier than ale.'

She looked up, astonished to see the young Campbell, tall in his swirl of green, blue and yellow tartan.

'I'll drink your mouth,' he said, and pulled her into his arms.

She kissed him gratefully, in vast relief that he had forgiven her. But he prolonged the embrace and she drew back abruptly, fearful lest Hugh notice.

Campbell tossed a crown on the ale keg. 'I'll see you Tuesday at eight above the Golden Hawk.'

Oh, God, she thought, as he bowed a merry farewell, he

might have waited outside the church. He had made the moment ill.

Dame Mary came up with Flutter; to Bess's surprise, they were old acquaintances. 'Indeed,' Mary said, 'Master Pfludder visits us at the convent twice a year, for I convinced the Bishop that news of the world need not be gossip. After all, we nuns manage a large farm and orchards. We should know how crops sell and what to expect of the weather and whether apple-troublers are about.'

Flutter nodded gravely. 'I never peddle you court frivol.'

'Though any news of the King is close to our hearts,' Mary said swiftly. 'We pray each night that he will banish his wench and cleave only to the Queen.' She looked up at Flutter. 'Is it true that Lady Bothwell parades a racoon leashed with rubies?'

'Amethysts,' he said.

'Imagine, and we poor nuns without a jewel for Our Lady's crown! Is it true that she—'

The bells rang out, tumbling like rolled silver, in such joyful cascades that Bess felt suddenly exultant. She ran to Hugh who caught her in his arms and lifted her to his shoulder. The crowd made way for them and they passed down the long aisle to cheers and quips. Bess saw the great oaken doors open to the rainlight, open slowly, fatally, as though to her own future. There was fog outside those doors but it did not grey her mood. She was Dame Dart, for ever, unto death and beyond.

* * *

Late that night while Hugh slept Bess rose from the pallet and sat on its edge, looking down at him through the pale lemon-gold of the taperlight. Amid the tossed coverings he lay naked on his back, deeply asleep from hours of love and wine. She bent and kissed his mouth; he did not stir.

She moved to the end of the pallet, shyly kissed a toe, and as he slept on, kissed the toe next it and the other three. She had the fancy that his left foot was forlorn, so she kissed it too, and both the ankles lest one be jealous of the other. Up the long legs she went, and the thighs. Gently, she nuzzled his stomach, nosing into the little creases there. Her head on his chest, she thought how soft and curly a pillow it was for all of its inner hardness, and the safest place in all the world for a woman to rest.

She pressed her lips to his throat, felt a little throb of pulse, and kissed its sleeping life. Stroking the wiry chest hair she found his heart by chance and marvelled, for never had she felt another's heart beat under her hand. For a long time she lay there until, despite his warmth, she grew chilled. She blew out the taper and pulled up the covers, curving her body to his.

She thought of the ravening world outside, of wynd-rats and robbers a-prowl, of the horrors abroad on this November night. Knifings, stranglings, corpses a-wash in the Loch under the cold-eyed stars. Only last week she had seen a drab pulled from the water, bloated, faceless, with hair like seaweed. And once near the city wall, the red-fleshed slime that had been a boy.

She cuddled closer to Hugh. Slowly, almost imperceptibly, the dawn stole in, thieving the darkness. She drowsed towards sleep on his shoulder, snug as a seed in an apple.

* * *

Yuletide came and Twelfth Night with its revels. Folk decked their houses with shrubs and the rich spread Flemish tapestries over their galleries. From the Canongate came the smell of roasting geese, spice and suet puddings, and on poorer streets women plucked kail from their gardens to stew with sheep guts. The city was linked by music – cithers, lutes, pipes, horns and drums. Through the open doors of St Giles the high, flute-like voices of choir boys soared to the golden roof. Kirks from both sides of the Loch joined in a rapture of bells.

In the new year of 1513 snow fell on sooted rafters and froze on gables in filigrees of ice. Each day the fist of the cold tightened brutally. There was scant firewood even for the rich since forests clear to Fife had been stripped to build the King's fleet. People burned turf and purls and bedded with livestock for warmth.

Early in January messengers rode from Stirling with news of the plague and on the 17th King James made a national proclamation threatening death to any pest-ridden person who mingled with healthy folk in public places. In Edinburgh, dunghills at the city gates were prohibited and incoming travellers halted until they and their goods were proven clean. Wynds and gutters and vennels were scrubbed, stray dogs and cats slaughtered lest they carry infection. But within a few weeks people had forgotten the alarm. After all, Stirling was thirty-six miles away. The evil vapour could not drift so far through battering winds.

But a graver evil worried Bess – the threat of war. She saw its omens as she roamed the streets – the *St Michael* anchored in the Forth, a great-gunned sea monster, the largest warship in the world. There were twenty-four ships at Leith alone, where French vessels unloaded cargoes of cannonballs and gunpowder. Night and day she heard the forging of cannon in Edinburgh Castle, saw sparks spitting red from the windy black battlements. In the taverns she heard rumours that if England invaded France, Scotland would attack England while Henry VIII's troops were engaged across the Channel. Flutter was gloomy.

'Our King is mired in chivalry,' he said, 'though the French would break our alliance in a whit if it proved advantageous. He tries to balance Louis and Henry like falcons on a jess but both are cannier than he. I think he has a love of war as a child plays at battle.'

Bess knew nothing of politics but she sided with the King in his hatred of England. On the Border she had heard bloody tales of Scots plundered, tortured, murdered. None could deny young Henry VIII's arrogance in permitting piracy of Scottish ships and refusing his sister Margaret her legacy of jewels and gold because she had married the King of Scotland. Worst of all, he had bragged that Scotland was rightfully his and King James his vassal. That, she felt, was near to blasphemy.

Because workers and foreign envoys crammed the city, Bess was never idle save for the hours she reserved for Hugh. She worked from morning until supper time and from nine o'clock, when Hugh slept, until after midnight. Dougal Campbell's clan and kin were faithful and he became her friend, though his disapproval of her trade was lively as any goodwife's.

'You gutter your life,' he said, 'I saw you today with that gorfy sailor—'

'Hush,' she said. They were in his lodgings above the Golden Hawk and she put her hand to his tightened mouth. 'You talk like a babe. You know what I am, why should you gash me so?'

'Women were meant to be virtuous.'

'I warrant God meant men to be virtuous too.'

'Man was created animal,' Dougal said, darkly sullen. 'But women are naturally virtuous.'

She shrugged. 'There's no great difference between men and women.'

'I mislike ignorance, especially when paraded.'

'I, too,' she said coolly. 'You've studied years, mayhap you'll be a great surgeon, but books don't tell you about men and women.'

'They don't, eh?' He got out of bed, stalked naked to the chest, pulled out a book and waved it as though it were a banner. 'Pliny, a great Roman writer. He says when a man drowns he floats belly up, but woman floats modestly on her stomach.' He tossed the book back in the chest and returned to sit beside Bess. 'Men and women are different as cod and cake. You know it.'

But she shook her head. 'I've known men as you have not. Aye, they are pawky yet often tender as women, plagued by the same doubts and dreams. I've known men so modest they'd not disrobe until the candles were out, and some have told me they broke their marriage vows only after their wives cuckolded them. . . . I have heard men weep, as women do, for a love lost or denied or never known. What is this vast difference of yours?'

'Why, in the lust of men. I walk the High Street, let us say, bemused by my studies, weary for my bed. I have no thought, no need of a woman. Yet some snisty wench comes by with her skirts a-flap in the wind and I am—'

'Perked.'

'– I am struck in the belly as though hammered. This doesn't happen to women.'

'It does. A woman's passion can be roused just as a man's, without word or touch. It needs but a glance.'

He was incredulous, outraged. 'Do you mean to tell me a woman can look at a stranger and feel as a man feels?'

'Not a belly blow, nay, but a strange sort of sliding of the belly as though she were drained or falling. All women may not feel this, but then, many would not admit to it.' Wind whistled through the crannies and she snuggled deeper under the blanket. 'Kate – she's a poor-penny bawd who walks the docks, the one with the harelip – told me of a man who comes into the Cock and Stag. She said she reels in her belly at his very glance, she would charge him nothing if he wanted her. She'd even feed him and work for him, yet he has never spoken to her.'

'Do you call that love?' he asked belligerently.

'It's the beginning, perhaps.'

'And what is love?' he asked scornfully.

She hadn't the wit to tell him, but she knew. Love was like a castle a-building. You could build a little castle from pity or affection as she had done for the beggar girl and the old man she had sheltered; or you could build a big one that towered towards the stars. Such a castle was based on the rock of passion which supported it so firmly that it held against the winds of the world.

'Love is more than lust between men and women,' she said, 'yet it is rooted in lust.'

'Which lasts but a few moments, at best an hour.'

'Ah, no!' She thought of her life with Hugh. Passion culminated on the pallet but it nourished on small intimacies – the touch of their hands as they carried the keg to the well, the sharing of an ale mug, the very look of their clothes entangled on a hook. Finally, too sweet to be borne, it was voided in one another's arms only to build again from the last satiate kiss.

She said, 'Lust is every lovesome thing one does for a man – plucking the lice from his beard, cutting his nails or mending his jerkin. You think of lust as separate but in true love it is not, no more than a stirred egg is yolk or white.'

'You're in thrillage to Hugh,' he said.

He could not disguise his contempt for Hugh.

'I am,' she said.

'The lust you share will end,' he said, 'and then what have you?'

But the lust would not end . . .

'A marriage needs two minds, not one, Bess.'

She bit back the retort, 'And what do *you* know of marriage?' It was strange that he had not married. He owned a tidy sum in Highland land, in sheep and oats, with gold to spare for the costly study of surgery here and abroad. But any woman would find him more than merely goldworthy, for he had the dark, haughty handsomeness of a gipsy prince. She liked his strong, proud straightness, the rough black hair and deep black eyes, with their stormcloud brows. Women looked at him as they looked at Hugh, sidewise, speculatively.

Often she wondered why, with his education, he mingled with common folk. Sometimes she didn't understand the words he used though she usually sensed their meaning. She respected his knowledge of surgery and medicine, astrology and astronomy but could not follow his simplest explanations. His studies set him apart in a realm to which she could not travel though he tried to bridge the chasms ofher ignorance.

'You are ignorant of love,' she said. 'Don't belittle it in others. There's five years between us, yet I know more of love than you.'

'You prattle of love for the very want of it.' Impatiently he rose, poured himself wine, drained it in a gulp. 'I marvel how women raise gods from dross.'

She did not understand but sensed criticism of Hugh. Abruptly she rose and began to dress. As she clasped her cloak she said, 'You owe me.'

He opened his coin pouch and flung her a shilling. As she started out he said, 'Wait,' and brought out a small canvas bag from under the pallet. Extracting coins from it he said, 'Here's sixty unicorns for your fish stall.'

She stood awed, unbelieving.

'Go to the Town Council in the morning and ask for my friend Provost Lawson. Tell him you want a fair spot near the Netherbow.'

She put the money in her waist purse and tried to thank him but he told her to stop chittering and go. Outside in the gusty dark she realized in sudden exultance that there would be enough for the stall without using more than half her savings. Her life would change, not swiftly, perhaps, but irrevocably. Perhaps a year from now she would be truly a goodwife, her hair up, her keys a-jingle, and the hours of darkness spent in her husband's arms.

She stood uncertainly, wondering whether to hurry home and awaken Hugh with the news or prudently continue her night's work. Wind moaned up the narrow alley, swinging the tavern sign behind her. In the light of the wall torch she saw a horde of rats sliding through refuse that lay on the street like a wet, splattered carpet. She watched them idly, thinking of Plump Paws, her cat, and wondering if Hugh had remembered to feed her.

Behind her, the Golden Hawk was virtually empty, so she decided to go to the Cock and Stag. If she met a man there, well and good; if not, she'd celebrate Dougal's gift with a cup of wine and a sweet. As she started towards the High

Street she saw a man approaching and unhooded her head to display her wanton, uncoifed hair. But as he came near she recognized Flutter and ran to him.

'Come,' she said, 'I'll pay for supper, I've fallen in luck...'

She told him as they walked. 'I'll never ken that Dougal. Sometimes he's so tiggy I could swear he hates me yet he does this! He must be mad from the stars.'

Flutter smiled from a corner of his string-thin mouth.

'Well, then?' she asked. 'How else could he part with sixty unicorns?'

'I'm a poor ballad pedlar,' Flutter said with mock humility. 'I've travelled only four countries and talked with but two kings. Therefore my opinion means little.'

'But what *do* you think?'

'I think Dougal Campbell's in love.'

If this were so (and Bess dismissed such nonsense for no man knowingly fell in love with a slut) Dougal's love bought wood, blue-painted canvas and the services of a carpenter who built the stall on Friar's Wynd. Due to the kindness of Provost Lawson it was a choice situation, for no one entering the city through the Netherbow Port could fail to see it, and many leaving bought salt fish to take on journeys. Mindful of such travellers Bess provided them pokes of cooked cod and shellfish and set up a small deal counter where folk might eat oysters or fishcakes. With her first month's profit she bought lady-stools, a nicety unknown in the brawling jungle of the markets. Ten booths south, MacNiff reduced his prices and kept the trade of the wretched poor; but Bess's booth attracted the rich, the comfortable and the wanton. The Countess of Bothwell and her ladies came to buy fat salmon and lingered over cod-cakes, sitting on the stools with skirts raised high from the gut-slime of the alley.

Since Hugh was unable to count or make change Bess worked at the stall all day. Her trades complemented one another, for the stall was a showcase for her beauty. She wore the bloody apron of the fishwife but beneath it, provocative bodices and slashed sleeves tied into points. Her hair was adorned with blue or cherry ribbons or plaited under ruffled coifs. Men flirted, were encouraged, and arranged trysts behind Hugh's back.

Bess taught Hugh to gut, to shuck clams and oysters. Relieved of those chores, inured to the stench, she enjoyed her work and the town gossip which swirled around her. The Bishop had hanged his cat for killing a mouse; Robin MacTause, punished for purse-snatching, lost his hands under the Tron axe. In the West Bow the Douglases and Hamiltons had feuded to the death of twenty men, leaving a pond of blood. Shop and stall keepers were warned to have cudgels handy to subdue fighting clansmen.

But such trivia was lost in the tide of war rumours. Interminable peace negotiations between Scotland and England had failed. On June 30th Henry VIII in personal command of his armies, sailed to attack France. As France's ally, Scotland was pledged to war; and across the Border England lay vulnerable.

Yet as the summer flowered without further incident, Bess indulged in hope. Henry would likely be beaten on French soil and frightened into truce with Scotland. She mocked Flutter's prediction that King James would invade England at any hour. Even if he did she assured herself that Hugh would not be conscripted. Surely foggies, like women and children, would remain at home.

July was oppressive. At night, lightning forked and sizzled without rain. By day the sun was murderous. Travellers reported strange omens – comets that rushed down the northern skies and stars rimmed with green light. In Jedbergh a cow dropped a pig-snouted calf and midwives marvelled at the number of babies born with cauls. Court astronomers studying the moon from Calton Hill saw a fiery cross far to the south which blazed 'with the burn of hell'. Tarans were said to be abroad, the souls of unborn children, and taneawas were found in the fields, boys and girls decayed by the devil.

The slow-creeping plague reached the village of Dean, a mile from Edinburgh, Guilie sold hundreds of charms, amulets and pomanders to prevent infection. Flutter's 'Ballad of the Pest' comforted tavern-tarriers with the assurance that the plague would deflect from Edinburgh and spread to England by sea.

Despite the heat with its threat of drouth, Edinburgh revelled. The court masqued and jousted, the common folk crammed the taverns and everyone mingled at cock fights and bear-baitings. Save for a few old people the kirks were empty and the clergy exhorted in vain. St Giles's unlit candles melted in the heat; poor boxes were scarcely pocked with pennies. Children played Pi-Cow, chasing one another down shadowy aisles.

On the High Street vendors sold all their stalls could hold, even to outmoded merchandise – chastity belts and linens yellowed with years. Bess's sign 'Honest Fish' became true, for she had to order it fresh from Leith each day. It seemed to her that God smiled on her and on everyone she knew. The omens seemed distant and unreal as ancient tales.

So she told Flutter as they strolled towards the docks one dawn in late July. 'I've ceased to fret about war.' She skipped along the cobbles, grateful for the cool air. 'I'll not heed second-talk.'

'Then you err. Yesterday the King sent Lord Lyon to France with an ultimatum for Henry that's a virtual declaration of war.'

'How can you be sure? We've heard such tales since spring.'

'Lady Bothwell told me.'

'Perhaps she dreams her wish, perhaps she longs for war to rid herself of her husband.'

'Nay, I've told you – the King thirsts for war, partly for sport, but he covets the English crown. And he must move now while Henry's warring in France.'

'Why does he delay? He's had near a month and he's not moved an inch. I doubt he ever will.'

'Now who dreams her wish? You're giddy as a jackdaw.'

They walked on, sniffing the sea. Mist seeped between the dumpy wooden houses that led to the docks. Tall warehouses loomed ahead standing in small parched yards. Cats and stray pigs moved among bales and barrels, rubbing and snuffling. The sky paled slowly towards a hot pink sunrise.

As they came within sight of the harbour wind swept the fog and scattered the grey, screaming gulls. Flutter grasped Bess's arm and she followed his glance.

Far out in the Forth nine or ten ships moved north-east towards the Isle of May, gold and crimson banners whipping in the breeze.

'The *Michael*,' she said wonderingly. 'The *Margaret* . . . What can it mean?'

'War,' he said. 'Our fleet bound for France to fight Henry.'

She drew in her breath on a sigh. 'And our men will march on England?'

'Aye,' he said, 'and the price of woe-weeds should rise.'

* * *

On a sultry August night Bess met Dougal Campbell at his lodgings and found the room stripped bare of his books and clothing. Baskets and chests were piled near the door. He said, 'I'm going home.'

She knew he needed a holiday from his studies but his decision seemed sudden. 'When shall you return?'

'Never.'

There was black storm on his face and she asked, 'But why? What's amiss? What of your studies?'

'I'll study at St Andrews in the fall.'

'But why?'

'Perhaps I mislike my teachers here.'

'Ah, no. You've some other reason.'

He was silent, glowering.

She moved close to him, put her hand on his arm. 'Tell me.'

He slapped away her hand.

'Have you brawled with someone? Are you in trouble? Is that why you must leave?'

He cursed and turned away. She thought, likely he's had some message and is blood-bonded to return to the Highlands on clan mischief. A wild breed, these Campbells, spawned of a violent land. He had told her tales. About Ian Campbell, who killed his wife's lover and forced her to eat the heart; about Nancy, who jumped to her death in the sea rather than wed a man she despised; about Duncan, who kept his enemy's eyes in a velvet case.

She said, 'Why did you send for me if you won't talk to me?'

He spun around. 'Is a tawpy drab for talking? Take off your gown.'

She obeyed mutely, troubled and bewildered. On the rough pallet, naked in his arms, she tried to fathom his fury, his bitterness. She had done nothing to offend him, indeed last week she had repaid ten unicorns on the fish stall. Could that have disturbed him? Had he intended the gold as a gift? Perhaps . . . yet he had accepted it calmly enough. She had spent an hour here last night, had brought him a haddock and cooked Livery-Downey here on the hearth. He had seemed cheerful . . .

Suddenly his body in hers forbade thought and fevered her into feeling. Her arms tightened about him, her lips pressed his throat. She felt him in her womb, thrusting and beating, engulfing her in a warm, monstrous wave. And then the wave receded and she lay spent and gasping like a woman washed ashore on a strange beach.

She closed her eyes. Tears trickled down her cheeks.

'Bess.' He moved to lie by her side. 'Are you weeping?'

'Aye.'

'Why?'

'No matter.'

'Because I'm going away?'

She hid her face in her hands.

'Why, Bess?'

Her guilt was too heavy, too deadening for speech. She had betrayed her husband by returning another man's ardour. She had broken the spiritual chains that bound her to Hugh and by which she desperately needed to be bound.

'Come, lass, I'm sorry I was ill-humoured.' He stroked her hair. 'I'll tell you why I'm leaving – I've had the foul-fated luck to love you and I'm not standing by to torment myself. I've been cuckolded long enough.'

'*You've* been cuckolded?' It was almost comic.

'Love gives me that right,' he said grimly. Then, in sudden eager hopefulness, 'But you love me too, else you'd not weep for me.'

'I'm weeping for myself,' she said.

For the death of pride in herself, and for the birth of loneliness.

She remembered an evening in St Giles soon after her wedding when she had knelt before the image of the Virgin to ask forgiveness of her trade. Looking up she saw the tall white candle grimed by many hands but burning purely, serenely. I am like that, she thought, my spirit flowing clean above the dirt of wax and wick, my love for Hugh inviolate.

She had felt part of Hugh, close as his skin, part of his sweat and sweetness, body and blood and breath. But now, briefly and fatally, she had responded to another man, diffusing the peace and the passion of belonging.

'Come with me, Bess,' Dougal said. 'We'll start anew. We'll pretend to be wed and no one in Argyllshire will be the wiser, no one here would ever find us. Nay,' he said, as she shook her head, 'let me tell you of my glen.'

He described a glen gold with gorse, surrounded by towering mountains. The river which ran through the valley was sluggish with fish, and the slopes were brown with cattle. Dougal had a small stone hut snug to the winds. The garden, grown to weeds in his absence, would flourish again under her care. The place was desolate in winter, made impassable by heavy snows, but no Campbell or his kin bowed to the freaks of the weather. They slogged through snow or mud or swam the swollen streams of spring to merry at one another's hearths, to dance and pipe and drink and tell the old, wild tales that were no wilder than the folk who had lived them.

'I know your heart,' Dougal said, bending to kiss her hair. 'It longs for peace and plenty. I'd stock your larder with beef and moorfowl, rabbits and squirrel and deer. You'd have firewood to warm you all of your days, not this stinking purl. A few months at St Andrews, then I'd be back to the valley – we need a surgeon among us. You'd need me for your birthing.'

She turned and raised her head. 'Birthing!'

'You'll birth in time – all women do. And merry-made or not, our sons would be Campbells. Some night I'd tumble you and you'd think it only another joust but the seed would bloom. Our sons and grandsons would spread like balefire, God knows how far, into what country or what century. And you'd live in each of them – the gold of your hair or the spook of your smile.' He pulled her close so that she lay with her head on his shoulder. 'You'd be safe, safe as these arms can make you. Why, even the thought of death is bonny when you know that kinswomen will shroud you and kinsmen plant you; when you know where you'll lie. And you'd live on in your sons and in the land – moor and mountain, apple blossom and heather honey . . .'

But she could think only of Hugh, alone and innocent on their pallet, sleeping with one hand curled under his cheek. He would never know about tonight, but she knew; and nothing would ever be the same.

'Come with me, Bess?'

'Oh, God,' she said, thinking of Hugh.

'You loved your Border hills. You would love these more.'

'I love Hugh,' she said. She could not wait to lie near him, though she might never feel close again.

He was asleep, as she had known he would be, naked in the heat, a stub of rushlight smoking the iron holder. She undressed and lay down beside him, loving him most at these times when, childlike, he snuggled into her shoulder pushing his curls against her throat. 'Bess?' he said, and her 'Aye,' was his bridge back to sleep.

She knew it was the cruel, body-soaking heat that forced him to move away and seek a cool place on the pallet, yet she felt intense rejection. She listened to his even breathing, to the stir of rats in the wall, to the far sound of hoofbeats. She thought of her first night in Edinburgh at the dismal lodging house, alone and despairing. She was more alone now, for the Virgin would not help her. Or perhaps . . .

She prayed, admitting her lust for Dougal 'which will never happen again, for I'll never bed with him'. But the prayer brought no solace.

She raised her sweating hair to cool her neck. She had no right to a goodwife's cap nor a key cord, not even in private. Flutter said that the mind was a fool, for ever tricking itself, but she could not trick hers. I am a slut, she thought, deep to my very soul.

She knew other sluts who were married – the only two, beside herself, in Edinburgh. Their husbands beat them and forgave them, beat out the guilt, hurt and kissed them in unending love and brutality. She wished that Hugh were like those men, strong in mind as in body.

But the evil must stay in me, she thought, to be borne alone with a love beyond tears.

She thought of the drab she met in The Cock and Stag, with her eternal chant: 'I'll quit next year.' Flutter had mocked, 'She has said that since 1500 – and she nearing forty.'

'But she *will* quit,' Bess had said.

'Ho! They'll bury her with painted tits.'

I've the night-frights, she thought. Nothing is changed with Hugh and me. And in a year, if the stall continues to prosper . . .

The tears came, flooding, choking, silent.

And in the strangest moment Bess had ever known, Hugh turned, still sleeping, and took her into his arms.

* * *

Bess paused at the Netherbow while the sentry examined a train of carts, questioning the drivers about the plague. A mile away the Castle hulked like a black mountain against the burn of the sunset. In the gutter dead rats stenched in the windless heat and bony dogs fought over the carcasses.

The last cart lumbered through the gate and the watchman called, 'Move on, lass. I know what pest *you* carry.'

She did not mind; it was an old jest between them. 'You'd never guess where I carry it tonight.'

'To the King?' he mocked.

'To Sir John Gordon.'

'If you're going to lie, why, then, lie in higher company.'

'It's no lie! He accosted me today in the Lawnmarket and asked me to come to his house.'

The watchman offered bawdy advice and she laughed and passed on through the gate, lifting her fresh green skirts clear of the dust and the rubbish. She hurried up the High Street with the red sun in her eyes, and its glow reflected on the grey houses turned them pink. Again she noticed dead rats; there seemed to be a fever among them and she thought it a pity, for, with the pigs, they kept the city from towering filth.

At the Cowgate she turned into a quiet wynd of elegant stone houses and paused at the one Sir John had mentioned, marked by its marble sundial in a patch of garden. A man-servant lighting torches at the entrance bowed as she approached and conducted her inside to a small parlour. His respect delighted her; he had mistaken her for a lady.

She fluffed her skirts and looked about her. The room was bare save for a bench by the hearth and a case of elaborately worked dags. On one wall a tusked boar's head grinned down at her, a monstrous thing with strangely vacant eyes. Perhaps, she thought, the eyes had been plucked . . .

'Sir John will see you, mistress.'

She followed the servant into a larger room rich with crimson draperies and massively carved furniture, then up a flight of stone stairs, through another room, into a bedchamber.

She had an impression of almost feminine luxury – a rose-painted ceiling, mirrors framed in silver, damask-covered chairs and a bed posted by porcelain nymphs and curtained in flowery silks. A servant was drawing the window draperies and Sir John sat reading in the light of a tall silver candlestick. Seeing Bess he dismissed the servants and put down his book.

'You are late,' he said.

She bobbed her humblest curtsy and murmured that she had been detained at the Netherbow. 'I am sorry, Your Lordship.'

He smiled. 'When in doubt of a man's title, always exalt it. My maidservant called a Bishop "Your Holiness" and won a place in his bed.'

There was something in his smile that made her uneasy, and a feline malice in his voice. Yet he was young and fair, indeed, as handsome as Hugh in a thin-faced golden way. Above the wavy blond beard was skin like the down of a peach and his mouth was pink as though painted. He motioned her to sit beside him on a cushion at his feet and she smelled the thyme and rosemary that emanated from his clothes. His hand on her hair was gentle as a woman's.

In a corner of the room she saw a small table laden with food and drink and she hoped to share it. Meals of fish and turnips were tiresome, with only a costly pear or a handful of peas as occasional luxuries.

For a while he said nothing, his fingers idling through her hair. Most men grabbed and pounced. This, she thought, was the way of gentlemen, an unhurried dalliance.

'Are you hungry?' he asked.

'Aye, sir. Almost always.'

He laughed. She wondered how laughter could have so cold a sound, like the colour of pewter.

'Eat, then. And bring me aqua vitae.'

She brought him the drink in a filigreed goblet. Then she filled her plate with roasted neat's tongues and boiled swan. She ate slowly, cherishing each bite.

'You'll be too full to bounce,' he said, suddenly querulous.

Reluctantly she wiped her hands on a linen strip. She had so wanted to try the violet-leaf omelette. . . . Quickly she came to his chair. 'I thank you, sir. I've not had such food in my life.'

'A merit, for you'll blowse soon enough. Fat folk die early.'

She knew – she had heard Dougal say so.

'And if the pest comes, they die first. So do sluts. Venery is death in pest time.'

But Dougal did not believe that. He had studied, and he knew. Copulation or no, folk died of the pest, nuns as quickly as whores. First they ached in the head, shivered in fever. Boils erupted on the neck, under the arms or thighs and swelled to the size of hen's eggs. Black spots appeared on the body, blood was vomited. And folk were dead in three days – goodwives and pursepricks and bishops shared the same agony and often the same bursting grave.

'I have seen the plague in Italy and Germany as well as France,' he said. 'It is caused by a meeting of Mars, Jupiter and Saturn under Aquarius.'

But Dougal said the cause was some strange, unknown miasma that poisoned the air.

'Sluts and satyrs die first.'

Why must he repeat that? She eyed the bed, wishing to fall to business and be gone. Gentlemen did not realize how they talked away time and sometimes resented paying for it, as though they flattered a lass by prattle.

'Are you not afraid?' he asked.

'Aye, my lord.'

'Of plague?'

'Aye.' He wants me to be afraid . . .

'You are safer here than in most places.' His speech was softly slurred. 'I've urns of wine and vinegar to purify the air, and I burn herbs.'

She could smell them. Silver pots hung from the walls, some curling with smoke.

He held out the empty goblet and she filled it. Perhaps he was mizzled. That would account for the strange unease she felt. Wine mellowed men, but this raw brew feyed them.

'It is not the plague you fear,' he said as she resumed her place on the cushion. 'You are afraid of me.'

She looked into the ash-grey eyes and forced a steady glance. 'Why should I be, and you so kind?'

He sipped, watching her over the rim of his goblet. He put the glass down, bent and caught her in his arms. She felt his cold, moist lips on her throat.

On the bed in the candle-snuffed darkness she heard the stir of trees in a sudden breeze, the whir of a weathervane. She thought beyond his embrace to the sweat-steamy sanctuary of the Cock and Stag where she hoped to find Flutter later tonight. He had promised to have news of the Spanish Ambassador's arrival. D'Ayola's entourage was gallant and generous.

Pesk take him, Sir John was dulled by drink, slow to rouse, slow to surfeit. At last he turned and sighed and lit the candle, and she was free to dress.

He put on a dark satin robe and resumed his place in the chair, watching as she tied the points of her sleeves and coiffed her hair at a mirror. Turning, she saw him pick up his book and begin to read.

She waited, reluctant to interrupt. Finally he looked up. 'So? Why do you tarry?'

'Your lordship owes me.'

'For what?' he asked gently. 'You ate, and I did you the honour of bedding you.'

'But, sir—'

'Was it not an honour?'

'Indeed—'

'Then go.'

She could not believe it. Sometimes a gentleman argued, but this had never happened.

'I asked you here to pleasure you. Haven't I done so?'

'Aye, sir, but I need the pay.'

He raised his thin gold eyebrows. 'Is that my concern?'

She could only think that he was accustomed to the favours of fine ladies, that he had never known a slut before and did not understand what was expected. As she pondered what to do he rose and went to the table and gulped a goblet of aqua vitae as though it were ale.

What's amiss, she wondered, that a wealthy young gentleman could be so unworldly? Or was it arrogance? She assembled the bits and pieces of gossip about the nobility she had heard from Flutter. Aye, many were haughty but surely none stupid in matters like this.

'Sire,' she said.

He exploded in laughter. 'Now you exalt me to royalty.'

'Sir, I think you mistake the matter. A whore is paid in money.'

'By those who chose to do so.'

He had wasted nearly two hours of her time. Wordlessly she walked to the door.

'Wait,' he said. 'Come here.'

She came to him slowly.

'You sulk.'

'Oh, no, sir.'

Again his smile, the teeth china-white against the pink lips.

'Do you know,' he said, 'you are very beautiful. Perhaps too beautiful.'

'Sir?' She waited hopefully.

'There is no imperfection.'

She shifted uneasily.

'I have studied art, and I am an excellent judge. There

should be some imperfection as contrast, else the beauty lacks.'

Such talk bewildered her. If only he would pay her, but he pattered on about Greeks and Romans and beauty while the sand-glass trickled another quarter-hour.

She had the fancy that he was talking more to himself than to her, and he drank as he talked. Finally she broke in. 'It's late, sir. I must go.'

Not in despair, but in release. She would gladly give a crown to be down those embellished stairs and on to the street.

'But you'll not go unrewarded. Come.'

He led her to the tumbled bed. A little gold casket lay on the table beside it.

'Sit down,' he said.

She sat on the edge of the bed while he unlocked the casket. She tried to peer in, but the tall raised lid obstructed her view.

'This will make you more beautiful,' he said, 'by providing contrast.'

She dared not hope for anything of real value, but she longed for a bit of coral or a trifle of jet. The only ornament she possessed was the waist cord Flutter had given her.

He withdrew a slender, cruelly-edged knife hilted in diamonds. The white flashing fire of the jewels dazzled her.

'You will thank me,' he said softly.

She was too overwhelmed to speak. Then she looked into his face and was seized with such horror that she sat as though paralysed, unable to move. As his hand reached out and tore her bodice she felt her lips jerk in a soundless scream. Then the steel slashed her right breast. There was a moment of searing, scalding agony before her eyesight blurred and she fell into darkness.

When she regained consciousness she was lying face up on the bed, her body bathed in blood. She vomited and called out weakly but no one came.

Again she fainted and awakened. Time was measured in

pain beyond tears. Finally she rose and crept to the door and down the stairs and the house was silent as a vault. Through a red fog of torment she had one thought – to reach St Giles and die on hallowed ground.

Father Duncan found her on the High Street and took her to the surgeon.

* * *

The long, slow twilight had deepened so that they could scarcely see one another. As she finished her story, Father Duncan said, 'You must not think on vengeance.'

He had read her mind.

'You must leave his punishment to God.'

Bess started to tell him that Guilie planned to cast a spell, then remembered his horror of witches. Instead she said, 'He may be killed in battle.'

'Such a thought is vengeful. You must find it in your heart to forgive him.'

He blessed her and left. She groped for a candle to light, then decided against it. Her thoughts were best left to darkness and the beat of rain and the high, womanish scream of the north wind.

2

Margaret Stuart

August 3rd, 1513

WIND WHISTLED THROUGH the tiring-room at Linlithgow Palace, moving the thin silk draperies and fluttering the candles in their oaken sconces. She stared into the mirror, hearing the soft chatter of her women as they assembled unguents, paints and pins for her hair.

Her hair was her pride, a pale silver-blonde, straight and luxuriant, falling to her knees. But her face did not please her. Her nose was snub, her cheeks too round, and her ruddy complexion required frequent bleaching. Now Lady Crawford was preparing a new remedy learned on a visit to Rome. Its base was the familiar white lead, but there were other ingredients – oil of bird lime, mashed radish, swan fat, hare's gall, veal marrow and lemons. With a final stir, Lady Crawford set the bowl on the dressing table.

'If your Majesty pleases, it is ready.'

Margaret leaned forward in her chair and smelt it. 'It stinks. The meat's rotted.'

'It's the rot that helps whiten the skin, Madam.'

'Add oil of jasmine,' suggested Lady Argyll.

Lady Crawford was reluctant, for one should follow a recipe exactly, but the Queen insisted. The mask was sponged on and Margaret sat back with her eyes closed, waiting for it to dry.

'I wish you all to gather dew for me,' she said. 'Queen Anne uses dew and asses milk. 'Tis said it makes a fine varnish.'

The ladies-in-waiting exchanged dismayed glances.

'Indeed, Madam,' Lady Buchan said, 'but it will take a heap o' dew—'

'Then set the maids and pages to help you.'

'But how does one gather it?' Lady Huntley asked.

'How should I know that?' Margaret asked pettishly. 'It's surely gatherable. You don't suppose Queen Anne rolls in the grass for it?' She touched her face. 'This brew still stinks.'

Lady Huntley placed a vial of civet to her nose.

'See to my hair,' Margaret ordered.

Lady Crawford combed out the lice and brushed three hundred strokes. The mask was removed and egg white applied. When it dried the face was bathed in white wine and patted dry with a scented cloth.

It did look paler, Margaret agreed. She called for burned rabbit's head powder, applied it to a strip of pomegranate peel, and brushed her teeth. Now she was ready for painting.

Her brows were plucked and darkened. Kohl and belladonna made her blue-grey eyes seem larger, brighter. There was cerise for her small pouting mouth and a patch to accentuate the dimple there. Her hair was parted in the middle and drawn back into a smooth, shiny helmet.

She rose and they removed her robe and dressed her in a blue silk gown stamped with silver, the square neck bordered in seed pearls, the sweeping sleeves lined with silver cloth. Then they set a half-moon of silver far to the back of her head. Lady Bothwell brought the jewel chest.

Margaret chose a string of pearls and pearl earrings, regretting as always how little selection there was. James had been generous with rubies and emeralds and diamonds during the first years of their marriage, but of late he had given her only trinkets of amethyst and gold. And her brother Harry still refused to send her dowry of jewels, though James threatened war.

Of course, there were other reasons for war. Harry had always been arrogant. It was monstrous that, not satisfied to be king of England, he trumpeted himself king of Scotland as well. Still, she saw no reason to battle over a mere concept. And if Scots ships had been pirated, well, Scots had pirated in turn. Despite the peace treaty Border warfare had never ceased, only diminished through the years.

'Your majesty is beautiful,' Lady Argyll said.

She accepted the compliment as her due. Wryly, she thought, there has never been an ugly queen in all of history – court painters and court poets see to that. And she was not precisely ugly nor even plain, but merely sightly. She wished that her mouth were larger, her chin a fraction of an inch longer, her cheeks less babyish. At twenty-four she had a voluptuous body married to the face of a petulant child.

'This gown is a trifle tight,' Margaret said. 'Perhaps I am with child.'

She saw Lady Bothwell wince, catching the barb full-force. The other women exclaimed in delight.

'I am not sure,' Margaret said. She looked at Agnes Bothwell and drove the barb in deep. 'But it is more than likely, considering . . .' She assumed a secret smile and let the sentence trail off.

She wanted a child, not merely to spite Agnes, but to provide another heir. She had lost two sons and two daughters. Only James, Duke of Rothesay, survived, blessedly healthy at sixteen months. 'God grant Your Majesty is right,' Lady Bothwell said, her smile set as a gravestone. She held out a crystal vial. 'Does Your Majesty wish myrrh?'

Margaret took the bottle and scented her throat and hair. Then she moved to the door, the blue train sweeping the rushes. Despite her perfume and the spices burning in the braziers she could smell those rushes, permeated with bits of rotting food, dog-droppings and cat urine. James loved animals and they had the run of the place.

A page with a wind-flickered candle led her down a long corridor to a small oak-panelled oratory, her private chapel. Her confessor, the Bishop of Tutberry, knelt at the altar. He rose as she entered and kissed her hand.

'You summoned me, Madam?'

'Aye.' She knelt briefly, crossed herself, then motioned

him to sit beside her on the stone bench. 'I require your counsel.'

He did not look like a wise man, she thought, for wise men were dour, ascetic. His face was lined with smile wrinkles and his mouth in its folds of fat, seemed always ready to laugh. He looked younger than his fifty years, with a pink skin and white teeth. A waggle of grey hair fell from a curly cockade over a low, broad forehead.

'Whatever Your Majesty requires of my poor mind is yours to command.' He bent his head, resting his third chin on his collar, prepared for listening.

'More than ever, the King is set on war,' she said. 'Somehow we must prevent it. I have had evil dreams, dreams of such disaster they can only be omens sent to warn us, but when I tell him he laughs and bids me mind my own matters. You know how wilful he is, how hard it is to deflect him once his course is determined.'

'I had hoped the threat of excommunication would suffice,' the Bishop said. 'But if he will not heed the Pope, Madam, how will he heed other counsel?'

'Even in his holiness, the Pope is but a man. And James fears no man. Sometimes,' she added softly, 'I do not even think he fears God Himself.'

The Bishop was silent, plump hands caressing his crucifix.

'What of a pilgrimage? What if he went afar, not to St Ninian's or St Duthac but out of the country? Perchance I could persuade him to journey clear to the Holy Land, for he has often talked of it.'

'He's not talked of it in more than a year. You could never budge him from Scotland save to war with England. I think he hates my brother more than he fears hellfire. He cannot bear to be named Harry's vassal.'

'The sin of pride,' sighed the Bishop.

'But a king cannot humble himself. We cannot persuade him through logic.' Tiredly she touched her forehead. 'I have been thinking, thinking, until my head wears bands. I scarce can eat, I toss in sleep, and my dreams drip blood . . .'

She told him about the dreams. Her astrologer said that Mars ruled James this month, and the influence would last through August into September. '. . . Yesterday, stitching an altar cloth, my finger was pricked, and blood ran. Another omen.'

'I think the King requires such dreams as you have had, Madam. But since dreams are not available to all of us, why, then, a vision. A vision of doom.'

Such visions were common to the Scottish kings, she remembered.

'But James seems impervious.'

'Then a vision must be created, Madam.'

'Created of what?'

'Of a ruse. I do not approve trickery, Madam, but when the matter is of such gravity, I see no other way.'

She waited for him to explain, watching a moth flutter in the altar light.

'Long ago there was an Eastern prince who was persuaded from a foolish murder by a vision of a god who warned him that if he dared the deed, the knife would be turned on himself. It was later found that the god who appeared to him was a human imposter hired by his brother.'

Margaret nodded. 'It is something to think on. Where did the vision take place?'

'At night in the prince's chamber.'

She thought of the crowded palace. 'Our chambers are too full.'

'There is the church.'

Again she nodded. No one came to the royal chapel save by invitation, and God knew it was dark enough there of a night, so dark that she never entered unless accompanied by a stream of taper bearers. 'But who shall appear as the vision?' she asked. 'He must be a stranger to the King, yet we dare not trust a stranger.'

They sat in thought. Finally she said, 'Surely you could find some discreet monk who has never been to court.'

'There are many in my diocese, Madam, but I shall not ask one to lend himself to a hoax.'

'We must think on it,' she said. 'There must be some-one . . .' Finally, wearily, she rose, dismissing him. 'I shall pray for guidance.'

Alone, she prayed, but futilely. Perhaps she should re-linquish the scheme altogether. It was too dangerous. If James learned of her meddling, his contempt would be flaying.

She turned from the altar; prayer was beyond her mood. She needed gossip and gaiety, a break in sombreness. Following the page she climbed to her tower apartment and summoned Master Pfludder.

* * *

Her bower was as grim as the rest of Linlithgow. Tattered grey hunting tapestries barely covered the dank rock walls. The furnishings, of odds and ends brought from Holyrood, were old and shabby. There were only two chairs, and the rose velvet cushions on the floor were splitting with age. Here, high in the tower, there were no window draperies to repel draughts, for she had not expected such weather after the heat of Edinburgh. She had brought thirty-seven carts of summer clothes but not one fur cloak.

Huddled in a woollen shawl she sat at the fire with her ladies and listened to the wind thudding the palace like a battering ram. Of all her castles she liked Linlithgow least, but none were ever completely furnished nor quite home to her. James was restless, moving from here to Edinburgh, from Stirling to Falkland. Thus she was constantly uprooted, but she never complained. When he asked her to accom-pany him on his travels she felt honoured; when he did not, she worried that he had found a new mistress in some country retreat. Better Agnes Bothwell than some unknown menace. Better a light love than a true love.

Her ladies admitted Flutter and she dismissed them. 'You are a boon in this dismal place,' she said.

He bowed and smiled. She wondered if he filed his teeth, for they looked rat-sharp. She had heard strange tales of him, that he killed for pleasure in inns and brothels, but she did not believe them. Or, if by chance they were true, they had nothing to do with her. He was her friend, her confidant, her spy; even, at times, her adviser.

'I've no fresh news for Your Majesty,' he said apologetically. 'Little has happened since yesterday, save an occurrence on the Border. You mind the Laird of Lurie who lives near Ninestane Rig?'

She remembered him well – a bully, a wife-beater, rich of land and sheep. Once at Falkland he had over-drunk, vomited on the table and been banished from court.

'Aye,' she said, 'an ill-gaited man.'

'He thrashed a stable boy near to death.'

Margaret yawned. She hoped Flutter had a story, not an incident.

'The boy recovered and took vengeance.'

She perked. 'Against his *master*?'

'Aye, they say he was mad. In any case, the boy contrived to lock the laird in the dungeon. It's deep underground, with walls ten feet thick, and no one heard his cries. For three weeks his household searched the countryside. Then a maid and a page, seeking privacy for love, descended to the dungeon and found him.'

'Dead?'

'Aye. He had eaten both his hands.'

She shivered delightedly. No one was so amusing as Flutter. 'Perhaps rats ate them.'

'The flesh was still in his mouth.'

Their talk turned to personal matters. She told him that she suspected Lady Bothwell encouraged James to war.

'She tells me it is impossible to dissuade him.'

'Has she tried?'

'She says she could scarcely succeed where Parliament has failed.'

'But has she *tried*?'

'So she says, Madam, and I believe it. With his death, she stands to lose everything.'

'With his death! Surely he'd not fight in the field!'

'You know him, Madam.'

'But that would be madness! That would be—'

That would be fully in his character, knight-errant as he was, fool that he was, dupe of a queen he had never met nor likely ever would.

'May Anne of Brittany be damned to hell!'

'Amen,' he said. 'But if it were not Queen Anne, some other cause would sway him. There is provocation enough.'

She said, 'I have argued with him point by point to no avail. I have schemed and plotted.' She told him of her conversation with the Bishop. 'But a hoax is too difficult. We cannot trust a stranger to impersonate the vision, and a stranger it must be.'

For a while he sat in thought, softly plucking his lute. 'If Your Majesty will forgive me, I think the Bishop's idea childish.'

She frowned.

'But I do not say it should be dismissed, for in many ways the King has the pure heart of a child.'

'This is true.'

'To effect such a ruse you require a man who will not bungle, a man of subtlety and experience. There's a player named Jock MacDermod, waiting below in the kitchen, hoping to entertain Your Majesties at supper.'

There were always strolling players, tumblers, gipsy dancers anxious to perform, grateful for bread and meat or a bed in the straw. Most of them were not worth lodging.

'The fellow has talent, and I'd stake my life he can be trusted.'

'You know him well?'

'We've drunk and gamed together for years. There's no better way to know a man.'

She hesitated.

'What vision do you have in mind, Madam? The spirit of the King's father? Or perhaps some saint?'

'A saint would be safest.'

'The King would listen to St John,' Flutter said.

'Aye, so he would. . . . What of the man's looks?'

'MacDermod? He's a tall, lank fellow with yellow locks and beard. In a flowing robe and sandals he'd make a credible saint.'

'Send him to me after supper,' Margaret said, 'and make certain he remains out of sight of the nobles.'

'Spare your worry, Madam. May I beg a favour?'

She waited.

'I should like to write the lines he speaks.'

'Good,' she said. 'Make them fearsome. Warn against war, and tell the King to trust no women, nor dally with them.'

Flutter hid a smile.

* * *

The following night in the Church of St Michael, Margaret and the Bishop stood in the deepest shadows, concealed behind a pillar. They heard the flap of bats high up in impenetrable darkness and the harsh cry of rooks through the open window. Presently, lights bobbed at the entrance and footsteps sounded. Margaret reached for the Bishop's hand and held it tightly.

The King entered, followed by Sir David Lindsay and Sir John Forman. Tall in a pale gold doublet, he moved past them to the royal stall, genuflected and sat down with his head bowed. The two courtiers stood in the stall behind him.

Five minutes passed, ten. Candles sputtered at the altar. Far off in the hills Margaret could hear the barking of foxes.

Silently, almost imperceptibly, a blue-robed figure moved from the side of the church to the altar. Over his robe he wore a white linen girdle and he carried a tall staff.

'Sire,' he said.

The King looked up.

'Sire, I am come to warn thee.'

James rose. His hand slid to his dagger. 'Who are you?'

'My mother has sent me to thee desiring thee not to pass into that country thou covetest, for if thou dost, neither thee nor any with thee will fare well. Few will return . . . Further, she bids thee not to dally with women or use their counsel else thou wilt be confounded and brought to shame.'

'Who are you?' James repeated.

'I am John, adopted of the Virgin Mary.'

Slowly he moved away and was lost in the shadows.

The King remained standing. It seemed to Margaret that she could hear his breath, even his heartbeat, so still he was. Then he went to the altar and knelt in prayer. The two courtiers stood rigid, unmoving. When the King turned they followed him out of the door in silence.

After their footsteps had died away on the cobbles Margaret and the Bishop crept out of the side entrance where Jock MacDermod stood waiting, muffled in a black cloak.

Margaret handed him a little bag of gold. 'You did well. Now swear you will tell no one of this.'

'I have sworn, Madame.' He bowed deeply. 'I am honoured to serve you.'

She was suddenly exultant, sure she had succeeded where James's advisers had failed. The shrewdest brains of men were no match for a woman's wit. Likely tonight she had saved Scotland and England from war, perhaps even the lives of her husband and brother. It was a pity that the world would never know. She thought of the first Queen Margaret of Scotland, canonized a saint. *She* had never done so wondrous a thing, only puny goodnesses, yet her chapel on Edinburgh Rock was a holy shrine. It wasn't fair . . .

The Bishop was bumbling absolution for the actor's sin.

'Come,' she said to him, 'take me to the palace.'

She had hoped to find James alone in his oratory, shocked and humbled by what he had experienced, but he was in the Great Hall surrounded by courtiers. Close to him on cushions below his dais sat his favourites – Lindsay and Forman, who had witnessed the vision; young Alexander Stuart, Archbishop of St Andrews, James's son by Marion Boyd (dear God, Scotland crawled with the King's merry-made progeny!) the poets William Dunbar and Gavin Douglas. And of course Agnes, Countess of Bothwell.

Agnes shared a large cushion with Adam, her red-headed husband, but her body was arched towards the King. Save for the swell of bosom it was a girl's body, slender of waist and wrist and thigh, not befitting, Margaret thought, an eighteen-year-old woman who was mother of a child. The child was not the King's, God be praised, but legitimate – a red-haired boy born last year. No doubt the slut longed for a son by the King, for this brought honours and estates and a deep, sometimes permanent closeness.

It was scant comfort that Agnes wore modest jewels. (Jewels, she had told Flutter, were for hags of twenty-four who needed such adornment to perk their plainness.) Her smooth black hair was braided with strands of gold and turquoise, her smooth white throat was bare. She flaunted a gown of turquoise silk under a kirtle of mauve, the skirts spilling over her husband's lap. Her pet racoon, leashed with amethysts, slept at her side.

The poet Dunbar called her 'the black kitten', for she was all whim and mischief and grace, black of hair, with black eyes that were long and slanty. Her hands, quick and deft, toyed with an ivory fan – surely an affectation in this draughty hall. Margaret thought, she looks like a cat, red-lipped, avid for prey.

There was no way to fight her as yet. Margaret could not dare the King's displeasure lest, Stuart-like, he prove reck-less and make a choice between them. She must hold what she had of him, though it be only love brewed of loyalty.

The court rose as she entered but she motioned them to be

seated and took her place on the dais beside James. The four Italian musicians resumed a pavane with viols, cithern and gamba. She noticed that James seemed abstracted, drumming his fingers into the palm of his hand, staring up at the heavy oaken chandeliers, then off into some private dream. Good, she thought. The vision has shaken him.

The music tumbled, ending in a flipping cartwheel of gaiety. The Italians retired and a Scots minstrel sang of the death of love and the death of the year.

Aye, Margaret thought, the autumn is nearly upon us. A few tarnished leaves already fluttered on the banks of Linlithgow Loch. She had heard the click of crickets. And now through the open window wind carried the smell of earth mould and dying fern.

How dismal these Great Halls were, barren of colour save for the dress of the courtiers. As in her tower chamber, the faded arras barely concealed three of the rock walls; the fourth was hidden by poor painted cloths, mere rags to repel the cold. Above the great stone fireplace hung rusty hunting spears crossed above an ugly, dog-mangled elk's head. Fox brushes hung at one end, mangy from the years. Now after supper the long oak tables had been trestled and the benches set flush to the walls. Wooden candle holders stood in each corner, fastened with rushlights. The floor was carpeted with stiff, browning hay.

The King left his chair abruptly and took Margaret's hand, drawing her to her feet. The courtiers rose and the singers broke off in mid-note. A trumpet shrilled.

As Archbishop of St Andrews, the King's son blessed the court. Taperbearers lit Margaret and James up the narrow stone stairs. She paused at the landing, hoping that he would invite her into his apartments or follow her up to her tower. But as always she said, 'God rest you, Sire.'

'Come,' he said, 'I must talk with you.'

A fire burned in his chamber which was the largest and pleasantest in the palace. There were lion tapestries, thick and tawny, and heavy bed curtains of dark yellow velvet.

At the window she saw the moon cruising over Linlithgow Loch and a scattering of wind-driven stars.

'Be seated, Margaret.'

She sat on a hearth cushion. He took the chair.

'There was an odd occurrence at St Michael's tonight.' He told her what had happened. 'I think it a hoax.'

She was dismayed. 'Why?'

'Forman and Lindsay agreed that the figure seemed human in voice and gesture.'

Damn Forman and Lindsay to everlasting hell! Both shared her horror of war (or so they said) and now they failed to grasp a rare advantage.

'I, too, sensed it was no spirit, but flesh and blood. Someone arranged this – perhaps the English, seeking to intimidate us.'

She could only listen to his speculations, helpless to change his mind. What a waste of effort, and what a waste of gold! Her money was meagre and she had given MacDermod more than she could spare of her month's allowance.

'Yet if it *is* an English trick it bodes well for us. In this way, Henry reveals his fear.'

She said, 'Love, I have battered you for months, and I know I weary you. But if you will allow me to speak just once more—'

'I was warned,' he said smilingly, 'not to heed the counsel of women.'

'Please, Sire. The question I raise is this: what loyalty should you have for Anne of Brittany? Why should you fight her battles?'

'Our long alliance with France—'

'Does not provide that you should go to such lengths! Ever since you received her letter you've behaved like a man bewitched. Don't you see what she is doing, using your chivalry to her own ends?' Margaret mimicked, paraphrasing Anne's letter which had contained a ring and a scented glove. '"I send you these tokens to be my knight-errant, to ride three feet into English soil and strike a blow for my honour." *Her* honour, not ours. And who should defend her honour but her own husband? Why doesn't King Louis invade England? I'll tell you why – he is too shrewd, too prudent of money and men—'

'Peace,' he said gently. 'We'll not talk of it further.' Bending, he stroked a spaniel that nuzzled his shoe. 'Mignon has burrs in her coat.'

You fool, she thought, you stubborn, romantic fool! She felt at times like a loving but exasperated mother helpless to stem the recklessness of youth.

'Next week,' he said, 'I go to hunt at Falkland, then to St Duthric.'

His annual pilgrimage, north to the Highlands.

'I shall come back here to escort you to Edinburgh in mid-August. But when we march you shall return here for safety.'

'If it goes against us there will be no safety anywhere in Scotland,' she said grimly. 'Harry will not be content with victory on English soil. He'll invade us and plunder. It will be ghastly.'

He chuckled. 'Why do you think your brother so formidable? Why do you even consider him a worthy opponent? Mark you the disaster he suffered in France last year – even in league with Spain he was routed ignominiously. His troops, highly paid as they were on sixpence a day and Spanish wine, mutinied. They'll do so again.'

She appealed to his most vulnerable point. 'Since we are bound by treaty not to war with England we should not declare war at all, but particularly not while my brother is fighting in France and unable to accept your challenge. To take such advantage is not the act of a true knight.'

'He has made the treaty a farce.'

The spaniel jumped into his lap and he pushed it off. 'Look you, Margaret, we have the greatest fleet in the world, new French arms and an invincible army.'

She echoed the counsel of his advisers. 'Harry's army,

being split, may be small but his men are trained. Ours are raw recruits.'

He still spoke gently though she knew his patience was fraying. 'We have a cause they believe in. The people are with me in all I do. You forget that men fired by love and loyalty will fight even beyond their normal abilities.'

'And shall you lead them into battle yourself?'

'Of course. Do you think I play at war?'

He rose and paced the room, tall, slender, finely proportioned in his golden doublet and long grey trunk hose. Aye, she thought wryly, Queen Anne's gallant knight, even in looks. His face was lean and strong with glowing dark eyes and a wide, firm mouth. In repose the face was merry, the mouth up-tilted, the eyes ready to crinkle in amusement. Now he was frowning.

She went to him and caressed the silver-flecked dark red hair that fell to his collar. 'Please, my treasure, I only fret for your safety. You cannot fathom this because you fear nothing.'

He was instantly mollified. 'I'll not widow you.' He kissed her cheek. 'Not even to pleasure Archie Douglas.'

She knew he was teasing but she blushed. A woman – especially a woman unloved – must have an admirer, just as she had lap dogs and jesters to amuse her. Douglas was young, near her own age, with the same love of masques and dancing, a playmate with whom to pass the hours when James was away. Often when she strolled the gardens at cock-shut he accompanied her. It was pleasant to be adored . . .

She shrugged. 'Douglas behaves like a swooning lover, but it is only pretty pretence. He loves his wife. But it is fashionable – and romantic – to worship a queen.'

'You under-estimate your charms.'

Always gallant . . .

'But since we're on the matter I've certain thoughts – nay, commands. In the event of my death you shall marry a suitable noble as soon as the mourning year is over. To have but one heir is too great a gamble with fate.'

'I feel I am with child again,' she reminded him.

'But we are not sure, and there's many a slip betwixt womb and crown. What if Jamie be suddenly stricken?'

'Aye,' she said softly. 'That could happen.'

The sweating sickness, the strangling disease, the plague . . .

'Before I go I shall leave papers appointing you Regent until Jamie is of age to rule. He must be crowned the instant my death is confirmed.'

She nodded, head bent. Always she had wanted power but the supreme power of Regency would be gall in her mouth with James gone. Still, she would do as he bade her.

'You've never found me remiss in my duty, Sire.'

'There's a good lass. And now you've another duty.'

She looked up.

'Come to bed.'

It was not duty. But it was sad delight to lie in his arms longing for words of love that had never been spoken, and likely never would be.

* * *

At dawn on August 8th James left Linlithgow, riding north to Falkland and Tain. From her tower Margaret watched the cavalcade of horsemen until the last gold banners were lost in the mists.

She had not reminded James that he was leaving her on their eleventh wedding anniversary nor had any courtier remembered. Rather than stir a pale flurry of celebration she said nothing. It would be just another day, more dour than most, for ragged clouds gusted down the north sky and the Loch was obscured in fog.

She dined as usual at ten in the morning, visited little James in his nursery, embroidered a headdress, read a bit of Douglas's translation of Virgil. Bored, she called for her female jester but Daft Ann was ill of the Quacks. Archie

Douglas and Master Pfludder had left in the King's train. She could not hunt in the fog. There was nothing to do.

Restlessly she wandered the palace, even down to the kitchen. The dinner dishes were spread about the floor and a dozen hounds were licking them clean. For a while she stood at the boiling hearth and watched a chef make soup. Another, at a table, was cutting off a boar's head, and she left hastily, sickened by the sight of blood. Assuredly, she was with child . . .

Finally the endless day ended. The palace fires were banked, the candles snuffed, and Margaret lay in her silk-sheeted bed behind musty blue curtains. But she could not sleep; she feared sleep. There might be the blood-dripping dreams again, the red horror of battle re-enacted. But dreams, she thought, were not always trustable. As a young girl betrothed to James she had dreamed of Scotland many nights, seeing herself robed in ermine, a jewel-heavy beauty moving past worshipping courtiers into fantastically golden halls. Those dreams had seemed more real than Harry's warnings.

Even as a boy, Harry was savagely opposed to her marriage with James, hating Scotland, its people and its king as only a child can hate. She remembered his malice on that November night at Westminster when the Scottish ambassadors had paid their first visit on the long, delicate matter of marriage negotiations. It was a gusty night much like this, with the wind rattling the leaded panes of her bedchamber. She saw herself as she paced the floor in a patched wool nightrobe, the rushes tickling her bare feet. She heard Harry's strident laughter as she stubbed her toe on a footstool . . .

* * *

'I've hurt myself!' she said angrily.

He laughed still harder.

'You little fart!' She rubbed the wounded toe. 'Is it not enough I'm in such suspense? Why should I be excluded from the conference? Why should a clatter of old men decide my marriage?' They could hear music from the Great Hall below and she said, 'I should be down there. After all, I am twelve years old.'

'Perhaps Father keeps you hid for good reason. Your portraits flatter you.'

She lunged at him and he tried to trip her but she regained her balance and he ducked her slap. 'What an irony,' he said, 'that the marriage is meant to bring peace for ever. If the Scots knew you they'd think better than to tie with a shrew.'

'I am not,' she said icily. 'You plague me to fury.'

'I am only a mischievous boy,' he mocked.

So their parents thought, but she found him cruel. She never considered him as younger than she, for at ten he was precocious beyond his years. Everyone spoiled him, everyone admired his tall, strong body, his dimples, his gold-red curly hair. Silly maids sighed over his eyes, not noticing how hard and narrowly shrewd they were, like glitters of blue glass. Yet, she admitted, he could be, if it suited him, charming beyond belief.

His moods changed quickly. Now he was smiling and his voice wheedled. 'Be nice to me, Mag, and I'll gossip you.'

'You know no more gossip than I.'

'Ah, but I do – from keyholes. And from Scots in drink.'

'Well, then? What do you know?'

'That King James never wished to marry before because he did not wish to relinquish his mistresses. There are two.'

She shrugged. 'I'm above such rivalry. I am not interested.'

'You lie vehemently, sister.'

'Well, then, who are these trollops, if you know so much?'

'Janet Kennedy and Margaret Drummond, but there are others as well.' He smiled. 'Most of his gold goes to support their brats. He leaves litters like a tomcat.'

'If I marry him, he could change—'

'Ha! As a cock changes when a new hen appears.'

'But,' she said, 'you told me he had not wished to marry before because he did not wish to relinquish his tarts. Now, obviously, he *does* wish to.' She was triumphant. 'Do you see?'

'The difference now,' he said, 'is that he'll hide the wenches. That's a man's way. But of course, you don't care . . . however, you might care to know that he wears an iron belt of penance.'

'For what?'

'For having led a rebellion that ended in his father's murder.'

'Oh, that,' she said scornfully, 'that was years ago. He was only a boy duped by wicked lords. Why must you bring up the dregs of scandal? Have you never heard that he is good and gentle and beloved as no other king in Europe?'

'Aye. It is curious, but I've heard that only from Scots.'

'Then see for yourself.' She went to an oaken chest and removed from its linen wrapping a miniature framed in gold. 'Is this the face of a murderer, a lecher?'

She had studied it for many weeks and each time she felt like telling it her troubles. A man with such a face would be sympathetic, tender, immensely protective. Strength lay there like a sword sheathed in silk. The dark eyes were direct.

'I've always thought so,' Harry said complacently. 'And he's old, too – twenty-eight. Christ, Mag, will you never sit down? Here, have a sucket.'

He offered a velvet box but she refused. Her physician had advised her to eat as little as possible lest she burst her gowns. Not that she was a pudding-filler, but roundly developed. James must find her beautiful . . .

'Why do you hate him so?' she asked.

'Because he is beneath us, because Scotland is a barbaric land a century behind any other. In the isles, men still wear bear pelts—'

'They do not!'

'They do. And I hate to see a Tudor mate with a Stuart.'

'Harry,' she said, 'have you ever heard – I mean, do you know how men and women mate?'

'Don't *you*?'

'Nay, I think I do but I am not sure.'

He snickered and told her.

For a while she was silent, reflective. 'That is what I thought. I am not surprised.'

He bit into a sucket. 'A pity you'll not know a young lover. Old men stink.'

'My God, Harry, what choice have I? I must wed someone, and if James will not have me, all Europe will know and laugh.'

'And count you lucky.'

Ann Luke, Henry's old nurse, poked her nose in the door. 'Your Highnesses, Prince Arthur is here.'

Their elder brother came in and Margaret ran to him. 'What happened? What did they say? Is it settled?'

'Not yet.' He was a tall, emaciated boy of fifteen, hacked by a cough. 'It may take time. This is not merely a marriage negotiation, but a peace treaty. With your union hundreds of years of war would end.'

'I know,' she said impatiently, 'but when will it be settled?'

'Weeks, perhaps months. They have only begun to haggle terms and whenever they reach towards some point of agreement, Father or Lord Bothwell or the bishops raise another splinter. They eat and drink and argue and flatter – God knows when it will end.'

'Damn!' Margaret plumped down on the bed, stretching her legs, arching her arms behind her head. 'I can't bear the waiting.' She stared up at the oak beams. 'They have no thought of what I'm enduring.'

'You must endure,' Arthur said. 'Mind you, even if it is agreed on, the marriage cannot take place for two years.'

'Or until I bleed,' Margaret said.

'Or until then.'

'Marriage, marriage, I'm ill of the word,' Henry said. 'I'll never marry, I'll just big them.'

'And forget your duty as a prince?' Arthur asked, shocked.

'You'll do your duty, brother. Why must I? Catty will foal in time, and by the look of her, often.'

Arthur's pale cheeks flushed. He had been married to Catherine of Aragon only nine days.

Ann Luke reappeared. 'Come, love,' she said to Henry. 'Get you to bed. It's near ten o'clock and I have me orders.'

Henry dawdled to the door, clutching his box of sweets. He turned a sugar-smeared face, shrugged, grimaced, and clowned out humming.

Arthur sat down on the bed beside Margaret. 'You must learn patience, and for your lifetime. You are too impetuous, too quick to speak before you think, you must study to curb your tongue. If all goes well you will meet James's ambassadors and you must impress them by your prudence and good sense. Their ears will miss nothing, nor their eyes.'

'For a princess,' she said, thinking of the other royal ladies of Europe, 'I am comely.'

'So you are.'

'But Harry says I look like a bloody blooming milkmaid.'

'Be glad. I've seen more beautiful wenches on the farms than at court. No man wants to kiss a paintbox or caress a corset.'

'Do you? Does Catty paint and pad?'

He groaned. 'Now, that is what I mean. You must not ask such questions, nay, not even of me.'

'Then how am I to know anything?'

'By observing. By listening. You've natural wit, and you have been taught.'

'What am I taught?' she asked sullenly. 'Do I have Erasmus, Skelton, Tom Moore? Harry studies philosophy and mathematics while I know only a smattering of languages and a whisper of history.'

'You study embroidery, music, mythology—'

'Will these help me to rule a land?'

'Rule? Such responsibility is not required of you. You need only to emulate our mother – rear children, greet guests with grace, do pious works.'

'I'll not live such a life! I'll not be hidden in a bower between Masses, I'll not withdraw from revels at nine, I'll not mix with monks and nuns 'til I go grey! And I'll not wear grandmother's cast-off gowns!' She thrust out the skirt of her woollen robe. 'Ugly, scratchy, and twenty years old! Do you know that I wore torn hose to your wedding and shoes with holes? Do you know that at the tournaments I shivered in a furless cloak? With all his store of gold and lands Father is a miser.' She pointed to the turf fire. 'He does not even allow me logs and I've had no wax candles since Whitsuntide. Princess!' She spat the word. 'Merchant's daughters fare better than Mary and I. She's wearing a gown I wore at five, patched in the seat. Edmund is wearing Harry's old smocks and bibs. And what did you gain for your marriage clothes? Only one new robe, two hats and a doublet refurbished.'

'That's true. But you'll not find luxury in Scotland.'

'Nor will I find a man so frugal he grudges the very shift off my back. I heard James goes magnificently attired, that his chambers are hung with gold cloth, that he spends more on masques and jousts in a month than we do in a year.'

'I am not sure . . . there are the clever falsifications of his ambassadors, and second-talk at that.'

'But I must marry.'

'Then go to it with sense, not dreams. The less you expect, the more you may be pleased.'

He bent his head, and the fair hair drooped over his forehead. For a moment he shook in a paroxysm of coughing. When it eased she asked, 'What of your marriage? Are you pleased?'

'You should not ask.' But he was smiling faintly. 'It's as I thought it would be.'

He was living with Catherine at Ludlow Castle and

Margaret had not seen him alone since the bridal festivities. 'Our court seems more Spanish than English, for she brought such a vast train of servants and priests. I must hasten to learn her language, for it's awkward to speak through interpreters.'

'But does she please you?'

'As you saw, she is modest. She has a great dignity. She spends six hours a day in prayer.'

'But does she *please* you?'

Again, the paroxysm of coughing.

She could not please any man, Margaret thought. At fifteen Catherine of Aragon was a puffy, heavy-chinned girl with a greasy skin and protuberant blue eyes. At the wedding, with her auburn hair down her back, she had seemed like a peasant masquerading in white-pearled damask.

'I am told you and Catty eat off the same plate.'

'In public.'

She said, 'That is a pretty fancy. I shall take care to do the same with James.'

'Christ,' he said, 'you are not even betrothed! And you must not seem too eager lest your servants bear tales to the Scots. Remember, you are an English princess; you confer a favour on James by even considering the match. No man wants a bride too easily won. There is a certain strategy. When – and if – the ambassadors finally seek you out, you must appear only cordial, not effusive. You must seem remote . . .'

She was impressed. She had never thought of pretending inaccessibility, superiority. Thus far no one had advised her. She had only been commanded to stay out of sight until summoned.

'What does James expect of me, aside from ensuring a peace treaty?'

'He expects a virgin breed-sow and a dowry.'

'Oh, God! Will Father *pay* a proper dowry?'

'That is one of the matters they haggle.' He rose, awkwardly tall in ill-fitting hose that wrinkled on his thin legs.

'Sleep, sister. And remember what I've told you. Confide in no one. Be patient. And walk in pride.'

He kissed her cheek and left her.

Outside she heard the change of the guard as the hall clock struck the hour. The music below had stopped and she pictured the commissioners dispersing, wine-slogged, to their quarters.

Walk in pride . . .

She stood erect, barefoot in her ugly robe, and went to the guard in the corridor who summoned her five maids-in-waiting. Usually she asked only one to attend her at night for there was nothing to do but remove her robe, open the bed and blow out the light. Tonight she demanded that they brush her hair and oil her with flowers. She wanted a psalm read, and a verse of scripture. There must be a hot brick in her bed. She wished a cup of ale.

When she could think of nothing else she bade them go, and lay alone in the darkness hearing the flap of a broken shutter and the bark of a dog across the windy gardens.

James would be fortunate to wife me . . .

Her hands slipped down on her naked breasts.

I am soft and full and firm.

She touched her hair and traced her face. *I am smooth. I've no pock-arrs.*

I am an English princess.

She smelled sheep grease from the dead, smoking rush-light and turned her face into the lumpy goose pillow she had known as a child.

* * *

Twelfth Night passed into the New Year of 1502. On January 25th Margaret knelt in her mother's chapel at Richmond Palace and pledged herself to take James Stuart as her husband.

In the shine of tall white candles the old Earl of Bothwell knelt with her at the purple velvet altar. Serving as proxy for James he swore to honour and cherish her for the rest of his life. Rings were exchanged. The couple was blessed, and trumpets sounded proclaiming Margaret Tudor Queen of Scotland.

To Margaret it was unreal, the thinnest edge of dream, unreal and disappointing. Because of her mother's pregnancy the gathering was small. Because of her father's parsimony the banquet that followed was modest. She knew that he begrudged two months' lodging and entertainment for the Scots commissioners but she felt cheated of her rights. The golden loving cup which she shared with Bothwell contained only Lamb's Wool, a brew of hot ale and roasted crab-apples. Compared to Arthur's wedding feast the meal was scant – grey goose, sparrow and lamprey pies, mullet and mutton and perch. The sweets were meagre – cream of almonds, baked oranges and a citron cake with slender battlements of sugar.

Later in the courtyard, knights jousted in her honour, thundering across the field in a clash of scarlet and silver, their lances gold shafts in the sunlight. The gallery was draped with green and white ribbons that swirled in the wind. Her hood ballooned from her head as she rose to end the contest, presenting favours to the winners – a strand of her hair, a primrose, a blown kiss.

As they left the gallery she walked beside her mother hand-in-hand, equally a sovereign. For the first time she preceded Arthur and Catherine. In her father's glance she sensed a new deference. She had provided a peace treaty which he had bought cheaply for the price of her dowry – 10,000 angel nobles for three successive years. He had arranged that if she died barren during that time he need not pay the balance.

At supper she shared the dais with her parents, Lord Bothwell and Scots ambassador Andrew Forman. She watched a sword swallower and a band of Moorish dancers, listened to madrigals in her honour. But the entertainment was brief. At nine o'clock it was over. Bothwell, followed by her brothers, escorted her to the entrance of the bridal apartments where he knelt and kissed her skirt. He had served his purpose as proxy, and she dismissed him.

Arthur and Henry stood in silence, and she said, 'What's amiss?'

'Nothing, Madam,' Arthur said.

She looked at Henry, all merriment gone, all guile. 'Well, Harry?'

He inclined his head. 'Madam.'

'What is this jest between you?' she asked suspiciously. 'Why are you mute, what do you keep from me?'

'Nothing, Madam,' Arthur said. 'It is for you to dismiss us, or keep us, at your whim.'

She was suddenly aware of her position. She was Queen of Scotland, imperiously, regally a queen. It would be amusing to give them a haughty nod, turn her back and let them go. But it was early; she was wide awake, over-excited and anxious to talk.

'Come in,' she said graciously.

One of her ladies admitted them into the large oak-panelled bridal chamber. To her astonishment a log fire burned brightly – imagine Father providing wood! Apricot silks hung the walls, matching the bed draperies. A white damask robe, heavily pearled, lay across the coverlid.

Her brothers sat stiffly on the seats she indicated and she sat across from them on the loveseat. She talked of the day, but her chatter sputtered out in the chill of their courtesy. She had never felt close to Arthur, but she admired and trusted him. Harry, for all of his teasing and malice, had been an amusing playmate. Now she felt cut off from them as though she had already journeyed five hundred miles to the north.

She found herself wooing them. 'When I go to Scotland you must accompany me. Think what freedom we'd have, away from nurses and tutors.'

Arthur said, 'Madam, my place is here with my wife. And Harry cannot go a-gadding from his studies.'

'But it will be almost two years from now.' She appealed

to Harry, always adventuresome. 'You will come with me, won't you?'

For a moment she saw the old, sullen look always precipitated by mention of Scotland. 'If your parents permit, Madam.'

She looked at him sharply. 'Are you ill?'

'Why, Madam?'

'You are flushed and eye-bright.'

'A slight fever, Madam. I caught a chill in the wind.'

'Then get you to bed.'

He rose, bowed deeply and left them.

Arthur said, 'He brought on the fever by a fit of rage, Madam. For two hours before supper he ranted about his chamber like a madman, frightening the servants near out of their wits. Our mother called her physician who finally quieted him with a potion so that he could appear at the revels.'

'What caused this rage?'

'Your marriage, Madam.'

She shook her head in bewilderment. 'His hatred is unnatural. James has never harmed him, nor indeed has any Scot. I might think it jealousy of me, but Harry has always scorned me, baited me – there is no love in him where I am concerned.'

Arthur said bleakly, 'There is little love in our family, but there is great passion.'

She thought of her father's passion for gold and lands, of her mother's religious ecstasy, and of her own obsession for power. Only Arthur seemed bloodless.

'And what is your passion?' she asked.

'To cling to what I have.'

'Catty?'

'She is part of it.'

He was being evasive and she found herself bored. They drank a glass of sack, and he left her.

Her ladies bedded her, and she lay for a while watching the applewood die in the hearth. She wondered what James was doing now, thinking now. Perhaps he thought of her across the wind-flogged miles, reflective on this strange and lonely bedding.

Close to the fringe of sleep she imagined the lean, dark, merry face turned, like her own, into the silk of a pillow.

Goodnight, she told him, across the hills and the wild, briared bracken and the years that separated them. Goodnight, and may God rest me.

* * *

That April Prince Arthur died. Now she knew what his passion had been – the need to cling to life.

The following year she attended her mother's funeral, immeasurably shocked, yet secretly elated. She was the first lady of the realm now, taking precedence before everyone but her father. She ordered her mourning robes trimmed with mink and sable. She commanded perpetual Masses for the Dead.

On June 25th Henry was betrothed to his widowed sister-in-law, Catherine of Aragon.

'It is not seemly,' Margaret told him. 'You know as well as I that the Bible warns against a man taking his brother's wife.'

'But she says she was not his wife,' Harry said blandly. He was twelve now, taller, more strikingly handsome than ever. 'She vowed to her priest she is virgin, that her marriage to Arthur was never consummated.'

'Do you believe that?'

Harry grinned. 'No, Madam. I've a long memory. Several gentlemen of the chamber told me of Arthur's remark on the wedding morn when he called for wine. "Marriage is a thirsty pastime," he said. "Last night I was in Spain." '

'You will rue this,' she said. 'I fear some disaster will fall upon you.'

'Do you, Madam?' he asked. 'That would be sad, indeed, but you would rise on my corpse.'

Margaret prepared for her journey to Scotland. For once

her father was liberal of clothing and she was also allowed an impressive escort which, she learned later, was paid by the Scots. When she bade him goodbye at Colesworton in Northamptonshire she was trailed by peers of the kingdom led by heralds, guards and musicians and guided by the greybeard Earl of Surrey, Lord Treasurer of England. Their horses were caparisoned in green and white brocades, her litter was a nest of embroidered silks cushioned in down. She had a train of sixteen tiring women and twenty ladies.

At first she found her progress exciting. Sheriffs of villages throughout the north were commanded to do her honour, providing pageants and entertainments clear to the Scottish Border. Thirsty for pomp, she drank it eagerly, greedily.

Yet a few miles beyond York she began to tire of the hot-beating July sun, of the change from saddle to litter as they entered important towns. Village entertainments proved tiresomely similar and the speeches of provosts welcomed her towards sleep.

When they stopped at castles or manors overnight she was forced to stay awake through interminable banquets and pantomimes. At dawn the cavalcade was off again, swelled by ladies and gentlemen who joined them from town to town.

Almost imperceptibly the soft green cushions of England were turning to cruel hills and wild wastes. Rain poured down, forcing them to take shelter in mean cottages or dismal monasteries. Finally after three weeks they reached Berwick and crossed the Border to Lamberton Kirk where they were welcomed by the Earl of Bothwell and the Archbishop of Glasgow.

'Our Queen has come to Scotland . . .'

Her hands were full of heatherbell as the litter swayed over nearly impassable roads. This was a land of bogs, of treacherous peat hags and rain-swollen burns. A land that changed from mile to mile beneath unending grey skies.

She rode through turnip fields, and violet heather, up rough slopes and down into valleys soft as bosoms. In grey stone villages children brought her wreaths of flowers, priests and provosts welcomed her with eulogies, fountains in market squares flowed wine. She sat her palfrey through endless toasts.

Fast Castle . . . Dunbar . . . crash of sea, cry of curlews, creak of leather, plop of hooves, grind of wheels. Sun, dust, drizzle, thunder that shook the hills.

As they left Haddington the Countess of Surrey rode up to Margaret and asked permission to halt a few miles from Dalkeith Castle so that the ladies might change their grimy gowns.

Margaret thought wearily of more entertainment at another country castle, of amateur jugglers and singers, clumsy dancers. Jesu. . . ! Why dress for provincial company, why bother herself so needlessly? But she was hot, sweating and itching under her robes. The fleas were torturing. So she called a halt, allowed her women to undress her behind the curtains of the horse litter, to change her oaken corset to one of lighter wood. Laced with leather, in a fresh shift and gown, she mounted her white palfrey and the cavalcade moved on across the moors to the blare of trumpets and pipes.

At the gates of Dalkeith the Earl of Morton and his lady knelt and presented Margaret with the keys of the castle. She was conducted to a chamber hung with purple tapestries woven with gold. Before supper, refreshed by a cup of wine she sat with her favourite lady, Avys Browne, whom she had brought from home. Avys was a pert, pretty brunette, gossipy as a magpie. This evening she had news a-plenty.

'Begging Your Majesty's leave—'

Thus the gossip always began.

'Aye, girl?' Margaret stretched her saddle-sore body on the couch.

'I heard today that Margaret Drummond is dead.'

'Dead!' Margaret sat up. 'How do you know?'

'Lord Surrey told his wife, who told me. They think it providential that the mistress dies before the wife arrives.'

It was a happy omen. 'How did she die?'

'No one knows, Madam, but it seems like poison. Lady Drummond had dined with her two sisters, and soon after the meal all three were mortally stricken.'

'Who would have poisoned them?'

Surely not the King . . .

'The Surreys think they were murdered by Scots nobles who feared the King might never consummate your marriage as long as the slut lived.'

'That is absurd! He would not have gone so far as to wed me by proxy and accept my dowry if he intended to break the alliance.'

'No, Madam.'

'The King knows of this?'

'Aye, Madam. He has had her buried at Dunblane Church and Masses said . . . her little daughter is at Stirling Castle.'

Margaret mused on this long love of James's. Some said that he had wanted to marry his mistress and legitimize the child; that it had taken the combined force of his council to prevent the match. In any case, she need not trouble about the matter.

Lady Morton tapped on the door and Avys admitted her. She knelt before Margaret, and gasped out that the King had arrived. 'We did not expect him . . . he gave us no warning!'

'Jesu!' Margaret summoned all of her ladies, Lords Surrey and Bothwell. There was no time to do more than tidy her hair, for she could not keep the King waiting. Thank God, her dress was clean, and her shoes. But she had wanted to wear her most magnificent gown and here she was in plain brown velvet.

At the sound of a trumpet she hurried to the entrance of her chamber and awaited the King on the stair landing. He ran up the steps swiftly as a boy, slender, buoyant, graceful. Behind him by taperlight she saw the shadowy mass of his attendants, the black and white of bishops and monks, silver crucifixes, golden beads, glowing brocades, feathered hats. His own head was bare and his hair, a dark auburn, streamed loose to the collar of a green doublet. Over one broad shoulder swirled the Stuart tartan.

Margaret knelt as he approached and he said, 'Rise, child,' and smiled at her. His beard was untrimmed, he still wore a hunting jess on his wrist, he smelled of horse and sea-wind and fresh, wild grass.

She extended her hand. He touched the tips of her shaking fingers, then leaned forward and kissed her cheek.

She tried to reply to his words of welcome but could manage scarcely a murmur. Envying his poise, she watched him pass among her attendants, lightly kissing her ladies, welcoming the old Earl of Surrey and thanking him for protecting Margaret on the long journey. Then he returned to her, took her hand and led her to the end of the room where he seated her on a window bench.

He ran a hand through his tangled hair and smiled ruefully. 'I should not have come to you thus, but we were running a stag in these moors and being so close I took the liberty of a visit. Will you forgive my appearance?'

'Of course, Sire.'

'You are trembling.' His hand on her sleeve was a gentle caress. 'Am I so fearsome?'

'Oh, no, Sire.'

'You must feel free to tell me anything,' he said, 'for I am your friend as well as your husband.' He sat down beside her. 'You must be weary of travelling.'

She murmured that she was not weary now.

He inquired of her father's health. He hoped she would not be homesick in Scotland, he would do all he could to provide her amusement. He could imagine how it must feel to be uprooted.

She had never encountered such charm in any man. But as they supped together in the bannered Hall and listened to minstrels she was aware of his condescension, as though she were a child to be humoured rather than a woman to be respected. Aye, he showed respect by remaining hatless throughout the evening, but that was mere courtesy. She longed for a sense of equality but he treated her with a twinkle-eyed gentle affection such as an uncle might afford a little niece.

Late that night he returned to Edinburgh where he said ceremonies were being prepared for her arrival and for their marriage. The townspeople were wild with anticipation. She was already enthroned as Queen of Hearts.

Alone with her ladies she listened to their coos of admiration for so handsome, so gracious and gay a sovereign. Lady Surrey said, 'I vow he is not real. When he leapt on to his horse and rode off into the mist I had a fancy he was returning to the pages of a romance.'

Margaret agreed. He was the perfect knight of legend, polished as pearl. Compared to him she felt awkward, blundering, even crude.

She lay awake in the darkened bedchamber vainly trying to revive her pride. He had certainly made it difficult for her, invading her privacy in such a casual manner, denying her the privilege of proper adornment. The most experienced queen would have felt at a disadvantage. It wasn't fair . . .

At the foot of the trundle couch she could hear Avys's even breathing, and envied her.

An hour passed, Margaret sank into fitful sleep, on the thinnest edge of dream. Suddenly she was jolted awake by cries of 'Fire!' She sprang out of bed, dragging a sheet over her nakedness. From below there was a pandemonium of shouting, stomping men. Avys, shaking, finally lit a candle and Margaret's ladies poured through the door just as Lord Bothwell appeared on the stair landing.

'The stables are afire,' he said, 'but the castle is safe. Calm yourselves – there is no danger.'

Now they could hear high, agonized whinnying, terrified bellows and barks. Margaret thought of her two favourite palfreys and put her hands to her ears. One of her ladies retched in the fireplace and Lady Surrey sent hastily for aqua vitae. Lord Morton brought the brew himself and tried to comfort Margaret.

'It will soon be over, Madam. They'll not suffer long.'

But the screams continued until finally there was no sound but the dirging howls of castle dogs safe in the courtyard.

No one slept further that night, and breakfast was early. Margaret demanded of Lord Morton full recompense for the loss of her palfreys.

'I'll not ride a nag,' she said, 'and I'll not ride pillion like a common drab. What horses are left?'

'None, Madam. But something will be arranged for you.'

That afternoon the King sent Margaret three white palfreys.

He made another unscheduled visit and found her playing cards, uncoiffed and unpainted. That evening she and Lady Surrey danced for him and he played the clavichord and lute. He told her of the many repairs he was making on country castles and of how he had rebuilt and refurbished Holyrood Palace in her honour. She thought, he dangles sweets before a child; he does not woo a woman.

He spoke of his interest in medicine and surgery and told her that he was often physician and chemist to his nobles. He experimented in curious fields.

'Did you ever wonder,' he asked Margaret, 'what was the original language spoken by man?'

She had never wondered. 'Indeed, Sire.'

'So had I. To plumb the mystery, I sent a deaf and dumb woman and two orphaned infants to the Isle of Inchkeith, which is uninhabited. Thus these bairns heard no speech. As the months passed I was impatient to know what language they would speak, but I bided my time until they were five years old. Then I sent a learned friar to the Isle. He told me that one bairn spoke good Hebrew. The other bleated like a goat.'

'Or a dumb woman,' Margaret said.

'Aye. The whole matter was very strange.'

James visited her two more evenings, but now she was

prepared for surprise. Laced tightly, her body was beguiling. Properly painted her face emerged from childish softness to the dignity she desired. She would never achieve beauty, but she was no pudding. And she moved with conscious grace, though she felt, in his presence, gawky as a colt.

For all of his impeccable courtesy, and the shine of worldliness she detected something of wildness in him. He jumped on to his chargers, ignoring the stirrups. He revelled in foul weather, preferring storms, his courtiers said, to sun. Folk worried when he jousted for he took the game savagely. He broke the fiercest horses and tamed his hawks himself. She was not surprised to hear that his priests prayed for his life. As yet she was too timid, too awed, to chide him for his recklessness. She thought: I must first change myself. And when I am confident (perhaps in a year) then I shall change him.

On September 7th Margaret journeyed towards Edinburgh by horse litter. Anxious to look mature, she wore a severe blue gown stamped with gold and a long cloak of gold cloth, but her hair was down her back as befitted a maiden. She wore no jewels on her hands but the betrothal ring.

James met her on a rough path half-way to the city. Gone was the careless beard, the hunter's clothes. He wore a jacket of gold cloth faced with purple velvet over a purple satin doublet and a shirt embroidered with gold and pearls.

He had brought Margaret a hart, and as he swung off his horse and went to her litter he made a little jest. 'The hart is tame as my own, Madam. You must course him.'

Surely he would not insist on hunting now, on a state entry into Edinburgh!

'In time,' she said, glancing at the red deer, 'I should love to. But please, Sire – may I just ease myself until we reach Edinburgh?'

It was her first request and she wished she could have retracted it. James had brought the hart for the pleasure of hunting. And she had spoiled that pleasure.

'Madam,' he said, 'this is your day to use as you please. Do as you will with it.'

As always he was gentle, smiling. But she felt that she had erred. He had benignly put her in the wrong.

'Please, Sire, if you wish to hunt—'

'No,' he said. 'You are right. We shall travel in leisure.'

She had wanted to enter the city in the comfort of the horse litter but James did not want her curtained from the people, so she mounted a palfrey and sat behind him. She wondered if he had inquired of her ladies what clothes she meant to wear, for the horse was caparisoned in blue and gold. Plumes bobbed at their ears, matching the tiny plumes that curled about her hat.

Trumpets sounded and the Horse Guard moved forward. Lances formed a forest about her, glinting in the sun. Behind her, as far as she could see, trailed nobles, ambassadors, bishops, priests, ladies and gentlemen moving like a long strand of multicoloured jewels.

Long before they reached Edinburgh she could hear the bells of moor kirks and monasteries, and as they entered the city a thunder of bells chimed welcome and guns boomed from the Castle. The grey, steep-piled city was massed with colour – every gallery, every stair and balcony was draped with tapestries and painted cloths or garlanded with greens and flowers. Children pelted her with rose petals. The mobs were so thick they seemed welded in embrace, and looking up she saw folk crowding the rooftops.

Slowly, slowly, they inched towards the south of the city where the pageants began. On a green clearing, two armoured knights jousted for love of a lady. Progressing, the procession was greeted by groups of Cistercian and Dominican friars who gave Margaret and James holy relics to kiss. Farther on, little girls robed as angels presented Margaret with keys to the city and sang praise of her virtue and beauty. The cavalcade wound up the West Bow to the Market Cross and halted. City provosts brought from the flowing fountain a ruby cup of wine which Margaret and James shared.

Unlike her father, James permitted the people to crowd close – too close, she thought. Tanners, fleshmongers, fishmongers, all had their smells, and she wanted to hold her nose against the general stench which, she thought, was far worse than London's. She found it disgusting that James was so familiar – even intimate – with the rabble. A cobbler put out his hand and touched James's shoe, chiding him for neglecting the sole. A woman kissed her hand to him and thanked him for sparing her the ducking stool – punishment for scolds. A baker held high a great cake, and James admired the gift and asked a page to take special care of it until tomorrow's banquet. Jesu, she thought, every chandler and ironmonger and brewer in town regards him as friend. Every kailwife and shepherdess and milk-woman looks on him with love. They even asked about his ague, and suggested amulets and cures. And James – good God! – chattered away as though each were a member of his own family.

Everyone smiled at her; no one spoke to her. She felt that she was cheered for James's sake, that they would have tolerated any bride he chose, be she the ugliest crouchie. Aye, tolerated was the word; she found no genuine warmth in their welcome. She was appraised and accepted. That was all.

In a flash of self-honesty she remembered that the London crowds had been much the same. She had not Harry's magnetism nor had she her mother's grave (some said saintly) sweetness. And for the mere sake of popularity she could not lower herself to beg favours of her inferiors.

They watched a morality play which ended with a Te Deum of the bells of St Giles. At the Netherbow Port they were welcomed by beautiful women representing the Four Virtues who descended from golden thrones to sing Margaret's praises. Beyond, in the Canongate, the banners of Scotland and England fluttered from every house.

Now she could see Holyrood Palace like a toy French château cuddled below the wild Salisbury Crags and Arthur's Seat. From the abbey to its left came a long procession of priests headed by the Archbishop of Glasgow, with the high clergy of Scotland in gold and crimson robes. James lifted Margaret from the palfrey on to a carpet of heather. The abbey bells seemed to burst their throats as she knelt, kissing the archbishop's cross and an image of the Virgin wreathed in roses.

She followed James into the abbey and took her place beside him. During prayers of thanks for her safe arrival she looked up through a hundred streaming candles past tier after tier of saints up to the vast vaulted roof. From an open window she could hear the coo and flutter of wood doves.

James sat with bent head and closed eyes. She had heard that he was deeply religious, but no Stuart heart had ever been tame, despite his jest. She knew his origins as well as she knew her own and she shivered in the warm, cedar-scented darkness.

The Stuart line had started in 1316 when Margery Bruce married Walter, High Steward of Scotland. A fey woman, Margery, restless as the winds she loved. Three days before her child was born she rode out on the moor, was thrown by her horse and killed. Will o' The Simples, her father's surgeon, found her and cut the baby from her body. It lived to become Robert II, and from this birth came the Stuarts – reckless, fascinating, strangely ill-omened. Margaret could not think of one whose life had not been violent and blood-haunted.

Even James, embroiled as a lad in the rebellion that had led to his father's murder. As yet she knew James only superficially but she could not believe that he had been more than a tool in the hands of ruthless, power-hungry nobles. To imagine that he would deliberately harm anyone was inconceivable to her. Even his discarded mistresses were kept in comfort and their children honoured. She had witnessed the almost inordinate love of his people. His bishop, Andrew Forman, had told her. 'If he has a fault, it is overgenerosity.' For once she was beginning to believe a diplomat.

The ceremony ended with trumpets. Margaret and James moved slowly towards the door, through the great entranceway into the cloistered walk that connected with the palace. In the inner courtyard household servants knelt in long rows. James bade them rise and introduced her as 'your queen, whom you shall love and protect as you do myself.'

She was about to pass on when he whispered, 'Smile, Madam.'

She did so, flushing. Such camaraderie was absurd. Why should she curry the approval of cooks and pages, stableboys and kitchen wenches? And she was weary of smiling. She had smiled from Newbattle clear to the abbey. Tomorrow she must smile through hours of wedding revels.

James conducted her to a staircase on the left. 'Your apartments are prepared for you, Madam. May you rest well . . .'

She followed the Mistress of the Household up three flights of stone stairs. As she entered the anteroom, preceding her ladies, she saw that the mantelpiece was banked with flowers and the floor carpeted with fresh green leaves. The walls were tapestried in yellow and window seats were upholstered in the same colour. Turkey-work embroideries covered tables and chests, and she saw with approval that there were chairs as well as cushions. It was not quite the elegance she had expected, but it was not shabby, and everything seemed new.

'Your bedchamber, Madam,' said Lady Argyll.

The walls were hung with hyacinth and crimson velvets. The bed, canopied in gold cloth, was topped with a gold coronet, and the draperies lined with crimson. She had never seen a more exquisite room, but she must not show the Scotswomen that she was impressed.

'It is small,' she said grudgingly, 'but it will do.'

She sent her tiring maids to unpack her wedding clothes, her paints and pomades and other immediate necessities. Alone with Avys, she sank on to a hearth cushion and removed her hat. She asked for a cup of wine.

'You must be weary, Madam.'

Not weary, she thought, but depressed. She had been the centre of the day. Now the day was ending in strange apartments in a strange country; she was soon to wed a stranger. She felt trapped as the little merlin that swung in its cage by the window.

"I am *not* weary,' she said.

'Mistress Deane has ordered you a fine capon stuffed with prunes and currants.'

Margaret shrugged. James should have provided a banquet with music and jesters. Instead he had packed her off to her apartments as if she were six years old. And where was he on this last night of his freedom? With one of his wenches? Or in the abbey, hearing Requiem Mass for the soul of Margaret Drummond. . . ?

A black restlessness was on her and she went to the window and looked out over the courtyard. Beyond the guarded gates a group of soldiers rode out of White Horse Close and pounded up the Canongate. A woman threw slops from her window. Urchins played in the gutter. To the west the sky was streaked with the first gold light of sunset. The abbey bells tolled for vespers.

'Send for my priest,' Margaret said. Perhaps Father Ives could lift her grey mood. In any case she required confession before tomorrow.

But Father Ives was at vespers. A little Scots maid, blushing and curtsying, suggested that the Bishop of Tutberry was available.

A small oratory adjoined her bedchamber to the west and Margaret awaited him there. Here, indeed, was a room for discontent. There was a shabby oaken altar and plain cloth, a scarred prie-dieu. Avys lit the cheap rushlights, which smoked, revealing wooden saints naked of jewels.

I shall make changes, Margaret thought grimly, no matter what it costs him. There shall be figures of porcelain and ivory, cloths of lace and silver brocade, silver sconces for white tapers, a font for holy water. She had heard of some savage group of London students who worshipped God in barren places, mad creatures all. Surely James did not subscribe to such heresy . . .

She was still sulking when Avys admitted the Bishop of Tutberry. At forty he was plump, dimpled, rosy and smooth-faced as an ageing cherub. He wore a robe glittering with red and gold embroidery. His fingers were heavy with rings.

She said, 'I am deserted on the eve of my wedding.'

He clucked soothingly. Surely Her Majesty was jesting. Her ladies . . .

'I've no need for their frippling. I should have been entertained, made to feel welcome. But the King does not – has not' – she could feel tears massing – 'cared to provide me with more than food and shelter.'

'His Majesty presumed you needed rest. Perhaps he did not take into account the spirit of Your Majesty's youth. He meant not to forsake you, but to cherish you.'

'There's a Great Hall below to cherish me in. There's the Castle, big enough by the look of it to cherish a thousand guests.' She went on, listing her grievances. 'I have never felt so lonely in my life. And he treats me as a babe.'

He listened sympathetically with an occasional cluck which encouraged her to further confidences. Already she felt eased, if not happy. And after she had confessed (the sins of pride, of vanity, of jealousy) he absolved her gently. He did not scold.

'It is hard,' he said, 'for a woman to place herself in the mind of a man. But think – the King is more than twice your age. He knows you only from brief meetings, and seek as he may, he has no chart of your heart. I feel sure that what you consider neglect is, from his viewpoint, consideration. He thought you in need of rest.'

She pouted. 'Perhaps . . . but where is *he* tonight?'

'No matter, Madam. It is not seemly that a betrothed couple see one another on the very eve of marriage.'

'Catty – Catherine and my brother Harry shared a love-cup.'

'But Scots custom,' he said vaguely, and let the sentence trail. 'You've no true complaint, my child.'

'Are you never restless, despondent?'

'Aye, Madam, there are times.'

Priests never admitted to such foibles, and she was intrigued.

'What times?'

'When women come between me and God.'

She stared in startled silence.

'I left home because of women, Madam. My mother and sisters' tongues were a-clack from cockcrow to cockshut, my aunts were always a-pluck and a-pull, my granddame – heaven rest her – rattled her mouth without taking breath – or so it seemed. As a lad I was meditative, searching for truth in quiet and finally I found it in the Monastery of St Cuthbert. And all would have been well had I been content as a simple monk.'

'But you were not content?'

'I was fired by the Devil of ambition. I learned to read and write. I rose in the Church only to find myself besieged and sore beset by women.' He sighed. 'Nuns.'

He shook his head. 'I ride the circuit of my diocese from convent to convent to hear confession, to oversee the planting or harvesting of crops, to administer and advise monetary matters. And no sooner is my mule in sight than the entire sisterhood, every one from novitiate to prioress, rushes to her cell to recall the year's grievances she has saved for my ear alone. Believe me, Madam, they raise such a yackle as would drive a worldly man to the yims. Does one hide a ruffled shift, another will tell on her; does one over-eat, the entire convent will list her sins, down to the very duck or mullet bones; does one receive special favour because of illness, others contrive to catch the same malady. They are allied on one point only – all of them harbour little pets, which is against church law, and none will tattle on another in this matter. Spaniels, poodles, pompoms, terriers, cats, marmosets—'

She tried not to laugh. He was so clearly distraught.

'– even turtles. Almost every time I approach a convent I see budding gardens, I marvel at the peace of kirkyards and the holy silence all around. Then, as my trumpeters announce me and a sister pokes her head out of the window and sees my retinue, there is a sudden spurt of sisters out of the cloister to the rear, and a yipping and shushing that can only mean little dogs sent to hiding. *I like* little dogs,' he added plaintively. 'It is not *my* ordinance . . . I pretend I know nothing of the infractions but the matter sits heavy on my conscience.'

'Did not St Francis love all living creatures?'

'Aye, but his was a different age. There were no prohibitions, and besides, birds in special circumstances may be permitted. Madam, you've no conception of the slyness of prioresses! Dame Mary at St Catherine's – in many respects an admirable lady – descended to sophistry in defence of a kitten. One night while visiting there I retired to my cell and was no sooner dozing than the creature sprang upon my bed and mischiefed about so that I was forced to stumble out of bed in the dark and toss it out the door. Next morning I chided Dame Mary for harbouring the animal. "If it was dark," said she, "then how do you know it was a cat?" She asked me to describe it, eyes, coat and tail. I could not. She suggested I had dreamed it. When I denied this, she insisted it was but a rat. You may imagine my indignation.'

'Did you inform your superiors?'

'Nay, for Dame Mary told me that if I reported the matter she would write the Archbishop of St Andrews explaining that through my holy influence a rat had turned mild and merry as a kitten. She and the sisters threatened to establish a miracle.'

Margaret laughed. 'You might have risen higher in the Church.'

'On the back of a kitten? I have begun to ponder on how many miracles may rest on the evidence of nuns, and I fear I have begun to question . . . but enough of my troubles,

Madam. We should dwell on the happiness of your wedding.'

She said, 'I've looked forward to it for years, yet now it is imminent I am fearful.'

'That's true of all maidens, Madam.'

'So I am told. But to be in a foreign land, to scarce know one's husband—'

'His Majesty will prove the most devoted of husbands.'

She looked him squarely in the eye. 'What shall I do if he persists with his wantons?'

'Your love will banish them.'

'Love?' she said scornfully. 'Do you imagine I marry for love like a peasant?'

'Of course not, Madam, but in time you may come to love him.'

She dismissed the thought as absurd, a priestly platitude. Yet she liked him, for he was more amusing than Father Ives and less generous with penances. She felt that she had made a friend – her first in Scotland.

* * *

Robed in white damask she knelt on a gold cloth cushion, the crimson lining of her train spreading like fire across the grey abbey stones. Beside her James, in robes of white and gold, bent his black-bonneted head. The taperlight caught the deep glow of rubies, diamonds, emeralds shining clear to the back of the church where black-clad nuns formed a dark curtain.

The Archbishop of Glasgow performed the ceremony and she thought resentfully that his mitre was handsomer than her crown, which was made from gold coins without a jewel among them. Head bowed, she heard the Archbishop of York read the Pope's bulls, permitting and sanctifying the union. The Litany . . . The Mass . . . her anointment. She accepted the Sceptre of State and raised her head to look into James's luminous dark eyes. They rose and kissed as the choir burst into song and the bells rejoiced.

Margaret had no criticism of the dinner that followed in

Holyrood's Great Hall. There were over sixty dishes served, including great boars with gilded heads, moor fowl adorned with their feathers, jellies and pastries embellished with the arms of Scotland and England in coloured sugar. From the dais she shared with James she looked down on eight long tables. Closest to her were members of the Scots and English nobility: archbishops, bishops, knights, clan chiefs and their ladies. At the far end, below the great salt cellar, sat humbler folk – monks, tiring women, the Master of Horse and Mistress of Household. On each table there was a honey ring to lure lice, and a stone trencher for beggar-scraps. Musicians played from behind screens decked with heather and broom.

She noticed considerable drinking of aqua vitae and unwatered wine. Manners relaxed as flagons were emptied. Food was spilled, goblets were overturned. The Scots, she decided, were uncouth compared to the English. Instead of daggering their meat they tore it with their fingers and wiped their hands on their breeches. They stomped accompaniment to singers and fiddlers and roared bawdy jests. Yet it was gay, gayer than banquets at home. When wrestlers appeared, stripped to the waist, she thought of her brother Harry, who loved nothing so much as a contest of brawn and muscle.

Two hours passed, three. Some of the Scots slept, heads on the table between platters of food. Others sang with the musicians, quipped with the jesters, cuffed the snarling, scrap-hunting dogs. At a signal from James, trumpets blew, drunken guests were prodded awake, and the court rose, cheering the bridal couple as they left the hall.

In her bedchamber Margaret was bathed by her ladies in a wooden tub and attired in a white nightrobe embroidered with pink and silver roses. Over this went a hooded silver-cloth cloak. Gentlemen of His Majesty's Chamber escorted her to James's apartments on the floor below.

In the anteroom, archbishops and bishops bowed low, then followed Margaret into the bedchamber where James awaited them, robed in dark damask. The gold cloth curtains of the Bed of State were stamped with the arms of Scotland and England, embroidered with roses and thistles of silver thread. The Archbishop of Glasgow blessed the bed and sprinkled holy water on pillows and coverlid. Bride and groom knelt to receive a final blessing, and the priests left them.

James smiled at Margaret. 'Be seated, and tell me your thoughts. Were you pleasured today?'

She chose a little oaken chair. 'Indeed, Sire.'

He sat on the bed, shook off his sandals and leaned back against the bolster, crossing long legs. 'You seemed marvellously calm.'

'I am not unused to ceremony at home.'

'Aye,' he said. 'My ambassadors told me of your poise. I am more delighted than surprised.'

She thanked him.

'Margaret,' he said, using her name for the first time. 'Last night I lit a candle to St Ninian. Can you guess my prayer?'

'For peace?' she asked.

'For your happiness. I asked him to show me ways to assure your comfort.'

She was pleased. 'That will not be difficult, Sire.'

'You must tell me whatever you lack.'

She started to mention the re-decoration of her oratory, but thought better of it. She must move slowly lest he find her greedy.

'I have a surprise for you.' He moved from the bed to a dark corner and uncovered from a nest of blankets a sleepy black poodle puppy which he laid in her lap.

A gift for a child, she thought in disgust, then she saw that the dog was collared with rubies.

'Dear God!' she said. 'They are beautiful!'

'I bred her myself,' he said, 'delivered her, weaned her but yesterday.' He was eager as a boy. 'Do you like her?'

She had unclasped the ruby bracelet. 'Magnificent!'

The little dog whimpered and he picked it up, stroking

the silky coat. 'If she takes after her mother you can teach her to dance and leap through hoops.'

She fastened the bracelet on her arm. 'Thank you, Sire.'

'What shall you name her?'

She looked up. 'Name what?'

'The puppy.'

'Oh.'

'No matter.' He returned the wriggling fluff to its bed. She removed the bracelet and held it to the light, marvelling at the blood-red of the stones. It must have cost half her dowry . . .

He was standing at the table which was laden with sweets and wine. 'Would you care for refreshment?'

'No, Sire. Unless— I should like to taste aqua vitae.'

'Aqua vitae?' He spoke incredulously. 'It's a brew for men.'

'I have seen women drink it. And I am not a child.'

He poured her a few drops, adding water. It tasted like the smell of stale peat smoke but she concealed her revulsion with a smile.

'Long ago, Sire, I stopped playing with dolls.'

Or puppies . . .

'But you are not fourteen—'

'Nay, but my tutors called me precocious.' She lifted her chin. 'Child-talk wearies me, always I feel happiest among older folk.'

He said with a wry twinkle, 'Then you should be happy with me, a virtual greybeard.'

He had shaved his beard and she thought he looked astonishingly young. 'I'd not guess you to be more than twenty-three, Sire.'

'My diplomats could learn from you.' He held out his hand to her. 'Come here.'

He slipped the silver cloak from her shoulders and tossed it on a chair. For a moment he held her closely, his mouth on her hair, then released her. She climbed into the great, high bed, smelling the fragrance of oil of roses.

He blew out most of the candles, then pulled the bed curtains. Presently she felt his weight on the mattress. She lay rigid, tense, mindful of all the woman-talk she had heard in the past two years. Men were brutal or, at best, clumsy...

He smoothed her hair. 'You've lovesome hair, Margaret. I find it a shame you must cover it tomorrow.'

She murmured that she longed for the dignity of bound hair.

He turned and put his arm around her. The darkness was soft, scented, secret. He said, 'I should not spoil Master Dunbar's surprise, but he has written an ode for us which you shall hear tomorrow. He asks me to honour you as "the fresh rose of colour red and white, the queen and sovereign of all other flowers".'

She relaxed a little. 'He is court poet?'

'Yes.' James chuckled. 'I do not fare so well as you in the verses. I am the bristly thistle to your gentle rose. I am warned to be discreet and virtuous.'

'As indeed you are, Sire.'

'As I intend to be.'

He turned her into his arms and kissed her lips.

For a few moments she felt only gratitude that he was not forcing her. Then, slowly, she sought his mouth and her arms tightened about him. He pulled down her nightdress and kissed her breasts and she pressed her body to his, plunging her fingers into the thick, rough mass of his hair. Suddenly, thrust fiercely into pain, she cried out but his lips silenced her and she ceased to struggle and lay limp in his arms.

He felt her tears on his face and brushed them away, murmuring as he would to a child in some strange language that she presumed was Gaelic for she did not understand it. Then he released her and swung off the far side of the bed. She heard the silken swish of the curtain as he pulled it open and the room sprang softly into candlelight.

She sat up, blinking. He had put on his robe and was pouring a cup of ale.

'Will you join me?' he asked.

'No, Sire.' She drew up the sheet and leaned back against the pillows.

'What is your pleasure?' he asked, smiling at her. 'No wish shall go ungranted on your wedding night.'

'I wish ...'

But she dared not tell him lest he think her bold.

'... nothing,' she said.

'Then you must sleep,' he said. 'The celebrations begin at eight.'

There would be four days of festival – music, dancing, masques, jousts. Bonfires would rage above Arthur's Seat, fireworks would burst in white stars from the wild crags to the east.

'I am not weary, Sire.'

But she was lonely. She wanted him close, close in the curtained darkness. She wanted his arms about her again, and his lips on hers. She wanted to curl into sleep with him.

He came to her and kissed her hand, patted her chin and plumped her pillows. Then he took a book from the table and moved to the end of the room. She watched him light the tapers there, settle on a couch and open his book. The little dog awakened and wobbled over to him and he scooped it into his arms.

Talk with me, she implored him silently, notice me.

He continued reading.

Love me ...

So it was the next night, and the next. He was unfailingly gracious, considerate, remote.

She assured herself that she was merely excited by being fulfilled, but her need of him was too deep to reject, too sharp for self-foolment.

She paraded her pretty dresses. She read his books, hoping to lure discussion but he never shared his thoughts. He gave her jewels at Christmas, on holy days, and on her birthdays, but she waited in vain for inscriptions of love. When he wrote her from some country retreat, or on pilgrimage, he signed his letters with a formal seal.

Bereft of love, her need for power remained, but she soon realized that he neither wanted nor followed her advice in matters of state. He listened with charmed attention when she suggested means of quelling rebellion in the Western Isles, but enforced peace in his own way. He agreed with her that his gifts to favoured courtiers and citizens were extravagant, and continued them. He nodded when she said that the craftsmen working on his various castles were overpaid, and raised their wages. She touched him only as a bird bills against rock.

She forgot that she had been frustrated and unhappy in England and roused nostalgia for her family that was part desperation, part pretence. She wrote Harry long, loving letters, praying that his betrothal to Catherine would lead to happy, fruitful union. Learning that her widowed father was seeking a bride she cautioned him against swift decision. He was negotiating for the hand of Juana, whose father was King Ferdinand of Spain. Ferdinand wrote to Henry VII:

'I shall never consent that she wed with anyone but the King of England . . . but you must know that the said Queen, my daughter, still carries about with her the corpse of King Philip, her late husband. Before I arrived they could never persuade her to bury him and since my arrival she has declared that she does not wish the said corpse to be buried.'

When her father forwarded the letter to Margaret she showed it to James. 'Jesu!' she said. 'She is green-mad!'

'Lovesick,' he teased. 'Would you, *ma joie*, afford me the same consideration were I to die?'

'You jest cruelly!'

'You'd not haul my corpse about, then? What a woeful lack of wifely devotion!'

'You must write to my father at once, advising he withdraw his suit immediately.'

But he only laughed and pinched her cheek and told her not to frown lest she wrinkle at sixteen.

Her English courtiers were returning to their homes and she could not blame them nor did she try to stop them. She would miss Avys Browne. On the day she left Margaret entrusted her with a letter to her father:

'Give ear to the lady who will bear this letter, for I have showed her more of my mind than I will write at this time . . . God send me comfort . . . I wish I were with Your Grace now . . .

'Written with the hand of your humble daughter
Margaret.'

* * *

When James was away on state business Margaret remained at her dowry castle of Stirling, gateway to the Highlands. Tier upon tier of pale stone towered to the immense battlements. She could look across the world from there, where eagles skimmed mountain peaks. She saw the fogged valleys and flooded waters of spring; the autumn blaze of oaks and tarnishing gorse. In winter snow iced the castle like a wedding cake, spilling from the upper slices as the sun melted it.

Her days were spent hawking, her nights dancing or dicing. She was friendly with the poets Dunbar and Douglas and warmed herself in the glow of their flattery. She kept women at a distance, for she was mistrustful of the young beauties her own age and bored by those older than she. Seeing them hedged by children or awaiting confinement she grew increasingly uneasy about her own condition. After two years of marriage she was still childless.

She could not blame James – God knew, he sweated for an heir. But his seed, proven with many mistresses, failed to meet her need. Her physician assured her that she was healthy. The palm of her hand was oily, always a sign of heirs. Next month they said . . . next month.

She licked the crumbs of affection that James let fall. Surely with child she could win his love. At least she was certain he loved no one else. In the chattering, often drunken court, no whisper of scandal came to her. Perhaps his heart had died with Margaret Drummond; yet if she could conceive he would forget his lost love like a broken toy of his youth.

Marking time, she played with her own toys – Highland ponies, hunting dogs, hunting birds, toss-balls, bows and arrows. As James strengthened and improved old castles she decorated them, buying ells of Flemish tapestries, Spanish fringes and Turkey work. Her taste was garish. The walls of Holyrood were frescoed with lush red grapes, swollen roses, breasty Venuses – and above all, fat, overblown cupids, the unborn princes of her dreams.

On a chilly night in May 1504, Margaret waited for James in her bed at Holyrood, rabbit fur covers drawn close. Adam Bothwell, a lad of ten, went soberly about his duties as Gentleman of the Chamber, laying out his master's night robe and sandals, slipping a warming pan under the sheets. She glanced at the sandglass. It was nearly midnight.

The boy moved restlessly from draughty door to window, warmed himself by the fire, then roamed again. He had none of the giggling sportiveness of the young pages, nor their fawning manner. Already he seemed conscious of his position as heir to his father's earldom, holding himself with grave dignity. Usually calm, he seemed exceptionally nervous tonight and Margaret asked, 'What ails you?'

He hesitated a moment. 'My stepmother is ill.'

'Oh!' This was news indeed. Janet Kennedy, Lord Bothwell's second wife, had once been James's mistress. 'What's amiss?'

'She chills and sweats.'

A small satisfaction, for Janet was no longer a rival. Yet it was galling that her children by James were honoured and pampered. Little Lady Margaret lived in royal apartments at Stirling until the queen took residence there, when she moved to lodgings in the village. Alexander, James's eldest son, was studying under the finest tutors at St Andrews. However, James was not without tact. He never mentioned any of his natural children to Margaret, though she knew he visited them often and gave them costly presents. For weeks at a time she forgot their existence.

'Is your father with her?' Margaret asked the boy.

'Aye, Madam, at Darnaway. He is much distraught.'

Her jealousy of Janet, banked for so long, flared out in thought. Perhaps James still loved her, visited her secretly, cuckolded the old earl. She must be beautiful still, for it was said that Bothwell kept her shut up in his strongest keep lest she attract younger men.

Lady Argyll came to the door and announced the King.

He entered in a flurry of leaping hounds, gave Adam a rough pat on red curls. 'Pack you a fardel,' he said, 'and meet me in the courtyard. We go on a journey.'

The boy bowed and backed hastily from the room. Margaret sat up against the pillows.

'Where are you going?' she asked.

'To Darnaway.'

He went to the hearth and stretched his hands towards the fire.

'You go to your slut!'

He did not turn.

'You still love her!'

'Be still,' he said. 'Be still.'

Her silence was enforced by the entry of two gentlemen who inquired what His Majesty would need for the journey and hurried off to pack. Finally she said, forcing her voice to gentleness, 'Is she dying, Sire?'

'Perhaps. It's the sweating sickness.'

Even in death she would triumph, Margaret thought, adored by her husband, her children, her lover . . .

James strode to the window and opened it. Now she could hear the sounds of departure – men and horses, the tuning of pipes. She sprang out of bed and went to stand beside him. In the torchlight she could see a little group in the outer courtyard – his escort in wind-driven cloaks, his big bay, saddled and stomping, held by a groom.

He put his arm around Margaret. 'Be generous, try to understand. I owe her old allegiance . . . I have sent physicians and medicines. Now I must go myself.'

She was rigid with fury.

He spoke so quietly that his voice was almost a whisper. 'I need not have told you of this journey, but I've honoured you with the truth. I've not lain with Janet nor any other since we were wed.'

'But if she recovers, you will!'

He removed his arm. 'I cannot reach you through the bones of your selfishness.'

'If you loved me—'

'What is love to you? To consume a man like a lioness? Do you think of no one on this earth but yourself?'

She spat venom. 'What of my pride? How shall I feel for the whole court to know you're in Darnaway with your wench? I hope she dies screaming, aye, in agony, and sucks the Devil's tail in hell!'

He left her abruptly and went to the door.

'Sire!' She followed him. 'You cannot leave me like this.'

'There is nothing I cannot do.' He spoke slowly, distinctly, as though she were deaf. 'What I shall do now, whether Janet lives or dies, is to acknowledge my natural children. They shall bear the Stuart name, they shall be treated as princes, taking precedence over all others in Scotland.'

'Oh, no! You cannot taunt me with my barrenness—'

'It is no taunt. I should have acknowledged them at birth, Madam, for they are my pride.'

He left her.

* * *

Shamed, helpless, she confided in the Bishop of Tutberry who advised her to bide her time and wait for James's anger to subside. The King held no grudges. But when he returned from Darnaway she must display a new tolerance, a new gentleness.

'So I must play-act,' she said bitterly.

'The act of forgiveness may become genuine. If we practise love, we attract it.'

Pious platitudes . . .

'Very well,' she said, '*I* am the wronged one, but I shall seek his forgiveness.'

Word came from Darnaway that Janet was better but James remained there a week. Margaret rode from Holyrood to welcome him on the moor, her arms full of roses. As she saw his cavalcade approaching through the dust she found herself trembling. If he refused reconciliation, then her life was over at sixteen. She would wither alone in her apartments, childless for ever, stripped of even the illusion of power, while other women . . .

He waved to her and spurred past the archer guard, then checked his horse. He took the flowers she offered and kissed her hand. At a signal from him, his escort stopped a few yards away. As the dust cleared she could see a horse litter curtained in the Royal Stuart tartan, tasselled with crimson fringe, roofed in crimson velvet.

James said, 'I have brought the Lady Margaret Stuart.'

Later, fury would engulf her. Now she was mercifully numb.

'Will you welcome her, Madam.'

It was a command, not a request. Margaret hesitated, then turned her horse and rode to the litter.

James followed her and drew aside the curtains. 'Madam, may I present my daughter.'

The little girl peered out from a nest of silver cloth pillows, smiled and inclined her head. A tiny gold coronet rested on brown curls. She was dainty as a hawthorn bud in a gown of pink tissue.

Margaret murmured, 'Your ladyship.'

'Is welcome to Edinburgh,' James said.

'Is welcome to Edinburgh,' Margaret parroted.

'I thank Your Majesties,' the child said, and offered Margaret a broken daisy.

She took it, careful not to crush it in her fist. James said, 'The Queen brought you these,' and leaning from the saddle, placed the roses in his daughter's lap.

Again the child thanked her. James smiled approvingly and patted the pert brown head. 'We've only another hour of travel, then you shall eat and sleep. And tomorrow Alex shall join you.'

Both bastards! And then, likely, his brats by Marion Boyd and Margaret Drummond and God knew what others. Holyrood would become a nursery.

They moved along the blossoming moors towards the city. Margaret thought, I have mistaken James. Under his gallantry lay a will of granite, and despite his fair words, he was deliberately humiliating her because she had borne no heir. Holyrood was their smallest palace; she would never be free of his children. And how many had he fathered? Seven, ten, eleven? God damn them, nurtured on royal privilege while she skimped on a meagre allowance. James could not afford such a household. His sons and daughters would strut in clothes and jewels deservedly hers.

As they approached Holyrood he said, 'I shall leave you here, Madam, and conduct my daughter to the castle.'

She had not considered that possibility. Edinburgh Castle, up the Royal Mile from Holyrood, could house a life-full of brats with all their nurses, tutors, servants, priests, pets.

'Alexander comes to study theology,' James said. 'I have granted him the See of St Andrews.'

The richest Archbishopric in the land! But in her relief that she would not have to live with the children she managed a polite murmur. 'Whatever Your Majesty deigns shall please me.'

He bowed from the saddle and rode ahead.

Two weeks passed. Outwardly James was unchanged, taking part in the jousts, hunting with Margaret, accompanying her to Mass. Only Adam Bothwell and her tiring women suspected that he did not come to her bedchamber at night. She listened vainly for his steps on the private stairway that linked their apartments.

One midnight in June she shed her pride and crept up to his room in her nightrobes. James was seated at a table, maps spread before him. He looked up frowning.

'What is it, Madam?'

She had no plan, no words prepared, only her desperation. She went to him and knelt with her head on his knee. 'Forgive me, Sire – I love you too well.'

He said nothing but he did not draw away.

'Sire, it is our duty to have' – she paused – 'legitimate heirs.'

'True. But a man cannot summon passion at will.'

Humbly she said, 'He does not need to love.'

'But he needs to desire.'

She spoke over a sob. 'And you do not?'

'Impotence, Madam, is often created of women's words.'

Did he refer to her outburst over Janet Kennedy? Jesu! Her rage had been only natural, only wifely, and she felt it flooding back. Here she was begging for her sacred rights while he sat like a god in judgement.

'And how long shall this impotence continue?'

He shrugged.

She rose. 'Very well. If you deny me children, then I shall return to England and shame you before the world, as you have shamed me! What then of your peace treaty? Do you think my father will not take vengeance in my behalf when he learns you have scorned me – who am its very symbol?'

'Margaret,' he said, 'when will you learn that you are not the heart of the universe?'

'God knows I'm not the heart of yours!' She ran to the stairs. 'I'll write my father this very night. You'll stew in a scandal worse than any you ever made!'

In her chamber she wrote far into the night detailing her grievances. She begged her father to send an escort for her immediately and placed herself on his mercy. She asked him to inform the Pope and to work on her behalf for an annulment, 'as I have never been wife to the said King of Scotland but am still a maid.' (Had not Catty also lied, and successfully?)

Spent of anger she went to bed. In the morning she destroyed all she had written, burning the parchments in the fire.

James came to her two nights later. It did not matter that he was moodily silent and she enjoyed his roughness. This time, she thought exultantly, I have conceived . . .

But the barren weeks passed, and the months, and the years.

* * *

On a May morning in 1506 Margaret awakened at Linlithgow Palace. The day was fine and James was already out with his falcons. Her ladies dressed her in hunting attire and she ordered a large breakfast – strawberries, eggs and game pie. As she accepted the tray from Lady Buchan she looked at the food and was violently ill.

All day following her hounds through the swamps, releasing her merlins, she treasured the hope that she was pregnant. But she dared not consult her weary, now-cynical physicians. Too often she had run to them with her painted calendar and spurious symptoms. She would curb her impatience and wait.

Daydreaming, she planned how she would tell James. Through the years she had changed the scene a dozen times, from bed-chamber to garden to castle turret, as she had changed her gown. She would wear Madonna white or pale, romantic blue, or flamboyant crimson. She would say, 'Sire, I am with child.' That phrase never varied; it was dramatic beyond embroidery.

She hugged her secret through another week of recurrent nausea. At last the physicians confirmed her guess. When she left them she danced up the stairs to James's study, unheeding the dogs that barked and frolicked after her, uncaring that she wore a simple kirtle. She was about to burst in when the guard said, 'His Majesty is in Council.'

She had forgotten. Pest take the ten old men up from Edinburgh with their long faces and longer sheaves of papers, their secretaries and scriveners. If she were to sit in council, matters would rush to conclusion, not waggle along in endless debate. How men loved the music of their own voices, how they prolonged the simplest decisions! Women could solve a problem in seconds, but men gnawed it for hours, like dogs a-boning.

Resentfully she returned to her tower. Now she would have to wait, perhaps for hours if James entertained the men through first and second suppers. There might be the longer delay of fireworks in the garden or night-fishing in the Loch. And he might retire without coming to her.

Suddenly she was seized with an idea – nay, an inspiration for the drama she craved. She summoned her ladies and changed into a magnificent purple gown laced with gold, stamped with pearls, a gown worn only on state occasions. Her crown was brought from its white velvet casket with her diamond necklace and earrings. She sensed the women's surprise and made no explanation but the current of their excitement fused with her own.

Arrayed and perfumed she sent for Adam Bothwell. 'Go to Council,' she said, 'and inform His Majesty I must see him at once on a matter of grave national importance.'

For was it not? A matter to make history!

The lad left on his errand. She dismissed her women and stood hesitant. Should she stand by the sun-streamed window, her jewels a-dazzle or move into the oratory? To please James's piety she rustled into the dim little chapel where a candle burned beneath the image of the Virgin.

She considered kneeling in gratitude but was reluctant to wrinkle her skirts, for it took a maid hours with the sleek-iron to press twenty yards of brocade.

Would he never come? She passed the time by envisioning the evening ahead. In the Great Hall she would announce her pregnancy to an awed court. It was fortunate indeed that the Council was here to dignify the occasion. If only there were important ambassadors and papal representatives . . . for once she longed for the King's bastards to be present so that she might see blank shock on their smug little faces.

There would be bonfires lit from hill to hill, crackling the news towards Edinburgh as couriers raced throughout Scotland. She would dance until cockcrow, aye, even with the grooms and stableboys as was customary on high holidays. Oxen would roast at the palace gates for the townspeople, wine would splash from the Market Cross. James would throw largesse . . .

She turned at his step. He looked apprehensive and even in the dim light she could see white beneath his sunburn.

She said, 'I am with child.'

He shook his head in wonderment.

'It's true,' she said. 'Master Penhurst says there can be no doubt.'

His face lit suddenly; he gave a great shout and clasped her in his arms, lifting her off the floor. Then he released her and knelt at the prie-dieu.

She stood beside him, head bowed, waiting. Then, softly she began to tap her foot. He was sometimes an hour at his devotions, aye, even longer. And now in his thankfulness he was apt to set a precedent for prayer. She too was grateful, but now she wanted a cup of spiced sack and a sugar fig and discussion of the evening's celebration.

Silver-belled horns shivered in the distance. Hunters were after boar and she hoped they would bring one to be royally garlanded and roasted. She must send the maids to gather acres of flowers.

James rose, genuflected, and taking her hand, led her into the bedchamber. He kissed her and she clung to him. Then, blinking in the sunlight he smiled and said, 'Are you gowned for his christening already?'

She went to the mirror and preened. 'I am gowned for the celebration tonight.'

'But, dove, we cannot make it public now.'

She whirled. 'Why not?'

'It's unseemly, undiplomatic. Our ambassadors must be summoned to carry the news abroad.'

'But I want—'

'The princes of Europe are our family, and our family must be the first to know. How would it be for His Holiness and for your father and King Louis to hear this matter as second-talk?'

'Do you mean,' she asked fiercely, 'that I may not tell anyone? There will be no revels tonight?'

'We'll revel in private, you and I. We'll have a swan and maybe a furbished boar. The chef shall build you a honey cake. There's a new soothsayer below. And we shall play Fox and Lambs as long as you like.'

She stripped off her crown and tossed it on a chair, kicked off her pearl-heeled shoes. 'I shall summon my maids to disrobe me – there being no need to peacock.'

'Margaret—'

'Am I one of your whores to be hidden in child-sickness?'

'For the love of God—'

'And pacified with playthings, honeycakes?' She tore at the fastenings of her gown. 'Nay, you were *proud* of your spawn. I warrant you held high revel when Meg Drummond told you, and Marion and Janet.'

'Quiet!' His voice struck her hard. 'I return to Council. I shall join you here for second supper. Be ready.'

Ready for what? It would be only the usual supper, a clutch of thin-singing minstrels and a vagrant soothsayer. As Lady Crawford laced her into a simpler gown she asked, exasperated, 'When you were first with child, my lady, what did your husband do?'

'Why—' Lady Crawford considered. 'He was equerry to His Majesty.'

'I mean, how did he feel?'

'He was overjoyed, Madam, and caught the toothache, aye, he did, and within the fortnight.'

It was a certain sign of love when a husband responded with pain, and the other ladies nodded, discussing the matter. Lady Argyll said that her husband was plagued by boils for the full nine months. Lady Huntley's had conceived a tumour.

'*My* husband,' Lady Buchan said triumphantly, 'died.'

Margaret spoke through a respectful silence. 'But what does a husband do or say on the very day he is informed of the child?'

Lady Crawford said, 'Mine was hunting but when I sent the news he returned immediately. And he got drunk.'

'And mine,' said Lady Argyll, 'tumbled me that very night.'

'Mine,' said Lady Buchan, 'tumbled me twice and gifted me with a brooch set in pearls.'

'But did none of them provide feasts?' Margaret asked. 'No revels, dancing, fireworks?'

'For a *first* bairn, of course,' Lady Crawford said. 'I was minding the thought of my third.'

'For my first-born,' Lady Argyll said, 'we invited the whole of the shire and we danced from bird-shut to dawn.'

'We danced near a week,' Lady Buchan said. 'I wore out my slippers.'

Lady Crawford sprinkled flea powder on Margaret's gown, rubbing it into the hem and train. 'Aye,' she said softly, reminiscently, 'a man is gay on first-birth. But then he loses interest, as one does at an oft-told tale.'

Margaret thought so that is it. James is child-weary. He cannot summon the first excitement.

The women spoke of the horrors of labour. Aye, they agreed, it was a myth that the pain was forgotten as soon as the child was birthed. They never forgot. There was the threat of death, the malice of the fairies. If the child were plump and fair the fairies stole it for their own while the mother slept unattended. Many an ugly imp had they substituted in place of the true heir. This explained hare-lipped daughters and witless sons. A child must be watched constantly from womb to cradle until it was two months old. And sometimes the bonniest midwife turned out to be a witch in disguise . . .

James appeared and the women left her. He was followed by servants bearing a supper service. They set places for three and she spoke sharply. 'Sire – you have invited a guest?'

'Aye, there's a lady arrived from the Border – an Englishwoman. I thought to make her welcome.'

If she could not have a public celebration, she wanted a private one. Sullenly she said, 'At such a time I should think you would wish to be alone with me.'

He shook his head warningly, mindful of listening servants and she said, 'Very well, but I trust you'll dismiss her early.'

She knew these Border women – cloddy, sun-browned, smelling of sheep; too awed to speak, or when they did they talked of their eternal plantings and harvests, making a fuss of the dullest cabbage patch. Oh, God – and it must be tonight, when she and James could be close as ever they could be . . .

James filled her wine glass and clinked it with his. To the Prince, said his eyes. To the future King of Scotland.

For the moment she was appeased. They drank and hurled their glasses into the fireplace where they shattered, sending the spaniels yowling into the oratory. A servant announced Lady Heron.

She knelt, rose in a puff of dark silk skirts and lifted a thin white face. She was severely groomed, brown hair tightly braided into a plain linen coif, slender brows plucked to elegant arcs. Her eyes, a curious brown-green, were long and languorous, her mouth ripe. Margaret thought her beautiful, but strange as a painted nun.

Margaret said little at supper but James was talkative and Lady Heron responsive. They spoke of the skirmishes that still took place between Scots and English on the Border, mocking the treaty of peace. Lady Heron saw no political implications, rather the wild mischief of youth. Scots and English lads behaved precisely as their forebears had, stealing horses, sheep, goats.

'You assume the lads are natural enemies, like cats and dogs?' James asked.

'In a manner, Sire. I think they fight for thrill more than for gain. There is scant amusement on the Marches – it is not like Edinburgh or even Dumfries.'

As James asked about conditions in Dumfries, Margaret watched the candles lower, the shadows deepen. She was uneasy not merely because she sensed James's interest in this lady (he admired many) but because the quality of his admiration was different. He was not gay, nor did Lady Heron coquette. In their mutal attraction there was tension and gravity, a sombre force she did not care to fathom. Often they were silent, eyes locked.

She is older than I – more than thirty. Doubtless she is ashamed of her hair else she would not conceal it so . . .

Against her will she imagined the coif removed, long, wavy hair spread over a pillow, red lips open to James's kiss.

'My lady,' she said harshly, 'did your husband permit you to come to Edinburgh unattended?'

'I have attendants, Madam.' The voice was soft and cool. 'I shall meet my husband in Berwick, after Justice Court.' She turned to James. 'I was there four days. My husband tried a dozen horse-thieves, sheep-stealers, wife-beaters and a few corpses.'

'Corpses?' Margaret asked.

'Aye, dove,' James said indifferently. 'It's Scots law if a man be murdered by a mob, his kinsmen may bring the cadaver to court and have it tried legally – as is only fair.'

'It is fair,' Lady Heron said, 'so fair that we have taken the custom into north England.'

'And were the corpses judged innocent?' Margaret asked.

'All but one who had stolen another man's wife. We are mired by provincial morals.' Lady Heron smiled. 'We are primitives.'

Servants removed the bony remains of quails and larks and brought the honey cake. A silence developed and deepened. Behind a screen minstrels played softly.

Margaret asked, 'Do you have business in Edinburgh, my lady?'

'To buy clothing. I have been here two days. Before I left I wished to see my king.' A glance at James under lowered lids. 'And my queen.' A shy smile. 'I've not been to court since I was a wee lass, with my father. We did not seek audience then.'

James said, 'You should have.'

'We were countryfolk. The tall ports and houses frightened us both. Now they are even taller – I marvel how the city has swollen.'

'But now you are no longer frightened?' James asked.

'Aye, Sire – but only a little. Sometimes fright can excite one.'

Their silence again, and the long-held glance over the failing candles.

Margaret curbed her impatience – it was James's place to dismiss her. Another half hour passed, and Margaret summoned the servants to clear the table. Pointedly she said, 'We were happy to meet you, my lady. You must return with your lord.'

Lady Heron rose. 'I thank you. Should Your Majesties ever journey our way, Ford Castle shall be honoured to receive you.'

James accompanied her to the door. 'Ford Castle – is that east or west?'

Her reply was muted.

Presently James returned to the table. 'Fox and Lambs?' he asked.

'As you wish, Sire.'

A page brought the perforated board and wooden pins. James set up the painted animals.

He will play until he thinks me sleepy. Then he will go to her.

When they were free of servants he took from his belt a

small golden box and gave it to her. Inside was a bouquet of diamonds on an emerald stalk and she exclaimed at its loveliness. He pinned it to her bodice and she leaned to kiss his mouth but his lips were cool and resistant. He had paid his price for a prince, she thought; he feels he owes no more.

'Come, dove.' He patted the board. 'I shall best you.'

Usually she battled but her mind was not on the game. He won twice. She glanced at the sandglass, wondering how she might keep him with her.

'Shall we send for the soothsayer, Sire?'

'Nay, it's late. I must sit in Council all day.'

'Must you leave me?' she asked desperately.

'No,' he said.

Still, even as he lay abed with her she wondered if his sleep was assumed. She dozed fitfully, awake at his slightest movement, fearful that he might part the curtains and slip away. But at dawn he was still there.

While a servant brought ale and bannocks she stood at the window and saw Lady Heron's little retinue ride south through the mist.

* * *

In November she wrote to her father, 'I am seven months with child and it kicks hearty as a man-child should . . . May God love Your Grace, as I do.'

Did she? Henry VII was a shadow in her memory, a thin wraith. He would be greyer now, perhaps totally bald, his lips a crooked string. She tried to summon some spark of affection, tried to bask in remembered warmth. But she could remember best the night she was lost in the mazes of Westminster Palace.

It was six of a stormy night. Anne Luke, her nurse, had sneaked off to some private darkness with one of the man servants. The corridors stretched ahead, amber and oaken, pricked by prongs of lightning.

'Anne!'

The beamed ceilings echoed her call.

She stumbled on stumpy legs past darkening doors. She remembered that the palace was virtually empty because her parents and brothers were at Richmond.

On and on she went in the fading light. She turned a corner. Dimly, she could see oaken chandeliers, unlit. Young as she was she knew her father wasted no illumination, neither tapers nor fire.

'*Anne!*'

The halls were silent save for the wind that shivered the leaded casements. Eager for light, Margaret ran to them and looked out on dark, leaf-tossed gardens. A crash of thunder sent her running down the corridor. She blundered from door to closed door, unable to reach the high latches, but she pounded on them with her little fists, calling Anne's name.

Rats creaked in the wainscoting and she flew down another panelled hall. Somewhere there was Anne, there were other servants, there was the hot, meat-smelling kitchen where she had eaten supper at four. Somewhere in this nightmare was the sanity of her own room.

Finally, exhausted past terror, she sat on the cold checkerboard floor, her knees drawn up and her skirts pulled down for warmth. She slept. Sometime during the night a guard found her and carried her to her apartments.

Blinking the sleep from her eyes she saw Anne standing in a huddle of frightened maids. Behind them, to her astonishment, she saw her father.

'Papa!' She squirmed out of the guard's arms and ran to him, clutching his legs, hiding her face in the stiff damask of his tunic. He bent down and pulled away her hands. He examined her with cold, pale eyes. Where had she been? Why had she strayed? Weeping, she tried to tell him but he turned away to question the guard. Then he whirled on Anne. 'Should this happen again you shall be tried for neglect of your duty.'

Anne whimpered that children strayed no matter how carefully one watched.

'She is no child. She is the Princess Royal.'

Anne began to sob and Margaret joined her. The King stepped back, hands to his ears. 'For the love of Christ, have done with it! Must my sleep be broken on negligence and whim?'

He strode towards the door. Margaret pattered after him, seized his hand and clung to it. 'Papa—'

He thrust her aside. 'Stop your mewling and get to bed.'

But had he not ridden from Richmond on her account? She fell asleep on that comfort.

Next day she learned that he had been at Westminster four days. He had not wished to be disturbed.

Now, in later years, she could understand his need to be alone for Europe lay heavy on his shoulders and he played a lonely game. She understood, but she could not forgive.

More and more often at Holyrood or Falkland or Linlithgow she retraced the past as one winds torn threads on an old spool. Her father had not loved her, her mother's love had been given to God. Her tenderness was remote, as though Margaret were not quite visible through the clouds of holy incense that burned wherever she went. Elizabeth of York shared the Tudor passion, but hers was the lust of religion.

Margaret remembered the compassionate words and the soft, pink-palmed hands. It pleasured her to be feverish for Elizabeth would come to sit at her bedside, stroking, soothing. But she never remained long, for she was insatiable of altars. When Margaret was injured by a pony she left the doctors to attend her and sought the chapel. Always in hours of crisis she abandoned her children to pray for them.

Awake in the night at Stirling Margaret thought, But I *was* loved.

She was loved at ten. John Graves, a page, followed her about in thrall, bearing her shawls, toys, pomanders, sunmasks. He brought her baskets of berries, wreaths of cowslips, necklaces of Canterbury bells.

Practising coquetry she smiled on him, stamped on his

devotion, wooed it back, teased, sneered, sulked. She lured him to kiss her mouth, then slapped him. One day, in a summerhouse near the palace of Greenwich, Anne Luke found them embracing (God knows, Margaret thought, like a pair of cuddling pups) and told the queen. John was sent to serve a family in Northumberland. She never saw him again.

As her confinement approached she thought: I shall yet trick fate. My child shall love me.

Holyrood was prepared for her lying-in. When her first pain struck on the morning of February 21st she was hurried from the Great Hall up into her bedchamber. James and the high nobles assembled in the anteroom. Archbishops, bishops and priests crowded the little oratory. She lay between the two rooms with her physicians, midwife and wet nurse.

Sinking into a delirium of pain she clawed under her pillow to make sure that bread and iron were there to bribe the good will of the fairies. She clung to Janet MacKay's hand, digging in her nails, until the midwife gasped and withdrew it. She drank a cup of mandrake juice to drug her senses, spewed it out on the coverlid, drank again and retched. An hour later they gave her brandywine but she could not retain it.

She screamed for the Bishop of Tutberry, who took her confession. Candles were lit in preparation for the last rites. She saw her priests enter slowly, standing near the window like black crows, shutting out the light. The Archbishop of Glasgow came forward with a tall gold crucifix.

Five hours later the child lay on a cushion on Janet's lap. She heard the chanting, the blessing of the priests, then the thud of guns booming from Edinburgh Castle and from the courtyard the roar of a thousand voices as the people rejoiced.

She had borne a son.

Margaret could scarcely let him out of her sight. He was plump and rosy with a fine fuzz of blond hair and round blue eyes. But she herself was wasted, skeleton-thin and feverish. The physicians bled her every day for weeks. James looked at her with near-horror and made a pilgrimage to pray on her behalf at the shrine of St Ninian on the west coast. She was too weak to leave her bed. She felt that she never would.

Gradually, almost imperceptibly, she regained her strength, and she found it, not in kail-broth or beef marrow but in the presence of the child who would be christened James. He was her triumph, her delight and an almost savage preoccupation. Once the wet nurse, out for a stroll, was a few minutes late in returning to the nursery, and the baby was clamouring for its milk. Margaret waited until the feeding was over and the child asleep. Then she struck the woman with all her force, loosening a tooth. None of her ladies dared approach the child, for Margaret was jealously possessive. Only James was allowed to cuddle him, and then only for brief moments 'lest he become excited and choke'.

Four guards, heavily armed, were stationed at the nursery day and night. Each morning the Bishop exorcized the apartments lest evil spirits harm the child. The windows were never opened. Crimson hangings were provided to absorb wandering fevers and the braziers smoked incense.

When ambassadors arrived Margaret regaled them with detailed descriptions of her son's amazing perception – every gurgle and coo was proof of astounding intelligence. James, too, was proud of the boy and in his gratitude for an heir, more attentive to Margaret and more generous than ever before. He gave her whatever she asked – new gowns, cloaks, jewels – so that her wardrobes and chests overflowed into Holyrood's storerooms. On journeys to country castles her horse litters were travelling palaces curtained in ermine or snowy, gold-crested velvet. Naturally avaricious, she was emboldened to the wildest extravagances. Her child's cups and trenchers were hammered of pure gold and studded with pearls. The little crucifix he wore was fashioned entirely of diamonds.

When the baby was nearly a year old he caught a fever at Stirling. For three days Margaret sat at his bedside, alternately raging at the physicians for not curing him and praying with her priests. She refused to sleep or eat and subsisted on ale and goats' milk. James could not budge her from her vigil.

On the third night she heard heavy boots tramping about the battlements that bordered the tower nursery. She told Adam Bothwell to remove the damned sentry or put him in velvet shoes – every step harried her head.

But the boy said, 'Madam, it is the King who paces.'

She went out on to the narrow stone terrace where wind caught her breath and tossed her hair. The stars were high and roving but the moon was obscured. She could scarcely see the dark figure that approached her but he called her name and she ran to him, resting her head against his shoulder.

Tired, tired to oblivion she felt herself lifted and carried along the south battlements, down steps. Servants hovered in a firelit room and James dismissed them. Swiftly he undressed her, letting the garments fall to the floor. She stared at the pool of brocade and fell asleep standing naked in his arms.

She awakened the following afternoon to find James seated by the bed.

'How is he?' she asked, sitting upright.

He put his hand on hers. 'Sleep, lass.'

Far below in the dungeon workmen hammered a coffin three feet long and women stitched a gold cloth shroud. The castle was draped with woe-weeds. Summoned by couriers, the high nobles of Scotland moved towards Stirling in wind-blustered robes.

For weeks after the funeral Margaret received visits of condolence. Foreign ambassadors reported her 'death-struck', 'shaken beyond belief'. James tried to comfort her but she lashed out in fury. Scotland had killed her child – the brutal climate, the low-lying fogs and the poisons that rose from the swamps below Stirling.

Could she not find solace in religion as he did? She evaded the question, reluctant to shock him. Religion was a mockery. Had she not been the most devoted of mothers? Yet God had tricked her. She confessed to the Bishop that her faith had perished with her child.

And that was a mistake. Heretofore so tolerant, he gave her pesky penances that kept her at her prie-dieu three hours a day. He admonished her to change her thinking lest she raise future tragedies. She began to avoid him, trying new priests as she had once tried new cosmetics. None suited her. They all required a faith she could not assume.

But in November her faith soared like a fire-ball. She was pregnant. Never, never again would she question God's goodness.

Her labour began at Holyrood while James was hunting at Stirling. Deep-slashed with pain she heard that he was on the way to her. He had sent gifts of venison and game birds. He arrived shortly before she bore a daughter. It died within four hours.

Again her convalescence was long, her body weak, her faith weaker. Recovered, she was restless and capricious. She began embroideries and put them aside, started plans for landscaping and grew bored before the seeds were planted. She fussed over her father's gift of caparisoned horses and groomed them herself but lost interest even before she rode them. She favoured new friends, toyed with them and dropped them. She was avid for gossip, and what Hans Pfludder could not report in true ballads, he invented. She constantly sought his assurance that James had no mistress, and was watchful of every new woman who came to court, however briefly.

She realized with triumph but with tenderness that James was ageing. He was still the handsomest man she knew but the thick auburn hair was beginning to silver and lines cornered the dark eyes. At night, when he removed the belt of penance she saw the slight thickening of the slim waist that was welted by iron chains. And yet, if he wanted another woman he had only to glance at her and she would fall into long love. That autumn the Earl of Angus came to court with his grandson, Archibald Douglas. James asked Margaret to entertain the young man while he took the earl on a hunting party to Falkland. She agreed. At least, a new face, a new voice, someone to break the familiar pattern.

She asked Douglas to sup in her apartments. Lest he prove too dull she could send him off later to wench in the town or dice with Adam Bothwell. She made no attempt to beautify herself but wore her simplest gown.

A guard admitted him and her ladies rose from cushions and window seats to welcome him. Their flutter of interest preceded him like a silken wind as they sank into curtsies. Jewelled fingers patted coifs, smoothed hips, unfurled fans. Then they parted and turned, creating a little aisle that led towards Margaret. And down the aisle swaggered a brown-haired boy with full, sullen lips and a hard chin. No man at court was so tall, so shouldered, so harshly, haughtily, virile.

Douglas knelt. She extended her hand and as he kissed it a little thrill ran up her arm. She said, 'Your lordship is welcome.'

As Douglas rose, Margaret said, 'The ladies will bring you wine. I shall return presently.'

She retired to change into a black velvet gown that emphasized her newly slender waist. After all, this was no young gawk but heir to a powerful clan. One must keep the friendship of the Red Douglases, one must think politically.

She painted her mouth and rejoined him.

They sat alone after supper. The room was pooled with ruby shadows from the Venice glass, the stained windows and the hangings brought from the sad, silent nursery.

He said, 'Forgive me if I am bold but you are so beautiful, far more so than portraits and poems had led me to believe.'

She smiled. 'Are you a poet?'

'Not as Gavin is.'

They spoke of Gavin Douglas's verse, then of music. He

sent for his ribboned lute and sang for her. His voice was too high, unsuitable to his manliness, but she was content merely to watch him. He looked about her own age, nineteen or twenty. His eyes were a deep, heavy-lidded grey. But it was the strong, full mouth that charmed her and, when he smiled, the white teeth. He moved with a nerveless grace.

She complimented his singing. Then she asked, 'Are you hand-fasted, my lord?'

'Aye, Madam. To Lady Margaret Hepburn.'

She knew the lass, daughter of the Earl of Bothwell. Sandy-haired, slender as a stalk – indeed, scrawny.

'And do you love her?'

He shrugged. 'I do not wear love lightly.'

'But shall you wear it?'

'Not with her, I think.'

'Still, it would be a suitable match.'

'So I am told,' he said indifferently.

'Perhaps in time you will come to love her.'

'I've had wenches since I was twelve, Madam. But I have never loved until now.'

The last two words were spoken so softly that she could not be sure she had heard them at all.

Quickly, she stammered a new question 'When shall you wed?'

'Next go-summer.'

'And where shall you live?'

'I'm not sure as yet, Madam. Perhaps Tantallon.'

She had seen Tantallon Castle on the east coast, bleak and grey as the sea it faced 'Would you not prefer to live at court?'

'Naturally, Madam, if the King wished it.'

She thought, I shall ask James. The Douglases, once rebels against James III, had spent their power-lust. What harm in this young man's presence at court? He would grace any revel.

'Come,' she said, 'let us go below. I've a whim for dancing.'

They joined the courtiers in the Great Hall. Dogs were chased out, fiddlers summoned. In the semi-darkness of corners, ambassadors seated on benches marvelled at the high spirits of the Queen. True, she was still in mourning, but the velvet skirts swirled high, the eyes glowed and her hair fell from her cap in a shining cascade. Hans Pfludder, probing for gossip, whispered to the Archbishop of St Andrews. 'Her Majesty is radiant. Perhaps she is with child again.'

The Archbishop, watching young Douglas, spoke abstractedly. 'He is no child.'

With James's consent, Archibald Douglas remained at court. He and Margaret danced through the Twelfth Night festivities, hunted together, roamed the Royal Park during the false spring of February searching for violets that would not appear for weeks. His presence comforted her, confused her, excited her.

If she had hoped to rouse jealousy in James, she failed. He beamed on Douglas and gave him two Irish hunters.

In early March Margaret was again pregnant and again overjoyed but in April her gaiety was subdued by news of her father's death. In June her brother, not yet eighteen, married Catherine of Aragon and was crowned Henry VIII in Westminster Abbey.

A few weeks later Flutter warned her that he had heard gossip about her and Douglas in England and on the Borders. 'I would not be your friend if I did not tell you, Madam.'

She was outraged by the slander. Why, she had not even allowed Douglas a kiss!

'I know, Madam. But if this came to the King's ears he'd likely send Douglas from court, would he not?'

'Without doubt . . . but who would dare tell James?'

'Some priest – perhaps his own son.'

Aye, the young Archbishop might well bear the tale.

'What shall I do?' she asked.

'Hasten his marriage to Margaret Hepburn.'

She hated the thought of his marriage, not, she assured herself, because of jealousy, but because his wife would break the close, gay relationship. Douglas, always available to her, would be trapped by a bride's demands.

'You must, Madam,' Flutter said as she hesitated. 'Such talk could presage a scandal.'

He was right.

She told Douglas the next morning as they hunted on Arthur's Seat. '. . . so to still the gossip, you must wed Margaret Hepburn this month, by my command.'

He cursed softly. 'Why tell me now, with people all about?' He looked back at the hunters who trailed them. 'Could you not have waited until we were alone?'

Humouring him, she spurred her horse and he galloped after her down the steep hill and into the heavy forest. She knew every trail, every turn and they lost the others easily. Presently, riding towards impassable brush, she dismounted and he followed her into the gloom of great oaks.

They came into a little clearing and she sat down on a rock, her skirts fluffed about her riding boots. He stood beside her, glaring down from his formidable height.

'I shall do as you command, Madam. But the marriage will be a farce.'

She was pleased. 'You think so now—'

'I shall not change. For I love you.'

She assumed a frown. 'You must never say that.'

'But I shall know it, and so shall you.'

She listened to the hunting horns, far off and ghostly. She must not let him speak of love but she cherished his every word. Presently he sat down beside her, leaned towards her and sought her lips.

She drew back. 'You must not!'

'If only in farewell.'

'But it need not be farewell. You may both live at court. You and I shall continue to meet.'

He clasped her hand and kissed it. 'Meet in secret?'

'No! We will continue as we are, only she will be our protection.'

'Shall you have no jealousy of her?'

She evaded that. 'Are you jealous of the King?'

'No.'

She turned cold. 'Why not?'

'Because he *is* the King.'

Unconsciously, she moved closer to him. 'You do not mind that I lie in his arms?'

Douglas spoke hastily. 'God, Madam, you've no thought of the agony I suffer! But what can I do?'

Take me, she thought in a sudden flare of feeling. Tear off my gown, silence my screams with your lips. No one will ever know, and I am safe with child.

'Kiss me,' she said.

He kissed her gently, almost reverently. The hunting horns were nearer now and he rose, pulling her to her feet. 'They must not find us here, Madam.'

Madam!

'What's amiss, Madam?'

'Nothing,' she said, and smoothed her skirts. They walked to the horses and he helped her mount. Slowly, she calmed, her passion diminishing. Soon she would be herself, thank God, with no sin on her soul, or such a small one it was not worth confessing. She'd be damned if she'd do penance for Archie Douglas's failure at rape.

* * *

Despite her disappointment in him she was still attracted to him and she resented Margaret Hepburn accordingly. The lass had sprouted tall as a weed. Her trousseaux gowns, though made in France, accentuated her colt-like awkwardness. The summer sun had deepened her freckles and robbed her hair of lustre. Margaret received her at Holyrood in August after the honeymoon. They minced through a formal interview. Thus welcomed to court, the new Lady Douglas was used as a chaperone for her queen and her husband.

If she found her role humiliating, she was too timid to complain, though often she was kept up until three or four in the morning while Margaret and Douglas gamed. When sneezingly ill of the New Acquaintance she rode doggedly through the wet mists of Liddesdale to hunt at Margaret's whim. Silent, unobtrusive, she sat and embroidered while Margaret and Douglas read love verse to one another.

James noticed the flirtation and teased Margaret about it. She insisted it was merely friendship such as had existed between queen and troubadour in olden times. It would have pleased her had he raged in jealousy but evidently he realized the innocence of the relationship – or did not care.

By the end of that year he obviously did not care, for Lady Agnes Buchan had come to court as tire-maid. She was fifteen.

At first Margaret scarcely noticed the girl. She moved quietly about the royal apartments, sloe-eyes downcast, mouth unpainted, hair down her back in black coils. She had assisted midwives in the past, so that she was present when Margaret's labour started on October 21st. It was she who washed the child and wrapped it in gold cloth for the Archbishop of Glasgow to take to Margaret's bed. It was a son, and again Margaret gave it her entire attention. The baby, a lusty redhead, was christened Arthur.

Margaret had little thought for Douglas these days; she spent most of her time with the child, and was too preoccupied to notice that James was paying marked attention to her tiring maid. Then one day she noticed that Agnes wore a ruby heart on a golden chain. Idly, she asked if it was a gift from her sweetheart.

Agnes went white. 'Aye, Madam.'

'Who is the lad?' Margaret asked, in good humour.

She stammered. 'Adam Bothwell.'

Margaret forgot the matter for several weeks. Then one evening, seeing young Bothwell in a moody gloom she asked if he had quarrelled with Agnes. Who, Madam – the tire-maid? Why no, he scarcely knew her. Indeed, he had never gifted her. He had no gold to buy rubies, he added angrily – his father kept him in virtual paupery.

Who, then, could afford such a ruby? And why had Agnes lied?

Thereafter, Margaret watched her, and gradually James's interest became apparent. They were discreet, but her eyes were open and her intuitions sharpened by suspicion. She told the Bishop, who begged her to ignore the matter for it could not be more than the frothiest folly.

Folly, aye – but she found the affair increasingly serious for James rarely came to her chamber though she was three months out of child-bed. Douglas was no solace – a spurious love at best, she thought. She told Flutter, 'For all his fair words and flattery I do not trust him.'

'Why, Madam?'

'I cannot explain . . . it is only a sense.'

Flutter did not tell her that her perceptions were correct. Archibald Douglas, unknown to his wife or the Queen, visited Lady Janet Stewart of Traquair as often as he could slip away from court.

Flutter said, 'Take heart, Madam. Your husband merely dallies. And Agnes Buchan is so unsure of him that she visits a witch in the town for love potions.'

'They are effective,' Margaret said bitterly.

'But you see, Madam, she has no confidence in her own charms. She is fearful of losing him. And that should cheer you.'

Nothing cheered her but her son's bouncing health.

On a hot day in July Margaret sought the stone-grey coolness of the Abbey garden. Idly she watched a nun tending the herbs there. Then Master Penhurst appeared to say that the baby was sweating. It might be merely the weather . . .

Margaret sprang up and ran along the arcaded walk up two flights of stairs to the nursery. Sweat beaded the little face. His forehead burned under her hand.

He died that night.

* * *

It was scant comfort that Henry VIII's first child, Prince Henry, lived only six weeks. It was deep comfort that James displayed a new tenderness, though she guessed that it sprang only from pity. She was pregnant again the following August. And she developed a sudden all-consuming piety that delighted the Bishop. She could not endure another tragedy and she took all possible precautions. At Linlithgow, the Loch of the Wet Valley bred poisons but they were shut out by heavy tapestries and blessed incense burned throughout her confinement.

On Easter Sunday another James was born. Margaret was frantic, for though several wet nurses were tried, he spat up their milk or refused it. Finally an Irishwoman was found whose milk was acceptable.

James was the most beautiful child she had ever seen, and she thought he resembled the infant Henry VIII, with red-gold hair and a fine, strong body. Yet all the others had seemed healthy too . . . She bargained with God. 'Let this one live and I shall never ask anything more.'

God was generous, Jamie flourished, and she was soon pregnant again. To complete her happiness, James told her that Agnes and Adam Bothwell wished to marry.

He spoke casually. 'It will be a suitable match – their parents are pleased, and in time they will both inherit riches. I have given my consent.'

So at last James was weary of the wench!

She feigned only mild interest. 'I shall think on some gifts for them. But it seems odd, I've not noticed them courting.'

'You've noticed little but the child, dove.'

True. And yet this marriage seemed strangely sudden.

'Is she with child by Adam, Sire?'

He turned away suddenly. 'No,' he said. 'No.'

His voice was splintered.

Minutes passed. He would not face her. Finally she went to him and forced him to look into her eyes.

'Is she with child by *you*?'

His eyes were dry and hard. 'How can you ask such a question?'

'Is she?'

'She is not.'

'Then why this hasty decision? Is it to stop the spread of scandal?'

Does he do what I did with Douglas . . . ?

He had assumed a bland mask. 'Scandal? I know of none. My God, Margaret, young folk fall into love and marry all the time without—'

'Aye, but heiress though she be, she's a bastard. And Adam overlooks this because of his love?' She laughed scornfully. 'And they are never seen together dancing, hunting – I am not blind!'

He shrugged and walked towards the door. 'I come to you with paltry news, and you puff it to the wildest drama. I can only assume that child-sickness has sickened your reason.'

He left her.

That night when Adam came to attend her apartments with his retinue of lesser gentlemen she studied him closely. He was twenty now, a long lad, long-faced, big-nosed, red-headed. Quietly, as always, he gave his instructions and her ladies came to lay out her night attire under his supervision. She thought, he looks no happier than usual. He is no blithe bridegroom-to-be.

She detained him after the others had left and congratulated him. 'I trust it is a love match?'

'Aye, Madam.'

He is well-instructed to lie . . .

But Adam, usually so reserved, blurted out, 'It is love on my part, Madam, but I doubt on hers, for she mocks me even as she kisses me. She is so beautiful, so quick and merry, while I' – he spread his big, stubby hands – 'I cannot match her in looks or wit. I've nothing to offer but my inheritance.'

'You are too humble. You've much to offer a woman.'

'What?' he asked bluntly.

'Goodness. Integrity. The dignity of your name.'

He smiled bleakly.

She had rarely felt compassion towards another and she had no means to express it now. 'She has chosen you from all the young nobles at court.'

He tipped his rough, curly head. 'That is true, Madam. I'd never have had the presumption to court her. It was she who sought me out.'

On James's command . . . In the tradition of royal lovers, he would marry off his mistress to a man who could offer no possible competition. In Adam he had chosen well.

'Madam, I cannot fathom why she—'

'Peace.' Impulsively she put her hand on his shoulder. 'When fate gifts us we should accept in joy.'

'I know, Madam. And I am grateful.'

Poor duped lad. But better off than I for not knowing how cynically he is being used.

* * *

That November Margaret's daughter was born three months prematurely and died in two days. But Prince James survived. Now that Henry and Catherine of Aragon had been married three years without issue, James was doubly precious for he was next in line to the English throne.

Margaret was fearful of loving him too much, of giving him more time and thought than she gave to God. One penance was self-imposed – she saw Douglas less and less frequently. He sent her romantic little messages and long, meaningful glances across the separating candles, tables, dancers. But she was anxious to remain in God's grace. She had the fancy that if she allowed Douglas the slightest liberty, Jamie would die.

Once searching for a quill in James's desk she came across an entry in the Treasurer's Accounts dated December 1503. 'Item: One necklace of pearls and gold. M L A.'

My Lady Agnes? Ah, no, the slut would have been a child

of nine. Unless he had chosen her early as one plucks a peach to ripen?

Agnes was more conspicuous at court now, with a wife's new dignity. She and Adam honeymooned at Hailes Castle but returned to court in the autumn. Agnes trailed new gowns. Her hair was worked with jewelled pins. She painted her mouth and eyes. When the old earl died and Adam inherited his title and fortune she assumed a hauteur that Margaret found infuriating.

Conceal it though he would, James was still fascinated. There was no gossip as yet, or else it was kept from her, but she noticed how often James invited the young Bothwells on long hunts to which she was rarely asked. Perhaps he and Adam had an understanding but she doubted it. She could not believe that Adam would be party to such connivance or knowingly share his wife – who was pregnant.

Agnes was confined prematurely and Margaret longed for her death. But the labour was easy and the baby healthy. One look at the small, square face and carrot-red hair reassured Margaret that Adam had fathered him. They named him Patrick.

Now, in 1513, her own son was safe in his nursery. James was travelling north. The country was balanced on the edge of war. And Margaret was fighting sleep at Linlithgow, fearful of red dreams.

A week later James returned from pilgrimage and escorted Margaret to Holyrood Palace in Edinburgh. Before dawn on August 19th the Bishop of Tutberry, accompanied by a priest, asked emergency audience and was admitted into James's antechamber where he and the Queen received them in nightclothes.

The Bishop said, 'Father Duncan brought me a strange story which I thought Your Majesties should hear at once. At midnight he witnessed a ghostly visitation at the Market Cross on the High Street.'

Father Duncan described a sepulchral voice that had announced the names of men who would die in battle, headed by the King's own. He told of blue corpse lights flickering about the graveyard of St Giles.

Margaret gasped in genuine horror but James smiled. 'I warrant it's another hoax perpetrated by the English. Evidently they've become desperate.'

'But, Sire,' Father Duncan said, 'even if it was possible to arrange for a man to lie concealed beneath the stone with a tube of some sort to speak through – what of the corpse lights? They were not of this world!'

'That could have been done by spraying the earth with pitch and lighting the turf. Were the people much affected by the death list?'

'Aye, there was much weeping, Sire, not only for yourself and your nobles but for the names of commoners mentioned.'

'Clever,' James said. 'The English think to panic the army.'

'There was no panic, Sire – rather, dismay.'

Margaret put in, 'To me, it has the ring of my own forebodings. Last night I dreamed His Majesty was hurled down a precipice. Later I dreamt that my diamonds changed to pearls – and pearls mean tears.'

The Bishop said, 'I agree, Madam, that such a hoax would be too difficult to have arranged, for the Market Cross is so public a place, and the High Street thronged from morning until night.' He turned to the King. 'I cannot take this occurrence lightly. I believe it to be a warning we dare not ignore.' He moved towards James and spoke softly. 'Have you no belief in visions, in the dark powers unseen to us?'

'Aye. But coming so conveniently as these do, I believe them most humanly contrived.'

Margaret said, 'Dare you risk thousands of men on so slender an argument?'

'I do not consider it slender.' James's voice was edged, and she turned away in silence.

'Comfort your flock,' he said to Father Duncan. 'Assure

them that I regard this visitation as inspired by Henry VIII – and so must they.'

He dismissed the priests, went to the window and looked out at the slowly paling sky. Margaret said, 'Sire, I do not mean to plague you but if you will heed me just once more—'

'What new plea could you possibly make?' he asked gently.

'It is not a new one.'

She reminded him that he had fallen into the trap of a rapaciously ambitious churchman, Andrew Forman. 'Is Bishop Forman ambassador to France in *our* interests? Nay, he pimps for Ann and Louis, he has tied you into an alliance with them hoping for a French Archbishopric as reward for persuading you to invade England.'

'No one persuades me,' James said. 'Only my conscience. You waste your words.'

He went into their bedchamber and she followed him, sinking limply on to a window seat. Gentlemen of the Chamber dressed him. Outside his doublet, as always, he wore his belt of penance, heavier each year with iron links. She thought, the entire clergy of Scotland has absolved him of his crime, yet he has never forgiven himself for rising to kingship on his father's corpse . . .

He had moods of melancholy, especially of late. Last night, on awakening from evil dreams she noticed that his, too, were troubled. He shivered and cried out unintelligibly. She moved to put her arms around him and he said, 'My love?' startling her into sudden, flooding happiness. Then he murmured, 'Agnes,' and she turned, heartsick, to her own side of the bed.

Adam Bothwell was attending James now, offering a velvet hat. Margaret said, 'Sire, surely you do not intend to go out before breakfast?'

'I'll breakfast at Boroughmuir Camp. Then I'll be back to Council. We must arrange for government of the town while the provosts are absent.' He took his gloves from Bothwell, then dismissed him and the other gentlemen.

'It's not yet cockcrow, Margaret. You should return to bed.'

She shook her head. 'May I not ride with you to Boroughmuir?'

'Why?'

'I want to spend every hour with you.'

'It's no place for a woman. I prefer you here.'

Miserably she left him, climbing the private stairs that connected their apartments. She summoned her sleepy tirewomen, dressed and heard Mass. At breakfast in the Great Hall she noticed that Agnes Bothwell was missing and inquired hopefully if she were ill.

'Nay,' Lady Seton said. 'The King commanded her to ride to Boroughmuir.'

The hours passed dismally. Then Flutter arrived with news. It was rumoured that Lord Surrey was massing an army at York and that Queen Catherine, in her husband's absence, was to join him with troops from London. Margaret thought, Perhaps if I rode south with our armies, Catty and I could patch a truce between us, for surely she comes on a peace mission. But when James returned that afternoon he forbade the journey on the excuse that if she were pregnant it would be too arduous.

Doubtless he would take his slut . . .

While he sat in Council she wandered the palace where women were polishing armour and spears, boots and breastplates and horse gear. No one knew when the King planned to march but preparations were completed.

Late in the afternoon Archibald Douglas asked audience. His wife Margaret was in child-sickness and had started labour. He begged the Queen's advice as to whether barley bread or iron should be placed beneath her pillow after the child was born.

'I tried everything,' Margaret said. 'Bread, iron, rowan – nothing pleased the fairies, for my bairns died soon or late. But when I was bedded with Jamie I had the Archbishop bless a rose noble. They took it greedily and all was well.'

'I thank Your Majesty.'

'Come,' she said, 'be seated. You look ill.'

His cheeks were pale, his grey eyes sunken and circled. But as always his hair and beard were impeccable and he smelled of oil of almond.

'The vigil is wearing me, Madam. I waited four years for an heir and now I've waited eight hours that seem aeons.' He smashed his fist into his hand. 'My entire life is waiting. God knows how much longer I must wait on my inheritance.'

'You are not without funds?'

'Nay, but you know how I feel.'

She knew that he wanted the Earldom of Angus. He was not unlike herself, ambitious for power, but frustrated, spending his energy as she did on hunting, dancing and gaming.

'And I've waited years for your love.'

'Archie, I have told you, you may not say such things—'

'You do not command my dreams. I love you.'

Perhaps he did. Perhaps he was sincere. Sometimes she thought so, but after a night in James's bed she felt that no man could want her save for breeding or as a stepping-stone towards power. If love was blind, then Douglas was dazzled by the light of her crown.

She returned to the safer subject of his inheritance. 'The title may come sooner than you think.'

'Your Majesty speaks in riddles.'

She told him about the roll call of the men who were to die in battle. 'Your father's name was listed.'

He shivered. 'And mine?'

'I don't know. But Flutter told me near a hundred nobles were warned.'

Douglas mused for a while, fingering the satin sleeve of his tunic. 'It's my Grandsire bears the title, and he is too old for war. So even if my father—' He let the sentence trail off. 'Tell me, Madam, who shall remain to protect you?'

'My archer guard, that is all. My pages under sixteen and the gentlemen of my chamber who are over sixty – a great defence, is it not? But His Majesty is determined to have the greatest army Scotland ever mustered.'

'I've heard we have sixty thousand men.'

'Even my husband doesn't know for sure, men are arriving hourly from the Isles, the Highlands, the Border. The English think we have forty thousand – or so our agents say.'

'And how many men have the English?'

'Only twenty-six thousand, but theirs are trained soldiers. Most of ours have never known more than a fist fight or a Border skirmish. And who knows at what moment my brother might not conquer France and hurl his other army across the channel?'

A page interrupted to ask that Douglas go to his wife, who was calling for him.

'Presently,' he said, and turned back to Margaret. 'Madam, you take too dismal a view. We shall not invade deep into England, only comply with Queen Anne's wishes and open a new front so that the English will be forced to withdraw from France.'

But she would not be comforted. He suggested a game of chess but she sat abstractedly, not studying her moves but thinking of Europe's chessboard and the strategy James might employ if he would only relinquish the idea of war. By breaking the French alliance he could remove the Pope's order of excommunication, and the Pope might then be counted on to patch matters between England and Scotland, even, perhaps, putting pressure on Harry to send her dowry . . .

Agnes Bothwell tapped timidly at the open door. 'Madam, I am sorry to intrude—'

'What is it?' Margaret asked sharply.

'Lady Douglas is dead, Madam – My Lord.'

Behind her stood a bloody-aproned midwife holding a white, silken bundle.

Douglas sprang up. 'The child?'

'Dead. It was a boy.'

He stared at the midwife and made a little gesture towards the bundle, but his hand fell to his side.

Agnes and the midwife stood in silence, awaiting instructions.

'Take Lord Douglas to her, send for his priest and her kinsmen.' Margaret put her hand on Douglas's shoulder. 'Poor lad . . . I shall order her apartments draped in woe-weeds, and a Mass said in the Abbey . . .'

And I shall do penance, she thought. But how could I know she was dying? And she would have died whether he were with her or not.

Margaret and James supped alone in his apartments. He said casually, 'We leave for England tonight.'

She jumped up from the table. 'Tonight!'

'As soon as I reach camp.'

'Oh, God! I had thought – I never thought—'

She had prayed for a miracle.

'Come, *ma joie*, you've nothing to fear. Tomorrow you'll ride to Linlithgow and I'll send you couriers twice each day telling you how we fare. Look from your tower at night and you'll see our balefire signals and be at ease.'

She sat down and looked at her food and pushed it away. 'James – do you have a premonition of death? Tell me, on your oath.'

He laughed and the candles reflected the dark fire of his eyes. 'I've a premonition of victory. We have every advantage – men, arms, supplies. Harry cannot even muster a fit commander.'

'Lord Surrey is an experienced soldier.'

'Aye, but too old. Seventy. Poor gentleman . . .'

James spoke of his instant liking for Surrey when he had brought Margaret to Scotland. She remembered how oddly close the two had been, the rough, foul-mouthed Englishman and the urbane Scot. It seemed ironic that they should now lead opposing armies.

James summoned a secretary who brought a locked chest

and gave Margaret the key. 'All is in readiness – my will, your authorization of Regency, instruction for the defence of our towns . . .'

Below she heard the shouting of grooms, the neighing of horses, the pound of boots and prance of pipes in the courtyard. James's gentlemen wrapped him in a thin, dark riding cloak and attached his emerald-glittered spurs. Lackeys carried out his weapons and armour, packed in waterproof boxes, his chests of clothing. The Master of the Household reported that his cases of wine, dried meats and salted fish were ready.

Margaret followed James to the prince's nursery where he bent and kissed the sleeping baby. Then he escorted her to the Great Hall where nobles and high clergy bade her farewell. Archibald Douglas was not among them. He would wait to attend his wife's funeral and ride to join the army in a few days.

Margaret whispered to the Bishop of Tutberry, 'See that the King does nothing rash.'

'Rest assured, Madam.'

The windows were open to the long, summer gloaming and candles burned in the hot dusk. Not a breath of wind stirred the arras or lifted the plumes, the feathers, the tassels and fringe that bordered capes and tunics. There was no sound but the weeping of women, as husbands, brothers, fathers embraced them.

Margaret saw Adam Bothwell clinging to Agnes and she thought, 'So the slut remains behind . . .'

But her triumph was lost in the desolation of the weeping. It shocked her to see the grief of nuns, whom she had thought to be braver than herself. There was Dame Mary, prioress of St Catherine's, head bent, hands clasped in prayer, tears staining the white prayerbook she carried. James's son, the Archbishop, stood beside her. When he moved forward to bless the congregation his cloak swirled like the black wing of a raven, and his face seemed skeletal.

There were hundreds of people in the room, and no sound

but weeping. She looked at the green and gold and scarlet of capes and doublets, the bright flash of breast armour and mailed sleeves.

She smelled death.

It is only the pesky smell of Edinburgh, she thought, carried on some wind that has passed to the sea. The smell of drouth-rot in the park, the smell of age from the Abbey vaults, the smell of the poor who crowd the gates and line the streets to watch the army depart. It is only the smell of my fear.

James commanded the musicians to play. As the pipes and cithers began he whispered, 'Come with me.'

He led her down the stairs to the cloistered walk and dismissed the guards there. They stood beneath oaks and dead, browning pear trees on a carpet of yellowing leaves. Above Arthur's Seat the sky was purple as a festered wound.

She noticed that he wore Anne of Brittany's turquoise ring.

James knelt and kissed the hem of her skirt. Then he gripped her close about her hips and she heard him murmur, but the words were muffled in folds of silk.

'What, Sire?'

He rose and cupped her breasts. 'I think you *are* with child. And I thank God for it.'

Tears dropped down her face, her throat. She pressed her body to his and raised her mouth for his kiss.

But he gave her a playful pat on her stomach. 'Take care you drink sweet cream and eat plenty of goats' cheese. Favour red wine and red meat—'

'Sire,' she said, 'you have never spoken of love, but now—'

'– and eggs. Above all, don't fret about me. I shall send Master Pfludder to you in a few days and he shall carry back your messages. That will pleasure you, eh, my treasure? And you'll find a surprise at Linlithgow – nay, I'll tell you. I've trained you a new merlin . . .'

So she was still the child, the kitten-queen to be offered a ball of yarn.

James kissed her lightly and sent a guard to summon his

retinue. As they streamed down the stairs she stood aside, pressing against a pillar of the cold, arcaded wall. Preceded by pipers, James crossed the courtyard, followed by his nobles and clergy. They were met at the palace gates by a cheering mob. She saw the bright, scattered toss of gold as James flung largesse. Then he and his men were lost to view as they entered White Horse Close where the war chargers waited.

Margaret turned and passed the two old halberdiers who guarded the stairs. She moved up past the Great Hall where the women were gathered and climbed to her own apartments. Wordlessly, with only a nod to her tiring maids, she entered the little oratory, a gloom of grey and violet where a candle burned under the agate eyes of the Virgin.

Far off she heard horses' hooves like muffled thunder and shouts along the High Street that grew slowly fainter. From below came the soft, sad pluck of a lute.

Sometime between the end of the long northern dusk and the brief fall of darkness rain came. It beat against Margaret's casement, drove the dust from the courtyard, filled the parched ponds of the forest and pooled the wynds off the Canongate.

In a hovel on Candlemaker's Row a child shivered in fever and spat blood. In a moor hut across the loch a woman stared at the boils on her husband's neck and caught his vomit in her apron. In lodgings above the Cock and Stag an old man gasped for breath and dug at the black spots on his arms.

The plague followed the army on the road south.

From her tower at Linlithgow Margaret looked out over the soggy moors. The Loch was stippled with rain but the sky was clearing. She left the window and returned to sit at her embroidery frame. At the other end Dame Mary was stitching on a long satin altar cloth. Her fingers, white and nimble, wove silver thread through blue pieties.

'I am glad you came,' Margaret said, hands aimless in her lap.

'I, too, Madam, though it is a luxury I scarce deserve.'

Margaret guessed that only a royal invitation would have budged Dame Mary from her convent, for the oat and apple harvests were imminent. Beans and plums must be gathered for drying and meats salted down for the winter. Then the turf cutters were due to lay in a supply of fuel, and carpenters must see to the repair of the roof before the autumn rains fell. All these matters required Mary's management for, as she said, the more devout the nun, the sillier in worldly matters. Not that she didn't have *her* faults. Finances, in truth, had been in a terrible snarl until the Bishop of Tutberry had examined the ledgers and put things right with the grant of additional land and fishing rights on the west shore of the Loch. She did not know what she would do if – God forbid – he were killed in battle.

Margaret said, 'I marvel you can keep your mind on your work. I cannot.'

'Your Majesty is sorely troubled.'

'But so are you. For in your way, you love the Bishop.'

Mary flushed. 'It is a love of the spirit, Madam.'

'I know. But suppose you had met before taking your vows. What then?'

Mary pushed a brown curl under her wimple. 'I'm sure he would not have cared for me, for if he thinks me frilly now he could not have abided me in my girlhood. Nay, Madam, I am only a trial to him.'

'How often does he visit you?'

'He used to come in April and September. But my accounts and estates are always in such muddle that the poor man rides to us five or six times a year. Once he spent an entire Easter ordering the planting and returned to supervise the harvesting himself, working in the fields like a common monk. His hands were briared, his face sun-scorched, he blundered into a beehive and was stung in the nose. We thought he would never return after that but he was back on All Hallows, at Yuletide and for the lambing. He travelled in the wildest weather. No road was ever too snowy or muddy. When he left me yesterday he said – he said he would be back if only to show me how to manage the buttery.'

She bent her head over the embroidery, taking careful little stitches on a rosette.

Margaret thought, she does not know it, but she is beloved.

At four o'clock they joined her ladies for First Supper in the Great Hall. Margaret noticed that Agnes Bothwell's eyes were red and puffed. She also noticed with fury that Agnes wore a new, if modest, jewel – a little golden heart arrowed by a diamond. She had a sudden, stunning thought: *If James dies, she will be at my mercy.*

Agnes raised her eyes across the glow of candles and met Margaret's speculative stare. The eyes were darkly remote, hooded by heavy lashes, and the face was calm. But a muscle twitched in her cheek.

She has read my thoughts. She is frightened.

Margaret smiled. 'How is your son, Lady Agnes?'

'Well, Madam.' The black eyes flickered.

'And yourself?'

'I have been sleepless.'

'Of course.' This could be amusing. 'I had forgotten that you are scarcely more than a bride. You must miss your husband sorely.'

Down the long oak table the ladies sat motionless, their food forgotten.

'I do miss him, Madam.'

'You must let me give you a potion to induce sleep.'

The black eyes opened wide. 'Oh, no!'

'A brew of poppy and milkweed.'

'Your Majesty is too kind. I am sure I shall sleep tonight.'

'Come to me before you retire, and I shall have it ready.'

'But truly, Madam, you need not—'

'Be at my bower at nine.'

Margaret turned and chatted with Dame Mary and Lady Seton, but all the while she was conscious of Agnes, sitting rigidly, white as her damask gown. Once she put out her hand for her wineglass but withdrew it. Her fingers clasped the little golden heart, then fumbled to her throat. She shook her head when a servant offered sweets.

Does the slut think I will poison her when a dozen witnesses have heard me?

After supper Margaret and Dame Mary spent a few moments in the chapel. On the gallery above – The Leper's Lair – creatures chittered and screamed as servants fed them with scraps through the holes. They made such a din that prayer was impossible, and Margaret and Mary walked out into the grey gardens. There was a musty, earthy smell of swampland. In ancient times Linlithgow had been called 'The Loch of the Wet Valley'. They could feel the dampness seep through their clothes, into their very bones. Shivering, they entered the palace.

For a while they read scripture in Margaret's tower. Then Mary retired; she must be up for prayers at two with the four nuns who had accompanied her. Margaret played primero with Archie Douglas, permitting him to win because he was still so tense and shaken. Tomorrow they would attend his wife's funeral.

Alone, she received a provost who had ridden the fifteen miles from Edinburgh – an old man in a mud-splattered cloak.

'There are six cases of the plague, Madam.'

She did not panic, but burrowed in James's chest and found 'Instructions on Alarm of the Pest'.

The stricken must be sent at once to isolation at Boroughmuir, where huts and tents had been vacated by the army. Clengers – professional cleansers – would be appointed to attend them and prevent their escape. Relatives and close friends of the sick should be confined to their homes for fifteen days, and might not mingle with clean folk on peril of their lives. Their quarters must be fumigated with burnt heather or peat, their clothing boiled in kilns or kettles and fresh gowns provided them if they were poor. All furniture should be scrubbed. Finally, the house was to be exposed to air and sunlight.

'After the rains there is only hot air and hot sunlight,' the provost said. 'The manual specifies cold.'

'We shall not fret about that,' Margaret said. She was oddly exhilarated, and with ideas of her own. 'Command the town callers to give these instructions when calling the hour and have the news proclaimed by herald at the Market Cross. Command what priests are left to exorcize entrances to the pest-dwellings and bid them say special Masses lest the epidemic spread. . . . Beyond all, do not allow a suspect traveller or cart to enter any city port.'

'An old man is dead,' he said. 'What shall be done with the body?'

'Have a clenger burn it outside his dwelling.'

The pest, she thought, was like a witch, impervious to all enemies but fire.

At nine o'clock Agnes Bothwell appeared. She had seemed wan at supper; now she was haggard. But her manner was icily calm as she took the chair Margaret indicated.

She is not really beautiful, Margaret thought. Her cheek bones are too high, her lips too full, and her eyes slant strangely. Yet the eyes were magnificent under the glossy arcs of brows and her skin a white dazzle.

I wonder what varnish she uses . . .

'The sleeping powder is ready for you,' Margaret said.

'Thank you, Madam, but I do not require it now. After supper I fell into so deep a sleep that my maids could scarcely rouse me to come here.'

'Oh? Then we shall dispense with the potion.'

She saw the girl's shoulders sag with relief. 'Then shall I go, Madam?'

'There is no haste.'

The shoulders grew rigid again and the eyes were brightly watchful.

'Tell me how you amuse yourself these dreary hours,' Margaret said.

'I tend Patrick. I – write messages to my husband.'

And mine.

'I long for a courier to pick them up and bring me news.'

'There could scarcely be news as yet,' Margaret said. 'They cannot be much farther than Selkirk, for the rains must have slowed them.' She rose and poured a glass of wine from the decanter on the table. 'Will you join me?'

'No, Madam, thank you.'

'I am instructed to drink red wine to build my baby's blood.'

Agnes's hand tightened on the arm of her chair. 'So – Your Majesty is sure?'

'Yes. I should birth in May.'

'God be praised.' But she could not manage a smile.

Doubtless James has told her that he beds me in duty of heirs, but no woman can bear the thought of her lover in another's arms, and no woman will ever believe that love-making is altogether a chore . . .

Margaret slid to another subject. 'His Majesty has the warmest regard for your husband.'

It was a lie, for James had never praised Adam Bothwell, though lately he had sat in Council.

'I am glad, Madam.'

Another lie. She wants James, in passionate love, to be jealous and fearful of Adam.

'Once I suggested that your husband accompany Bishop Forman on a mission to France but the King would not hear of it . . .'

So much was true. James thought the stolid young earl weak in diplomacy.

'He wanted to keep him here.'

'That is – gratifying, Madam.'

A long silence was broken by the sputter of the fire in the hearth. Margaret sighed and said, 'I, too, long for news. Especially from Master Pfludder. There's little he doesn't perceive or hear.'

'Indeed? I know him only slightly.'

And that was still another lie. Flutter was Agnes's most

intimate gossip and most of what Margaret knew about Agnes came from him.

'I have known him for years but he remains a mystery to me. He never mentions a family, and I wonder if he has ever been married, though with that ferret-face I doubt he'd attract any but desperate women.'

Agnes said, 'I've seen him on occasion with a wench who sells fish on the High Street.' She seemed grateful for a safe subject. 'She is young and very beautiful, with hair like primrose.'

'So Flutter has a sweetheart!'

'She is married to the fishmonger, who is equally handsome; but he's slow and sluggish. I think he is witless.'

'So Master Pfludder is involved in an affair!'

'I'm not sure of that, Madam,' Agnes said uncomfortably.

'Well, if he is, he will soon tire. Nothing wearies a man so much as the strategy of deceit – and an importuning woman. My brother, for example—'

'King Henry?'

'Aye, hadn't you heard about his women?'

'Nay, Madam.'

We match lies. 'He is merry and handsome, and women adore him, but because he is kind they invariably suppose him to be in love with them, whereas he is only toying. Of course it is his own fault, since he pleases them with praise and poems and gifts. But when he tires, it is difficult to be rid of them and he continues the sad masquerade until, at last, the woman realizes that she has wasted months or years of her life.'

Agnes said, 'If he truly loved his wife he'd need no other woman. Perhaps the lack is hers.'

So she dares to fence – and skilfully.

'You may be right,' Margaret said silkily. 'Queen Catherine is not one to rouse a man's passion – a veritable lump. And yet he must love her deeply for he always returns to her—'

'He must,' Agnes said, 'for she is his wife.'

'Ah, but you see, she is friend as well. He tells her of his women and she laughs and suggests means of his breaking the grip – kindly, of course – and he does so. It is a sort of male weakness that cannot bear hurting what it has enjoyed. Men are prone to sentiment as we are not.'

'True, Madam. But I wonder if the Queen is really amused by his confidence? I think she must play a part in order to hold him.'

'Most women play parts, do they not?'

'Perhaps in high places they must.'

She is clever, Margaret thought. Flutter has minimized her wit, perhaps through fear of offending me.

What do I really know of her? She knew that Agnes cared little for hunting but wandered the wavy hills of Liddesdale gathering plants and seedlings. She was virtually ignorant of literature or science but played prettily on the virginals and lute. She was fearful of the dark and would never enter Hailes's haunted dungeons nor sleep without a light. Over-emotional, she was always close to tears or laughter, mischief or melancholy. Perhaps these moods charmed the King, but Flutter felt that they had little in common and persisted in predicting that he would lose interest, yet the affair had survived nearly four years.

Due to Agnes's position as king's mistress the women of the court dared not offer her friendship for fear of risking Margaret's enmity. Thus Agnes had sought Flutter as confidant, trusting him with her secrets. These were the obvious ones – jealousy of Margaret, worry that she might lose the King to another woman. She was fiercely possessive and quarrelled with James each time he honoured a lady with the most casual notice. She treated her husband abominably, with bored impatience, often with malice. Adam, like a great faithful dog, received the kicks and licked her hand.

Agnes stirred uneasily and glanced at the slow-sifting sandglass. The long dusk was ending and gold light pooled the far corners of the room, glistening on the rock walls. The little golden heart glittered on her breast.

Margaret felt herself sinking into deep depression. What had begun as cat-mouse play had ended painfully. She had not triumphed, only exposed her own raw nerves and fed her jealousy. Hate was like an appetite that required the food of vengeance. And she starved.

She said, 'I shall look for balefires tonight.'

'I, too, Madam.'

Perhaps James had some secret signal for her . . .

'You may go, my lady.'

Agnes rose, tiny waisted in her huge-skirted damask. Curtsying, she emerged from its petals of lace and embroidery. 'May God send Your Majesty good rest.'

Margaret stared through the window that faced south. She knew that watchmen were stationed on mountain tops and castle battlements ready to light fires at the slightest glimmer of another. They started at the King's camp – wherever he might be – and each had its message. One fire signified that all was well; two, that the enemy was in motion; three, that the enemy was advancing; four, in a row, that they had great strength. Probably Hume Castle would give the first alarm, then Dunbar, Haddington, Dalkeith and Edinburgh, spreading north to Stirling and the far Highlands.

But she saw nothing but the white roving moon. She heard nothing but the craiking of landrails and the boom of snipe.

She retired, but was up at four in the morning to resume her vigil at the window. There was utter silence on the loch, the moors, the far, rosy hills. Then a skylark sang, a blackbird, a willow-wren. Herons screamed harshly over the water. Plovers wailed, moorcocks birred. An owl plunged down from an oak to catch a frog. On the gargoyled ledge of the tower a nest of young rooks shrieked in a bedlam of cawing.

Otters played on the loch bank and plunged in, raising spray caps. A polecat stalked a woodchuck. A hawk dived on a rabbit and blood reddened the bracken. She heard the twirr of partridge flushed by foxes.

There were no balefires.

All day she awaited a courier. None came. She attended Margaret Douglas's funeral in St Michael's Church. The young face framed by sandy curls appalled her. The mouth was twisted in pain and though the eyes were closed it seemed the sleep of nightmare.

After the Mass was over she moved down to the vestry and stood before the carved stone altarpiece that pictured the Passion of Jesus. James had accompanied her here only a few weeks ago, kneeling in supplication. Perhaps even then he had not despaired that the Pope might rescind the sentence of excommunication. It was burned into her memory:

'By the authority of Almighty God and our blessed St Mary and all the company of heaven . . . and also by the power of the All Holy Church . . . we pronounce James IV openly and absolutely to be accursed and damned; so that he be departed from God and Holy Church, and have no merit of Christ's death, nor of sacraments, nor pride of prayers or good deeds among Christian people; but that he shall be of God accursed, sleeping, waking, standing, sitting, going, eating, fasting and in all other works; and shall dwell in the endless pains of hell for ever, without end. Amen.'

When she returned to the palace a courier came with word that the Scottish army was preparing to advance down the Valley of the White Adder to cross the Tweed. There were fourteen cases of the pest. The King was well and inquired of her health. He sent no personal message.

That evening she invited Archie Douglas to sup with her and a few favoured courtiers. At her request he lingered after the others had left.

'I leave at dawn, Madam. I may never see you again.'

She shivered. 'Please—'

'But it is true. I must speak my mind to you. You must remember that I love you beyond hope of heaven.'

'Archie—'

'Madam, it is no time for tid-tattle. Let the truth lie between us.'

She said cynically, 'I know you had no love for your wife. Yet you are not a man to live celibate. What woman has amused you these past years?'

'None, Madam. I swear it.'

'The wenches of the town?'

'I'd not touch one.'

'For fear of the Yaws?'

'Nay, for love of you.'

Why can't I believe those forthright eyes, those swift and certain words?

'What is it you require of me?' she asked. 'I have no love to give.'

'I think you have. Or had.'

She flushed.

'Do you remember that day we hunted in the woods?'

'We've spent many days in the woods,' she said uneasily.

'Let us be honest, Madam, the hours grow short. I know you as I know my own pulse. I have watched you when you thought yourself unobserved, studied you in every mood. That day in the forest you would have given love.'

'No!'

'But my awe was too great, my respect too deep. I was young, and youth's a fool. But now—'

He moved across the candles to her chair and knelt at her feet, clasping her hands.

'May we be honest, Margaret?'

Her name on his lips excited her even as it startled her. 'Aye.'

'The King adores you as he worships his saints. I love you as a man loves, hotly and jealously. I could cut his heart to collops!'

'But that is treason-talk!'

'Nay, it is love. And love is all I have to give.'

She thought of Agnes Bothwell and of all the other

humiliations she had suffered at James's hands. 'But I love the King. I could not betray him.'

'You would have – that day.'

'It is not that day.' She withdrew her hands from his. 'You must go. I command it.'

But again he caught her hand. His lips burned her open palm.

He rose. 'Very well. But think on what I have said. You know where I lodge?'

She knew. Below her tower in the west corridor.

'Come to me, Margaret.'

'You are mad!'

'Is love sane? I shall be waiting.'

Slowly, she prepared for sleep. But when the last lady had left, closing the bed curtains, she lay open-eyed in the darkness.

It was unthinkable that she should go to Douglas. First, there were guards outside her chamber whom she could not evade. There was her terror that if she broke her marriage vow God would take her son in reprisal. And she did not love Douglas.

But she wondered how it would be . . .

Next day the weather turned raw. The huge-mouthed fireplaces blazed from cellar to turret but the palace corridors were tomb-cold. From her tower Margaret looked out on white murk over a swampy wilderness. The wind screamed incessantly.

She jumped at small sounds – a dog's bark or the tumble of a log. She saw inexplicable shadows and freaks of light. One of the lepers died and servants refused to bury it for fear of contagion until the captain of the guard threatened them with the lash.

Margaret slept fitfully. In dreams she saw Margaret Douglas rise from her coffin in St Michael's vault, climb the castle's turnpike stairs and float through the barred door to stand accusing with white, hollow eyes and twisted mouth. In terror, Margaret aroused the guard at the door and the ladies who slept in the adjoining chamber.

On August 22nd she saw the glare of balefires from the south. The Scots army had crossed the Border. The next evening a courier brought word that James's forces had attacked Norham, an English fortress commanded by Captain Ainslow. The Scots, battering the castle, faced strong winds and heavy rains, but the King expected the siege to be a brief one, for he had French guns as well as the great ordnance of Edinburgh Castle.

The Scots captured Norham after six days. They advanced up the right bank of the Till, destroyed Etal Castle and captured the castles of Wark and Ford. Slowly, through lashing storms and rivers of mud, Surrey was advancing towards Newcastle to meet his northern troops. Couriers reported that agonizing gout forced him to ride in a horse litter.

On September 5th Flutter arrived at Linlithgow and told Margaret that the King was at Ford Castle and had made it his headquarters for three days.

'Why does he linger there?' she asked.

'I don't know, Madam, I am no military expert.'

'He is not ill?' She plucked at his sleeve. 'Pest-ridden?'

'I vow he's not, but in merry mood, for it has been victory all the way.' He took a letter from his pouch. 'He sent you this.'

It was a hastily scrawled note that trusted she was well and promised his safe return.

Margaret sighed. 'He gives little thought to me. Do you know if he writes to Lady Bothwell?'

'He gave me no messages for her.'

'What does he do at Ford?'

'He studies his maps and charts.'

'Has he taken captives?'

'Aye, a few. Lady Heron and her servants.'

'Lady Heron?'

'The chatelaine.'

The name was familiar. Suddenly she remembered the

beautiful Borderwoman who had supped with her and James at Holyrood.

'Lady Heron begged on her knees that His Majesty spare the castle, and he did so.'

'Is her lord at the castle?'

'Nay, captive of the Scots on the Border.'

'So she and His Majesty are alone at Ford?'

'There is her young daughter and His Majesty's nobles.'

'Tell me truly, is His Majesty enamoured of her?'

'Truly, Madam, I do not know.'

She smiled wanly. 'You, who see everything, are suddenly stricken blind.'

'I see them at table, at cards and at chapel. I have not seen them abed.'

'What do you hear?'

'There is always rumour when folk are idle.'

'You shall take this rumour to Lady Bothwell. Embroider it lushly.'

He smiled. 'Very well. But you know the King's heat is for war. Is he likely to dally with a woman at such a time?'

'I see no other reason why he lingers there. Time is a-wasting as Surrey approaches and strengthens his forces.'

'But the weather, Madam—'

'The weather has not deterred the King for two stormy weeks. Why should it now?'

'Perhaps he is sobered to realize that due to the weather and pest-fear there have been many desertions.'

'Desertions *now*?'

'Aye. I passed more than a hundred Scots struggling north across the Border.'

'Yet surely that would not stop the King from meeting Surrey's forces?'

'No.'

'How many English are advancing?'

'Twenty-six thousand, Madam. But we far outnumber them.'

'Do you return to Ford?'

'Aye, Madam, in a few hours. Likely he will have left there for a new encampment.'

'When you find him, give him this.' She handed him a sealed letter. A love letter, she thought, that James will read and toss aside. 'Go to Lady Bothwell, tell her your news. Determine if she has heard from the King. Then come to me.'

Agnes had received three brief but loving letters from James. On hearing of Lady Heron she had laughed scornfully. A thirty-five-year-old woman! Preposterous! And an ill-dressed provincial at that. It was obvious to Agnes that after six days of exertion in battering Norham, and the storms, he was resting his troops at Ford so as to spring them fresh on the long-marching English. It required no military wisdom to figure *that.*

But she had returned to the subject of Lady Heron. Did she pad? How long was her hair? Did she have all of her teeth. . .?

News came to Margaret from Edinburgh. The plague seemed under control, but the Council was wroth at the appearance of deserters, and women stoned them in the streets. The Nor' Loch had flooded its banks and ruined the harvests there. Due to impassable roads food was scarce and expensive. But word of the King's victories had heartened the people and candles of thanksgiving lit St Giles.

Couriers came and went. Then, on a wet midnight, Francis Cray, the King's equerry, brought Margaret official news.

James had left Ford with his army and crossed the Till to a high ridge two miles north-west. About a mile in area, it was an unassailable position protected by marshland and hills, with access to plenty of water. Its only approach was up a steep slope. At its foot, cannon guarded a ditch. Other guns were entrenched above. There were curtaulds, culverins, sacres and serpentines amounting to seventeen great pieces.

Spears fifteen feet long, together with shields, arrows, yew-bows, claymores and battle axes were piled with swords in water-proofed cases. The cannon-balls, of lead, were also boxed against the weather. On the heights the royal pavilion was raised under the wind-flapped banners of Scotland. There were tents for the nobles, others for the common soldiers. Horses and Highland ponies roamed the wet grass.

Save for a few folded hills, the countryside spread out in clear view of watching eyes. There were the magnificent Cheviots, towering to the south, and to the west the Eildon Hills. The Tweed silvered in the distance, and on its far banks rose the fires of Coldstream. Little villages cuddled nearby – Branxton, Blinkbonny, Sandyford. Through them and beyond them ran turnip fields and land plump with harvest.

At the hill's foot, beyond the ditch, oxen roamed, freed from their burdens of guns and supplies. There were mules, donkeys, sheep, goats and cattle which had been driven from the captured castles. Here was a tented carnival camp, numbering hundreds – whores, pimps, palmists, astrologers and gamblers who had followed the army from Edinburgh. Gipsies had set up fortune-telling booths. Renegade priests sold the bones of St John and St Ninian for a shilling apiece, and threads from Christ's robe at a crown. Holy silver medals could be had for a groat each. Vendors shrieked their wares – aqua vitae, sack, muscadine, flea salve, scratch-backs, fresh meat and fish, barley cakes, gingerbread, blankets, tooth mastic, cooking pots, drinking mugs, rushlights, bowstrings, visors, breastplates, satchels. They sold talismans against plague, witchcraft, infidelity, blindness, scrofula, fever; love potions, heart protectors, crosses made of rowan twigs to insure long life.

Beggars were permitted for good luck; there were laundresses, scriveners, harpers, pipers, jesters, jugglers, armourers, goldsmiths. The pimps sold their women with willow whips, Spanish ticklers, yaw-cooler and strategically cut shifts. Nobles and common soldiers came down the hill to stand in line before their tents, and the soothsayers did a lively trade.

The camp on the hill was well provisioned with ale, beer, mutton, beef, salt fish, cheese and wine. Spies reported – and accurately – that the English had been short of food for three days, and unable to buy it. There was only water to cheer them through days of marching through mud and driving rain. From Alnwick on September 4th Surrey sent a herald to James offering battle and two days later received a message from James suggesting that the armies meet at noon on Friday, September 9th.

Surrey marched his hungry, exhausted men through the rain to Wooler Haugh, six miles from the Scots encampment on Flodden Hill.

3

Bess Dart

September 2nd, 1513

GUILIE SAID, 'I have watched his house these six days. There are no servants left there but an aged man and a girl – all others have gone to war. The man is sodden drunk by seven of the evening, when the girl goes to the well, where she lingers to gossip. She never locks the doors so nothing bars my entry.'

'You risk too much,' Bess said, 'and you may find nothing.'

'I am sure to find hair on his pillow or chair backs, a bit of his beard on a razor.'

'And if you are caught?'

'Then I'm hungry, searching for food or a trinket to sell. I'll get no more than a shilling fine and a scold from the magistrate.'

'Sir John may be killed in battle.'

'But if he is not, I'll never have so good a chance to enter his house.'

She glanced at the edge of Bess's bodice where the bandage showed. 'Do you want him free to do the same to another woman? Do you want him to live unpunished?'

Bess shook her head.

'Then I go to his house tonight. I shall return by eight.'

Bess waited. The watchman called the hour of eight and the name of a house closed for the pest on Cap and Feather Wynd. She listened for Guilie's footfall on the stairs. The watchman's voice echoed along the worn grey streets.

The sky darkened. A cat cried. From the window hole she

ooked out on the eaves of houses across the way, black gainst a slate sky.

I should never have let her go. I should have taken my wn vengeance in my own time.

The cat wailed again. She heard a woman's curse, the plash of thrown water and a screaming scurry up the wall. ess's own cat curled in sleep on the pallet.

Rain began, drumming on the pointed roofs. The torch bove the arch at the end of the wynd hissed and drowned n the downpour.

The room chilled and Bess put on her shawl. She set herelf little needless tasks, scouring the clean deal table, stiring a sheepgut stew long since cooked and cooling. As she ightened buttons on Hugh's old doublet she heard footsteps nd opened the door. Flutter stood there.

He laughed at her astonishment as she clasped his outtretched hands.

'Is the war over?' she asked.

'Nay.' He told her about the captured Border castles. He ad no news of Hugh but would inquire when he returned. he served him food and while he ate he recounted court ossip. Then as she moved about listening abstractedly he sked, 'What's amiss?'

'I fret about Hugh.'

The shrewd gold eyes pinned hers. 'You can scarce leave hat window. Are you awaiting someone?'

She smiled wanly. 'What men are left?'

He went to her and tipped up her chin. 'Why did you void me before I left?'

'I was ill of the Quacks.'

'So Guilie told me. But why did you shut me out?'

'When I'm ill I want no one about.'

'You're a poor liar.' He spun her about and she cried out n pain. The shawl came open and he saw the bindings.

'What happened?'

Reluctantly she told him.

'Why were you silent? Why should I not have known?'

'Because you have killed men for less. And I want hir alive.' She explained Guilie's plan. 'It is safe and secret

'Safe! For the love of Christ, if she's caught she canno plead hunger or housetheft – were you green-mad, the tw of you?'

He picked up his cloak that dried by the fire.

'Where are you going?' she asked.

'Where should I go? To watch the house. To seek new of her.'

'You must not inquire at the house—'

He cursed. 'Do you think me mad, too?'

He left and again she waited, waited. At midnight h brought word that Guilie was celled in the Tolbooth on th charge of black witchcraft.

* * *

On September 5th Sir John Gordon rode back to Edin burgh at the summons of Chief Magistrate Donald Gloon The next morning the trial began at the old turreted Tol booth on the High Street.

The grim stone room, ill-lit with cressets, was windowles and bare save for the jury's bench, the magistrate's chair a table and a stool for witnesses. That area was roped of and behind it spectators shoved for a better view. All trial provided free amusement but the trial of a witch was covete as the most rewarding of all.

Bess stood with Flutter. At first he had refused to allow her to come. It would be dangerous further to entangle her self with John Gordon, and Guilie would never betray her But Bess had insisted that she could not endure the suspens of waiting at home. She swore that she would keep silent

I have broken vows before. I will help her if I can . . .

Flutter's sharp elbows and sharper tongue manoeuvre them closer to the rope so that by standing on tiptoe the could see the jurymen and two dark-robed inquisitors Magistrate Gloon rapped for silence and called the court t order. The jury of old men was sworn. A clerk read th charge 'against Guilie McIver for entering the house of Sir John Gordon with intent to practise the odious arts of black witchcraft'.

Bess gasped as Guilie hobbled in slowly, assisted by a guard. In a scant few days she had aged twenty years. The once-thin body was skeletal. The bare arms were bruised purple, one eye was darkly puffed and her unbound hair was a long white snarl. She started towards the stool but Gloon frowned. 'That is reserved for witnesses.'

Dear God, she can scarce stand!

A clerk read her recorded history. Aged twenty-eight. Born Kelso. Unmarried. Trade, Healer. Plea, not guilty.

She was not sworn lest the Bible be mocked by her hands. She was not permitted counsel.

The first witness was called. 'Jean Reekie.'

She was young, plump, pert in her Sunday kirtle.

David MacBride, the first inquisitor, asked, 'You are housemaid to Sir John Gordon of St Mary's Lane?'

'Aye, sir.'

'What happened at his house on the evening of September 2nd?'

She and her father had supped at five. At six-thirty she had gone to the well to draw water and returned to the kitchen about seven-thirty, where her father slept at the inglenook. She had been sure no one else was in the house for the Master and young menservants were off to war. But soon after she put down the water pails she heard footsteps on the floor above. Alarmed, she roused her father and they went up the stairs.

'And you found this woman?' He pointed to Guilie.

'Aye, sir, in the Master's bedchamber.'

'What was she doing?'

'She was at his bed, sir. She was bending under it.'

'What did she say when she saw you?'

'She begged for mercy. She said she was hungry, that she had hoped to find food but saw my father in the kitchen and crept upstairs to search for something of value to sell. She said she had heard that rich folk hid their gold under beds.'

'And what did you do?'

'I ran out and called the watch while my father held her.'

Jean's father, the gardener, corroborated the story. He said, 'As I held her I felt a burn on my hands clear to my heart . . .'

Guilie said, 'He was mizzled with drink! It took all his strength to hold me.'

'Quiet! You are not to speak unless questioned. Master Reekie, had you or your daughter ever seen this woman before?'

Aye, they had seen her at the fleshers. And on the street from time to time. But she had never come to the house before.

'Was there aught missing from the house? Had she thieved?'

'No, sir. We found all in order.'

'And nothing was disarranged?'

'No, sir.'

'You may go.'

Sir John Gordon was called and sworn. As Bess shuddered, sick with loathing, the women grouped around her murmured in admiration. He wore a brown silk doublet worked in silver. His hair streamed gold to the edge of the velvet collar. The clerk placed a cushion on the stool and he sat down, crossing long, brown-hosed legs. For a brief moment he looked at the crowd, then down at the floor.

'Do you know this woman, sir?'

He glanced at Guilie obliquely.

He fears the Evil Eye . . .

'I do not know her. Once I saw her on the street. The bairns ran from her, calling her a witch. God knows she looks like one.'

'Can you imagine, sir, why she would enter your house and search under your bed?'

'No.'

'Would she have aught against you?'

'Why would she? I do not know her.'

'Have you enemies who would hire her to witch you?'

He hesitated. Bess held her breath.

'Aye, I have enemies. Thousands.'

'Who, sir?'

'The English.'

The spectators tittered, applauded, were hushed.

'Do you believe she searched under your bed for gold?'

'The tale is unlikely.'

'Did you find aught missing?'

'Naught missing. But I think she had meddled in my dressing closet where I keep unguents, salves, razor, pomades and such.'

'What is the value in the closet?'

'Nothing.'

'Thank you, sir. You may remain.'

The clerk scribbled, the inquisitors conferred. Guilie moved towards the wall to lean against it but was ordered back to stand before the jury.

Bess thought, folk must have seen us together, Guilie and I. Once we shopped in the Lawnmarket when, hoping for Robert Lawson's attention, she bought sleeves of Flemish lace. Once we picnicked on Arthur's Seat. But the town is large and busy about its own affairs. Our meetings, though not deliberately secret, were not in public. We washed at the Loch apart from other women. We visited at one another's homes.

If no one knows she worked in my behalf, no one can prove her a black witch.

Another stool was brought. The clerk called, 'Betsy Gudge.'

A pocked woman was sworn. Aged 72. Born in Dublin, widow of a chandler.

'Do you know the defendant?'

She peered at Guilie through rheumy eyes. 'Aye.'

'Tell the court, Dame.'

Six years ago Betsy had lived in the same close as Janet Merton, a black witch. She would often see Guilie enter Janet's house.

'Did you ever talk with Guilie McIver?'

'Aye, she gave me a sack of turnips and brought me food when me husband died. She gave me a healing herb for me shoulder—'

'But you feared her gifts as coming from the Devil. After Janet Merton was burned as a witch did not Guilie McIver move into her house?'

'Aye.'

'And thereafter you moved from the close for fear of Guilie McIver?'

'For me health. The air of Leith—'

'She made evil the air in the close, did she not?'

'I don't know, sir. The pigsties—'

'Enough, Dame, You may go.'

Robin Annin, a grave-digger, testified that he had seen Guilie place a mark on Janet's grave on Calton Hill. By day it seemed a simple cross of rowan. By night it cast hell-light.

Gloon read from a paper sent by the Provost of Kelso. Sixteen persons had perished of the plague induced by Guilie and she had been stoned out of town.

The crowd muttered angrily. Likely she had brought the plague to Edinburgh.

MacBride questioned Guilie. 'Do you admit you visited Janet Merton?'

'Aye, sir. I learned white witchcraft from her and the arts of healing.'

'You learned white witchcraft from a black witch?'

'Aye, sir.'

'And the odious arts as well?'

'Oh no, sir. One learns only what one wishes to – as you know.'

He flushed. 'Why did Janet Merton leave you her house and goods?'

'She was grateful. I nursed her through her last illness before she burned.'

He consulted a paper. 'John Piper, aged 81, and unable to attend this court, states that he saw you emerge from her house in guise of a cat on All Hallows Eve, 1508.'

'How did he know it was I?'

'Quiet! You are not to ask questions.'

The court recessed for noon dinner. Bess sat with Flutter at the Cock and Stag but she could not eat.

'I must do something,' she said.

'You cannot. If Gordon knows you and Guilie are friends he will sense a motive for witchcraft.'

'But he cannot speak without revealing his crime against me.'

'In his position a crime against a slut is no crime. And the court will believe any story he chooses to tell.'

'There are dozens of folk who could rise to her defence. Lady Bothwell—'

'Do you think she'd admit to buying love potions and make a public jest of herself? And even so, do you think she'd trouble?'

'But there are others who come to Guilie for amulets and healing potions. There are mariners for whom she quiets the winds, crofters who seek sun or rain – why should they not come forward?'

'No one cares.'

'Do you?' she asked angrily.

'Aye, but you are my principal care. I warn you again, one word from you in her defence will doom her. Gordon is no fool.' He leaned towards her and clenched her arm. 'Should you start forward in that court or even open your mouth to speak, I shall knock you senseless. And then – since you have "fainted" – I will carry you out.'

They returned to the Tolbooth and the trial resumed. Ian Sinclair, the second inquisitor, addressed the court.

'On the 3rd day of September we examined the defendant in the manner prescribed by civil and ecclesiastic law. She was stripped naked and her body prodded by a bodkin. Sh pretended to feel pain when her limbs, arms and belly wer touched. When her private parts were lightly lanced sh screamed and assumed a swoon. But we knew she fel nothing, for in these regions no witch is sensitive.

'During the examination she was found to be no virgi and admitted to sodomy with the Devil. Later she was lef alone in a closed cell and he came to her in the guise of a fl which lit on her shoulder.' He turned to face Guilie. 'Ca you deny this?'

She swayed a little. 'I have denied all traffic with th Devil. I do not remember admitting guilt, but under tor ture—'

'Examination!'

'– I may have confessed to gain respite. Under tortur folk will admit to anything.'

'Quiet! I shall read your confession. "I, Guilie McIver did enter the house of Sir John Gordon to cast a glamou upon him at the behest of my master, the Devil." '

'But why?' Guilie asked. 'I did not know Sir John, never met him. There would be no purpose and you canno prove one.'

'You know your own purpose but you will not reveal it.

'I have told you I searched for gold.'

'And we have searched your house. You have crowns a plenty in your pot, a snug house and a full larder.' He picke up a parchment on the table and read from it. 'You ow four gowns, two cloaks, a good pair of shoes . . .'

Guilie looked towards Bess for the first time. She straight ened and turned back to Sinclair. 'Very well, sir. I an shamed to tell you the truth, but I shall. Even under tor - under examination, a woman hates to admit to a truth s terrible.'

'What truth?'

'Her ugliness. Look at me, sir.' She spread her thin bruised arms. 'Never has a man looked on me in love though as a maid I was raped in the dark.'

'And so?' he asked impatiently.

'I have longed for love. I have seen Sir John often on the street and visioned him as my lover. Women come to me for love potions and I thought, I shall work a spell for myself. So I entered his house to seek some hair or nail parings and cast a glamour that would make him mine.' She turned to Sir John. 'Sir, forgive a stupid woman who has loved you vainly these three years. I meant no harm.'

Sir John ran a hand through his fair, wavy hair.

Sinclair said, 'Even so, you would have bedevilled him. You and your Master would have bestialized his body and destroyed his soul. That was your true design, was it not?'

MacBride joined him in a bullet-fire of questions. Guilie sagged, recovered, repeated, sagged again. Sir John stared down at his hands. Bess thought, in his vanity he might well believe her. By one word he can save her.

At four in the afternoon the jury retired.

'A farce,' Flutter whispered. 'Their verdict was made on the charge.'

He kept his hand tight on Bess's wrist. The crowd thrust about; neighbours greeted one another. Some had brought their suppers. In the close-packed room was a stench of cheese, herring, sweat and the sheep grease of the dripping tapers. Guilie stood with bowed head, her hands limp at her sides. Once she slumped and a guard caught her and forced her to stand upright.

The jury returned and the foreman whispered to Gloon. The room quieted. Bess hid her face on Flutter's shoulder.

Gloon said, 'As has been made manifest in this very court, and by her own admission, Guilie McIver is adjudged guilty of black witchcraft. The penalty by law—'

Bess took a deep, shuddering breath.

'– prohibits the shedding of blood. Therefore it is adjudged that the defendant shall be burned at the Market Cross at six of the morning if it be a fair day.'

The crowd cheered.

'She will make her peace with God and reject the Devil lest she burn eternally in hell.'

Bess lifted her head to see Guilie standing tall, aye, even proud, with a shine in her eyes strange as swampfire. She looked at John Gordon and said, loudly and clearly, 'It is a just verdict, for I have devilled you.'

He sprang up from his stool. 'How?'

'You will soon know.'

'Enough,' Gloon said. He motioned to the guard. 'Take her.'

'Wait.' Gordon raised his jewelled white hand. 'I want the truth. How did you devil me, and why?'

Guilie said, 'Once I spoke to you in the Grassmarket. Your look spurned me and you drew away as though I were leprous. Again I approached you in St Giles and you spat in contempt. So I have contrived an eye for an eye, manhood for womanhood.'

'What do you mean? You speak in riddles.'

Gloon also demanded an explanation but she turned on him in a fury. 'I am judged, doomed to death and beyond further trial. I speak only to Sir John.'

'In riddles,' he repeated uneasily.

'When you return to your home, look under your bed. There you will find the answer.'

He stared straight into the shine of her eyes. 'What will I find?'

'You will find an effigy of yourself, a doll formed of wax fixed with hairs of your own beard.'

His eyes flickered. His lips had drained of colour.

Gloon said, 'Take heart, sir, we know of such matters. The witch must treat the effigy for days, aye, weeks. She had no time. She was surprised in the act and forced to leave it behind.'

Guilie said, 'I left it for him to see, for the victim must see for himself. The image was treated, the pin thrust for weeks. All it lacked was the hair. Now the spell is fully formed.'

She spoke to Sir John. 'You will sicken within a week or

wo. You will deny your pain as fantasy but you will worsen
owly, slowly. You will seek physicians when the pain takes
old but they will be powerless and the pain will prosper
nd plunge. You will not die of it. You will live in pain to
he end of your days.'

His voice was shrill as a woman's. 'You burn, and with
our burning the spell is broken!'

'No,' she said quietly. 'It works upon you even now.'

He appealed to Gloon, 'Force her to remove it!'

Guilie said, 'I could not if I tried.'

Sir John stretched his hand towards her. 'For the love
f God—'

She smiled.

'– I will do anything you ask, pay anything, I will save
our life—'

'Nay,' Gloon said. 'You cannot save her now, sir. She
as confessed and she must die.'

Sir John's hand went to his heart. Guilie tossed back her
air and laughed. 'Not there,' she said. 'I will show you.'

She moved towards him but he drew back. She followed
im as he retreated to the wall.

'Don't touch me!'

She placed her hand between her legs.

'Here,' she said. 'Here.'

* * *

Bess begged Flutter to remain the night with her else, she
iid, she would go mad. She could not sleep as he did but
aced the room in bare feet, fancying that she wore a path
om pallet to hearth and back again. She was exhausted;
er breast ached, but each time she sank down to rest her
yes opened wide.

I have killed Guilie.

She argued around her conviction. She defended and ac-
uitted herself but moments later the trial began afresh. It
nade no difference that Flutter had absolved her, insisting
nat in the same circumstances Bess would have risked her

life for Guilie. Of what worth was Guilie's life, he asked An ageing spinster, barren of man's love, nor ever likel to find it.

She remembered Guilie's face when they had dreame their lives together before Hugh had altered the dream; th round-eyed face of a child on Yule Eve reaching for th plum high on the tree.

But there had been no plum, no tree.

Flutter had said, 'You gave her more than she ever ha before.'

Friendship.

No, Janet Merton gave her more than I. A trade. A house. Money.

So Guilie dies for my hours of gossip. For summer days a the Loch and shared food and a shared clothesline. Fo vision of a Border village, a cottage set in lilacs. For my futil sympathy that she loved the drunken Lawson. For pat goodnight, and cheek kisses. For sterile, womanish, mur derous friendship.

Flutter roused before dawn, ate the porridge she prepare and left to rejoin the Scots army. Bess went down the stai with him and looking out towards the High Street remarke in astonishment that so many people were astir in the wynd:

Gently he kissed her. 'Sleep, lass. Sleep all day.'

'But I wonder why all those folk—'

Then she realized.

Anxious to be as far from the Market Cross as possible sh walked to Leith and loitered there at the grey, sluggish sea One ship rested at anchor – from Spain, she surmised – bu its banner was heat-limp and she could not be sure. Th sun rose, burning across the far horizon. She wandered th docks.

Fishermen came to launch their cod boats. Presently th ship lowered a rowboat and she watched it skim shorewar through the sun-reddened water. Gulls screamed, divin above the cod fleet. The sun filled the sky with a harsh glare

She paced the length of the wharf, then back again, her shoes sticky with tar. Two sailors approached and flirted. At first she turned her back, then she thought, Someday I must. What better time than now?

They spoke Spanish and extended the equivalent of eight groats.

Humbly she shook her head. 'I am not worth so much.'

They conferred. '*¿Que quieres decir?*'

Better to show them now than risk their resentment later. She pulled down her gown to reveal the rust-coloured bandage. She took six groats.

'*Barato*,' said the taller one, caressing her hair. '*Para una chica tan guapa.*'

She led them to the empty warehouse near the north wharf.

Slowly she walked into Edinburgh, keeping to the clean high crown that rose in the middle of the street. In the gutters on either side ran a turgid tide of slops dammed by a dog's head. Poor houses sagged into browning weeds. As she passed through the Canongate beggars picked through the rich rot of vegetable parings, swollen fruit, bones, a rusted horseshoe. Red wine spilled like blood from a shattered jug.

She approached the High Street and stopped short.

Then she turned and ran, ran back as she had come, past the fine houses and the broken shacks on and on until she reached the fresh salt of the sea but even then with her kirtle over her face she could smell the rank sweet char of flesh.

4

Margaret Stuart

September 10th, 1513

THAT NIGHT AT Linlithgow she sat by James's cradle where he slept under a spread of lace. Dame Mary said, 'He is so plump, so bonny. Our prayers are answered. Each time you lost a child we nuns made special petition.'

'Do not cease your prayers.' Margaret touched her stomach. 'I could lose this one, I am so harried, my dreams so fey . . .'

They spoke of dark omens reported throughout Scotland. There was an unprecedented flock of crows that surpassed belief, causing terror in the villages and even in Edinburgh where they fell like a black raucous cloud over Castle Rock and Arthur's Seat.

'Dogs howling are nearly as dreadful,' Margaret said. 'Last night I heard them clear from the village and ours in the courtyard joined in.'

'I heard them too, Madam. But I think it less an evil omen than a natural matter. What dog in Scotland does not miss his master?'

'Perhaps . . . but what of the fiery comet that passes from place to place as though warning each town? My astrologer says it presages a great tempest and that His Majesty should be on guard.'

'As indeed he is,' Mary said cheerfully. 'Has he not set his army on a fine impregnable hill?'

Margaret nodded. Cannon thick as bluebells from slope to slope clear to the summit.

'I could almost feel pity for the English, Madam.'

Vastly outnumbered, exhausted from a long day's march

through swamps made hellish by the roaring Cheviot winds; bereft of food, with only brackish water to drink. Surrey, their old commander, agonized by gout and forced to ride in a litter.

'In their weakness, Madam, I doubt they could take that hill were it merely a mass of thistles. You may soon wear the crown of England.'

It was an exciting speculation. Margaret would be merciful to Harry and Catty, banish them to some remote country manor. She visioned herself riding in state through London, flashed in jewels, mistress of all the gold in Harry's coffers. And oh, to be free of Scotland, to dally in the frequent sun of Richmond or Westminster, to walk the soft, flowering fields of her birth, to be queen of two lands at peace and prospering! James would have little excuse to take Agnes Bothwell to England. Surely he would not dare remove his nobles lest trouble arise in the Isles . . .

Abstracted, she did not hear Mary shift the subject. 'He wore such a thin tunic. Of course in his position a leather-jack would be inappropriate but I *told* him of the autumn storms and he paid no heed.'

'Who?' Margaret asked.

'The Bishop. He should at least have worn a cutting scarf and carried a target to protect his chest . . .'

They moved up to the tower. At midnight neither was sleepy and Margaret sent for wine and suckets. A page announced the King's equerry.

Haggard, grimed, he spoke his news on a sob. 'A disaster such as I cannot describe. There was no one to give me dispatches . . . a chaos . . . few left alive who can write.'

Margaret sprang up from the table. 'The King?'

'Oh, God, Madam – dead.'

She cried out and Mary ran to the anteroom to summon her ladies who rushed in to surround her lest she faint.

But she stood steady though her voice cracked to a whisper. 'Tell me.'

'His Majesty was in the fore of the fighting and none

fought more bravely. He killed five men with his spear before it shattered. Then he grasped another and was within a thrust of Surrey's litter when he was arrowed, then slain by an English bill . . . The hillside was so slippery with mud and blood that we took off our shoes and fought in our hose or bare feet. It was madness, mire . . . And at the end a pile of corpses as far as I could see, most naked, despoiled of armour, clothing, weapons. I saw the King naked, his dead nobles circled around him.'

Stunned, questionless, she sank into a chair. She could not believe the unbelievable, face the incredible. Even red dreams had not prepared her for this.

Finally she asked, 'What happened to his body?'

'I don't know, Madam. The last I saw he lay there stark and bloodied.'

Agnes Bothwell spoke over the sound of weeping. 'My husband, Lord Bothwell?'

'He too is dead, my lady. He commanded the fifth division, and gallantly. He sought to capture the English standard, but—'

Margaret interrupted. 'Archibald Douglas?'

'I know not, Madam. But his father and uncle perished – the clan was cut to shreds. His grandsire, the Earl, quarrelled with His Majesty and returned to Scotland.'

Old enmity, but Margaret could not imagine Angus quarrelling with James on the very edge of doom. But she accepted it as part of the horror.

Dame Mary asked about the Bishop of Tutberry. 'I do not know, Madam. I only know that clerics perished like common soldiers. The King's son and the Archbishop of Caithness. I saw an abbot with his head bashed by plunderers and another whose hand was severed for the silver cross it held. Monks, friars . . .' He appealed to Margaret. 'For the love of God, Madam, I can scarce stand or speak or think.' He eyed the brown bottle on the table. 'I need wine.'

More wine was brought and shared. Rumours ran like

ats. From the kitchen, the buttery, the laundry, the stables, he Great Hall, servants and courtiers came unbidden to he tower chamber, half-dressed with no thought of proto-ol. They crowded out into the corridor and one by one ook courage to come in.

Over and over again Francis Cray was made to tell his tory. He was not ill-educated; he had spent a year in study t St Andrews, but he could not be lucid. It had been so wift . . . he could not fathom what had happened in the errible tangle of battle. It had been less than three hours – r so he judged. Panic through smoke, arrow-fire, cannon-re and the bloody gashing of English bills and halberds.

He knew that James, responding in chivalry to Surrey's ourier, had agreed on the day of battle. That Surrey had noved the main part of his tired troops from the marshes o the banks of the River Till, crossing by way of Twizel ridge.

'At dawn they were in full view of us. We saw the long nes of men, a-horse and a-foot. We had no thought but it vas the entire English army moving north to Berwick to cut ff our communications and to prevent our retreat to Scot-and. Only Lord Angus suspected a trick but His Majesty efused to heed him and said, "If you are afraid, then return o Scotland." And Angus rode off in a rage.

'Then the mists fell, the heavy mists of morning. Under heir cover Surrey turned back and forded the Till but as e recrossed the bridge our scout saw him and galloped back o report to us. His Majesty ordered us to break camp, to escend and give battle. We burned refuse on Flodden Hill nd under screen of the smoke went down to the lower slope f Branxton. Surrey struck at us from the rear. We engaged im at past four in the afternoon. Before darkness fell it was ll over.'

In three hours, the most devastating defeat in Scots istory.

'Can you' – Margaret's tongue seemed too thick for peech – 'judge our losses?'

'No, Madam, it will take weeks.'

Heedless of interrupting, Lady Huntley came forward to inquire of her husband.

'Dead, my lady.'

Lady Argyll and Lady Crawford approached him, clinging together.

'Dead . . . dead.'

Cray took a gulp of his wine. Margaret moved from the chair and shivered across to the cold-ashed hearth, beckoning Cray to follow.

'What of English losses?'

'Few, Madam. It was a complete victory.'

'Our fleet?'

'No help came by sea. I've heard of King Henry's triumph in France.'

'So there is nothing, no fleet, no army to defend us?'

Mutely he shook his head.

The room, full of weeping, was real and unreal as nightmare. Like a sleepwalker she groped to the window. In the moonlight across the calm grey loch rose vapours of white mist. There were no balefires as yet. No signal of English attack. But Surrey would assuredly press his advantage, march into Scotland and take Edinburgh. For the city was helpless. It held only women, children, greybeards; soon, cripples struggling in from the south.

She thought, what would James have me do? And then her tears came in flood. She wept for James, for herself, for their children born and unborn. Strangely, she wept for the lost men, for her ladies bereft of their lords, aye, even for a serving wench who stood forlornly near the door, and for the child in her arms. And she wept for those who must live in fear for weeks until the dead were counted and known.

She raised her head and looked at faces she had seen for years yet never perceived with her heart. Pages, grooms, cooks, stableboys. The old Master of Horse – did he not have four sons at war? She remembered that the washermaid was newly married.

One by one they came to Francis Cray asking a name, begging news, however scant.

'Henry Mackenzie. He tended the dovecote here.'

'My brother, James Doon?'

'Do ye ken, John Ritchie?'

'My son, Jock Armstrong . . .'

And the equerry shaking his head, shaking the blood from his memory.

What must I do?

She could not stand here gazing for ever southwards. When the balefires glowed it would be too late. She must gather her wits.

Her voice knifed through the weeping. 'Go to your quarters.' She bade the guards return to their posts and ordered their captain to arm all men and women and all lads over ten. Should the palace be attacked, vats of boiling water were to be poured upon the invaders. Broken glass must be spread upon all sills and turrets.

She would leave for Edinburgh at first light to confer with the Burgh Council on defence of the town.

What defence? She thought of the city wall. Started in the twelfth century and extended two hundred years later, it had crumbled to fragments. All that remained was at Wellhouse Tower at the northern foot of Castle Rock near the West Bow. It crossed the ridge at Netherbow Port and ended east of the Nor' Loch between goose houses and hog sties, a ruin of turf and scattered stones. In past years folk had demolished it and rolled away the big rocks for house-building.

I must start a wall. There is no time and few folk fit for the labour, but I must start a wall for the future. I must crown James. I must take the Oath of Regency, I must . . . sleep.

Yet she stood at the window, looking south.

Edinburgh was shrouded in deep, ochre mist. It was quiet, church-quiet, dead quiet. Doors were barred against

English attack and few folk walked the streets. There was no sound but the tolling of mourning bells from the Abbey, St Giles and the moor kirks across the Loch. A few houses were draped with white cloth on gallery or forestairs, signifying the plague. Margaret glimpsed them through the yellowish, ill-smelling haar.

In the Tolbooth, seated with the Council, she asked, 'How did it happen?'

No one knew. The few survivors who had reached the city were simple folk hedged in horror, maimed or blinded. Each hour swelled their ranks.

She drew up a proclamation: 'Forasmuch as there is a great rumour now lately risen within this town, touching our Sovereign Lord and his army, wherefore we charge and command in the King's name that all manner of persons having ready their arms of defence and weapons for war appear therewith at the tolling of the common bell for the defence of the town against them that would invade the same.

'And we also charge that all women, and especially vagabonds, pass to their labours and be not seen upon the street clamouring and crying, under the pain of banishing of their persons . . . and that the other women of the better sort pass to the kirk and pray for our Soverign Lord and his army, and the townsmen who are with the army.'

She learned that Randolph Murray, captain of the City Guard was the first man to return. He had ridden through the Cowgate Port, one mailed hand holding a bloody banner. Though trailed by a questioning mob he remained mute. Margaret commanded his presence at Holyrood and asked news.

His eyes were aware, his lips moved, but he could not speak.

At Holyrood Abbey Margaret ordered and attended a Solemn High Mass for the dead. The church was crowded and the doors left open. In the courtyard hundreds knelt on the hard stones.

At St Giles on the High Street candles lit to the saints streamed out through the dark shadows. Those who could not afford a groat for a candle brought offerings to lay before the Virgin – a flower, a toy, a green bough. A priest exhorted his flock to pray for storms to prevent English attack.

The mist lifted. The night was clear and starry, the moon full. On the battlements of Edinburgh Castle, bereft of cannon, sentries paced. From the Border to the far north Scots watched from hill tops and castle turrets.

At Holyrood, Margaret sat alone in her anteroom. Lady Huntley and Lady Argyll, putting aside their own sorrow, tried to comfort her but nothing availed. Words were only words. They could not lift black grief.

Restlessly she moved down to the Great Hall, empty save for the guard at the entrance. She went aimlessly down the stairs to the arcaded walk, then realized she had been drawn to this place where James had told her goodbye.

A guard bowed and she moved on into the inner courtyard. It was warm, dark, fragrant of dying heather. Moths fluttered about the cressets set above the door. In the woods an owl hooted.

Where was James now? The poor mutilated body tossed in the charnel pit under the hill or granted decent burial? She would demand to know and to have the corpse brought to lie in state at the Abbey. The people would want that, for they mourned him as their own kin. Today at Mass the candles lit to James's favourite saint had gleamed brightest of all. But even St Ninian could not save him from hell. The writ of excommunication had doomed him.

I could not reach him in life, nor shall I find him after death.

There was a way if she chose to take it. She remembered the story of Lady Fraser whose husband had died excommunicate a hundred years ago. She had deliberately committed the mortal sins of adultery and blasphemy, and died unrepentant so that she might join her lord in hell.

Margaret thought wryly, if I did that I would find Margaret Drummond there before me.

Nearby she heard light footsteps and the whisper of silk. A woman moved towards her into the torchlight. At first she seemed as startled as Margaret. Then she curtsied, dark skirts sweeping the cobbles. They looked at one another for a long moment across a gulf of silence. A breeze rose and leaves fell from the oaks.

'Goodnight, my lady,' Margaret said softly.

'Goodnight, Madam.'

The silk skirts rustled past, the footsteps receded. Margaret watched until she was part of the darkness. She found that her hand was outstretched.

* * *

For three days the city waited, certain of doom, but Surrey did not attack. Margaret heard various rumours – that he dared not drive his men into the teeth of expected storms; that he had no provisions; that he waited for troops to be released from Henry's victorious forces in France; that despite his triumph at Flodden his army was exhausted and pest-ridden; that Henry, in mercy, had ordered Surrey to disband. None of these explanations satisfied her but she took hope with the passing of each day. If he had intended invasion he would have invaded immediately while the surviving Scots were in panicked flight and Edinburgh defenceless.

She took the little prince to Stirling where he was crowned James V of Scotland. The chapel was filled with noble women, their children and old priests. In the absence of De La Motte, the French ambassador who had died at Flodden, his kinswoman brought gifts for the child in the name of King Louis and Queen Anne.

Margaret would adhere to the old alliance for James would have wanted it. But she raged at thought of Anne.

'*Go three feet into English soil for my honour . . .*'

And now he was six feet under English soil – or was he? Perhaps they had not troubled, but left him to the corpse-fat vultures that ranged the peaks of the hills.

Margaret left King James at Stirling for safety. She was returning to Edinburgh when Father Duncan limped into the West Bow on blistered feet; when Archibald Douglas rode past Holyrood Gate holding his horse's reins with a bloodied gauntlet; when the Bishop of Tutberry hobbled through the Netherbow on tree stump crutches; when Robert Lawson spurred his lame mule to the doors of the Cock and Stag.

An awed crowd gathered about Lawson, remembering that he had defied the Devil's warning at the Market Cross. Thus far, of all the men marked for death, he alone had returned.

Plied with brandywine, he was drunk within the hour.

* * *

Gradually Margaret learned something of the truth which she found more terrifying than the rumours had been.

Only four Scots lords survived – the Lord Treasurer, Lord Hamilton, Lord Herries and Lord Murray. Eleven earls were dead, and fifteen lords. Hundreds of fleeing men had crossed the Tweed at Coldstream and been drowned in its flooding waters. Others retreating by way of the dry marshes had lost their lives and their horses to the bandits of Tynedale and Tweeddale.

Andrew Pitcairn of Pitcairn was, like many another laird, killed with his sons, which numbered seven. Two hundred Douglases were dead. Over seventy men left the village of Selkirk. One returned. For thousands of families the male line was for ever broken.

She asked, repeatedly, How did it happen?

No one agreed upon the size of the Scots army save that it vastly outnumbered Surrey's 26,000. Even allowing for thousands of Scots camp followers who did not fight, and for deserters, it seemed incredible that the English could have wiped out the flower of Scotland in three hours and lost only 1,500 men.

Margaret said to Archibald Douglas, 'We had the advantage of numbers, of position, of provisions, of open communications, of artillery—'

'Aye, but our artillery was a jest for our gunners were green. Who do you suppose manned one of the "Sisters"? Patrick Paniter!'

The king's clerk.

'The cannonballs flew aimlessly, making a great noise, causing fright but harming no one. Then even the fright diminished. But the English had expert gunners and their guns were more numerous and more manageable than ours.'

'But we were better armed in other ways!'

'Not for hill fighting. Our spears are eighteen feet long, clumsy in close combat and useless against the English brown bills.'

'A bill,' she said, wondering if she had ever seen one.

'It's part hatchet, part sword, Madam, only eight feet but murderous in close quarters, and God knows our quarters were close. Against the bills our spears and broadswords were useless. So was our armour.'

Yet still she asked, How did it happen?

The Bishop, lying abed with his hip strapped received her at his palace on the high ground above Holyrood.

'I cannot tell you how it happened, Madam – it was all so swift. But Surrey with his sons and Stanley and Dacre seemed to work to plan, each division supporting the other, whereas with us there was no leadership.'

'The King led you,' she said angrily.

'You forget that he flung himself into battle like a wild lad. Huntley and Lindsay begged him not to expose himself to fire but to co-ordinate our forces. He would not listen. Thus there was no brain behind us, no one to direct us. We fought like blind men.'

'Did you fight on horse or afoot?'

'Afoot. Most of the horses were unarmoured so we tethered them down the hill. The English did the same.'

Later Dame Mary bustled in followed by a nun bearing refreshments. Mary smoothed his coverlid, clucked at a maid who had neglected to pat up his pillows and scolded him for over-exertion.

'Madam, last night he walked clear to his oratory, *imagine* walking ten yards on a broken hip?'

He smiled. 'I walked from Lauder when my horse mired.'

'Well, no horse has mired *here*.'

Margaret left them wrangling sweetly and she thought, with a tinge of envy, though they never clasp hands they will love one another to the end of their days.

Flutter arrived at Holyrood unharmed save for an arrow-graze on his cheek.

'I cannot answer your question, Madam, for it was madness . . . But Surrey was cool and precise as His Majesty was impetuous. He had expert archers and gunners. The ground was jagged and hilly so that we could not form solid columns and use our spears to advantage. We attacked individually, each man for himself, and the bills smashed us as if we held toy pikes. At the end we drew our swords but their halberds were longer and heavier – we couldn't counter.'

She sighed. 'If only I knew where the King rests. I have written Queen Catherine but have had no reply.'

'Perhaps she herself does not know. There are rumours—'

'What?' she asked eagerly.

'That before dawn on September 9th he removed his penitential chain so as to fight unencumbered. He was wearing a purple tunic and armour. It's said that a corpse wearing purple and royal armour was carried off to Berwick for embalming and thence to Richmond Palace for burial.'

'But several people had seen the King stripped naked.'

'There are dozens of stories. One thing we do know, that at least ten men of the King's age and stature were dressed in purple and armour so as to confuse the English and en-

courage our soldiers. Any one of these may lie at Richmon
if there *is* a corpse there. Since His Majesty died excommunicate King Henry would not be likely to grant hir
Christian burial.'

Her tears came and he said, 'Forgive my bluntness
Madam, but even if the Pope sanctioned such burial, woul
your brother build a tomb on English soil for a man h
hated? So that Scots pilgrims, through the years, could com
to honour a martyr's grave?'

She was silent for a long while. Then she said, 'A kin
does not vanish and rot in an unmarked grave. He could b
identified. He was wearing Queen Anne's turquoise on hi
finger and there would be chain-marks on his waist.'

But then, she thought, the scavengers were busy, th
hawks and the humans.

Douglas sat with Margaret at chess. Leaves gusted at th
open window and he said, 'It will be an early autumn.'

She stared down at the ivory chessmen – a bishop, a
knight, a king.

He took a sip of wine from a tall, ruby goblet. 'I hear th
boars are running.'

She tapped the edge of the checkered board with a pale
polished fingernail.

'Yesterday Hamilton ran a stag in the park but lost it i
the thickets. He said it was the largest he had ever seen.'

Her thin white mourning veil moved in a sudden breez
and she shivered.

'Do you wish a shawl, Madam?'

She shook her head.

'Shall we end the game?'

'Aye,' she said, 'I've no heart for it.'

For there was the intricate game of politics to play. Sh
must hold Scotland against England, against French oppor-
tunism and Scots greed. Power-lusts would rise even from
the ruin of Flodden. She could not remember a year o
recorded history when a Scots ruler had not been on guard

against rebel clans or Borderers or Islesmen. James had subdued the Islesmen earlier in his reign, but the fragile pattern of peace could fray in her hands.

She said, 'Jamie is strongly guarded at Stirling, I hear. But we are not as safe as the poorest family in a moor hut.'

Douglas reached across the chessboard, covering her fingers with his bandaged hand. 'You have me.'

She smiled wanly. 'But the world is ravening.'

'Margaret.'

Her hand fluttered under his but she did not withdraw it.

'Listen to me.'

She looked into the smoke-grey eyes, at the full, sullen mouth she had once desired.

'My grandsire is failing – he cannot live long. As Earl of Angus I will head my clan. Many have perished, aye, but there are young lads a-building, a new generation to defend you.'

What was the old adage? 'A Stuart is born to the crown. A Douglas is born to thieve it.'

Yet she could not, in fairness, suspect him of intrigue. It was only natural that a man of his age should be ambitious. . . .

He kissed her hand. 'I love you.'

Why should I not trust his love? Perhaps because James made such a mockery of fidelity that my pride in myself is shattered. But I cannot judge one man by another's follies.

'I ask nothing now,' he said. 'Only that you consider that my life is at your disposal. I no longer live for myself, but for your happiness.'

And what was happiness but to be treasured in a man's arms? To rule one man's heart, she thought, is to rule a world.

She rose and he rose with her. Against her conscious will she was drawn close, closer until their lips and bodies met. Her arms tightened about him.

Faint, far away, she heard warning drums from the lighthouse of Leith.

5

Bess Dart

September 21st, 1513

SHE WENT OUT each day to stand at the Cowgate Port inquring news of Hugh from the men who were returning, some piled in carts, others shambling afoot through rain, mud, dust. Sentries paced the turrets of the great fortified gate.

The faces around her changed from day to day as women found their men, left the gate in despair or returned in new hope. They brought kegs to sit on or spread cloaks in the high grass. Babies were nursed, clothing mended, meals eaten. Some lingered until midnight staring down the dim grey road; listening for hoofbeats or footfalls. Bess waited with them.

It was nine o'clock when a sentry called down. 'The King is crowned!'

Now they could see the signal fire burning on the Castle battlements. A faint cheer went up, but the people had loved the father too deeply to rejoice for James V.

Mists rose. Bess could not see farther than the cressets above the gateway. Beyond lay darkness. In her mind's eye she saw the road from Flodden littered with corpses, from which half-dead men rose to stumble on to Edinburgh.

Sometimes, listening for wheels or hooves she heard sounds that murmured off to nothing, ghost wagons, ghost steps. Sometimes voices seemed to approach on the road only to silence in the mourn of the wind.

But now she was sure she heard cart wheels and she left the grass with the other women and hurried to the archway.

The watchman called, 'Who goes there?' and swung his lantern.

'David Craik.' A cart creaked to a stop.

Bess ran forward. There were likely several David Craiks in Scotland, but perhaps . . .

It was he, his face grimed, his beard tangled. She called out, 'Master Craik!' and he gasped as he saw her, and stared as though she were a spookie.

'Bess Andersen?' He reached out his hand and she clasped it tightly. Then he said, 'Come with me.'

She climbed up on the seat beside him. The watchman examined his papers in the lantern light, and passed them on through the gate.

'We'll go to my house,' she said. 'You can lodge with me tonight.'

Rain fell in a sudden drenching downpour, making talk impossible. They clattered through the narrow streets as fast as the tired horse would go. Bess directed Craik to a stable where they left the horse and cart. Finally, alone in Bess's room she brought him ale and he sat down, easing his travel-sore body on to a stool.

She said, 'Thank God you are unhurt.'

He knew she referred to Flodden and he told her he had gone there as apothecary in the train of the laird of Threave. 'Sir John was killed,' he said, 'and I'm saddened to say, so was his ward.'

So Giles Thorn was dead. . . .

'I'm sad to hear, but my love for him too is dead.' She asked, almost fearfully, 'What of my father?'

'He was wounded in the thigh, but it is mending. Only his heart will not mend.'

'What do you mean?'

'He has never ceased to mourn you, Bess. For months he searched the countryside, dragged the Solway and the burns. He never fails to have Mass said for you on your nameday and at Easter. For though you ken he's not much on kirk, he hopes for a resurrection.'

'He thinks I am dead, then.'

'Aye, what else could he think?'

She inquired about Moll and the boys, who were well. She learned that she had a little half-sister who was pert and patful. 'They call her Elizabeth, to honour your name.'

Touched, she said, 'I regret I hurt them.'

'Dame Moll keeps your room herbed and flowered as though any day you might return.'

Bess fought back sudden tears. 'I fear I misjudged Moll. I misjudged many things.'

'Aye?'

She felt that she could tell him everything for he had not changed in kindliness, only in looks. The curly cockade of hair was greyer, the dumpy body stouter, but the eyes were still soft for her. After supper she confided all that had happened since he had left her at Lucy's lodgings.

If he was shocked he did not reveal it. Only when she mentioned Sir John Gordon and her mutilation did he swear softly, and when she had ended her story he said only, 'Have you seen the surgeon since he treated your wound?'

'No.'

'Then I should tend it.'

He helped her remove her gown and shift and she cried out as he pulled off the bandage but he was deft and quick. From his fardel he brought unguents and a roll of linen. As he rebound the wound he said, 'You are healing well.'

She was trembling.

'Lie down, lass.'

Obediently she went to the pallet. Shyly she said, 'You may sleep here too, I'll not disturb you.'

But he made up a bed on the floor. She watched him as he moved about the room, clearing the table, feeding the cat. She felt safe and cherished and the thrashing rain lulled her to sleep before he had snuffed the rushlight.

For the first time in years she dreamed of the green hills of Galloway. She was home in her own room and the floor was strewn with broom and lavender. Magpies chattered on the roof and Moll admonished them: 'Hush you, for Bess is asleep. My daughter is asleep.'

At Bess's insistence Craik remained with her during that week while he replenished his supplies of herbs and spices, liniments and linens. On the fourth evening he returned from market with a tiny vial of powdered root of valley-lily.

'Give this to your husband when he returns. It's said to cure witlessness.'

'It will? I never heard of it.'

'It comes from France and is scarce and costly but I could think of no other gift for you.'

Delighted, she thanked him but she had no words for the gratitude she felt. 'How do I give this? In broth or ale?'

'Nay, you meddle it with a bit of grease and rub it on his forehead to stir the brain.'

She treasured the vial in her hand.

'But, Bess, we cannot be sure of it. Don't pin your hopes too high. I've found the most trusted herbs are not always effective. You mind the surgeon gave you mandrake to sleep your pain, yet you were cruelly aware. Even betony does not always heal . . . and it may be that Hugh's brain is beyond healing.'

'But I am sure—'

'You cannot be sure, you can only hope. Suppose the herb does not heal? What then?'

'Why, then, it will be the same as always.'

'You could go home with me.'

The thought had come to her, of course, but on softest tiptoe.

'I could not leave Hugh, witless or not.'

'Bess – he should have returned by now.'

'It is like him to have lost his way.'

'You must think on going home.'

'But what would I say to my father? How in God's name could I explain my long absence?'

'I think you'd need explain only that you followed Giles

Thorn to Edinburgh. Your father is no prude, he would understand and forgive a lass in first love. But,' he added wryly, 'you'd best spare him the rest.'

She would not consider it now, for surely Hugh would return. But to please Master Craik she said, 'I will think on it.'

At dawn, in driving rain, the watchman at the Cowgate Port halted a group of men.

'Who goes there?'

'Wardell MacKay . . . Father MacAllister . . . Hugh Dart . . . John Kirbie . . .'

Bess roused at sound of a knock but did not get up. She could not admit a man now. Whoever it was would return later.

'Bess!'

She sat upright.

'Bess!'

Craik heard too and plucked his blanket from the floor. Thank God he was fully dressed . . . He tossed her her gown and she called out, 'Wait!' and went to the door, tying the points of her sleeves.

Then she was close in Hugh's arms standing on tiptoe to nuzzle his soft, wet curls, kissing his lips and rain-cold cheek, holding him off to marvel that he was unwounded, unhurt.

'Hugh,' she said, 'this is Master Craik, an apothecary, an old friend from the Border.'

Hugh smiled, questionless. Craik took his dripping canvas poke and Bess started the fire for porridge. But before the turf was alight Hugh was asleep on the pallet.

Craik whispered, 'I'll find lodgings.'

She suggested the Cock and Stag and he agreed to go there. 'But mind, I'll be leaving tomorrow. And if the herb is useless you must set your mind to coming with me.'

Her 'Aye,' was weak and he said, 'I was soft with you before and my softness led to your ruin. You cannot abide here with a foggie. You cannot mire yourself in the life you've been leading.'

'I know,' she said, but she scarcely heard him, for Hugh was murmuring in his sleep.

Three hours later Hugh awakened and ate. He had marvellous tales of fighting in the ranks of the Islesmen who spoke a strange tongue. He had killed two men with his claymore, wounded others. And he had brought plunder from dead bodies.

'You did not rob Scots?' she said as he opened the poke.

'How should I know what they were? The dead lay there beside me, their boots scattered about with their legs and fingers.' He shook out the contents of the bag on the table. A blue sash stained with blood. A woollen cutting scarf. A pair of leather shoes. A fragment of chain mail. A dirk without a handle, a sword belt. A Highland bonnet.

'I told you I'd bring back plunder!'

She looked at the sad little pile. Perhaps he could wear the shoes, though they looked too small. The rest might bring a few groats.

'Shall we go down to the stall, Bess?'

'We closed it, remember?'

'Why?'

'Because – no matter. We'll open it later.'

She mixed the lily powder with sheep grease and rubbed it into his forehead and behind his ears. She told him that it would ease him and woo sleep.

'I've no need to sleep now.'

He put his arms around her and drew her down to his lap and kissed her. He pulled at the laces of her bodice.

'Nay,' she said, 'you must gentle me. Don't you remember before you left I fell upon a dirk in the street and hurt myself?'

His face clouded. 'Aye?'

'I stumbled and fell upon the dirk and hurt my right breast.'

'Ah, Bess. Poor Bess.'

'So I am bandaged. My breast is—'

Soon he would have to know. It took all of her courage to say, 'My breast is not there now.'

'*Not there?*'

She tried to smile. 'It was so small a part of me, it is not so great a loss. Love' – she kissed him – 'it does not matter so much, does it?'

'Aye, it does matter.'

She drew back as though slapped.

'You must feel half a woman.'

She had been prepared for his shock, for pity, for revulsion, for anything but perception. The lily powder had cured him!

She leaned against the cushion of his chest and clung there. Tomorrow at St Giles she would light a candle to the Virgin in gratitude for a miracle.

Hugh kissed her hair, her throat, her lips. He drew her towards the pallet.

'I do not want to hurt you,' he said.

He patted at her tears. He could not understand why she wept, for he was not hurting her at all.

They lay together on their rags, close in love and close to sleep.

'Bess?'

'Aye.'

'I brought back plunder!'

'I know.'

He sat up. 'Let me show you.'

He brought out his trinkets, one by one.

So the lily powder had not worked after all. Deeply depressed, she touched her breast. He will forget about this too. Each time he makes love I shall have to remind him, I shall have to explain over and over again . . .

He yawned and stretched.

'Sleep,' she said. 'You've had little.'

For a while he lay back quietly. Then he said, 'Bess, did you see the sash?'

She shuddered and bade him sleep. Perhaps in sleep the herb would reach his brain.

She moved about restlessly. At the window she saw that the rain had stopped, the day would be fair. She picked up Hugh's clothes and dumped them into the wash bucket. She must go to the Loch before the winter settled in.

Then she thought of Guilie and put the basket aside.

The watchman called the hour and added, 'At the command of Her Majesty the Queen, all able-bodied men and women, aye, even vagabonds, shall gather at the Market Cross at noon of this day ...'

Why, she wondered in terror. What news impelled such a gathering? If the English were attacking there was not so much as one cannon to defend the city.

Quickly she dressed, roused Hugh and fed him, rushed him into his clothes. They had nearly two hours to spare but she needed him awake, needed the comfort of his presence. Yet there was little comfort for he did not realize that the King was dead with the flower of the realm, that Scotland was like an apple for English plucking. He could not share her anxiety about the summons to the Cross nor its possible implications.

But he accompanied her obediently to the High Street where townspeople were gathering. Because she and Hugh were early they stood a hand's grasp from the high stone pulpit of the Cross.

The proclamation had specified 'able-bodied men and women' but hundreds of men surrounded them – men crippled and bandaged, blind men led by their women. There were old men and boys under sixteen, grey-grannies, and lasses too young to mate. The preponderance were women; many of them held little bairns.

As the Tolbooth clock chimed twelve the royal horse guard galloped down the Canongate through the Netherbow, and the crowd made way. Pipers preceded Queen

Margaret, who rode a glossy white palfrey caparisoned in silver brocade. She wore robes of mourning white bordered in silver and a lacy white veil hid her face. But as she reached the Cross she swept the veil aside and Bess, who had glimpsed her only from a distance, saw her closely for the first time.

The Queen's face was pallid and pinched as a bit of spent tallow, and her eyes were heavily shadowed. But the painted red mouth was firm and the scant chin was lifted. She spoke suddenly, grimly, without preface from herald or magistrate:

'I have summoned you here to tell you that we must build a wall against the English, against all invaders. There is no signal of attack, but we could be attacked at any moment. Never again shall we be vulnerable as we are now.

'It is only by God's grace that we have not been ravaged and vanquished 'ere this – I think only our prayers have saved us. But we must not trust forever in Divine Providence. For ourselves, our children and their children, we must make our city safe. We must build a wall.'

She reminded them of the crumbling condition of the city wall. 'It has rotted with age and use. Many of you have removed stones to build homes, for we grew smug through years of peace. I do not begrudge you the rocks of your walls and your roofs, but I command that those of you who have built fences or shelters for animals demolish them at once. Place the rocks in your yards, whence wagons will come to collect them. None shall be punished save those who refuse to comply.

'This will start us a-building. Later, the quarries shall be a-hammer when men are fit to ride to them and work them and cart the stone back. We cannot begin in earnest until after the storms of autumn and the floods of spring, and meanwhile more men will return or heal. All women under sixty are bound to help, and children too. Young bairns shall mix the mud and water and so lighten the task.

'Next week the wagons shall start to travel about the

town, so get you home and pull the stones from your fences and sheds. Men now able to work the quarries shall go to Master Lawson at the Tolbooth at dawn and register for labour. The pay will be one groat an hour, free bannocks at noon and free ale at the day's end.'

She surveyed the sea of people below her and pointed to Hugh. 'You, there – a long, strong lad – what do you say? I'll warrant you could build half the wall by yourself.'

Hugh removed his hat and smiled.

'Eh, lad? Is your tongue tied?'

Hugh slid out his tongue and touched it. Folk snickered and Bess put her hand protectively on his arm and looked up at the Queen in an agony of embarrassment.

The Queen's eyes pinned her like sharp blue lances. 'Well, lass? Is it your brother or your sweeting who stands there mute?'

'My husband,' Bess said. And then, in a surge of bravery, 'He's too shy of Your Majesty to speak, but he will work on the wall.'

Margaret said, 'And you? You too are young and sturdy. We'll have need of women like you to drive the quarry carts and help the loading.'

Bess tried to reply but she had lost courage. She could only nod and curtsy and stare at her shoes.

'You'd earn less than your husband, but four groats a day is no mean payment for a woman.'

I can earn more as fishwife and slut . . .

'Surely you'd help defend the town you love?'

But I loathe this town.

'Aye, Madam.' As Bess spoke she lifted her head. Their glances locked and it seemed to her that the crowd around them was excluded, obliterated, that only she and her Queen faced one another across the chasm of the Cross.

'I need you, lass.'

She means women like me. She uses me merely to reach other women. I would form the tiniest niche in her wall, humble as the turf, low as the mud. She does not need me;

she needs my hands and shoulders, my strong back. And I will not break my back for the sake of a town I hate.

Perhaps defiance or despair was plain on her face for the Queen said, 'I do not command any woman to such hard labour, only able men. But I ask you to do such work if you are childless or not with child-seed. Nay, I beg you to.'

The hard eyes were suddenly moist and Bess felt a curious closeness as though she herself sat the white palfrey and wore the pale robes of mourning. But that was only a fancy . . .

'I beg you,' Margaret said.

The mouth and chin were still resolute but loneliness looked out of the blue eyes, and grief.

For she must have loved the King as I love Hugh, and like myself, she will face an empty life without him.

Later as Bess and Hugh walked home she paused in a deserted wynd and stood on tiptoe to kiss him, pressing him close, closer to her breast.

She had no thought of the pain, only the need to cling.

'Love,' she said, 'I'll open the stall tomorrow and you shall work on the wall . . .'

'We'll prosper,' she said. 'I'll quit my – sewing. And when the wall is built, then you'll be back to help me buy and weigh and sell—'

'What wall?' he asked.

Next day at the Cock and Stag Craik rose from a bench and led Bess to a far corner. He poured her a mug from a bowl of sack and asked what she would eat.

'Nothing. I've no hunger.'

'Eat, lass. My pouch is full, for I've treated nine men today.'

'Nine!'

He ordered turbot for himself. 'If I remained here I'd not even need to raise a pole. Word of me spread before I was lodged an hour. Camp fever, raged wounds, cracked bones . . .' He smiled. 'Sir John Gordon sent for me.'

She put down her glass. 'For what?'

'For pain in the groin. He said he'd felt it two weeks ago and called in Geddes, who could not ease it.'

'And did you?'

He shrugged. 'I gave him a salve of mint.'

'But it will not help.'

'It will not help. He vows if the pain worsens he will kill himself.'

Bess drank her sack. Catherine the Pig came in, peacocking in a feathered hat. In the far shadows she saw Blind Robin drinking with a group of minstrels.

'Master Craik,' she said, 'I am sick at heart, for I tried the lily powder but Hugh is the same . . .'

'I warned you, lass.'

'I know.'

'Will you grope for ever through the mists of his mind only to find a further fog? Is it enough to love his body? Even so, how shall it be when you are no longer young?'

She was silent.

'A ha'penny whore?'

She drew herself straight. 'I have the fish stall.'

'But how will it fatten? Who were its customers?'

'Why,' she said, 'the nobility, the wealthy, the gentry.'

'And it is they who lie cold on Flodden. They followed the King like a pack of mad, devoted pups. I saw them, I tended them, I know.'

'But the men who survived must eat.'

'They will eat lentils and kale. Many will die of their wounds, others will never work again nor earn. Who is to buy fresh fish?'

'MacNiff has prospered for years. I can lower my prices to his.'

'And then he will lower his. Bess, there's no hope for two fish stalls on the High Street now. You do not ken what has happened.'

A song started in the far shadows of the room:

'You crave one kiss of my clay-cold lips
But my breath is earthy-strong
If you have but one kiss for my clay-cold lips
Your time will not be long.'

Blind Robin sang a verse alone.

''Tis dawn in yonder garden green
Love, where we used to walk.
The finest flower that e'er was seen
Is withered to a stalk.'

Craik said, 'Come with me in the morning.'

Bess stared out of the window, out into the future of age and poverty and loneliness of heart.

'Will you come with me?'

'Aye.'

She rose. Craik asked to accompany her to her door but she shook her head and he did not urge her, seeming to sense that she wished to be alone, aloof of men, even of him.

He said, 'I'll wait outside your house at sunrise.'

In the lingering twilight Arthur's Seat rose in slopes seamed with bracken patched in gold. Below the Crags crows cawed through the hazel trees of the Royal Park, and she smelled the death of alder and gorse.

She turned to take a last look at Holyrood Palace, grey with years, wearing its high conical caps. The west wing was lighted. In the courtyard above the door torches flickered in the wind.

In the South Back Canongate wind caught her breath, pranked her hair and swelled her skirts. Here was the only familiar desolation. Lucy's house was dark and forlorn in its weeds and she thought briefly of Lucy and her aunt with the coughing sickness but they were like images on a faded tapestry abandoned in the storeroom of her mind.

An abbot hurried by. A woman came out of a hut and called a child and the wind lost her words on a curse. Bess went on past cowsheds, pigsties, goat runs, geese pens, and turned into the Canongate.

She smelled the fallen fruit of an orchard. From a prim-curtained window she heard laughter and lute song; at another, the pibroch of pipes.

Here were fine houses surrounded by gardens. The lawns, still rain-wet, glistened green and gold with fluttering leaves. Bird baths and sundials were marble flagons for rainwater. From open windows she smelled burning oak and applewood.

As she came to the Netherbow the watchman greeted her as he always did when she approached from the north.

'And how is the King tonight?'

They both stood aghast at the old jest.

He stammered an explanation. 'It's just that I can't believe it. I can't believe he's gone.'

'Nor I.'

'No one does, I think.'

'No one.'

She passed on through the gate. The firewood smells changed to purl and peat, the houses humped in squalor. Here were no gardens, but tiny separating rigs of grass and gorse. The stalls began, row after row shrouded in canvas. At Friar's Wynd she hurried past her own without a glance.

The shops: Silversmith, chandler, cobbler, armourer, wig-maker, all with their wind-creaking signs. Adam Pirk, Baker of Bread. Adam had died at Flodden.

A man accosted her but she shook her head and continued up the High Street to the Church of St Giles. She tied her hair and entered.

Craik was right. The town was poor now, man-poor, candle-poor. Mourners knelt in the gloom of faint altar lights. She stared up into an infinity of darkness, unable to see the tops of the tall white pillars.

A thin cat rubbed her legs. Women wept. An old man coughed.

She went back down the aisle, pushing the great oaken door against the wind.

The sky was a wild brown-purple. Glimpsing the Nor' Loch through a wynd she saw boats tossed in ice-grey water. Leaves whirled in the kirkyard and grave-wreaths spun to the gutters.

She passed more stalls, their covering ballooned by the wind. In the Lawnmarket a boy approached and offered a groat. She said, 'I am going home.'

But she was far from home.

Outside the Golden Hawk she thought of Dougal Campbell and the many hours they had passed at his lodgings above. Dead at Flodden or safe in his glen? Likely she would never know.

In the Grassmarket she saw Greyfriar's in its gardens. Asters had spilled pale petals on the stone walk, a bride's path to the Monastery. And then she looked up at the Castle topped by its sentinel torches. Monstrous, ugly, yet a parent permitting the town to rest for ever on its rocky back.

In the West Bow she saw Robert Lawson lurch out of a tavern. Guilie would be glad he lives, even in the dark of drink. . . .

She turned and retraced her steps with the knife of the wind at her back. Why do I wander these streets bidding farewell to each lichened wall, each crow-stepped gable, almost as if I loved them?

A pest cart trundled by towards Boroughmuir. The driver grinned through his mask and shouted a bawdy greeting.

She walked on and on, up steep grey lanes, down crumbling, ill-lit steps. As she neared her house a man spoke from the shadows, jingling coins.

'What is your price, lass?'

As he drew close she saw a young face, newly scarred. A cat sidled up and rubbed her legs.

'I am going home,' she said.

Home to the soft, russet slopes of Galloway, home to the sound of sheep bells and the sea. Home to pumpkins fat in the fields and the plump plenty of geese and grain. Aye, wind knocked at the back end o' the year and storms battered but wood-fires burned in the cottages and juice-spitting apples runkled red on the hearths.

'I am going home,' she repeated.

'And where is your home?' he asked.

'Why,' she said, 'up younder wynd.'

And suddenly, simply, she realized it was so. Home was these worn cobbles on which she stood, this ancient wall on which she leaned, this wynd-cat which foraged the gutters. Home was where Hugh was.

'Someone awaits you?' the man asked.

'Aye,' she said. Hugh waited in love and trust, needing her as no one ever had.

'Tomorrow, then?'

And what of tomorrow, what of her future here? She and Hugh might hunger for a time, but surely the town would recover and prosper. Folk would buy fish as they always had. The new wall would rise on the ruins of the old. And in a year . . . or two . . . she could leave the streets, wear her key cord and bind her hair in pride.

'I'll meet you here at sundown,' she said.

He left her and she listened to his receding footsteps. Faint and far off down the darkening corridors of the town the watchman called the hour.

As she turned into her wynd and climbed her forestairs she heard drumbeats from Leith Lighthouse. Lightning ripped the sky above the Castle. Out on the Forth the little boats were coming home to harbour.

A LAMENT FOR FLODDEN

I've heard them lilting at our ewe-milking,
Lasses a' lilting before dawn o' day;
But now they are moaning on ilka green loaning –
The Flowers of the Forest are a' wede away.
At bughts, in the morning, nae blythe lads are scorning,
Lasses are lonely and dowie and wae;
Nae daffing, nae gabbing, but sighing and sabbing,
Ilk ane lifts her leglin and hies her away.
In hairst, at the shearing, nae youths now are jeering,
Bandsters are lyart, and runkled and grey;
At fair or at preaching, nae wooing, nae fleeching –
The Flowers of the Forest are a' wede away.
At e'en, in the gloaming, nae swankies are roaming
'Bout stacks wi' the lasses at bogle to play;
But ilk ane sits eerie, lamenting her deerie –
The Flowers of the Forest are a' wede away.
Dool and wae for the order sent our lads to the Border!
The English, for ance, by guile wan the day;
The Flowers of the Forest, that fought aye the foremost,
The prime of our land, lie cauld in the clay.
We'll hear nae mair lilting at our ewe-milking;
Women and bairns are heartless and wae;
Sighing and moaning on ilka green loaning –
The Flowers of the Forest are a' wede away.

Afterword

WHAT HAPPENED TO the body of the King?

R. L. Mackie in *King James IV of Scotland* says: 'Surrey knew that his victory had been overwhelming and that somewhere among the ghastly heaps of corpses lay the dead body of the King. Not until the following day, however, was it discovered. Dacre, who knew the King well, identified the body. It was conveyed to Berwick where it was recognized by Sir John Forman, the King's Sergeant Porter, and Sir William Scott, a member of the Council. But soon after the battle strange stories began to be whispered – that James had not fallen in battle; that he had been seen in Kelso on the night of the battle; that he had been slain by the Humes; that he had escaped and gone on a pilgrimage to Jerusalem. The corpse taken to Berwick, it was said, was really the body of someone who had been dressed in the King's coat-armour. . . . The persistence of the legend is simply the measure of his people's need of him.'

In *The Life of James IV* I. A. Taylor wrote: 'Though the King had died excommunicate Leo X gave Henry VIII permission to bury him in consecrated ground at St Paul's Cathedral but there is no evidence to show that this was done, and Stow asserts that on the dissolution of the great religious houses in Edward VI's reign the body was still lying, lapped in lead, in a waste room, amongst old timber and rubble . . . It has been a matter of grave doubt whether the body thus treated was indeed that of James . . .

'With regard to this legend of his survival it is a strange fact, that from a document amongst the State papers, it appears that Queen Margaret, when desirous of obtaining a divorce from her second husband, the young Earl of Angus, married by her within a twelfth-month of the Battle of Flodden, declared that James had lived three years after it and that her marriage was therefore invalid and void.'

Margaret bore James a posthumous son. Shortly afterwards, in a secret ceremony, she married Archibald Douglas, Earl of Angus. Her Council, infuriated by a Douglas brought to power, deposed her as Regent and appointed John Stuart, Duke of Albany, who had been banished to France by James IV. Margaret, disillusioned by Douglas's arrogance and greed, realized he had married her only for power. When she lost that power he urged her to make love to Albany in order to regain it. Divorcing Douglas, she married Henry Stuart, later Lord Methven – a handsome young opportunist curiously like his predecessor.

Douglas rose to supreme power in Scotland, with the young King his prisoner. At seventeen, the King escaped from Falkland Castle disguised as a groom and fled to Stirling. Douglas was driven into exile. Scott says, 'James V retained during his whole life an implacable resentment against the Douglases, and never permitted one of the name to settle in Scotland while he lived.'

After Adam's death at Flodden, Agnes Bothwell married three times, taking Cuthbert Ramsay, Burgess of Edinburgh, for her fourth husband in her mid-fifties. Strangely, her son and Margaret's, the two infants cradled at Linlithgow during the Battle of Flodden, were destined to shape one of the great passions of history. James V fathered Mary Queen of Scots. Patrick Bothwell fathered James Hepburn, who became Mary's third husband. Queen Margaret's daughter by Archibald Douglas married the Earl of Lennox and became the mother of Darnley, Mary's second husband – adding another link to the fantastic future chain of love and murder.

Few writers, military or historical, agree on the mystery of Flodden. You may read fifty different accounts and hear a hundred opinions. Contemporary writers were naturally biased. The fact remains that at least six thousand men perished in three hours on the mile-wide Flodden Hill.

In January 1958 I climbed that bleak Northumberland hill. Once slippery with blood and mud, it was slick with ice. Despite local legend of the clash of ghostly armies heard by night, nothing suggests the horror of that long-ago battle. Far below lie fields tidy with turnips. Sheep graze the higher slopes. The Cheviot Hills raise their great shoulders to the south. England and Scotland meet in a vast embrace of moorland.

As memorial there is a simple granite cross:

'*To the brave of both nations. September* 9, 1513.'

ELIZABETH BYRD

New York
September 1962